A PALM BEACH MURDER MYSTERY

The PERFECT 10

ERIC O'KEEFE

RIVER GROVE
BOOKS

Published by River Grove Books
Austin, TX
www.rivergrovebooks.com

Distributed by River Grove Books

Design and composition by Greenleaf Book Group
Cover design by Greenleaf Book Group
Cover illustration by Robert McGinnis

Publisher's Cataloging-in-Publication data is available.

Paperback ISBN: 978-1-63299-358-8

eBook ISBN: 978-1-63299-359-5

Hardcover ISBN: 978-1-63299-360-1

Trade Paperback Edition

To Tommy Lee Jones

"A polo handicap is your passport to the world."

—Winston Churchill

STUNNING, STRIKING, BOLD, BEAUTIFUL–these were the words that people in polo used to describe Juan Harrington. To his fellow Argentines, he was Juancito. But to the rest of the world, he was the Argentine Adonis—his tanned limbs, rugged jaw line, and trademark stubble instantly identifiable on six-story billboards that towered over Times Square, Piccadilly Circus, and the Ginza. Women swooned over his fiery good looks. Men gawked at his other-worldly talents and the ease at which he summoned them. His daily comings and goings as the honored guest of any number of world leaders invariably ran front and center in the tabloids that mesmerized Buenos Aires.

One summer, during the British Season, the long lens of London's paparazzi caught Juancito leaving Mark's Club with a duke's daughter one night and the Prime Minister's daughter the next. On the third night, the world's greatest polo player escorted both ladies off the premises. In the States, Juancito's unexpected appearance on the arm of one of the Best Actress nominees at the Academy Awards confirmed the ugly rumors that her on-again, off-again marriage was definitely off again. The final word belonged to the editors of *People*, who dubbed Juancito the World's Sexiest Man:

> **Polo's highest rating—a 10-goal handicap—is bestowed on a handful of exceptional horsemen. Juancito Harrington may well be the lone unanimous choice, the perfect 10.**

Which is precisely why Harrington always looked forward to playing in Palm Beach. The locals were so blasé. The ones with money knew it and couldn't care less. The ones pretending they had money? Too self-absorbed to pay attention to anyone else. Some might recognize his famous face, but for the most part, everyone let him be, including the Jamaican valet, who greeted him late Tuesday morning as Juancito arrived at the Brazilian Court in his silver Range Rover Sport, or the hotel's Kenyan gardener, who met Juancito's happy-go-lucky grin with a gracious bow and a long sweep of an arm as his hotel's most famous guest made his way through the lush Fountain Courtyard. The many pleasures of the Brazilian Court were always at his service.

The only one who paid Harrington any mind was a plump-cheeked turn-down maid. Late that afternoon, she began making her rounds, going from room to room in a bright yellow frock. She rang the bell to the Lancaster Suite but got no response. She unlocked the door, announced herself, and stepped inside. A quick pass through the guest bedroom revealed a throw pillow lying askew on the loveseat. She righted it and proceeded to the living room.

Then she spied shiny gold flecks on the beige carpet. She bent down to pick them up and recognized them as the remnants of the wrapper from a bottle of Champagne. More pieces littered the sofa.

An empty Champagne bucket?

She reached for her handheld and radioed Café Boulud to send a porter to come clean up the mess.

Wait—this doesn't make any sense.

Glancing down at her clipboard, her worst fears were confirmed. The Lancaster Suite was supposed to be vacant with a VIP check-in due that very evening. She took another step, and her heart sank.

Don't tell me!

The corner of a shirttail was poking out the door of the master bedroom. The rest of the shirt, a boot—actually, a pair of tall leather boots—a pair of socks, and riding pants lay scattered on the carpet.

"Housekeeping," she said in her firmest, friendliest voice. She peeked in the master bedroom. That's when Juancito startled her. The warm glow of the early evening light barely illuminated the suite, but it was still bright enough for her to see him clearly. He had the king-sized bed all to himself.

"Oh, pardon me, Mr. Harrington," she said, and she reached for the knob to shut the bedroom door. Then she paused.

The handsome man with the famous face had yet to stir. Slowly, she turned and took a second look. Despite the fading light, her well-trained eye was drawn to a beet-red stain on the Frette pillowcase. Then she caught sight of the entry wound on Juancito's temple.

Then the porter from Café Boulud heard her screams.

ON THE RUNWAY AND OFF, the leggy model with the raven-black hair was the ceaseless object of wide-eyed stares. That was definitely the case the moment she set foot in the crowded Buenos Aires steakhouse wearing a body-hugging number from Herve Leger. The sound of her high heels on the hardwood floor sent a ripple of silence through La Brigada—silence tinged with a heavy dose of testosterone.

"*Conmigo, mi amor,*" one of the regulars growled, welcoming her into the clubby male bastion. The portly chauvinist was lurking behind a stained napkin, his plate empty but his appetite still whetted. He was inviting her to share far more than his table. Throaty laughs pitter-pattered from table to table as the maître d', a chubby middle-aged man with a boutonniere pinned to his black vest, scurried from the kitchen to the front of the house.

The louts, he thought.

Solitary females such as this one were rare birds at the steakhouse, and he hurried to snare her before she flew the coop.

"Thank you for joining us this evening. By chance do you have a reservation?" He already knew the answer. *She's the one.*

"No. Perhaps my date does?"

She dropped his name, and he dutifully scanned the list of reservations.

"Ah, I see there is a request for something more private."

Much to the disappointment of the packed house, the maître d' escorted her to a secluded second-floor table. A trail of sighs followed the delicate taps of her high heels up the stairs.

Not ten minutes later, a second stranger entered their midst. Like the leggy model, he was young, in his late twenties. Thirty, tops. All eyes focused on the impossibly handsome newcomer. The light in his eyes, the drape of his stone-colored suit, his easy way of moving—all combined to create a quiet athletic confidence that none of them possessed. He was the lucky one, this confident man in his confident suit. He was the man the mysterious model was waiting for.

A waiter, one with a loyal following among the embassy crowd, gestured to the second floor. With a sharp nod and a quick wink, the stranger bounded up the stairs. As soon as he reached the top, he spied the maître d' seated opposite his date, pouring her a frosty caipirinha from an icy pitcher. As he stealthily approached the two, he nicked a napkin off a table, folded it over his arm, and assumed the guise of an attentive server.

"Is everything to the lovely lady's satisfaction this evening?" he asked in a sultry Argentine accent.

Anastasia's delighted laugh was all the answer he needed.

"And you, sir? What is the gentleman's pleasure this evening? Something from the menu or would you consider one of tonight's specials?"

"*Mi capitán*, my only desire is even one minute more of this angel's company." Hugo stood up, held the chair, and deftly poured a second caipirinha. Specks of shaved ice danced in the glass.

"To sunrise at Argentine Customs!" Rick Hunt said as he raised his glass.

Anastasia burst out laughing and joined him in the toast.

The two had met the night before on the American Airlines red-eye from Miami to Buenos Aires. Actually, they hadn't met on the flight. They had exchanged glances during the hour-long preboard process. By the time both were seated at opposite ends of the same row in business class, their eyes had met several more times and they knew each other by sight and by smile. But Hunt chose to stay put. When it came to international travel, he was a road warrior. The minute he got buckled in, it was lights out: no drink, no dinner, no movie.

Neither the time nor the place.

Anastasia, however, spent much of the flight shooing away a variety of pests. A CEO in first class had one of the flight attendants offer her a glass of Dom Pérignon along with an invitation to join him for dinner. Two teenage tifosi—young Ferrari fans—who glimpsed Anastasia on the podium at the Monaco Grand Prix, mustered their courage, snuck up from coach, and begged to have their pictures taken with her. Her chatty neighbor insisted on sharing the sad story of his two divorces. (Make that one annulment and one divorce from the same unfortunate bride.) By the time dinner and dessert had been served, Anastasia knew the poor woman's pain.

After touching down in Buenos Aires, the two found themselves standing next to one another in the foreigners-only customs and immigration queue at Ezeiza. Hunt had enjoyed a full night's sleep, and her yawns drew a sympathetic smile.

"Long night?"

The bleary-eyed Spaniard did a double take, her brown eyes blinking. Then Hunt saw the copy of *Spanish Vogue* in her tote.

"Buenos dias. Me llamo Ricardo."

With this simplest of greetings, he coaxed the tiniest of smiles from her lips. She yawned again and ran her fingers through the tangles of her bedhead.

"Hola, Ricardo. Me llamo Anastasia. Mucho gusto a conocerle."

The Madrid native volunteered that she was booked on modeling assignments in Buenos Aires through mid-May. All she could remember about the tall, tan American was that he had a quick smile and a quicker sense of humor, especially when it came to her in-flight fan club. By the time they parted ways, a dinner date was in the works.

At La Brigada, however, Anastasia was back on her game.

"Why didn't you tell me you were the President's right-hand man in Argentina?"

"Hugo does this every time I come here," Hunt said, shaking his head. "He lays it on thick about me and *el Presidente*. To hear him tell it, you'd think I was a regular member of the President's foursome at the Congressional Country Club."

"So Señor Hugo just lied? You don't work at the White House?"

"No, he's right about that," Hunt said. Out of a coat pocket, Hunt's White House ID materialized. Grabbing it, Anastasia playfully uncoiled the long blue lanyard and studied the laminated picture of Hunt in his service uniform.

"¿Es Usted un soldado?" she asked curiously.

"Sí, soy soldado."

"¿Un capitán?"

"Si, un capitán."

"And have you ever been in a meeting with the President?"

"Of course I have. Not that he would ever know I'm there. In a typical day, the President has dozens of meetings involving hundreds of people, rooms full of Cabinet secretaries and undersecretaries and deputy secretaries and all sorts of staffers. I promise you that most of us do nothing more than stand up when the President arrives and then stand up again when he leaves the room. Beyond that, not a word escapes our lips. That's the long and short of my presidential audiences."

"But you've met with him more than once, no?"

Hunt nodded.

"And if he gave you an order, you would follow it, wouldn't you?"

"Anastasia, he's my Commander in Chief. I've sworn an oath to follow him. It's my duty to uphold that oath, and I like to think I'm a man of my word. Maybe that's one reason I don't make many promises."

A smile made its way across Anastasia's face. "You're not doing a good job of convincing me you don't work for your President, Ricardo. I like that about you."

"You like men who know when to keep their mouth shut?"

She took a sip of her caipirinha and shook her head no. Then she took the stirrer and began swirling the tiny bits of crushed ice. "Most men I meet like to tell me all sorts of lies about themselves. They can't help it. But I know they could not possibly be telling me the truth. I don't know these men, but I know they are liars the moment they start to talk. They can't stand to be themselves. It's a curse that haunts so many men. It ruins them. I find them so odd, so unhappy."

Hunt found himself growing more and more curious about this beautiful woman.

"They want me to fall madly in love with someone who they are not. Maybe I need to not know that they are married. Maybe they think money is all that matters to me. Maybe they don't want me to know that they are scared to grow old. Do they think I can make them stay young? I don't know. I do know they are afraid to be themselves. But you, Ricardo, you are not afraid. You do not lie to me."

Hunt was smiling. And listening.

"But you don't say much about yourself, do you? And when you do talk about yourself, you leave some things out. Maybe you forget to mention a few things when we meet this morning? Maybe you are forgetting a few more tonight, no?"

Hunt was lazily stirring his own drink. He arched his eyebrows at her candor. And her insight.

"You like being yourself," she said, and touched her glass to his. "And I like that about you."

"THEY DID IT IN THE BED. They did it in the tub. Then he orders lunch, and she whacks him," the investigator said, as he pointed out each suspected point of entry.

His partner shook his head. He didn't buy a word of what he just heard. Standing directly over Juancito's lifeless body, he countered with his own theory. "Tub, bed, lunch; then the Mexican takes a siesta, and she lowers the boom."

"Pal, in case no one told you, the guy's from Argentina, not from Mexico."

"Who cares where he's from? He's dead."

"OK. One more time. How'd she lower the boom?"

"Tub, bed, lunch, siesta, BOOM!" he said, pointing his trigger finger at Juancito and lodging an imaginary bullet in the polo player's bloodied temple.

"You're both wrong," the crime scene photographer said. An older man with a few wisps of baby-fine hair clinging to his pate, he had systematically documented each of the suite's two lavish bedrooms, its spacious living room, and the cavernous bath with its oversized sauna, his and hers showers, and Jacuzzi.

"They started in the other bedroom. He sat himself down and got comfortable. You got to wonder what kind of show she put on for him in there. Then they do it on the sofa, and they do it over there—on that poufy ottoman. Next, they make their way to the master bath. They do it on the vanity, and they do it in the tub. But get ready for this. Not once did they do it in bed. This guy covered an awful lot of ground—just not in the sack."

Maybe that's why she killed him, he thought to himself and laughed out loud.

His colleagues' eyes darted around the room from point to point and back to Juancito.

"That's right. Got in there by himself," the photographer continued. He proved his point by taking his pen and singling out the perfectly folded sheets that cascaded off Juancito's chest. "Come look. Right here. Look right here. Not a crease. Not a thing out of place except for how he crawled in."

"And you know she's a she because?" the first investigator asked.

"Because the shoulder-length blonde hair in the tub matches the shoulder-length blonde hair on the robe that matches the shoulder-length blonde hair that got snagged on his watchband. Could be wrong. Been wrong before. But not this time."

The second investigator could not keep quiet.

"Ten bucks says it's shower, tub ..." and then he quickly clammed up. In the doorway of the master suite stood a cross-looking man in his mid-fifties with all the levity of a defrocked Catholic priest. His underlings knew the drill. All three immediately did their utmost to feign busywork.

Detective Raul Ramirez chose to neither greet his subordinates nor acknowledge their presence. Despite the fact that he had only taken the time to complete a single sketchy pass through the Lancaster Suite, the scowling detective with the frightful comb-over already had a bead on the killer.

The made-to-measure shirt, the well-buffed Faglianos, the saddle-stained polo britches, and the high-dollar watch on the nightstand—each piece of evidence hammered home the identity of the polo player's murderer:

Someone as self-indulgent as the victim.

4

NOT ONLY WAS ANASTASIA A STUNNER, but she turned out to be a witty raconteur and a wicked mimic. She jumped back and forth from English to Spanish, her quick-moving hands and expressive eyes mocking the mannerisms of her fellow models. The day's shoot had been staged poolside at the ultrachic Faena Hotel in Puerto Madero. She was the lone female; all the males were Argentine, and every one a diva. When they weren't preening themselves or badgering the stylists, they strutted around the pool like pigeons at a park, each with his head held high and chest stuck out. Anastasia shimmied in her seat from side to side.

"How did they strut?"

"I'll show you!"

Anastasia jumped out of her chair and began prancing around the dining room, her head held high, her eyes almost closed, her shoulders and hips swaying to and fro, her sun-kissed face glowing with excitement. She weaved among the empty tables with the grace and certitude of a bullfighter, effortlessly turning, twisting, and posing as she rid herself of the afternoon's exasperations.

"Bravo, bravo," Hunt called out and clinked a knife against his water glass in applause.

The couple had gone from caipirinhas to a crisp Sauvignon Blanc, which their host paired with an order of piping-hot empanadas, a specialty at La Brigada. Next up, a provoleta—grilled provolone bursting with robust flavor that disappeared in quick, greedy bites. Their appetites mirrored their energy, and the main course was already cooking.

The maître d' made his way up the noisy stairs and into their midst. In his arms he cradled a crystal carafe laden with a red wine. "The moment you made the reservation, *mi capitán*, I decanted this beautiful Cheval des Andes. It is from my private stash, my very best."

Hunt was beginning to feel the caipirinha and the wine. "Hugo, I have no idea why you are trying to convince Anastasia that I am the right-hand man of the President of the United States. Nor, at this moment, do I feel any need to disprove your theory that I am the President's wingman."

The proprietor slowly tilted the massive carafe. "My friend, it is such a shame that you do not have even the tiniest drop of Iberian blood coursing through your veins. For if you did, you would appreciate the importance of how a soupçon of storytelling or a dash of deception can change the course of an evening or perhaps even a lifetime."

He turned to Anastasia for confirmation. She nodded in agreement.

"That is not to say that the world does not appreciate you Americans for the many things you do so well. Your straightforwardness. Your openness. Your can-doism. And of course, you always get the girl!" he said, gesturing toward his lovely guest.

Hunt nodded in appreciation. Anastasia smiled demurely.

Their host was not finished.

"Try as you might, you cannot convince me otherwise, my friend. The way someone carries himself. The people he shares his table with. Day in and day out, I see these things. You operate up here, *mi capitán*," he said, waving his hand back and forth at shoulder level, "and the rest of us are down here," his hand by his waist. He paused. "Only now I insist you take my advice—enjoy this!"

The restaurateur poured a splash of the full-bodied red. Although he was still shaking his head at Hugo's flight of fancy about Iberian wiles and American ways, Hunt was determined to make the most of the moment. At a captain's pay grade, assignments such as this were few and far between. He swirled the grand cru round and round, opening it up. Then he lifted the light-filled goblet and gazed at its ruby red legs. The closer he looked, however, the less he liked what he saw:

FBI Special Agent Curtis Dean walking directly toward him.

Not an hour before, during the cab ride to La Brigada, Hunt received a quick heads-up, a text message on his personal iPhone. More often than not, he kept that line muted, and that was especially the case when he was on assignment. Although the call wasn't from Washington, it had everything to do with the White House. No particulars were mentioned. No details discussed. One point was stressed:

Be ready to hit the ground running.

Hunt snapped to. He was back on duty. Dean's visit would not be a social one. The FBI's legal attaché at the American Embassy in Buenos Aires only worked the biggest cases. Hunt nosed the supple red but set the glass down without taking a sip. Hugo was horrified, and Anastasia intrigued, but Hunt had reconciled himself to the fact that his picture-perfect dinner with this glorious girl was about to come to a close.

Neither the time nor the place.

"Care to join us?" he asked the FBI agent.

Dean chuckled at Hunt and turned politely to Anastasia. "Good evening, ma'am," he said. "Sir," he nodded to Hugo. Only then did his attention return to his colleague.

"As much as I'd like to accept your invitation, Captain Hunt, I regret to inform you that you have been summoned by the Ambassador. A car is waiting for us. Ma'am, my apologies."

Hugo became apoplectic. "Do you believe me now?" the restaurateur demanded of Anastasia. "Can you not see what is before your very eyes?" He gestured directly at Dean.

Anastasia nodded approvingly. The FBI agent looked slightly startled by the curious outburst. Hunt could only shake his head.

I can't win with this guy.

"This man does not come here because there is a passport problem on aisle three," Hugo said as he continued his tirade. "It is a command performance. Go ahead. Deny it. But I see the hands of *el Presidente.*"

Hunt rose to his feet.

"¡*Un abrazo!*" Hugo demanded.

The two gave each other a bear hug. Hunt turned to Anastasia. She was smiling radiantly. Like Hugo, she too had seen her point proven.

"I promise to call you," Hunt told her.

"Stay true to your word, Ricardo."

They kissed cheek to cheek, and Rick Hunt left La Brigada.

Hugo's voice followed them out of the restaurant. "You cannot fool me. I know who you are, *mi capitán*. You are up here, and the rest of us, we are down here!"

The Americans stepped out into the heavy night air.

"What the hell was going on back there? And how did you manage to hook up with her?"

Hunt laughed and shook his head. Some things were better left unexplained, especially ones he wasn't sure he could.

"We going back to the embassy?" Hunt asked.

"I am," the agent responded. He patted Hunt on the back. "You're not."

ESTADOS UNIDOS IS AT BEST a narrow street. Thanks to the convoy of armored black Suburbans idling in formation, it was claustrophobic in the dim damp light. Hunt shadowed the FBI agent to the second Suburban. A member of the Ambassador's security detail opened the truck's rear door. The back two rows had been configured executive style with four captain's chairs. Only one was occupied: by Ambassador Gannon.

"Sorry to interrupt your evening, Captain," the Ambassador said.

Hunt prepared himself to graciously accept this official apology when a sharp voice blared in over the speakerphone:

"I send you to Argentina to be a part of the jump team for the President's state visit, and you're out on the town your first night there?" the voice asked.

"No worries, sir," Hunt said, a tinge of embarrassment in his voice. He was on the firing line, and his only option was to fire back. "Special Agent Dean is doing a top-notch job of supervising me. He's already given me two Breathalyzer exams since I landed." The FBI agent smiled at Hunt's tap-dancing routine.

"Keep clowning around, and I'll have him put a GPS up your ass," the voice said.

The FBI agent mimed putting a rubber glove on his hand and popping it at the wrist. "Just say the word, sir," he said with a grin.

Only one man in Washington cracked a whip so sharply: the Chief of Staff to the President of the United States, Ari Auerbach.

6

LESS THAN A YEAR HAD passed since the Chief singled out Hunt at the G20 Summit in London. At the time, the Army captain was wrapping up a year's study at the London School of Economics. With England his gregarious host, Hunt, like thousands of American officers before him, was having the time of his life, especially after his two tours in the Middle East.

That is, until he was unceremoniously yanked out of class and summoned to Winfield House, the official residence of the American Ambassador to the Court of St. James. A State Department driver ferried him to the mammoth neo-Georgian estate, which sprawls over more than a dozen acres in Regent's Park.

Although Hunt tried his best not to stare, it was absolutely impossible. Winfield House was a sumptuous affair, more a palace than a residence, with priceless paintings, rich tapestries, and museum-quality antiques at every turn. A Marine guard ushered him directly to a small, hidden book-lined room. Hunt hadn't the foggiest idea who had summoned him or why he was even there. *This won't last long*, he thought to himself. But as the minutes stretched on, he found himself scanning the floor-to-ceiling bookshelves. Chaucer, Shakespeare, Pepys, Browning, Austen, Brontë, Dickens, Kipling, Waugh, Huxley—the greats of English literature were present and accounted for. *No doubt they're all first editions.* Hunt did a double take. *Agatha Christie?* He cracked a smile. Interspersed among the leather-bound volumes were masterfully framed black-and-whites of couples—fashionable couples, glamorous couples—and all of them from some bygone era.

Wait a minute. The couples are all different, but she's always the same.

Hunt compared the black-and-white on the first shelf to the one on the second. Both featured an immaculately tailored toff with the same dame. Hunt walked to the third shelf and instantly recognized a dashing screen star. *Cary Grant! And a young Cary Grant at that.* The fourth escort, like the first two, was a nameless face, one devoid of character or purpose. For her part, it wasn't the opulent jewels or stylish attire that stood out. It was the look she wore in every shot: perfectly bored, almost cursed, in a Wallis Simpson sort of way.

Hunt slammed on the brakes in front of the fifth shelf. Her sad smile? Gone. Instead, in this photograph, her head was thrown back. She wasn't just laughing. She was guffawing. One of her arms was around a polo player's shoulder, and in the other she held a stunning sterling trophy. *They don't make them like that anymore*, Hunt thought. He carefully picked up the golden frame and took a closer look at the dark-haired man in the tight-fitting shirt and snug britches. The match had just concluded. Clearly, this guy's team had won. His confident air was crowned by a dazzling smile. But what was more impressive was that he had won such a smile from the lady beside him.

How did he do it? Why was he the only one? What was his secret?

Hunt burst out laughing. "Rubirosa!" he cried aloud.

It has to be him. Who else could it be? She must be . . . *what's her name . . . the Poor Little Rich Girl.* Hunt tried desperately to remember anything he could about the dashing playboy. *It wasn't Haiti. He was from the Dominican Republic, and he married Trujillo's daughter. Then, during World War II, he married some French actress. Next in line was Doris Duke. What is her name?*

Hunt forced his thoughts back to an ancient conversation, the one where he first heard about the celebrated jet-setter. *"Larger than life"—that's what got everybody howling.* It turned out that dashing polo player boasted such a substantial male member that to this day Parisian waiters refer to an oversized pepper grinder as a Rubirosa. *What is her name?*

More than a decade had passed since that elegant evening when Hunt first heard this polo tale, but he had no problem recalling the setting: on a lantern-lit patio at Mar-a-Lago in Palm Beach. It was a year or two before he went to West Point, back when he still had hopes of becoming a professional polo player. *What is her name?*

Hunt was one of a handful of wide-eyed hopefuls selected to try out for the polo team that would represent the USA at the World Championships.

The weeklong training camp in Palm Beach gave Hunt his first glimpse at the gilded ways of the game of kings. It was a far cry from the hard-scrabble ranch polo he had known all his life. One of the many events was a lavish dinner at the great estate. The small talk at the far end of the long table where Hunt was seated had been beyond mind-numbing. But when a waiter approached the ladies at the table with a massive pepper grinder, someone chuckled, someone else mentioned "the Rubirosa," and the ice was broken. As it turned out, one of their hosts actually played polo with the Dominican playboy. He knew Rubi, as he called him, and he had also met the Poor Little Rich Girl. Somehow she and the owner of Mar-a-Lago shared a connection. *They were both heiresses, and they were related—but not by blood—and each filled her lonely life with far too many husbands. What is her name?*

A slight clicking sound at the other end of the room brought Hunt's sleuthing to a sudden halt. He turned in time to see a member of someone's security detail step out from behind a gilded bookshelf that swung out of the opposite wall.

Secret Service, Hunt thought as the agent coldly eyed him. *Who's next?*

Almost immediately, an energetic force burst into the room: the Chief.

Ari Auerbach was a lethal weapon: the iron fist the President kept cloaked in the folds of the Oval Office's velvet curtains. A former Congressman, Auerbach was equal parts surgical scalpel and blunt instrument. He walked directly toward Hunt.

"Captain Hunt? Ari Auerbach," he said, and the two shook hands. The Chief noticed the framed picture that Hunt was holding. "Who's in the picture?"

Hunt smiled at the happy couple. He turned the frame toward the Chief.

"Porfirio Rubirosa was his name. In addition to being an avid polo player, Rubi was a diplomat, a race-car driver, and the husband of who knows how many women. Most of them, I might add, were extremely wealthy. Back in Rubi's day, the term 'playboy' was a badge of honor, and Rubi was one of the greats, if not the greatest."

"What's her name?" the Chief asked, pointing at the woman.

Still stymied yet eager to put his best foot forward, Hunt remembered the counsel of Sun Tzu from a military history course at West Point:

Appear weak when you are strong, and strong when you are weak.

"She was one of his many wives," he said, choosing his words carefully. "In fact, at the time this picture was taken she was also one of the wealthiest women on earth. Does the nickname Poor Little Rich Girl ring a bell?"

"Don't tell me," the Chief said. "I'll get it. *I'll get it.*" He brought his left hand to his face and made a fist. He pounded it against his lips two or three times. The fist became a finger, one pointing directly at Hunt. "Hutton. Barbara Hutton. She's the Poor Little Rich Girl who built this damn place, and when she got tired of it, she sold it to Harry Truman for a buck. That's who she is."

"You are correct, sir. Good call."

That very same finger continued wagging in Hunt's face. "I'd appreciate it if you didn't go busting my balls right off the bat with such an embarrassingly easy question. But you know what? I like you already, Hunt. You're not some suck-up. 'Cause if you were, you wouldn't have made it this far. Now, how do you know so much about these jet-setting playboys and their rich wives, anyway? Are you some sort of blue blood?"

"Not at all, sir. I know a lot about horses—and horsemen—because I'm a cavalry officer. So was my father. So was my grandfather. We all played polo, but I can assure you we're definitely not blue bloods. We're Army officers. We play for Army teams. My grandfather played on the Army team that won the bronze at the 1920 Olympics. General Patton actually had him transferred to Schofield Barracks to play at Pearl Harbor. My father played for Squadron A at the Madison Avenue Armory in Manhattan. In fact, since I've been here in England this summer, I've been playing with the British Army team."

The Chief cut him off. "Got it."

Hunt smiled to himself as he replaced the photograph of the Poor Little Rich Girl and her Latin lover on the shelf where it had rested for who knows how long.

When he turned to the Chief, he found that same index finger wagging in his face.

"I need a military attaché this week. Just for the summit. My right-hand man—she is lights-out talented—but she's also lights-out pregnant. Any day now she'll be out on maternity leave. She doesn't know it, but I'm already working on getting a daycare center built in the West Wing. She's that good. But I need someone *now*—for the next five days. Can I count on you, Captain?"

"Sir, yes, sir."

The promptness of Hunt's response gave the Chief pause.

"You sure you don't need a moment to think this over?"

"That won't be necessary, sir."

"Why not?"

"If I don't cut it, you'll fire me just as quickly as you're hiring me right now."

Auerbach clapped him on the back. "Drop whatever you're doing and come with me. And by the way, this week, no polo, *kapeesh?*"

Hunt saluted smartly and silently.

For the duration of the summit, Hunt served as the Chief's eyes and ears, liaising with NATO counterparts as well as representatives of the European Union. As he soon learned, the highest levels of international politics proved to be as treacherous as the battlefields he had braved, a shadowy world full of subtle nuances and sharp edges.

Hunt found the Chief to be the sort of leader every soldier yearns to follow: demanding as well as rewarding. There was no denying that the man could be a challenge to deal with—he made no bones about that—but it was an incredible opportunity, one of the most memorable of Hunt's career. Their late-night downloads quickly became the highlight of Hunt's week as the Chief not only tested Hunt's powers of observation but opened his eyes to the chess match pitting global players scheming to outwit one another. The two were a good fit. The Chief played to win, and Hunt was bold enough to challenge him on matters he had never been privy to. Much to his surprise, the Chief encouraged his curiosity.

By the time Auerbach boarded Air Force One to return to Washington with the President, he had already set in motion a plan to orchestrate Hunt's reassignment to 1600 Pennsylvania Avenue as a White House Fellow.

From day one, Hunt was the Chief's go-to guy at the White House. He prepped, he fetched, he liaised. More often than not, he worked on special assignments, gathering intel and conveying his findings to the Chief. Hunt knew that as long as he could cut it, he had the best job in D.C. And the moment he couldn't, he knew the Chief would send him packing.

Almost a year had passed, and that hadn't happened. Yet.

7

THE CONVOY OF SUBURBANS WOUND its way through San Telmo and onto 25 de Mayo, but none of the passengers paid any attention to the route.

"Didn't you tell me you played polo at West Point?" the Chief asked over the speakerphone.

"Yes, sir. Not at the academy, though. We don't field a polo team anymore. But I was on the equestrian team all four years, and during the summers I managed to squeeze in a match or two here and there."

"Have you heard of a polo player named Juan Harrington?"

"Everybody in polo knows Juancito, sir. I'm one of the lucky ones. I've actually played with him."

"When was that?"

"During the British Season last year. Right before you and I met at Winfield House. While I was at the London School of Economics, Ambassador Catto invited me to Grosvenor Square for a reception honoring the commandant at Sandhurst. General Denaro is his name. He's the one responsible for bringing polo back to Sandhurst. During the reception, the General invited me to play with the British Army team out of the blue."

"What do you mean, 'out of the blue'?" the Chief asked.

"I have no idea how the commandant knew I played polo. I certainly never mentioned it," Hunt said.

"Doesn't matter. Go on."

"General Denaro invited me to practice with the British Army team, and Ambassador Catto insisted I accept. I ended up playing at a series of events, fundraisers against Royal Navy, things like that."

"Was that when you played in that match that the Queen attended?"

"No, sir. The match you're mentioning was the Westchester Cup. My playing in that was a total fluke. I shouldn't have even been on the field. But I'm glad you brought it up, because Juancito played earlier that day—in the Coronation Cup. Don't think for a moment that I'm in Juancito's league. There was an occasion, however, when we were on the same team."

"Go on," Auerbach demanded.

"At a fundraiser for the British Forces Foundation. We were both on the Prince of Wales's team."

A groan echoed over the speakerphone.

"You mind telling me why you've neglected to mention this to me?" the Chief asked.

"To be honest, I would have, but it never came up. The Prince of Wales and his sons are solid polo players, which is all I hope they ever have to say about me. But what about Juancito? I thought he was playing in the US Open this week. What sort of trouble has he gotten himself into?"

"The worst kind," Ambassador Gannon said, his easy smile gone. "His body was discovered a few hours ago in a hotel room in Palm Beach. A single bullet to the head. No arrests have been made, and the police have nothing to go on."

Hunt clenched his fists and closed his eyes. Silence enveloped the sound-proof Suburban. A smoky fog had blown in off the Atlantic. Tiny drops of condensation beaded up on the thick bulletproof windows. Hunt took a deep breath and soldiered up.

"This is a disaster—on so many levels," he said.

"You got that right," the Chief said. "The President's state visit to Buenos Aires is a month away, and an Argentine icon has been murdered on American soil. The guy's a damn UN Goodwill Ambassador. Who the hell knew that? He plays polo. Big deal. Turns out half the world thinks he walks on water, and the other half buys the clothes he shills. This is exactly what the President does not need right now. At my request, the police in Palm Beach have agreed to put off announcing any details about the crime, including the name of the deceased, until tomorrow. But when they do, I can assure you, gentlemen, it will hit the fan."

Ambassador Gannon shuddered.

"That's why I'm throwing you directly into the eye of this shit storm, Hunt," the Chief said. "With your background in polo, your West Point training, and what you've picked up working at the White House, your skill set could come in handy. Hell, it better come in handy. Who, when, why—I need answers, and I need them in time for the President's Daily Briefing tomorrow morning. Captain Hunt, as of this moment, I am designating you the White House liaison to the investigation of the murder of Juan Harrington. Anything and everything you need, you channel through this office, *kapeesh*?"

"Yes, sir," Hunt said. He glanced at his watch. "The last flight to the States left half an hour ago." He turned to Ambassador Gannon. "What about a charter? Who handles logistics at the embassy?"

The Chief's laughter rocked the Suburban. "Told you this guy would hit the ground running, didn't I?"

"That you did, Ari," the Ambassador said.

"Check in with me after you arrive in Miami tomorrow morning," the Chief added.

Hunt was about to respond, but the line went dead. He looked at the Ambassador.

"At my request," Ambassador Gannon said, "American Airlines is holding their nonstop to Miami until you board."

8

AT THE OPPOSITE END OF the hemisphere, a Falcon 2000 received radio clearance from the control tower at Teterboro. As its twin Pratt & Whitney engines revved up, the lone passenger, a silver-haired man clad head to toe in black Hugo Boss, studied a short text message on his cell phone.

Jack Dick grabbed his briefcase and pulled out his iPad. A stylized version of an ancient constellation graced its cover. He powered up the tablet and quickly accessed the lead story from the homepage of the *Wall Street Journal.* One of his underlings had just seen it on the newspaper's website and dutifully alerted his boss with a curt text message.

Jack Dick detested email. The man never took phone calls. His smartphone didn't ring. It didn't vibrate. Everywhere Dick looked, he saw people who were slaves to their technology, automatons whose entire lives were devoted to talking, texting, and tweeting. Not Dick. He answered to no one, and that was especially so when it came to mindless electronic devices.

It was a peculiar loathing because it was Dick's company whose proprietary software facilitated the mass migration of billions of bytes of data that ricocheted back and forth between iPhones, Androids, BlackBerrys, and every other gadget every second of every minute of every hour. This behavior he loathed had made him fabulously rich, but that wasn't the point. With Dick, the point was always about control. There was no way on earth he was about to let anyone or anything become his master.

Per his explicit instructions, each one of his incoming emails was boiled down to a one-line summary by one of his admins and then texted to him. Twice a day—at eleven thirty and at four thirty—he transmitted his responses

to his staff. Not that he ever spoke to them. Instead, he relied on voice recognition software to output his emails. Then, before his office sent any of his
outgoing communiqués, each was meticulously reviewed by his company's legal
department prior to transmission. Having clawed his way on to the Forbes 400
and joined the ranks of the world's billionaires, Dick was obsessed with his
company: its name, its reputation, and above all, its stock price. Any possible
downside was immediately excised, and that included employees as well as any
and all unflattering mentions in the press.

The article in the *Journal* took less than a second to download. Moments
later, as his jet climbed into the night sky, neither its gleaming interior nor the
New York City skyline merited Dick's attention. His only focus was the feature
story about his company slated to run above the fold on Wednesday.

"THE LAST OF THE HIGH-FLYING TECHS"

THE *JOURNAL* REPORTER HAD SPENT months researching the reveal-ing profile of Centaur Corporation. The company's shares not only ranked as one of the NASDAQ's most widely traded stocks; they were the most volatile as well. With daily trading volume routinely eclipsing 50 million shares and $10–$20 price swings typical in most sessions, buying and selling Centaur was like bodysurfing a tidal wave, which is precisely why so many day traders focused exclusively on it. And that was before Monday's first-quarter earnings report. By the time Dick's call with industry analysts wrapped up, the bulls were running wild. Centaur's shares spiked almost seven percent by closing bell.

An ever-increasing number of sophisticated traders—as well as scads of ordi-nary investors hoping to make a quick buck—specialized solely in the company's high-flying stock. The Centaur Phenomenon, as the *Journal*'s reporter labeled it, was one of the last vestiges of the Internet bubble and had grown into an enor-mous get-rich-quick racket complete with weekend seminars, webzines, blogs, trading software, and "risk-free" options schemes. This phenomenon was so pro-nounced that it attracted the attention of the Securities Exchange Commission, which regularly scrutinized Centaur's trading activity.

Like Apple, Amazon, ExxonMobil, and Microsoft, Centaur was a behemoth, the dominant player in a highly competitive, growth-oriented sector. Although many of his peers voiced their respect for Centaur's chairman to the *Journal*'s reporter, he was reviled by even more, a fact that had been thoroughly docu-mented in one of the year's best-selling business books, *Star-Struck: Surviving on*

Centaur. Written by a former C-level executive who reported directly to Dick, the tell-all rocketed to the top of the *New York Times* nonfiction bestseller list and was considered the de facto guide to Dick's secretive empire. Thanks in large part to the publicity it generated, *Star-Struck* earned itself a $10 million breach-of-contract lawsuit courtesy of Centaur's legal eagles.

The *Journal's* reporter devoted a considerable number of column inches to the lengthy list of legal battles that Dick's company was embroiled in, his hardball tactics in the boardroom, and the verbal fisticuffs that were standard fare at his company's annual shareholder meetings.

She also singled out striking similarities on the polo field, where over the course of the previous five years, Dick's polo team had morphed from "welcome newcomer" to "keen competitor" to "brutally efficient machine." As Centaur Polo grew increasingly successful, it too became more combative. Unlike other team owners, Dick didn't go along to get along. He didn't threaten lawsuits. He filed them: against his opponents, against polo clubs, and even against the sport's governing body, the United States Polo Association. Dick was not the least bit smitten by the camaraderie of polo's good-old-boy network. But he loved to win, and thanks to a brand-new lineup and a dream draw in the Open, he was tantalizingly close to claiming his first US Open crown. As the reporter noted, Centaur was the odds-on favorite in the country's most prestigious tournament. Only a victory in Thursday's semifinal separated Dick's polo team from playing for the US Open crown that Sunday. The reporter concluded by noting that "no matter the venue, Jack Dick almost always plays by his own rules—and wins."

Damn straight, Dick grumbled.

In just two days, Centaur's polo team would face its first real test in the Open draw against José Cuervo. It had been a long and tortuous rise, and a costly one too. Over the past five years, Dick had committed millions of dollars to learn the ropes at two of polo's costliest venues: Palm Beach and the Hamptons. Unlike other high-goal team owners, however, Dick didn't dip into his personal checking account to fund his polo team. Instead, it was a marketing expense for a publicly traded company, one with billions in revenue that he, as chairman, CEO, and largest shareholder, controlled outright.

The idea for Centaur Polo was the result of an afternoon's folly. At a charity dinner, Dick's wife bought her husband a polo lesson. Much to his surprise,

he enjoyed the experience of hanging on for dear life as a Thoroughbred galloped downfield. By comparison, racing Ferraris around an oval or bagging the
Big Five on safari in Zimbabwe seemed tame, almost staged. The moment he
heard his boss rave about playing hockey on horseback, Centaur's marketing
chief seized the day. The gist of his idea was that a polo team could become a
tangible symbol for a company whose product line was, for all intents and pur-
poses, very intangible. Polo's highly visual qualities made it the ideal vehicle to
convince Wall Street that the team's aggressive play and take-charge style were
in fact hallmarks of the company. The campaign went far beyond a narrowly
focused corporate sponsorship. Not only did Dick play on his company's team,
but Centaur Polo was celebrated by Hollywood's director *du jour*, who created an
arresting series of high-concept commercials. A slew of CLIOs confirmed the
pricey idea. It also convinced Dick to invest ever-greater sums in his polo team.
From a single lesson, a high-goal franchise was born, a publicity campaign was
created, and with them a tightly choreographed series of parties and press events.

But behind all the glitz and glamour, Dick's sole goal was a simple one: to
drive up Centaur's share price. Jack Dick was not just fixated on his company's
stock. It was his all-consuming passion. Winning was sweet, watching others
lose even sweeter, but beating the Street was the ultimate prize. And one of the
ways Dick scored Strong Buy ratings was by making sure financial analysts did
anything but analyze. At all of his team's matches as well as almost every one of
its practices, Centaur's marketing department set up a lavish marquee next to
the team's own tent. In the confines of this air-conditioned hutch, the business
press, institutional fund managers, and key influencers were plied with Veuve
Clicquot and a gourmet spread prepared to order by Bistro Chez Jean-Pierre.
Dick's ploy went well beyond the finest food and wines; his hospitality was
over the top: the blonder, the better.

It never ceased to amaze him how easy it was to stack the deck this way.
Whenever he barged over for a quick flyby—in between horses or after practice—none of his guests ever talked business. The minute those city slickers
saw eight Thoroughbreds charging down a polo field at breakneck speeds, they
forgot every bit of nonsense about pending litigation or what products were
making their way through the pipeline. The thunder of those horses' hooves
drowned out all thoughts in their minds save one:

Jack Dick is the hardest-charging CEO on Wall Street.

NIGHTFALL HAD COOLED PALM BEACH. On the bike paths and along the beach, couples were enjoying evening strolls, listening to the sound of the surf, or watching the sun's last rays disappear over the Intracoastal Waterway. A few blocks inland, however, the air was hot and prickly. A firestorm had erupted at the Brazilian Court, one that pitted the wheels of justice versus damage control.

"How can you claim to be in charge of this hotel when you can't give me a straight answer to a simple question?" Detective Raul Ramirez asked. "You had no idea what the hell was going on in this suite, did you?"

The hotel's general manager bit his tongue. As much as he wanted to admit the truth, he could not. A well-dressed publicist was making a game effort to justify her client's silence. "What Mr. Motsch means …" she began. She never got an opportunity to finish her sentence.

"That's it. Out of here," Ramirez said.

Everyone froze. Ramirez turned his gaze on one of his underlings. "She's contaminating my crime scene," he yelled.

"But this hotel is my client," she protested.

"And this suite is my scene," Ramirez fired back.

One of Ramirez's lackeys was about to escort the chastened PR flack from the suite when the hotel's director of security interceded and quietly ushered her out. Ramirez turned and set his sights on the general manager.

"One last time," the detective said. A threatening tone tinged his voice. "Was this suite registered in Juan Harrington's name, or wasn't it?"

Fred Motsch avoided any eye contact. The hotel's general manager nervously adjusted his Hermès tie. He tugged on his French cuffs. He pulled his Tom Ford suit jacket taut, cleared his throat, and rubbed the palm of his hand over his five-o'clock shadow.

"The room was most definitely not under Mr. Harrington's name."

A long pause followed. Ramirez's patience was wearing thin. "And?"

Motsch took a long breath, averted his gaze, and repeated the same precise series of nervous tics: tie, cuffs, jacket, throat, face. Then he pinched the bridge of his nose and tugged one ear.

"I am absolutely mortified to have to admit this. It is certainly not typical of the professionalism we instill in our staff here at the Brazilian Court, but Mr. Harrington was not registered at the hotel. The truth is the front desk has no record of any room reservation whatsoever for the Lancaster Suite."

HUNT PASSED ON THE DINNER service. Thanks to the embassy's intercession, American Airlines had not only saved him a seat but had bumped him up to the front of the bus. But he was in no mood for first-class frills. What he needed was a battle plan.

Based on what the Chief said, it was Hunt's task to figure out his highest and best use. A gentle ping broke his train of thought. The captain announced that the 747 had reached its cruising altitude of 39,000 feet. He looked around at the other passengers. Most were fiddling with their touchscreen TVs. A few were still ordering dinner. One thing was certain: There were no Anastasias on tonight's flight.

So close, and yet so far.

Working at the White House had nuked his love life. Actually, working for the Chief had vaporized the teeny bits that Hunt himself hadn't already dashed. He could still hear and see the raven-haired *madrileña* upstairs at La Brigada.

What was I thinking? Who on earth bumps into a beautiful woman like Anastasia and ends up with anything more than a hello-goodbye?

Hunt paused. He knew the answer. The only man who ended up with a woman like that was Juancito. For a moment, cushioned in the silence of first class, he let his guard down and lost himself in the emotions that came with such a sudden death. Suddenly, he knew what his assignment was. And it had nothing to do with Anastasia.

It had everything to do with that summer day in Surrey.

THE SCORE WAS TIED AT 12, *and the clock was about to run out. Play was stalled at midfield when Juancito Harrington, in his inimitable fashion, rode in, turned the ball, and took off for goal. If the match had been one of the major championships that Juancito typically contested and the 10-goaler had been going all out, there would be no question as to the outcome.*

But on this very English afternoon, it was a more laid-back affair, a fundraiser for the British Forces Foundation, and no one, it seemed, was playing for keeps—no one, that is, except the mullet who fouled the world's greatest polo player a few yards shy of the goalmouth. Although the game was as good as over, the referee obliged by calling a Penalty 3, which meant that Harrington's team would get a free shot on goal from 40 yards out. Given that Juancito routinely knocked in goals from beyond the midfield line 150 yards out, a 40-yard Penalty 3 was almost a waste of his time and talents.

Hunt rode over to where his team was gathered. As he approached their huddle, a strange humor was immediately apparent. Instead of confident smiles, puzzled looks were the order of the day. In addition to Juancito, who was obviously the de facto *captain, Hunt's teammates included the Prince of Wales and one of the prince's lifelong friends, a retired British cavalryman with a wicked back shot whom everyone referred to as Mr. Australia. That's what the Prince of Wales called him. That's what the Prince's sons called him. That's what the announcer kept calling him. And that's what Hunt delighted in calling him.*

The Army captain had befriended this notorious character in the not-too-distant past. Naturally, it was on horseback. The intriguing aspect to their introduction was that it hadn't taken place in England or, for that matter, in the States. The best description of the setting was that it was a no-man's-land, one found on the far side of the world at the front lines of the War on Terror. Each had been asked to risk his life, and both had done so without a second thought. Despite their many differences—age, rank, upbringing—they were kindred spirits, and the bond that they forged was grappled with hoops of steel. Since their great adventure, however, neither had seen nor spoken to the other till that summer day in Surrey.

Despite his strong riding skills, Mr. Australia looked like he was about to fall off his horse, he was laughing so hard. As Hunt listened to Juancito sketch out his plan, he soon learned why. It had everything to do with the speechless state of the Prince of Wales. Moments later, Juancito parked his grey mare well off the ball and sat motionless. In place of the world's greatest polo player, His Royal Highness rode out to take the penalty shot. Juancito not only insisted that the Prince take the penalty shot, but he also informed him that much more than just the game was riding on his shoulders. Blow the shot, and the heir to the throne would enjoy the privilege of picking up the dinner tab for both teams at the Ritz Club. Make the shot, and Juancito would top the bill.

The crowd grew hushed as the Prince rode a slow circle toward the ball. His sons were not so circumspect. Both were razzing their father in the low tones that military men use when they choose to be heard and not seen. The Prince paid them—and everyone else—no mind. He cantered easily on his buckskin gelding, eyed his target, and readied his swing. Without warning, his mount began to cheat a little bit to the left. In doing so, the horse veered ever so slightly away from the ball. A rank amateur would have continued his swing and shanked the penalty shot, but the Prince knew better. He gathered his horse and calmly began a second loop.

By this time, his sons had ditched their discreet tones and were calling for the umpire to cancel the penalty shot. Their father was approaching the ball twice, a clear violation of Hurlingham Polo Association protocol.

"Pops, you're breaking the rules," Will yelled.

"You're so out of touch, Pops," Harry blurted.

"Quiet in the ranks," Mr. Australia barked. "Stand down, man. Stand down, I say." It was a wildly absurd, wonderful moment.

Hunt took note of the eerie silence and the pallor of the summer sun in the late afternoon. The pounding of the Prince's horse's hooves on the lush green lawn stilled the other noises. This was polo as it was meant to be played: man and horse sharing a common challenge. Dead ahead, Sandhurst's stately façade towered over the goal.

On the sidelines, hundreds of spectators stared stone-faced at the solitary spectacle. So did all the players, including the Prince's two sons. Everyone was fixated on the conclusion of the match. Everyone, that is, except Juancito.

The mirth in the man's eyes—he was testing a fellow polo player as few would ever dare challenge him—spoke volumes about his love for the game. As the Prince's horse approached the ball a second time, Juancito piped up with some encouragement.

"Sir, mind the windows."

Moments later, a smart swing and a clean hit sent the ball directly into the goal-mouth. The partisan crowd broke into vigorous cheers. The savvy umpire wisely chose to overlook the Prince's two approaches and opted not to call the foul. It was a vintage Juancito moment, and the 10-goaler hadn't lifted a finger.

In the storied history of the game of kings, Juancito was one of only a handful of players ever to win polo's Triple Crown—the US Open, the British Gold Cup, and the Argentine Open—in the same year. Yet he was also capable of enjoying himself in a match of absolutely zero consequence. And that, as everyone who knew him recognized, was what set him apart from every other 10-goaler. That and his godlike talents.

Actually, the remarkable achievement of winning the Triple Crown belonged to both Harrington brothers: Juancito, the lightning bolt; and Cesare, the master-mind. Like his younger brother, Cesare also carried 10 goals, but he possessed an entirely different skill set. The elder Harrington was a field general, an all-seeing, all-knowing strategist. At any moment during a match, Cesare could pinpoint the exact location of every player on an opponent's side—as well as his own—and he could do this without so much as a glance. More importantly, he knew what each player was thinking. Most importantly, he knew what all were capable of. Bolstered by this matchless talent, he was able to plot the progress of the ball much like a grand-master anticipating an opponent's moves on a chessboard.

Neither Cesare's talents nor his looks were as showy as his younger brother's, but among their peers he was equally if not more respected. He was definitely more feared. Although he lacked the intuitive genius of his younger brother, he more than made up for it with clinical precision, be it his horsemanship or his stick work. Cesare wielded his mallet like a surgeon's knife—with brutal efficiency. By comparison, Juancito brandished his mallet like a conductor's baton—with effortless flourishes.

And as everyone who had ever challenged him quickly learned, Cesare was the fiercest of antagonists. Those who had never played against him knew nothing of this *trait, for he cloaked his intense competitiveness in the beguiling Harrington charm. Thanks to his ability to anticipate a play, most of his adversaries rarely challenged him or directly confronted him. Those who did, however, were ruthlessly dispatched by one of his handpicked teammates. Juancito could improvise. He was the artist. Cesare could organize. He was the engineer. The fact that the rest of the world concentrated on his younger brother's showier talents was a set of circumstances that both brothers took full advantage of.*

After the match, the players surrounded Prince Harry, who was tasked with le sabrage—*uncorking a magnum of Louis Roederer with everyone's favorite kitchen accessory: a sword. The Prince cautiously eyed his assignment. Then he looked at his brother. It was safe to say he was not at ease with guillotining the big bottle. Mr. Australia stepped forward.*

"Just pretend it's an unruly subject, man. Off with its head."

As executioners go, Harry was a natural. To the delight of the players and their guests, he whisked the blade along the seam of the bottleneck and cracked the cork off. Another round of cheers followed.

With Ambassador Catto present and Army brass from the Ministry of Defence in attendance, Hunt thought it prudent to abstain from a libation. The moment Mr. Australia spied Hunt's by-the-book behavior, he grabbed a Bass Ale off a waiter's tray and thrust it into his former charge's hand.

"This is the most important part of the match, laddie, the cannonade that concludes the 1812 Overture," Mr. Australia said.

"A thousand apologies, Colonel," Hunt replied.

A broad smile burst across Mr. Australia's face. "Thank you for remembering my once-lofty status. Since our return from the Khyber, I've been relegated to a more clerical role: running the polo operations of Tweedledum and Tweedledee."

"Seems as though you've found yourself quite the foxhole, Colonel."

Haynes raised his glass in a silent appreciation. "Plush? Yes. But nowhere near as challenging as the one you and I crawled out of. You are one of the privileged few who know of my service to the Lion of Panjshir. What should have been my darkest days instead became my finest hour. And you played no small role in that episode, old boy. Let that be a lesson to the both of us."

"Death or Glory," Hunt said and tipped his pint.

"Death or Glory," Mr. Australia replied in a commanding voice.

The Prince of Wales barged into the middle of the cavalrymen's conversation. He had changed out of his polo jersey into a Turnbull & Asser shirt featuring his signature colors, the Prince of Wales plaid. His double-breasted blazer he left unbuttoned. Hunt couldn't help but notice the distinctive insignia of its many gold buttons: three plumed feathers.

"For God's sake, man, don't tell me you believe a single thing this man says off the polo field, do you?" he asked Hunt.

"What makes you think we listen to him when we're playing?" Prince William countered as he and his brother joined the fray. So did the Harringtons.

"You'd be well advised to take my counsel," Mr. Australia said. "I have the high honor and distinct privilege of possessing the best back shot in the British Army, courtesy of Lord Louis himself, who schooled me at Guards in the lost art of backing the ball."

"Lost art is right. Are you incapable of using it anyplace but Guards?" Prince Harry asked. "Not one of us saw you put it to good use today."

Sharp laughs greeted the royal dig.

Mr. Australia looked at the Prince of Wales and slowly shook his head. "They're getting to be as bad as you were at this age." He paused. "I take that back. You were worse." The laughter grew louder. "On top of that, back in the day, Guy Wildenstein and Galen Weston were much too kind to you. They never should have let you play for Les Diables Bleus or the Maple Leafs."

"Is that so?" the Prince of Wales asked.

"Of course," Mr. Australia said with a wry grin. "If they had really wanted to win, they would have played me."

The mock indignation on his face was worthy of a Royal Shakespearean. Wales was laughing so hard, he literally leaned on his sons. Hunt soon found himself chatting with the young British princes and the fourth member of their team, the Saudi prince in charge of the Kingdom's defense ministry. All four of them had pursued military careers. With few exceptions, their polo playing days were over. Unlike their younger years, when each had thrived in competitive tournaments, their play was now relegated to charity matches, fundraisers, events like this very match. Deep down, their cutthroat instincts survived, and Cesare seized on this. He encouraged the sibling rivalry between Will and Harry and insisted on giving their polo manager his cell number.

"Anytime either of you two can break away and join us for a chukker, please, I insist, you call me. Don't call my brother. It's a miracle if Juancito ever looks at *his cell phone. Just call me. Even if it's just stick-and-ball. Juancito and I need to practice too."*

This bit of blarney was greeted by a chorus of mock laughter.

It wasn't long afterward that Hunt watched Juancito go for goal yet again. One by one the princes took off in their separate sports cars. Security tapered off, and bystanders began to mingle with the remaining players. Hunt was surprised by how welcoming the Harringtons were with complete strangers. Both were world famous, the game's elite. For over a decade, they had represented Argentina in international competition, including several triumphant performances in Coronation Cup play before Her Majesty on Cartier International Day at Guards Polo Club. Other monarchs routinely sought out the Harringtons for their services, including the Sultan of Brunei and his brother Prince Jefri, who paid them a multimillion-dollar retainer during the British Season.

The Harringtons were ferried around the globe on megayachts and private jets, yet Hunt watched Cesare enthusiastically pose with a group of giggling Pony Club members for a photograph. Juancito was in the midst of reminiscing with a country squire about a Best Playing Pony long since turned out to pasture. The two were swapping stories like old friends when a redhead in a sleeveless crinkle-cotton dress shyly stepped forward. The next time Hunt looked over, Juancito had an arm around her slim waist. The last time he saw them, the couple was driving off in Juancito's Jaguar.

As the XK convertible left the grounds of the military academy, an arm fell over his shoulders. It was Cesare, taking in the same scene. Neither polo player broke his gaze as the elder Harrington spoke:

"There's not a man on a horse who can stop my brother. Nor a woman who loves life who can refuse him."

THE MOMENT HE SAW HIS brother's lifeless body lying in a septic corner of the emergency room at St. Mary's Medical Center, Cesare Harrington broke into an inarticulate outpouring of grief that rendered him incoherent for the better part of half an hour. His demeanor gyrated from bitter cries to incomprehensible tantrums, yet there was one constant to his behavior. During the entire experience, he refused to leave his brother's side, pushing away nurses and even shoving a hospital staffer who attempted to coax him out of the emergency room. Afterward, when he gave his statement to Raul Ramirez at 9:45 p.m., Cesare refused to abandon his fallen brother. The bossy detective was annoyed at the affront, but secretly he admired the man's unshakable loyalty.

When he finally regained enough composure to answer the detective's questions, Cesare couldn't make sense of his brother's murder. Juancito was the most popular person in polo, quick to make a friend, a man of the people, *un don de gente*. To the best of his knowledge, his brother hadn't been the subject of any threats. Nor had he been involved in any legal proceedings or lawsuits. Cesare knew that point for a fact; their business affairs were completely intertwined.

On the polo field, the brothers played as a tandem—rarely for separate teams and never for competing ones. They commanded a single fee, shared all costs, and split all profits. Back home at their estancia in rural Buenos Aires, a sophisticated embryo transfer program was transforming their polo barn into a lucrative breeding facility.

After lapsing into what seemed like a normal conversational tone, Cesare suddenly broke down yet again. Pleading in Spanish, he begged Ramirez to let him remain that night in the chamber where the lifeless body of his younger brother lay. Much to his chagrin, Ramirez could not consent. By law, the remains had to be prepared for autopsy by the Palm Beach County chief medical examiner. The two argued, their voices escalating to a point that the ER nurses called for security. A uniformed guard arrived, ready to restrain the hysterical man. Much to everyone's surprise, Ramirez waved him off. Instead, he grabbed Harrington by his shoulders and implored him to listen.

"I will find your brother's killer. Justice will be served!"

"Justice can never be served," Cesare yelled back. As he sank to the floor, sobbing uncontrollably, he held on to the white sheet that cloaked his brother's remains. Ramirez covered up the corpse and then turned to an ER physician, whom he ordered to admit Cesare for routine observation overnight.

14

PER THE DETECTIVE'S EXPLICIT INSTRUCTIONS, the admissions clerk meticulously input the pertinent details. They had just come from the ER. There had been a death in the family. The man's younger brother was the victim of a violent crime, and the news dealt a frightful blow. Although Ramirez handled all the questions, the clerk could not help but notice the way Cesare kept chanting Juancito's name. The clerk jotted it down on a sticky note. Cesare only stopped mentioning Juancito when the clerk asked for the name of an emergency contact. Ramirez quickly volunteered his own. He also gave the admissions clerk his personal cell phone number. And he insisted that under no circumstances were any phone calls to be transferred to Cesare's room via the hospital's switchboard.

Ramirez not only waited for a nurse to arrive in the reception area, but he even went so far as to escort the grieving polo player to his private room, which the detective inspected before departing. Half an hour later, as his sleeping pill took hold, Cesare Harrington's agonizing evening came to a close.

And the longest night of Walter Ned's career was just getting under way.

HUSHED CALLS FROM BATHROOM STALLS had long been Walter Ned's stock-in-trade. Over the years, the *News of the World* reporter had woven a web of cops, clerks, deputies, dispatchers, barkeeps, valets, and housekeeping managers at police stations, in hospitals, at rehab centers, and in every name-brand hotel and resort in South Florida. Whenever a big story was about to break, the entire lot knew exactly who to call. As Ned readily admitted to *60 Minutes* when the newsmagazine sent Leslie Stahl to profile the sharp-tongued British journalist:

> "It's not highbrow. It's not critically acclaimed. It's just the stuff that life is made of, and that, dear girl, is what people can never get enough of."

Ned and his editors in East London knew that South Florida was ideal terrain for stalking Names—sports stars, rock stars, tycoons, politicians, and other bold-faced celebrities whose DUIs, divorces, and court cases sent sales of the *News of the World* through the roof. Trysts, tiffs, spats—all were fair game for Ned, who routinely doled out buckets of cash for tips, scoops, and tasteless snapshots.

Although the pay-to-play approach of the *News of the World* was typical of London's raucous tabloids, Ned's dog-eat-dog tactics were the stuff of legend. When the Bush and Gore campaigns duked it out during the 2000 election recount, Ned worked every possible angle at the Palm Beach County Courthouse. He even went so far as to have James Baker III and Warren Christopher tailed to and from their respective hotels.

Breaking the story of Anna Nicole Smith's death from an accidental overdose at the Hard Rock Hotel and Casino had been a massive coup, one Ned snagged courtesy of a dispatcher at the Broward County EMT service that responded to the 911 call.

Ned was beside himself over the news of the polo player's secretive death. Alone among the press in South Florida, he had witnessed the rise of the Argentine Adonis—at Britain's top polo tournaments and in its poshest clubs.

Raul Ramirez he didn't know, but he was more than pleased to get his hands on the private cell phone number of a Palm Beach detective. It was its own little bauble. Best of all, his snitch at St. Mary's Medical Center reported that Ramirez insisted on being present when Cesare was discharged from the hospital the following morning.

Churning out content as quickly as possible may be the mantra of the Information Age, but Ned was strictly old school: Fleet Street blood coursed through his veins. His journalistic training instilled a desire to generate gasps—of disbelief, of disgust and shock. Astonished readers meant empty racks at the newsstands and grocery stores where the *News of the World* enjoyed its greatest following. The greater the horror, the stronger the spike in sales. To that end, Ned nursed a Byzantine network of informants with everything from faux English charm to cold hard cash. The more he heard about Juancito's death, the more his intuition told him that this was *the* story, the one that could go all the way. Like the deaths of Elvis and Jacko, the loss of Juancito was sudden, tragic, and completely unexpected. Not only was the Argentine known and loved by the masses, but he was an intimate of the powers that be on every continent. In a world where news was not made but exploited, there was no telling what kind of media tsunami Ned could create with this story. And right now it was his and his alone.

At one o'clock Wednesday morning, only a handful of people on earth knew about the hush-hush homicide in Palm Beach. But if Walter Ned had his way, billions would remember where they were later that day when they first heard the news about the untimely death of Juancito Harrington.

THE RINGING BLACKBERRY SENT THE Secret Service agent lunging across her bed toward the blinking red light. That wondrous little feature, the one that personalizes a ring tone, left no doubt as to who was calling: the Special Agent in Charge of the Secret Service's West Palm Beach field office. The fact that it was four in the morning mattered not one whit to either agent. What mattered was that a breaking case required immediate action.

On her rare nights on the town, Cristina Cortés was invariably singled out as one of the silhouettes who made South Beach sparkle. Those who competed against Cortés in the triathlons she religiously trained for typically saw her taut body pulling away from them as she lengthened her lead. But to her higher-ups at the Secret Service, Cortés was a throwback who had more in common with old-timers in their fifties and sixties than with the current generation of Secret Service agents. She was definitely tech savvy, but her years with the Miami-Dade Police Department gave Cortés the sort of sixth sense that only a tried-and-true investigator develops from working case after case, interviewing witness after witness, and tracking down the despicable and the desperate.

Her boss quickly doled out her marching orders, including equipment to procure and liaisons to contact.

"Has our support been requested by local law enforcement?" Cortés countered.

"No."

"Is there a currency component that makes the case a natural for the Secret Service?"

"Not at all."

Cortés paused. "Is there a possible terrorist link?"

"Definitely not."

Cortés's last question was the most direct: a contact name at Palm Beach P.D.

"I'll get you that in a couple of hours. All I can tell you is that there's an Army captain inbound from Buenos Aires to Miami and someone *way* up the ladder has made it clear that it's our job to get him up to Palm Beach International ASAP."

A smile lit up her face.

No one in Washington bothered to answer any of his questions either.

THE WHITE HOUSE PRESS OFFICE issued a brief statement on its website and posted an extensive selection of photos featuring the unscheduled breakfast meeting between the President and the Argentine Ambassador to the United States, which took place prior to the Presidential Daily Briefing:

> *At a breakfast in the private residence of the First Family, the President and the Argentine Ambassador voiced their enthusiasm for the President's upcoming state visit to Argentina. "We had a wonderful discussion about our bilateral relations and the commitment of both our countries to free market principles. In advance of my upcoming State visit, I am happy to announce a new series of tax credits for US companies investing in Argentina as part of my National Export Initiative. Free trade among all nations is key to the strength of democracy in the Americas, and expanding foreign trade is an essential pillar to strengthening the US economy," said the President.*

The story was immediately emailed to every media outlet on the White House distribution list, and photos of the President earnestly engaging the Ambassador began to populate websites not only in the US but in Argentina as well.

18

HE MAY HAVE BEEN THE last to board in Buenos Aires, but Rick Hunt was the first out of the gate in Miami. Up the jet bridge and down hallway after hallway—he quickly navigated the bewildering maze that welcomes international arrivals to Miami International. Finally, he stepped out into the cavernous reception area and came face-to-face with a sea of sunburnt skin and loud tropical shirts. A charter flight from an all-inclusive resort touched down just minutes before, and the line would take at least an hour to clear.

Hunt switched gears, pulled out his BlackBerry, and punched in a text:

"Clearing Customs in Miami. Will report after I arrive in Palm Beach."

Hunt had no doubt the Chief had been up since five a.m. Nor would the Chief send a response. He pocketed his BlackBerry, pulled out his iPhone, and typed a second text:

"Anastasia—So sorry to dine and dash. Am confident Hugo and the guys took great care of you. Call you when I return to Bs.As. Ciao! ~ Ricardo"

Hunt put his iPhone away, grabbed his leather briefcase, and picked up the matching duffel that he had yet to unpack since flying out from the same airport two nights before. When he looked up, he noticed a swelling of the crowd. It wasn't going forward. It was . . . parting. Hunt expected a Customs agent with a drug-sniffing dog. Instead, a tall woman in a pinstripe pant-suit emerged. She wasn't a tourist. And she definitely didn't work for one of the airlines. He watched her wordlessly brush off a man in bright orange Bermuda shorts without breaking stride. Hunt eyed her Caribbean features and her dark hair, discreetly pulled back. The closer she got, the more he noticed her luminous brown skin tone. It was especially apparent when she came to a stop directly in front of him.

"Captain Hunt?"

"Yes, ma'am."

"Special Agent Cristina Cortés, Secret Service, West Palm Beach."

"Rick Hunt, US Army, assigned to the White House."

He nodded in the direction of the long lines. "Now get me out of here."

"Follow me, sir."

The Secret Service agent escorted the White House liaison to the head of the line and flashed her badge. Moments later, his passport processed, Hunt found himself following Cortés down several stairwells and through the bowels of the terminal to an unmarked door. Cortés lowered her shoulder, slammed into it, and heaved it open. Outside, sparkling in the bright glare of the Miami morning, one of the agency's Bell 430 helicopters sat purring.

"Pardon my asking, but do you always get shuttled around like this?"

JACK DICK GREETED THE MORNING with a bitter frown. It was well past dawn, yet almost everyone inside his Palm Beach estate was still asleep, which is why, he concluded, they worked for him and not the other way around. Still frowning, he heaved open the massive front door at Casa de los Santos, stepped outside, and yanked it shut with a resounding thud.

But as soon as he emerged from beneath the arched entranceway, it was an entirely different story. There, leaning against Dick's beluga-colored Bentley convertible, was the always eager, easygoing twit who served as his chauffeur, sidekick, and bird dog in South Florida.

"I'm not paying you to take it easy. I'm paying you to make it easy—for me," Rio Garcia crowed, as he repeated one of Dick's standard lines. It was Rio's tried-and-true greeting, the chorus he sang whenever he welcomed his *jefe* to Palm Beach.

A short man dressed like a tall boy, Garcia looked the same as an adult as he did as a teenager and as a child: a mop of black hair, a T-shirt, some jeans, and tennis shoes. Rio's command of English was equally slapdash. Hardly anyone could muster the courage to even speak to Dick, yet when Rio did—and he did so all the time in his broken English—the CEO beamed. Rio's Spanglish was an acquired taste. It required countless hours of intense training to comprehend, but once a fluency was gained, the rewards were many, as Dick himself learned.

Dick slowly made his way around his pricey ride, scrutinizing every detail from the sparkling chrome wheels to his own reflection in the power mirrors.

"How many times have you driven to South Beach since last weekend?"

It was his signature style, speaking in the form of a question. It enabled Dick to assert himself while simultaneously putting everyone else on the defensive.

Rio folded his arms and looked at Dick contemptuously. "Never," he snarled. "I thinks I take her to South Beach maybe twice times. And we never wenting more than 140."

Dick shook his head at the man's insolence. "I imagine I also paid for the gas you guzzled, did I not?"

"Is she my car?" Rio asked, his voice tinged with mock anger. "Why I buy you gas?"

Both men started laughing. The comic interlude was Rio's cue to open the passenger door for his *jefe*. Then he quickly scooted around the convertible, jumped behind the wheel, and pushed the ignition button. The Bentley responded with a roar. Rio pointed the convertible down the serpentine driveway. The crushed shells that lined the drive groaned and popped beneath the tires of the three-ton vehicle.

"What other transgressions do you need to confess? You'd better tell me now. You know I'll find out."

Rio pretended to look perplexed. The truth was he was perplexed. He had no idea what the word *transgression* meant—in any language.

"I very uncomfortable," he said as he turned on to North Ocean Boulevard.

"You should be. Now tell me why."

"Your wife, she calling me all the time. I tell her to not to, but she can't stopping herself."

Dick broke into a belly laugh. The thought of his high-maintenance trophy bride giving this little twerp the time of day was fiction at its finest.

Centaur's CEO had zero tolerance for brownnosers, yet this spark plug was unlike anyone he had ever met. Rio's entire focus was whatever his *jefe* desired. Or could dream of wanting. Many was the occasion that Rio intuited Dick's wishes before Dick even considered the proposition. Two weeks before, Dick casually mentioned that the Miami Heat were on an eleven-game winning streak. The following weekend, he found himself courtside at a sold-out game against the Orlando Magic. Day and night, Rio's lone motivation was to amuse, to entertain, and to facilitate his *jefe*'s every longing whenever he came to Palm Beach.

Restaurant reservations? Rio knew every maître d' in South Florida. Long line at a crowded nightclub? The wad of big bills that Rio kept stuffed in his black leather fanny pack put an end to any predicaments. A few chukkers of polo? Rio could get two teams and twenty ponies ready to play quicker than he could drive Dick to his polo barn in Wellington. Rio knew everyone in polo, not just the Argentines, and that in itself was a bit of an oddity because no one in polo could recall ever having seen him throw a leg over a horse, let alone play a single chukker.

Although his English needed a complete overhaul, Rio's work ethic was case-study material. Without so much as a word from Dick, Rio called ahead to Cucina and ordered Dick's standard breakfast: an egg-white omelette served with asparagus, feta, Greek olives, and arugula. Listed on the menu as "The Rossellini," Rio ordered it with grilled tomatoes, not potatoes; a piece of toasted ciabatta; and a double espresso.

Dick didn't lift a finger. When they pulled up and parked on Royal Poinciana, he didn't walk into Cucina either. Instead, he made a beeline for Main Street News and bought every copy of the *Wall Street Journal*. As an afterthought, he grabbed the local papers. By the time he took his seat at the patio table that Rio snagged, his heart-healthy breakfast awaited him. Not that he touched it. Instead, he flashed the front page of the *Journal* to his sidekick. Rio immediately picked out the stipple portrait of his *jefe*.

"Did you seen him?" Rio asked.

"Do I look blind? Of course I saw my picture, you idiot. Last night. On the Internet."

"¡*Mozo*!" Rio yelled out to their waiter. "Champagne!"

By the time their waiter arrived, Dick was oblivious to Rio's babble about some sort of celebration. Instead, he was entranced by his own press, feasting on his many quotes, savoring the repeated references to his company, and nonchalantly leafing back to the *Journal*'s front page and the sight of his picture above the fold in the official scorecard of American business.

Minutes later, Rio gunned the Bentley over the Intracoastal Waterway and into West Palm. As he floored it down Forest Hills Boulevard, a bottle of Piper-Heidsieck bounced around on the floorboard of the backseat. Dick didn't even notice. He paid no attention to the fact that his breakfast tab was north of $300. What he did notice was that Rio's cell phone was vibrating nonstop in the center console.

Of the many rules his indentured servants were required to observe, *numero uno* was not to use a communication device in Jack Dick's presence—unless, of course, it was to better serve his needs. Texting, taking a personal call, or worst of all, initiating a personal call in his company was no ordinary lapse. It meant that your priorities were not Jack Dick's priorities, and as such, there was no need for you to be on his payroll or in his universe.

As the phone rattled in the cup holder, call after call came in. Both men knew such behavior was taboo, verboten, a mortal sin.

"Does the whole world need to talk to you this morning?" asked Dick.

Rio's forced smile was more a cringe. "I turn her off," he meekly volunteered. He picked up his phone and sneaked a peek at the list of his callers: everyone in polo. Most of his *paisans*, the Argentines, were never up this early. Chastened as he was, Rio couldn't contain his curiosity. With a quick click he accessed the phone's texting feature. There were dozens of unopened messages awaiting him. Before he could even consider reading one, the blaring horn of a speeding 18-wheeler scared the wits out of Rio—and his passenger—as he blew through a red light on Military Trail.

"Put that phone down before you get us both killed!"

Dick was on the phone with his lead secretary. Not that they spoke. Dick dialed directly into her voice mail and left a detailed message doling out the day's marching orders. On those rare occasions when he actually wanted a living, breathing human being to answer the phone, he speed-dialed his private office line. One ring. That's all he would tolerate.

Dick was still on the phone leaving a message for Centaur's marketing chief when the Bentley pulled into Centaur Polo. With two full-sized polo fields, a stick-and-ball pitch, a training track, and a seventy-two-horse stable hewn from massive blocks of Vermont granite, the eighty-acre estate was a stunning showplace, one surrounded by acres of lush green grass, sprays of blooming flowers, exotic plants, and groves of fruit trees. In the center of this complex stood the magnificent barn. At almost any hour of the day, pricey Thoroughbreds poked their heads out of their stalls, eyes ever watchful.

It was here that Dick had closed some of his biggest deals, finessing buyouts and going one-on-one with hedge fund managers itching to invest in something, anything. Just a few months earlier, *InStyle* orchestrated an elaborate photo shoot for the magazine's New Year's issue, featuring Dick and his fellow teammates from Centaur Polo at the barn's *palapa*-style patio. Centaur's marketing department had been pushing the project to the magazine's editors for ages. They had even gone so far as to fly several of the magazine's staffers to Palm Beach, put them up at the Four Seasons, and conveniently overlook the plush robes and the other tchotchkes that they absconded with. The missing items were direct-billed to Centaur marketing. In Dick's mind, the two-day shoot had been a complete waste of time, but to everyone else, the results were a public relations coup. The article, which trumpeted the beginning of the season in Palm Beach, ran ten pages and included grip-and-grins of Centaur's CEO with anyone and everyone. All of Dick's cronies at the Yale Club claimed to have read it. Or so they told him.

On most mornings, the showcase property was a beehive of activity, and that was especially the case when the boss came to town. That's when the players and the grooms did their best to convince Dick what dedicated, hard workers he was overpaying. Today, however, was an exception. Although the barn had been buzzing well before six, a strange quiet greeted Dick and his charioteer. Not a soul hurried out to welcome them.

Dick had forked out more than $50 million to buy this stretch of the Everglades and build his polo complex. Landscapers ripped out acres of melaleuca trees and transformed the overgrown swamp into a lush wetlands preserve. Cash bonuses were paid to Italian stonemasons who toiled through the torrid heat of South Florida's endless summer. Expensive hardwoods were imported to line the stalls and tack rooms. Craftsmen were flown in from England to do the finish work. High above the grounds flew the team's standard, a hand-stitched silk flag that featured the stars of the company's namesake constellation. Everything beneath it belonged to Dick, reported to Dick, and was bought and paid for by Dick, which is why he was so perturbed to see two strangers milling about.

"Can I help you?" Dick asked in a tone that was anything but helpful.

"You certainly can," one said. "Tell us who you are."

"I own this barn," Dick announced in a mean-spirited boast. "I own this property. My name is Jack Dick, and I'm the chairman and chief executive officer of the Centaur Corporation. Who are you?"

"We're with the Palm Beach Police Department, Mr. Dick, and we're here to investigate the homicide of a man who worked for you," one of the plain-clothes detectives responded.

Dick rolled his eyes. He was not the least bit surprised. There was no telling which one of the team's grooms had gotten himself killed at one of those god-awful dives off Okeechobee Boulevard.

With his *jefe* distracted, Rio seized the opportunity to power his phone back up and discreetly scroll through the long list of people who had been calling him. There was no end to the names, and the calls had all come in during the last fifteen minutes. At that very moment, his ringer blared again. Dick's head snapped, his eyes ablaze. Rio pushed the mute button and sent the call directly to voice mail. He put his phone in his pocket. As soon as Dick's attention returned to the police officers, he pulled it out again.

"So sorry to hear this," Dick said, not a trace of sorrow in his voice. "Who was it?"

"Mr. Dick, did you know a . . . ."

Before the detective could finish speaking, Rio's eyes widened as he let out a high-pitched squeal:

"*Juancito!*"

20

AFTER A TURBULENT NIGHT, Cesare Harrington was gently awakened. Following a light breakfast and a cursory checkup by St. Mary's chief physician, the grieving man was escorted by Raul Ramirez, several nurses, and an orderly from his private room to an unmarked vehicle. Unfortunately, any hopes of a low-key departure were shattered by a crack squad from the *News of the World* that had been lying in wait since before dawn.

One team was on foot, and the other, with Ned in command, was in a minivan. Ned also planted lookouts in the hospital lobby: a redheaded bartender and the waitress with the short bob. Both worked at Ned's favorite watering hole. Although the ladies pretended to be visiting a family member, the true nature of their mission was to scrupulously monitor the departure desk.

Thanks to a surreptitious text from the pair, Ned's minions pounced the moment Cesare stepped outside, cornering their prey and cutting off all escape routes. The brazen attack was featured at the *News of the World*'s website in real time. Less than a minute later, just after eight o'clock, an avalanche of email alerts deluged inboxes on six continents. Crowning Ned's email blast was a truly tasteless achievement: a clandestine photograph of the world's most famous polo player . . . in death.

Juancito's expression was beatific, his long locks cascading off his brow. This saintly study was marred by a single, unsightly detail: the blood-encrusted bullet hole that marked the end of his life. A second photograph, snapped from directly overhead, was a more jarring image, one conjured up by Dali himself. It featured the Jekyll-and-Hyde distortion caused by the force of the bullet slamming into Juancito's skull: half his face rested in peace; the other half, a contorted portrait of his violent death.

The lure of a six-figure sum was all Ned needed to induce the admissions clerk to sneak into the ER and document Juancito's corpse with his iPhone. Ned even agreed to pay the man's legal bills—not if but when the hospital's legal team terminated his employment.

The shocking images and breaking news generated a response that exceeded Ned's own lofty expectations. At television stations in South Florida, Great Britain, and Argentina, previously scheduled programming was interrupted with live reports of the Palm Beach polo murder. On talk radio, announcers read Ned's post word for word. The *News of the World*'s report also included links to an elaborate photo gallery that featured Juancito's life from youthful polo prodigy to international icon and UN Goodwill Ambassador. In an effort to stave off sleep during his all-nighter, Ned himself added a treacly voice-over that included personal accounts of witnessing Juancito in action: on the field and off, in London, in Hollywood, and of course, in Palm Beach.

Per Ned's explicit instructions, the *News of the World*'s website went live with the story the moment Detective Ramirez and Cesare Harrington exited St. Mary's.

It was this online assault that alerted almost everyone in polo to Juancito's death. It was this barrage that made Rio's phone ring nonstop as he and Jack Dick were driving down Forest Hills Boulevard. And if anyone in Dick's organization were capable of contacting him directly, this would have been how he would have learned of Juancito's death. But they couldn't. So they didn't. And he hadn't. His only heads-up was a terse text message from one of his underlings that remained unopened until long after the police finished questioning him at his polo farm.

Not ten feet from the hospital's main entrance, Ned greeted Cesare Harrington and Raul Ramirez with white lights and a boom mike. Still feeling the effects of the sedatives, Harrington appeared wounded, almost helpless. The shell-shocked man attempted to respond to Ned's questions but was quickly hustled past the cameras.

Ramirez was livid. The tasteless nature of Ned's intrusion didn't bother him in the least. But getting caught off guard made his blood boil. A shouting match erupted, with Ramirez threatening to handcuff any member of the *News of the World* staff who hindered his progress. Ned refused to be bullied.

"This is not a police state, and from what I can tell, you're not much of a policeman," Ned said as he taunted his foe.

In the ensuing melee, one of the *News of the World*'s videographers was shoved to the ground. An elderly patient lost her footing. Hospital personnel scattered as the police peeled out. And every detail was captured on a pint-sized Sony camcorder.

Ned may have lost the battle, but he won the day. Not only was his scuffle with Ramirez featured live at the *News of the World* website, but it instantly went viral. Just as importantly, Raul Ramirez had been "Waltered," a designation that Ned and his henchmen used to describe earning themselves a place on someone's Enemies List. Unlike other newsmen, who endeavored to stay in the good graces of the law, Walter Ned did exactly the opposite. It was not enough for him to outmaneuver his adversaries. He had to outsmart them. Raul Ramirez now knew his name. The Palm Beach detective now knew his modus operandi. Best of all, Ned had succeeded in turning the hunter into the hunted. His ultimate goal?

To entice the detective to join his long list of informants. Ned had no idea how this would happen. He didn't know if this would happen. But as the two tussled, he made a point of shoving his *News of the World* business card in the breast pocket of Ramirez's suit.

Now the man who detested him most knew exactly where to find him. The only question that remained was whether or not Ramirez would be savvy enough, or desperate enough, to call him.

21

LIKE EVERYONE ELSE IN SOUTH Florida, Jack Dick had been privy to the first reports of the high-profile homicide. A sanitized version of the events surrounding the murder ran in the Local News section of the *Palm Beach Post*, one of the many papers Dick paged through that very morning. But no one—not even those familiar with the crime itself—could have possibly deciphered the terse report, which is exactly what Ari Auerbach intended when his staff convinced Palm Beach P.D. to muzzle the story:

PALM BEACH REPORTS HOMICIDE

10:15 PM EST on Tuesday, April 15

PALM BEACH (AP)—An unidentified man died from a single gunshot wound in Palm Beach Tuesday afternoon. Palm Beach Police responded to a 911 call at a local business shortly after 6:00 p.m. and found the shooting victim unresponsive. According to a police spokesperson, the individual was transported to St. Mary's Medical Center and pronounced dead a short time later. The man's name was not released pending notification of relatives. There were no arrests.

The Chief's subterfuge, coupled with Walter Ned's sneak attack, caught everyone flat-footed, including Juancito's employer as well as his sidekick.

"*Juancito!*" Rio screamed again, his eyes glued to the grisly photograph on his smartphone. Without so much as a word to his *jefe* or the detectives, Rio hurried toward the barn and his *paisans*.

"Hold on, sir. We may need to ask you a few questions."

Rio paid no attention to the policeman.

"Sir," the detective yelled.

Rio broke into a run.

"*Come back here, sir!*"

As one of the detectives hustled after Rio, the other continued questioning Dick. In a complete role reversal, the Grand Inquisitor was demoted to answer-man status on the front steps of his own barn. Jack Dick spent the next hour explaining the intricacies of Centaur Polo as he responded to a long list of the detective's questions, including the exact nature and extent of his financial ties to the deceased.

"So on those occasions when Mr. Harrington played for your team, were he and his brother compensated by you personally, by Centaur's parent company out of New York, or by some other entity?"

"I have no earthly idea."

"Mr. Dick, you just finished telling me that you had final say on every aspect of your polo team."

"I don't write the checks."

"Not even multimillion-dollar ones like you just described? Sounds a little odd, don't you think?"

Dick wasn't thinking. He was fuming. No one ever talked to him like this. *No one.*

22

"CESARE HARRINGTON LAST SAW HIS** brother yesterday morning just before nine. He had a meeting scheduled with their polo manager at their polo barn in Wellington. Mr. Harrington was also there—this makes no sense—to school some green horses?" The Secret Service agent put down her iPad and looked at Hunt.

"No, it actually makes sense," Hunt replied coolly. Thus far, the police report Cortés was sharing was proving to be less than useful. No one at Palm Beach P.D. had any idea who Juancito was, what he did, or why his homicide was of international importance. Hunt and Cortés were seated catty-corner in the cabin of the Bell 430. Both wore noise-canceling headsets, which heightened the clarity of each spoken syllable to the point that Hunt picked out a slight accent in Cortés's voice.

"Fifteen minutes till touch down in Palm Beach," the pilot announced.

Out the east side windows, Hunt could see tract homes and garden apartments crammed into every available square inch of Fort Lauderdale. He did his best to pick out the few local landmarks he could recall from previous visits. But the last of the large citrus groves had been plowed under, and the one or two cattle ranches he remembered were now office parks or subdivisions.

Hunt's first visit to South Florida took place when he was a cadet at New Mexico Military Academy. Back then, his definition of big-time polo was loading up a couple of Quarter Horses and hauling them to a tournament in Midland or Santa Fe. By comparison, Palm Beach Polo and Country Club was otherwordly. Hunt was the teenage version of a green horse—full of talent but untested—and the week he spent competing for a spot on the national team was his initiation to the ways of the world of high-goal polo. After West Point, the few times he played in South Florida had been at Royal Palm Polo Club. Yet he couldn't locate it.

It can't be gone, he thought. But it was.

The absence of his old stomping ground hit home, particularly in light of Juancito's death. He had first witnessed the Argentine's dazzling abilities at Royal Palm. Hunt was shocked at how good Juancito was. He wasn't just better than the teenager himself. He was better than everyone else on the field.

"Was there anything unusual the Harringtons discussed?" he asked.

Cortés scrolled through the police report. "A lot about horses."

Hunt let out a laugh.

"What's so funny?"

"What else would two Argentines discuss in a polo barn? Climate change? No, they discussed which of their horses had been playing well, which ones needed to be worked, which ones they might sell, and who was selling good ones. They also talked about which horses they would play in tomorrow's semifinal game and the order they would play them in. That lineup is critical, especially in a key match, so I'm sure they touched on it. Polo players are horsemen. I promise you Juancito and Cesare talked about horses this way when they were ten years old. They talked about them this way the day Juancito died. It's just who they are. Please, go on."

"Then Mr. Harrington went out riding while his brother reviewed some paperwork with their polo manager, an Englishman."

"Haynes. Colonel Neville Haynes. Queen's Royal Lancers."

Cortés looked up. "Correct again, sir."

"Now you know why I was sent here. I have no investigative training. And my background in military intelligence may not be of any use. But I do know polo, and I know a lot of people in polo, and many of them are in Palm Beach right now. I assume the Secret Service is on the case because of Juancito's status as a foreign dignitary."

"That's right. Unfortunately, he wasn't on our radar until after his death. Beyond that, all I can tell you is that someone in Washington wants this solved *right now*."

"Not only is Juancito a national hero back home, but next month the President has a state visit to Argentina."

Cortés groaned over the headphones. "State visit? What a diplomatic nightmare."

"At the White House, my job is to get the right people the right information as quickly and concisely as possible. Can you hear the clock ticking?"

Cortés nodded.

"So can I," Hunt said. "Let's keep going."

"Tell me about this colonel," she asked.

"The ultimate insider. Neville Haynes has probably spent more time at St. James's Palace than most members of the Royal Household."

"Is that a good thing?"

"As assignments go, serving as polo manager to the Prince of Wales is as good as it gets. Haynes spent the better part of his career in that capacity. The two were schoolmates at Gordonstoun. Prince Charles went on to Trinity College, Cambridge, and Haynes attended Sandhurst. It's Britain's equivalent of West Point. Then he joined the Queen's Royal Lancers. A stout polo player too. Carried 5 goals. Longtime member of Guards."

"What's Guards, a military unit?" Cortés asked.

"No, it's a polo club at Windsor on Smiths Lawn in the Great Park. The Duke of Edinburgh was one of its founders. The Queen's Cup, Coronation Cup—all sorts of high-goal polo are played there during the British Season. High-goal polo is the best polo there is, the only polo the Harringtons play."

"What sort of a partnership did Haynes have with the Harringtons?"

"From what I gather, a very profitable one," Hunt said. "Want to buy a Harrington polo pony? Haynes is in charge of that end of the business. Traditionally, that's the way polo players make the principal portion of their income—buying and selling horseflesh. These days, there's not a world-class team that doesn't have half a dozen Harringtons in its barn. It's like ordering a Purdey over-and-under or a made-to-measure Hermès saddle. I can't imagine what they charge. Last I heard, they had gone into embryo transplants in a big way. But the key is the Harringtons themselves; they have the touch. Just the fact that a horse has been in their barn doubles its price."

"Any chance that Haynes might be a suspect?"

"Doubt it. I know the man. Served with him overseas. Like most Brits, he tolerates Argentines quite well. Has to. Nobody plays polo better, and the Brits consider polo one of their noblest traditions. On top of that, didn't you say the colonel was at the barn yesterday morning?"

Cortés nodded.

"I don't buy the idea of him hanging around the barn in Wellington with Juancito all morning and then trailing him twenty miles back to Palm Beach to murder him at some hotel. Anyone who has played polo as long as Haynes knows a dozen different ways to end a player's life, and almost all of them can appear accidental."

"For instance?"

"In a polo match, there's a highly dangerous maneuver called giving someone the back legs. Think of two Formula One drivers going all out down a straightway. Then, without warning, the one in front slams on the brakes. In polo, the guy in back is a goner. The only thing his horse can do is run right into the back legs of the horse in front of him. The back horse loses its footing and slams its rider into the ground. You don't walk away from a wreck like that. They cart you off the field in an ambulance."

"With all due respect, Captain Hunt, how would you have murdered Mr. Harrington?"

Hunt leaned back and crossed his arms. "Remember your comment about green horses?"

Cortés nodded.

"That's the term polo players use to describe a horse that's being schooled. Turning a green horse into a made polo pony takes years."

"OK."

"If I were out to murder Juancito, I'd make it look like one of his green horses was the culprit. They're young, headstrong, and incredibly powerful. As great a horseman as Juancito was, no one would think twice if a green horse kicked him in the head or dragged him to death. Haynes would have had every opportunity to set a trap like that at the barn. At a hotel? Has to be an outsider."

"Got it." Cortés turned back to her iPad.

"They finished chatting before nine, and Cesare Harrington never saw his brother alive again. He left the barn before his brother finished schooling his horses. Their polo team has a big game tomorrow, so in the afternoon he didn't return and had no way of noticing his brother's absence. Palm Beach P.D. tracked down Cesare at his office, one he shares with his brother. At the time, he was on a conference call with the director of the charity he and his brother jointly oversee. Prior to that, he had lunch with Jack Dick's chauffeur, a man named Rio."

"The one and only Dario Garcia. The world's greatest gofer. I can assure you he's in the middle of all this."

"Right you are, sir. What's his story?"

"In high-goal polo, team owners—they're called sponsors or *patróns*—pick up the tab for everything: the players, the horses, travel costs, lodging, and all sorts of other expenses. And that's where Rio comes in. He's an integral part of the Harringtons' organization. Always has been. Those three are from the same little sleepy town outside Buenos Aires. Their fathers were in the cattle business together. Rio's job is to make sure that whoever sponsors the Harringtons thinks that polo is the greatest thing that ever happened to them. Thanks to Rio, guys like Jack Dick get the best tables at the best restaurants, meet the most interesting people, and if they're so inclined, wine and dine the prettiest young things. The better Rio works his end of the business, the less Jack Dick notices he's dropped an extra million here or an extra million there."

Hunt stole a look out an oceanside window. For the first time since they took off, a break appeared in the endless parade of box-like condo complexes that crowded the beach from Miami and Fort Lauderdale to Boca and Delray Beach. Packed parking lots and crowded pools gave way to ever-larger seaside estates with guesthouses and beach houses and cabanas. One stood out above all the others.

"Bingo," Hunt said. Cortés unclipped her seat belt and scooted over for a look. Beneath them, a crescent-shaped Mediterranean villa was bathed in morning light.

"Mar-a-Lago," she said.

"Let me guess—you've been there a time or two."

"Dozens. And I was on the clock every one of them. You?"

"Only once," Hunt said. "For polo."

The twenty-acre private club looked just as enchanting as the night Hunt and his teammates enjoyed an elegant dinner there, one lit by lanterns and served with precision by liveried servants. Hunt shook his head at the memory of that showboat waiter presenting the Rubirosa. One mansion after another, each with high hedges and immaculate grounds, passed beneath them.

"Same story with The Breakers?" he asked.

Cortés nodded, and Hunt gazed at Henry Flagler's historic resort, its twin-towered façade dominating the view to the eastern horizon. Designed to evoke Rome's Villa Medici, the majestic structure rose seven stories above an enormous expanse of the vivid foliage, lush gardens, and manicured fairways that fanned out from the regal entrance off South County Road.

The pilot cut in over the intercom as the helicopter banked left over the Intracoastal Waterway. "Final approach to Palm Beach International."

Cortés scooted back and buckled her seat belt.

Looking down on West Palm, traffic was backed up for blocks leading up to a drawbridge. Its giant leaves were heaved open to allow a sloop with a towering mast to glide out. Only a couple of sailors were visible on deck.

"People in Palm Beach play by their own rules," Hunt said. "Every time I come here, I think I learn one or two more. But unless you're from here, unless you're really a part of things, you never learn them all."

"I get the idea that both of us are going to learn a lot very quickly," Cortés said.

The helicopter's forward momentum began to slow. Hunt and Cortés sat back.

Cortés picked up where she had left off.

"The two had a late lunch. Cesare and Rio called Mr. Harrington several times and left messages for him to join them at the Palm Beach Grill. Neither got a return call. At the time, Cesare didn't think much about it. That obviously changed after Palm Beach P.D. arrived."

The helicopter touched down and began to power off.

Cortés unbuckled her seat belt and was reaching for the door handle when Hunt held up a hand. "Pardon me, sir," she said and settled back in her seat.

"You never mentioned what he was doing there."

"Who? Where?" Cortés asked.

"Juancito. The Brazilian Court. Did Cesare venture a guess as to who his brother might be meeting?"

Cortés slowly smiled.

"All he would say was that his brother rode many mares."

23

AFTER SNARING CESARE HARRINGTON AND Raul Ramirez in their trap outside St. Mary's Medical Center, Ned and his unshaven cohort celebrated their massive coup on the short drive to his digs in West Palm Beach. His seedy flat also doubled as the South Florida editorial office of the *News of the World*. During the brief ride, Ned's retort to Ramirez achieved *Monty Python*–like status among the crew.

"'This is not a police state, and from what I can tell, you have the worst comb-over in three counties!'" the soundman crowed.

"'This is not a police state, and from what I can tell, you're a first-rate wanker!'" one of the cocktail waitresses added.

All eyes turned to Ned, who was riding shotgun in the front seat. To everyone's surprise, their fearless leader failed to join in the fun. Instead, he reached over and switched stations on the satellite radio. A few minutes earlier, they had erupted in cheers when word of their scoop was broadcast internationally on BBC World Service. Now Ned was silent, lost in thought, plotting his next steps, charting the course of the biggest story of his career.

Ned's two-bedroom flat was situated at the wrong end of Clematis Street, far from the hip restaurants and noisy dance clubs close to the Intracoastal. To its credit, the dingy end of Clematis was home to the Palm Beach County Courthouse as well as West Palm P.D. Ned touted this proximity and price as the drivers behind his choice of domicile, but the truth was he chose the blue-collar address for a single solitary reason: O'Shea's, the Irish pub that occupied the bottom floor of the building.

Like all London-schooled journalists, Ned knew only one way to end the day: by downing a pint. Guinness and Harp were on tap at O'Shea's. So were Stella Artois, Bass, and English cider. There were darts and billiards and nostalgic posters from the old sod, but it was the Guinness and the Harp that sealed the deal. At any hour of the day, a well-made Black and Tan could be had at the first hint of bad news. Or good news.

But not now. Ned and his motley crew made their way upstairs to his apartment. In the living room, cheap folding tables were stacked with local newspapers and glossy magazines. Computer monitors streamed stories from South Florida's leading news portals. Each was running the breaking news about the crime that was labeled "the Palm Beach polo murder." One even played the video feed from the *News of the World*'s YouTube channel featuring Ned and his band of merry newsmakers stalking Cesare and his police escort.

Ned could have cared less. He logged on to Skype and patched in to the news desk in Wapping, the tabloid's East London headquarters. The death of Juan Harrington had displaced a gruesome car bombing outside an Iraqi mosque as the world's number-one news story. The metrics at the tabloid's website had gone through the roof as thousands of websites linked to Ned's reports. His news director told him to drop everything and gave him carte blanche to pursue the story. Ned abruptly ended the call. He turned and faced his team.

"Do any of you have any earthly idea what's next on my list?" he asked no one in particular.

"A gin and tonic?" joked a videographer.

Scattered laughs broke out. A wily smile crossed Ned's face. He loved a well-placed cheap shot, even at his own expense.

"Already had it," he said. "At about three this morning. You know that bottle of Beefeater Dry that everyone pretends I don't keep in this desk drawer?" His colleagues chortled. Ned cut them off.

"What's next for me is not a drink," he said. "What's next for you and for me and for everyone at the world's greatest newspaper is to take this story all the way. We broke it. Now let's own it."

TWO DECADES. THAT'S HOW LONG Fred Motsch had been slaving away in the cutthroat South Florida hospitality racket. Finally, two years before, he rose to the top tier as general manager of a true gem, Palm Beach's Brazilian Court.

And now none of that would matter. Not the AAA Four Diamond Award. Not the Mobil Four Star rating. Not the rave reviews for Café Boulud. Not the record revenues that exceeded all forecasts and earned him a tidy bonus. Not anymore, now that his career was ruined.

Like the pro he was, however, Motsch was determined to go down with the ship. By seven Wednesday morning, he was back at the Brazilian Court, dressed in his smartest Brioni. He knew that the obnoxious detective with the ghastly comb-over would return much too early, raise more eyebrows, and continue to wantonly tarnish his property's sterling reputation.

Motsch was on the mark. The same two investigators who left after midnight were back at eight. Within an hour, five hotel employees had identified the female occupant of the Lancaster Suite the previous day. Thanks to her distinctive Gucci sunglasses, she was easy to pick out on the hotel's closed-circuit cameras. One by one the witnesses were escorted to the ballroom and their statements taken. Much to his dismay, Motsch was forced to endure this painful procedure as well. Afterward, he walked back to his office, shell-shocked by the crime and dismayed at the identity of the primary suspect.

As he passed the Frédéric Fekkai Salon and Spa, the manager caught his attention with an exaggerated wave. Motsch dreaded the idea of speaking to anyone at this moment. He turned away, but Cha Cha gestured wildly for him to come inside.

The moment he opened the tall glass door, she held a finger to her lips. Usually, Cha Cha was an absolute chatterbox. Now she wouldn't say a word. He stepped toward her, and she motioned frantically down the hallway to the treatment rooms. Motsch was clueless. He pointed a finger at himself and then toward the back of the salon. She shook her head, "NO!"

He had no idea what she wanted him to do and merely stood there.

Cha Cha looked like she was at wit's end. With a commanding gesture, she ordered him to her side. He made his way around the counter. She slid the appointment book in front of him and pointed to a client's name, one whose spa treatment was already well under way.

Like Motsch, Cha Cha had been one of the five witnesses who identified the woman behind the Gucci glasses. Now she knew where the woman was. So did Motsch.

As if to confirm the appointment book, a throaty snort emanated from a treatment room. Many a man found the laugh attractive in a Julia Roberts sort of way, but not Motsch. Not today. He raised a finger to his lips. Cha Cha nodded.

He left the salon and made his way back to the ballroom.

Fred Motsch knew his day was about to get much worse.

"NO WAY," RAUL RAMIREZ SAID.

The forensics technician nodded his head in disbelief.

"No one's got cojones that big—not even in Palm Beach," Ramirez said. The tech continued nodding.

"We've got her on tape arriving at 9:09 yesterday morning and leaving just after 12:15. In between, they do it in how many different places?" Ramirez asked.

"Sofa, ottoman, vanity, tub, plus a little hanky-panky in the guest bedroom."

"Not in that big bed?"

The technician shook his head.

Ramirez furrowed his brow. *What sort of lowlife does it on an ottoman but not in a bed?*

"And you're telling me she's right here, right now, at this very hotel where she murdered this guy?" Ramirez asked.

The technician nodded. "The manager said she requested a car to come pick her up this morning. The driver dropped her off before eight. Since then, she's had a deep tissue massage, and she's getting a manicure and pedicure right now."

"And she hasn't heard a word about the news?" the detective asked.

"The spa is phone-free. Some total relaxation thing. No cable. No news. Nothing. She'll be there all morning long."

Ramirez made the sign of the cross, kissed his thumbnail, and mumbled a word of thanks to his Savior under his breath.

"Seal off the spa." Despite the fact that the two were by themselves, he spoke in a steely whisper. "Cut off every bit of outside communication. Replace the hotel employees with crime scene investigators, and remove every other guest as quickly and quietly as possible. You got it?"

The technician nodded.

"By the time she's finished getting primped and pampered, I want hair, I want fingerprints, I want DNA. I want every shred of forensic evidence you can get your hands on. This is our one chance. Don't blow it."

This time, the technician nodded emphatically.

"When you've got everything we need under lock and key, then it will be time to take her on a little tour."

As the tech hurried off, Ramirez stood absolutely still. For the first time since being informed of Juan Harrington's murder, he felt real emotion, and it had nothing to do with the crime or its victim.

His stomach grew queasy. He knew what he had to do, but he couldn't stand the thought of doing it. He absolutely detested the idea. But only one individual was capable of inflicting the level of punishment he had in mind for this spoiled brat.

Ramirez reached in the breast pocket of his suit coat and retrieved Walter Ned's business card. The thought of calling the man pained him. But in his gut, he knew he had little choice. Personal likes and dislikes mattered little compared to his vendetta, avenging the wrongs perpetrated against him, wrongs he could never right, wrongs where justice would never be served, wrongs where the judicial system itself was the perpetrator.

In his mind, Walter Ned was a thug who violated every standard of professional decency. On top of that, Ned somehow managed to snag Ramirez's cell phone number. The cretin actually had the gall to call the detective and ask him to confirm specific details about the murder—with Cesare Harrington sitting right beside him. Ramirez swore to himself that when next they spoke, he would be arresting the slime ball. And now he was about to go back on his word.

26

IT ALL STARTED WITH A call from one of the regulars at the county jail, a shopworn prostitute whose career had topped out a few years earlier at a strip club off I-95 called Rachel's. She knew who to call—a good-looking vice officer who regularly dropped any charges by letting her cop a plea in the backseat of his cruiser—and she told him the basics.

A high-profile financier had been schooling her stepdaughter and a few girlfriends in the ways of the world. The guy was no ordinary whack job. At his private pool parties, naked schoolgirls were the party favor of choice. All were underage. All were in over their heads. On several occasions, he and his pals had taken the show on the road by flying the harem to the Bahamas on one of his private jets.

"Did they have sex?" the cop asked.

She hesitated.

"Did they or didn't they?"

"She won't tell me."

"Then why are you wasting my time?"

"Because she's making more money playing Marco Polo in the nude than I'm getting working all night on Dixie Highway."

The cop had already hung up.

Child Protective Services was too busy dealing with dirtbags they knew about than to waste time with one they didn't. Her last best hope was Palm Beach P.D. It should have been her first call. The moment Raul Ramirez learned about the $500 teenybopper bump-and-grind routine, the chase was on. This would be no ordinary takedown. It took time and manpower, but Ramirez had both. He spent months building an airtight case: subpoenaing cell phone records, staking out the huge mansion behind a maze of twenty-foot-tall Ficus, tracking the arrival and departure of the man's Boeing Business Jet at Palm Beach International, surveilling the comings and goings of the teenage girls, and videotaping their detailed descriptions of the perpetrator, his digs, and his pool parties.

Ramirez's investigation was some of the best work of his career—thorough, meticulous, and by the book. Too good, in fact. When he was done, he didn't think twice about submitting his probable cause affidavits and case-filing packet to the State Attorney's office. He should have.

In Palm Beach, money talks loudly in hushed tones. Ramirez knew this, but he had no way of knowing the depth and extent of the financial and other ties that his perp enjoyed with local power brokers on both sides of the aisle. But the Assistant State Attorney who reviewed the case did. So did his boss. So did the select few who manipulated the inner workings of the judicial system.

Days turned into weeks, yet nothing happened. As weeks turned into months, Ramirez realized he had been gamed. Instead of going directly to trial, hidden hands skillfully derailed any chance of a successful prosecution. Rather than letting Ramirez's ironclad police work speak for itself before a petit jury, select evidence was carefully presented to a grand jury. When an indictment was handed down, the perpetrator was charged with none of the sex crimes that Ramirez uncovered: statutory rape, unlawful sexual activity with a minor, and an endless number of Mann Act violations. The lone indictment, a misdemeanor charge of soliciting a prostitute, was quickly dismissed, a point the press gleefully trumpeted for days and weeks.

Ramirez knew about Palm Beach's addiction to money and power. But it had never talked down to him before. It may not have always respected him, but it never blew him off like a nobody. He wasn't the nobody everybody had read about. And he would prove that this very day.

27

AT PALM BEACH INTERNATIONAL, HUNT and Cortés made their way off the heliport toward an unmarked police cruiser. The plainclothes officer behind the wheel waved them over. As they got in, dispatch broke in over the police radio.

"Suspect is being transferred to Palm Beach P.D. 10-22 to headquarters," the dispatcher said.

"10-4," the driver said. He turned to Hunt and Cortés.

"Looks like we've got our shooter."

28

EVERY JOURNALIST, EVERY PHOTOGRAPHER, and every camera crew in the Palm Beaches was arrayed on the front steps of the Palm Beach Police Department. No one had any idea what captured beast was about to be paraded before them, but the odds-on favorite was Juancito's murderer.

Typical police procedure mandated that all suspects be transferred to headquarters via the building's discreet basement entrance. It was less provoking, more professional, and altogether cleaner. But professionalism no longer mattered to Raul Ramirez. Clearing his name did.

It had been ages since a felony suspect had been so regally received, and a carnival-like atmosphere instantly sprang up on the steps. All three northbound lanes of South County Road were clogged with news trucks and closed to traffic. There was barely enough room for Ramirez's Expedition to thread the gap between the sidewalk and the TV trucks. The feeding frenzy began the instant the detective pulled up in his SUV.

"Oh my God!" one reporter shrieked.

"Look who it is!" another exclaimed.

"It's Kelly!" another screamed.

Ramirez emerged from the passenger side of the front seat, flung open the back door, and yanked his platinum-haired captive out of her cage. In her short tennis dress, tight top, and ponytail, his thirtysomething prey was picture perfect, fresh from her spa treatments, her new spray tan aglow.

"Is it true, Kelly?" one reporter yelled. "Did you kill Juancito?"

Hands cuffed behind her back, she defied her captors and chose to remain silent.

"Kelly, how long have you and Juancito been lovers?" another howled.

She didn't flinch. Her seething stare was focused on the detective.

"Why did you kill that beautiful man?" another screeched.

In the midst of dodging cameras, microphones, and cheap shots, Kelly misjudged a step, caught the tip of her tennis shoe, and fell down. The detective didn't lift a finger to break her fall. He made a point not to help her up either. Instead, he assumed a boastful stance over his suspect and posed for the cameras. When he finally looked down, he noticed that her tennis dress had come to rest in a revealing manner.

It was Raul Ramirez's finest moment—watching his victim grovel as she attempted to regain her feet. He eyed the feeding frenzy with delight. Like carrion, the press was closing in on another's kill. Not one of them thought to reach out and offer a helping hand. But they were helping him, all right. That bungled case was already forgotten.

Bare-assed and bruised, Kelly was forced to roll to her knees on the concrete steps. Tiny bits of rock bit into her soft skin. Yet she didn't wince. She stood up. She was taller than he was. Looking up at her, he expected to see tears in her eyes. What he recognized was fiery determination. The detective grabbed her by the arm. He led her up the steps to the broad porch that led inside.

She taunted him under her breath. "Too bad your stage show is over."

Ramirez's cruel smile returned. "Not yet, my dear."

He shoved her toward the front doors.

There, ready to have his way with her, stood an overeager Walter Ned. Kelly hesitated. Ned's camera crew blocked every entrance—and behind her the pack of reporters were stampeding up the steps, yelling more questions. Ramirez grabbed her cuffed wrists and thrust her toward Ned, who had launched into another Internet exclusive: a live interview with America's most beautiful murder suspect.

"We don't have much time, Kelly dear, so forgive me if I cut to the chase. Was the Brazilian Court where you and Juancito usually rendezvoused, or did the two of you have sex in all sorts of different hotels here in Palm Beach?" he asked.

You lousy ingrate! she thought to herself.

"Kelly , are you familiar with the 7UP Club? It's a scavenger hunt of sorts."

I knew I never should have let that slip!

As Ned's questions continued, all she could think about were the countless occasions when she had shared juicy bits of gossip with the man now mocking her. And this was how the thankless bastard returned the favor.

A *News of the World* cameraman captured crude close-ups of Kelly's public shaming: Ned, gleefully poking his microphone at her mouth; Kelly, dodging, glaring, wincing, biting her lip, and all the while not saying a single word. When Ramirez finally hauled her inside, Ned's last cheeky question hung in the air:

"Is it safe to say that you and your husband have an open marriage?"

29

"FOUL PLAY TRIPS UP CENTAUR'S POLO-PLAYING CEO"

THE SELL-OFF BEGAN THE INSTANT the *News of the World*'s email alert
went out: Jack Dick's wife had been arrested for the homicide of polo superstar
Juan Harrington.

At the tabloid's website, users could download a 10-minute podcast nar-
rated by Walter Ned, complete with photos of Kelly Dick arm in arm with
Juancito, Juancito with Dick, and a tawdry shot of Kelly sandwiched between
her dead lover and her cuckolded husband in a cozy pose that ran in *InStyle*. It
would be a record-setting day for the tabloid's online portal.

Centaur's stock set new records as well, the kind that gives corporate boards
nightmares. Day traders feasted on the unending stream of online bulletins
and email alerts from Dow Jones and Bloomberg that chronicled Centaur's
tanking share price. The bulls fled the ring, and the company's stock, which
opened at $157 and had enjoyed an early rally, skidded to $147 by early afternoon. And the bad news only got worse.

The Harrington murder was not merely the lead story at the *News of the
World*'s website. It was the biggest story at every news site. *CNN World News*
broadcast footage of the stage show on the front steps at Palm Beach P.D.
every half hour. The massive sell-off and Centaur's tanking price dominated
CNBC, particularly once Centaur's plummeting shares began to drag down
the NASDAQ. *Entertainment Tonight* asked viewers to go to the show's website and cast their vote on whether the beautiful blonde killed the polo player
in a lover's quarrel, over money, or because she was an Aquarius.

In London, BBC World News pieced together an extensive retrospective on the legacy of the greatest player in the history of the game of kings. In Argentina, the 24-hour news channel, Todo Noticias, canceled its regularly scheduled programming and began broadcasting special reports complete with exclusive interviews and updates. By sundown in Buenos Aires, there was no news, no weather or sports.

It was all Juancito.

30

WITHOUT A WORD, THEY BEGAN to congregate. No one told them where to go. No one told them why to go. Shortly after the first news broke, thousands of *porteños* thronged to Palermo, the colossal stadium in Buenos Aires that is the epicenter of Argentine polo and the site of some of Juancito's most memorable triumphs in the world's greatest polo tournament, el Campeonato Argentino Abierto—or, as the Argentine Open is more commonly known around the world, *el Abierto*.

Shops were shuttered. Schools were closed. Police diverted traffic along Avenida Libertador. Security at the American Embassy was heightened "strictly as a precaution." A police spokesman estimated that the crowd of mourners numbered in the thousands.

The live television broadcasts from the polo grounds only made matters worse. Thousands more began to stream into Buenos Aires, taking the train to Estación Retiro, crowding Plaza San Martín, and joining the ranks of the faithful. By nightfall, all of Argentina was in mourning. By then, the President's afternoon meetings were canceled, and she returned to Casa Rosada. At nine that evening, she stepped out onto the balcony of the north wing to address the teeming crowd in the Plaza de Mayo. In a dramatic speech, one widely considered to be the best of her Presidency, she lamented the loss of their country's greatest hero. Like angry children, the crowd reacted with a tantrum-like outburst, one the President did nothing to interrupt.

By the time her speech concluded, the nation's flags were flying at half-mast.

31

"WELL, WELL, WELL," HUNT MUTTERED. "Someone has come a long way since the Indoors at the Garden."

Hunt and Cortés stood side by side before a long glass window. On the other side of the one-way glass in a very empty interrogation room sat a shapely blonde in a Stella McCartney tennis outfit. From her flawless fake bake to her perfectly unscuffed tennis shoes, it was clear that she had mastered the art of self-presentation.

"Sounds like you two go back a ways," the Secret Service agent said.

Hunt nodded. "That we do."

"Should I consider you a material witness?"

Hunt's eyebrows went up. "Let me put it this way. Once upon a time, *everyone* in polo had the hots for Kelly."

"What's her story?"

"A dressage rider, and a damn good one. She was still competing when I first came to town. Didn't meet her. Just saw her training. A bunch of us were here prepping for a tournament. We were all so green—I think the oldest guy on our team might have been seventeen—and Palm Beach was way beyond anything we had ever experienced. It could have been another planet. It *was* another planet."

The Secret Service agent smiled.

"And watching this gorgeous brunette train in the ring quickly became the center of our universe."

"Do you mean she's not a natural blonde?" Cortés asked with a smile.

"I can't remember the last time Kelly was a brunette. Or the last time she competed. It didn't take long for her to figure out that the ones having the fun didn't ride horses. The ones having the fun owned horses."

"Sounds like she's a smart cookie."

Hunt nodded. "Polo in Palm Beach is all about upgrades: better horses, better teams, and in Kelly's case, richer men. I gather she was a charter member of the 7UP Club."

"What's the 7UP Club?"

"A not-so-secret society of enthusiastic young ladies. In polo, players are rated on a 0-to-10 scale. A 0-goal player is a rank amateur, and a 10-goaler is the best of the best."

"So a 7-goaler is …?" Cortés's voice trailed off.

"A professional polo player. Definitely upper echelon. The best players—Adolfo Cambiaso, the Harringtons, the Heguys, the Piereses—they're all 10-goalers. So the members of the 7UP Club only slept with polo players who carried at least 7 goals, if not 8, 9, or 10."

"You make it sound as though they collected them."

"From what I gather, they traded them like baseball cards."

"Were you a 7-goaler?"

"I wish."

"Oh, *really*, Captain Hunt?"

"Perhaps I should rephrase my answer."

"Perhaps you should."

"As a lifelong polo player, earning a 7-goal handicap was beyond my wildest dreams. You need *so* many lucky breaks to go that far. As it turned out, my highest rating was 5 goals. I was eighteen. That was the year I went to West Point. Now I'm a 3-goaler, the same rating I had when I was sixteen and first saw Kelly."

"How'd she end up marrying one of America's top CEOs?"

"Don't know. I don't know anything about him, and I definitely don't know how they met. I do know that she graduated from the 7UP Club to *patróns* early on. I wasn't around long enough to follow her trajectory—we flew to Paris a week later—but the following season she moved in with a Greek shipping magnate. In the next couple of years, I remember her dating a wildcatter from Calgary and a Swiss currency trader. I can't recall which one was first. Every few years, we'd run into each other at a cocktail party or a polo event, and she'd have a new beau. And no matter what his business was, she always seemed to know it inside and out—she's amazing that way. Don't be fooled by the pretty packaging. She probably knows more about Centaur's projects and deals than its board members."

Cortés stared at Kelly through the one-way glass. "Why hasn't someone told me about this magical kingdom where women get to put their social life first and foremost?"

"I guess that's not the lifestyle the agency stresses."

"Stress is the lifestyle the Secret Service stresses, which is why my ex-husband's second marriage was to a kindergarten teacher."

"All you've got to do is make your way down Lake Worth Road and you'll arrive in the Promised Land."

Both gazed through the glass at Juancito's lover.

"They bought her cars, paid for her implants, sent her and her friends on shopping sprees to Fifth Avenue, to Highland Park Village, and to Rodeo Drive. Kelly may never have swung a mallet, but she sure can play this game with the best of them."

ONLY THE SLIGHTEST HINT OF worry clouded Kelly's bronzed face.

But beneath the placid façade, her mind was racing at Mach speed.

He's going to kill me.

No, he wouldn't possibly do that.

He'll bail me out first, and then he'll kill me.

No, that's not how he'll do it.

First, he'll prove I'm innocent. Then the prenup will kick in. Then he'll kill me.

She looked at her watch.

Maybe he'll never show up. That's it. He'll send one of his hatchet men. That's who'll bail me out. He'll be the one who puts me in time-out.

Her mind ricocheted back to the Brazilian Court, to the Lancaster Suite, and to Juancito.

No one, NO ONE can ever know.

RAUL RAMIREZ STORMED INTO THE observation room without so much as a glance through the one-way glass at his suspect. Instead, the enraged detective marched directly up to the Army captain with the plainclothes officer from the heliport in tow.

"This, as I mentioned, is Special Agent Cortés with the Secret Service," said the officer hurriedly. Ramirez ignored both the comment and the agent. Hunt began to introduce himself, but Ramirez cut him off.

"I know who you are," Ramirez said, "but what I don't know is what the hell you're doing here." This time, Ramirez wasn't going to let anyone get in the way of his investigation. Not from the Army or Argentina or wherever the hell Hunt was from.

Hunt didn't flinch. He didn't tense up.

"To answer your question, I was sent to assist in any way possible."

"What can I expect from someone who knows nothing about the crime?"

"Special Agent Cortés was briefing me on the way up—"

"You call that assistance?

"I've got my orders, sir—"

"Don't you dare compromise my investigation, Captain."

Hunt met the detective's stare with an easygoing smile.

"That's not how we work, sir. And I'll prove it to you right now."

Hunt walked past Ramirez toward the room's only exit. Instead of reaching for the door, however, he reached for a wall phone. He accessed an outside line and began dialing a number. Once the call connected, Hunt placed it on speakerphone for all to hear. The icy quiet gave the ring tone a tinny peal.

Cortés was enjoying the show. Hunt had yet to bat an eyelash. Neither had Ramirez. She sensed what Hunt was up to—this sort of bureaucratic posturing was standard operating procedure at the Secret Service—but she didn't know him well enough to know how well he played the game.

First ring. Hunt turned and took another look at Kelly. From what he could tell, she was even better-looking than the last time he had seen her. There was no second ring.

"White House."

"This is Captain Hunt calling for the Chief of Staff."

"One moment, Captain," the operator said and put the call through.

Cortés did her best to stifle a smile. *Going to be hard to trump that one.*

"Office of the Chief of Staff," a second voice said.

"Checking in, ma'am," Hunt said casually.

"There you are, Rick," a pleasant voice said. "The Chief told me you'd be calling in this morning. I'll put you right through." She placed the call on hold.

Hunt turned to the plainclothes officer who had picked him up that morning. "Officer, would it be possible for you to grab me a bottle of water?" he asked. The officer nodded agreeably.

"One for you too?" Hunt asked the Secret Service agent.

"Thank you. I'd appreciate that."

"How about you?" he asked Ramirez.

The detective offered no response.

Now you're pushing it, Cortés thought.

Just then a voice broke in.

"Look who made it to Miami," the Chief said sarcastically.

Hunt smiled. "The kind folks at American don't normally hold flights for me like that. And they don't bump me up to first class either. That's actually why I'm calling, sir. Would it be too much to ask you to handle my travel arrangements from now on?"

Auerbach ignored Hunt's chitchat. "What have you got?" he asked.

"I'm here with Special Agent Cortés of the Secret Service and Detective Ramirez of the Palm Beach Police, who is heading up the local investigation."

"Sounds like there's a break in the case."

"There most definitely is. In fact, the detective is ready to give you an update, sir. And of course, anyone else at the White House you'd like to bring in on this call."

Ramirez slowly stepped forward, slightly shell-shocked. "Thank you," he stammered; only now he couldn't remember Hunt's name. A deathly silence followed as Hunt let Ramirez swing in the wind. Auerbach's patience ran out in a millisecond.

"Did she do it?" he asked point-blank.

"She's not just the principal suspect," Ramirez said, regaining a measure of his composure. "In fact, she's the only suspect. Her prints are all over the crime scene: doors, furniture, even his belt buckle. I'm sure the rest of the evidence will match too."

"How did you track her down?" Auerbach asked sharply.

"Hotel personnel identified her as being present in the suite at the time of the crime. On top of that, a close personal friend of Mr. Harrington's identified her as the individual he was going to meet at the Brazilian Court. This morning, the hotel's general manager notified us that she had returned to the property. I guess her curiosity got the better of her. She couldn't have been nicer when I first approached her. I asked if she'd help us on a little matter, and she followed us right to the room. No hesitation at all. When I took her inside the suite and showed her the crime scene, that's when she clammed up. She said she wouldn't say another word until she had spoken to her husband or his legal counsel. We've had her isolated ever since. That's where it stands."

"I'm glad to hear so much progress has been made this quickly. The President will certainly appreciate it. He met with the Argentine Ambassador this morning and went to great lengths to express his profound regret over this tragedy. He personally penned a note of condolence to Mr. Harrington's brother. What's his name?"

"Cesare, sir," Hunt said.

"That's right. Captain, I know I speak for everyone here at the White House when I say how much we appreciate your dropping everything and flying back from Argentina at a moment's notice to assist on this. I'll pass your report along to the President. Don't hesitate to call on us if we can support the investigation in any way. My thanks to all of you. Keep me posted," he said.

The line went dead.

CRIS CORTÉS WAS BESIDE HERSELF. She had never seen someone lay down the law as smoothly as this White House Army captain. She stepped down onto the sidewalk in front of Palm Beach P.D. No sign of Hunt. Squinting into the glare, she could barely see him making his way down South County Road. She set out after him. Then she started laughing.

As soon as his boss hung up, Hunt congratulated Ramirez and genuinely thanked him for "keeping the Chief posted." Then he left the room. Just walked out. Didn't wait for an apology. Didn't piss on the guy's leg. Didn't ask him to kiss the ring. He just left.

After listening to Detective Ramirez feebly attempt to justify his behavior, Cortés offered a standard agency sign-off and made her exit.

It took her two full blocks to catch up with Hunt. When she finally did, her stride slowed and she began to match his, step for step.

Hunt was sipping his water and eyeing the eastern horizon. It was a cloudless day, and the wind was blowing in off the Atlantic.

"So do I gather interagency cooperation is your forte?" she asked.

"Getting the job done is my forte, Agent Cortés. Doesn't matter if it's hopping on a redeye, shouldering a service rifle, or keeping my mouth shut."

"You honestly think Detective Ramirez will keep you posted on any developments in the case?" she asked with a smile.

"That's a moot point."

"How so, Captain Hunt?"

"Do you honestly think Detective Ramirez will offer any insights into this case?"

Cortés laughed openly, and it brought them both to a stop. Hunt looked at her glossy lips, her sparkling white teeth, and her coffee-colored eyes, so deep and dark and dancing. A single thought came to mind:

Neither the time nor the place.

He liked Cortés. She wasn't coy, but she wasn't overly familiar either. There was a hint of an accent that barely crept into her voice, and it had been driving him crazy since he first picked it out on the flight up from Miami. Try as he might, he could not place it. Cuba? That made no sense. She was way too young to be a Castro refugee, in her early thirties at most. He'd figure it out.

"No one at Palm Beach P.D. gives a damn about the death of Juancito Harrington. So I've taken the liberty of contacting someone who actually knew and cared about Juancito. More importantly, he actually knows a thing or two about what Juancito was up to lately and what may or may not have precipitated this crime. Most importantly, he's going to facilitate our attendance at a polo match this afternoon. You good with that plan, Agent Cortés?"

"Sir, yes, sir!" she said enthusiastically.

35

HUNT WAS BY HIMSELF ON the back patio at Bice, navigating a maze of bright yellow umbrellas as he trailed the maître d'. From young fashionistas to the island's old guard, not a chair was empty, and judging from the lineup of Mercedes, Bentleys, and Aston Martins at the curb, the same could be said for every other establishment on Worth Avenue.

At every table, a single topic was being discussed: Juancito's murder.

"What surprises me is how long it took her husband to have him killed."

"They're savages, those polo players are. Every one of them should be gelded."

"No doubt about it. Drug money. The cartels control Wellington."

The maître d' guided Hunt to a shady spot beneath a long green awning in a corner of the patio. At a table by himself sat a bear of a man in his mid-fifties. Unlike the restaurant's other guests, he shunned tropical colors and designer labels. Instead, he wore khakis, a white polo shirt with a tasteful monogram, and a gimme cap with the same logo. He stood up, smiled broadly, and extended a mitt of a hand. Hunt clasped it tightly.

"Picked a hell of a day to come to Palm Beach, my man," Joe Bigelow said.

The maître d', his task completed, turned to leave.

"Sir?" Hunt asked.

The maître d' performed a quick about-face.

"Do me a favor and have our waiter bring the lady a Pimm's Cup," he said, gesturing to the empty seat. "What about you, Joe?" Hunt asked Bigelow.

"What kind of beer do you got?"

"Amstel Light, Coors Light, Miller Lite," the maître d' began.

"I said beer, not soda pop."

Hunt grinned. "Bring the man a Budweiser. No glass."

The maître d' nodded. "And you, sir?"

"Club soda with lime."

"Yes, sir."

Hunt turned to Bigelow. "I knew the lure of a cold one might get you to come to town—even on game day."

"Why the hell not? Our horses are primed. The team is locked and loaded. Rio Bravo is ready to go. The only thing a coach like me can do right now is screw things up before we take the field. Who's joining us?" Bigelow asked.

"Federal agent assigned to Juancito's murder investigation. A lot of people are watching this case."

"I'd say. Been sitting here by myself about ten minutes and that's all anyone can talk about. I figure I'm the only one in this joint who knew the guy, but that hasn't stopped any of their yammering. What have you heard?"

Hunt leaned back and stretched. "Just the headlines. Sounds to me like Kelly finally got caught with her pants down."

Bigelow let out a laugh. "Actually, she's been caught on several occasions. Only this time around there was a dead man in her bed, not a live one."

"You got any bright ideas about who, what, when?"

"Nah. Everybody's still in mourning. No one can think straight, see straight, or imagine high-goal polo without him."

"Same here," Hunt said.

Several moments passed. Neither spoke.

"What about this federal agent? The Pimm's Cup lady. What does she know?"

"Only what Palm Beach P.D. knows, and that's not much."

"What about you? You know enough about our crowd. What do you think?"

Hunt nodded. "This is how I see it."

"Hit me."

"Scenario number one: somebody wanted to kill Juancito."

"Check."

"Scenario number two: someone wanted to set up Kelly by killing Juancito."

"Check."

"Want to take a stab at scenario number three?"

"Don't try that fancy stuff with me, boy. I taught you everything you know and a whole lot that went in one ear and out the other."

Hunt grinned.

"So in scenario number three, let's kill Juancito *and* set Kelly up."

"Fine. Let's start with poor old Juancito. Must be half a dozen husbands on this island that wanted to throttle his ass."

Hunt nodded in agreement.

"And that's not counting the dozen or so in England and the two dozen in Argentina and everywhere else he played polo."

Hunt nodded again. "You with me on the fact that Kelly is a patsy?"

"No question. When Kelly's kind gets mad, they max out credit cards. Or they go wreck a new car. Some of them go sleeping with strangers, and others sleep with their husbands, friends. But killing the likes of Juancito? That's a tall order. This is high-goal polo we're talking about. There's always next season. You know that. I know that. And Kelly damn sure knows that. She's been in this game long enough to know better."

"No argument there. Now tell me about her husband. How did she hook up with him?" Hunt asked.

"Caught him on the rebound," Bigelow said. "His first wife left him for another woman, so he had to go out and show the world it wasn't his fault. Went off and married the first gal he slept with. Turns out he was in Palm Beach. You know what that means."

"Kelly was the short favorite?"

The two smiled as a server arrived and set down their drinks.

Bigelow raised his beer and nodded. Hunt reciprocated.

Bigelow leaned in. "Word in the barn is she's been sleeping with Juancito all season long. And last summer in the Hamptons, after the British Season, Cesare was her boy toy. Who knows what no-good those two got up to."

Hunt lowered his voice. "You just nailed scenario number three. Was it her husband?"

Bigelow tabled his beer. "Why not? Be a hell of a *quinela*: Kill the man screwing your wife and get her ass thrown in jail. Only problem is, you don't kill a Harrington the same week you're trying to win the Open."

Both pondered the possibilities.

"So who else would want Juancito out of the picture?" Hunt asked.

"How about everybody in polo? The guy's been unstoppable. Won the Queen's Cup and the Gold Cup in England last summer. Hell, what am I telling you that for? You were there."

Hunt nodded.

"He and Cesare followed that up by sweeping the Argentine high-goal season: Tortugas, Hurlingham, and the Abierto. And Centaur has been tearing it up here in Palm Beach. Pretty solid run, if you ask me. When the guy's on, no one can touch him, and there are plenty of teams that don't stand a chance on one of his off days."

"What about Cesare? Any bad blood between those two?"

"Can't say there was or there wasn't. But wouldn't you wait till after the Open to kill his ass? Hell, I'd want to pocket that bonus check, wouldn't you? Then I'd kill his ass."

"Touché," Hunt said.

"The truth is I can't figure out how Centaur will field a full team for their semi final match tomorrow afternoon," Bigelow said.

Hunt started to do the math. "Not a lot of 10-goalers sitting this tournament out, are there?"

"10-goalers?" Bigelow said. "Hell, I can't think of a 9-goaler or an 8-goaler who could fill in at such short notice. Is there somebody I'm not remembering down in Argentina? None that I recall."

"You're right. Doesn't make sense for her husband or for his brother to sabotage their team like that. Not right now," Hunt said.

The patio door opened, and the maître d' reappeared. He was escorting a willowy brunette in a floral dress with long wavy hair, a pair of bold black wraparounds, and a perfectly sublime smile. The two walked directly toward the men's table.

Hunt stood up and assumed she knew Bigelow.

Bigelow stood up and assumed she knew Hunt.

It didn't take long for the two men to realize that neither one did.

"Captain Hunt?" she asked.

JACK DICK STEPPED GINGERLY INTO the interrogation room at Palm Beach P.D., taking in the barren chamber as quickly as possible. His eyes were everywhere but on his horndog wife, who jumped to her feet the instant he entered. Arms extended for a hug, Kelly hurried around the table only to be brushed off by her husband. She started to speak, but he brought his index finger to her lips. Dick was sizing up the overhead video cameras that monitored their every move. Hawk-eyed and purse-lipped, he scanned the one-way mirror that ran the length of the back wall.

"I trust you have kept to yourself?" he asked in an icy tone.

Kelly's hands dropped to her side. *This is going to make Guantanamo Bay look like Six Flags.* Chastised and childlike, she tucked her chin in and nodded.

"Would that be the only thing you've done right all day?"

Her eyes dropped to the floor. She began looking from side to side.

"Let me congratulate you. In my entire life, no one has ever cost me as many millions as you did this morning. And when I say no one, I'm talking about people with honest-to-god talent, with brains and drive and education and ambition. I'm talking about people who do something for a living besides fall on their back with their legs in the air."

A wave of dread swept over her.

"And I guarantee you this: You will pay me back every red cent I have lost today, every single red cent, with preferred interest."

Her stomach started to turn.

"If I so much as hear that you have spoken a single word to a soul today, I will have that pathetic wretch who gave birth to you in a charity hospital out of wedlock tossed out of that high-priced hotel you call an assisted living center."

"I take that back." For a moment, Jack Dick actually looked his wife right in the eye. "Your mother won't be the first to go. It'll be those damn cats of yours. I will personally escort them to my polo barn and have them fed to the alligators in the canal."

Kelly couldn't hold her husband's gaze. She averted her eyes and reached back to steady herself on the table. Before she could move, Dick placed his ice-cold hands gently around her throat.

"I have committed *every* resource at my disposal to clearing your name. As we speak, a check for one million dollars is being couriered to the offices of South Florida's top trial attorney just to get him to look at your case. At this very moment, members of the team I am assembling to save your hide are flying in from across the country. And until your legal counsel arrives, you will play the quiet game and you will not lose. Have I made myself clear?"

Dick was no longer glowering at his wife. He was staring at the long mirror over his wife's shoulder, trying to pick out who was watching him. But no matter where he looked, all he could see was the reflection of the pathetic creature he had married.

Dick felt a hand on his chin, his wife's hand. Shock registered in his eyes as she guided his gaze back to hers. He saw the same fiery determination that Raul Ramirez encountered not two hours before, when Kelly picked herself up off her knees.

"I dare you to lay a hand on my mother or anything else that belongs to me. If I so much as find a hair out of place on one of my Persians, I'll cost you more millions than you can ever count. When I finish torching you and your company, you'll think this morning was a good day. Now get my ass out of jail. Have I made *myself* clear?"

37

"CAPTAIN HUNT?" JOE BELLOWED.

Hunt was caught completely off guard. Gone were the Ann Taylor pinstripe suit and the Nine West pumps. In their place, the Secret Service agent was decked out in a new Michael Kors shift dress and some Jimmy Choos.

"What's wrong with you, boy? How on earth could you not recognize this gorgeous gal?" Bigelow asked.

The Secret Service agent was quite proud of herself. She swiveled left. She swiveled right. She turned a tan leg and showed off her Jimmy Choos.

"Is this too much, Captain Hunt? Will I blend in with your polo friends?"

"Blend in? Hell, you'll stand out!" blurted Bigelow. He doffed his cap, grabbed her chair, and offered her a seat.

"Joe Bigelow, ma'am. It's a pleasure."

"Cristina Cortés. My friends call me Cris. Is that OK by you, Captain Hunt?"

"Whatever works for you two works for me, Agent Cortés."

"Cris it is."

Joe was shaking his head. "I don't know how you managed to hook up with Einstein here, but you've probably already figured out he's not the sharpest knife in the drawer. And don't let him go telling you that it has something to do with mortar rounds in Afghanistan or wherever the hell he's been that he can't ever talk about 'cause he wants you to think his whole life is so damn top secret. He's been pulling stunts like this all his life. Nobody in polo lets him use that Defense Department routine to cover up any of his shortcomings. And don't you either."

The Secret Service agent started laughing. She took off her new shades and looked at Hunt. "This one is a little tougher than the last fellow you sparred with."

"I promise you, Cris, José is just getting warmed up."

Bigelow continued. "It's this big bucket of his, and he throws everything in there: slacking off on the job, not following through, running late like he does all the time. Hell, I had to drive twenty miles to make it to lunch, and I still got here before he did. What's that about?"

"Come on, Joe. I was on foot. You got to drive."

"You had to walk four whole blocks. Man, you're getting as bad as SOB."

"No one is as bad as SOB."

"Who's SOB?" Cris asked.

Hunt and Bigelow looked at one another. Then each pointed at the other.

"He's on your team," Hunt said.

"He was your teammate," Bigelow countered.

Hunt turned to Cortés. "Remember I told you about the first time I came to Palm Beach? SOB was one of the guys, and Joe was one of the pros who was coaching."

"It worked, didn't it? You boys won it all—world champions."

"Rick, you never mentioned that you even made that team. Why didn't you tell me you were a world champion?"

Hunt waved his hand dismissively. "That was once upon a time in a tournament nobody remembers."

"Once upon a time? How about last year?" Bigelow asked. "Did *Captain Hunt* tell you he won the world's oldest and most prestigious championship in England last summer?"

"He most certainly did not."

"I cannot believe I invited myself into the middle of all this," Hunt said.

"That's because you'll never learn a thing about Rick from Rick. Want to know the President's favorite restaurant in Washington? He's the guy to talk to. He'll tell you his favorite table, what he orders off the menu, and who his favorite waiter is. But ask him what he's been up to, and before you can blink an eye, he's changed the subject."

"I've noticed that about him, Joe. Half the time he ignores whatever I say."

"You're getting off light if it's just half the time. So just tell me what you want to know."

"Time-out," Hunt said, holding up a hand. "I'm going to make this short and sweet, so you can go back to saying whatever you want to say about me, Joe, but Special Agent Cortés is handling the investigation of Juancito's murder for the Secret Service out of their West Palm Beach field office, and her status as a Secret Service agent is not to leave this table."

"Didn't I tell you?" Bigelow asked.

"Tell me what?" Cris asked.

"That he'd try to pull the wool over your eyes with this secrecy B.S."

"You definitely did. Now tell me more."

"Don't you see what he's trying to do? He's not telling me to keep my mouth shut about you. Hell, I won't be talking to anyone today. I'm going to be yelling at four players in two languages for six chukkers while Rio Bravo plays Piaget in the mother of all polo tournaments. What old Ricky Ricardo here wants is to make sure that you play your role to perfection."

"My role?" Cris asked.

"You mean, he hasn't told you?" Bigelow asked.

"I can assure you he's making this up as he goes," Hunt said.

"Your role, if you decide to accept it, is to be the arm candy that Mr. Westchester Cup here will parade back and forth directly in front of his former fiancée, her family, and everyone else in polo. Are you willing to accept this assignment?"

"Most definitely," Cris smiled. "I've been told I parade very well."

"He did tell you about his former fiancée, didn't he?" Bigelow asked.

"No," Hunt interrupted. "*He* did not tell her about *his* former fiancée. For some inexplicable reason, *he* chose to confine *his* discussions to matters pertaining to a homicide investigation for which *he* traveled overnight from Argentina. Believe it or not, that is the same topic *he* brought up with *you* several minutes ago when *we* sat down together."

Bigelow ignored Hunt's statement. He swiveled in his chair and looked directly at the Secret Service agent.

"You're going to love this."

38

RAUL RAMIREZ WAS ANYTHING BUT happy. He eyed the barmaid, looked at the barstool, and forced himself to sit down. He was now uncomfortable and unhappy.

"Coffee. Black."

The Irish barmaid grabbed a stained ceramic mug and filled it to the brim with the foul brew burping on a hot plate. Then she placed the cup on the badly scarred wooden bar. The detective turned and stared at the man in the rumpled pink button-down and plaid trousers who lured him out of Palm Beach, across the Intracoastal, and into the Irish pub beneath the *News of the World* office.

"Another Black and Tan, love?" the barmaid asked.

Ned placed a hand over an empty pint glass. Ramirez was not surprised that the journalist was a day drinker.

"I never drink on the job. My work won't allow it," the detective said.

"I always drink on the job. My work requires it," the journalist replied.

Never one to let an aspersion go unanswered, Ned looked up at the redhead and tapped on his glass. The barmaid obliged and began crafting a proper Black and Tan.

For Ned, the biggest story of the year was still his and his alone. He knew the victim, he knew the chief suspect, and he was intimately familiar with the world they inhabited in ways none of his peers could fathom.

But Ned wanted more, and there was only one way to get it: by enlisting Raul Ramirez in his cause. After Waltering the detective at St. Mary's Medical Center, it took less than two hours for Ramirez to extend an invitation to his nemesis for an encore performance on the courthouse steps. Ned turned

Kelly's perp walk into a theatrical production worthy of Covent Garden. He followed up his courthouse triumph by inviting Ramirez to peace negotiations at his West Palm headquarters.

But the detective's tone was anything but collegial.

"I have an officer outside waiting to haul you in for the way you ambushed me this morning at St. Mary's. Would you mind telling me why I shouldn't?"

Before Ned could answer, the barmaid presented him a freshly minted Black and Tan and gave him a wink. He looked at her. He looked at his pint. With a wide smile, he grabbed it and inhaled the creamy foam with a loud slurp.

Setting the pint down, Ned stood up and walked out of O'Shea's. From inside the bar, Ramirez and the barmaid watched him cross Clematis and knock on the window of the unmarked police car. He and the officer chatted ever so briefly. Then Ned turned away, and as he walked back across the street, the police car drove off.

"What the hell did you just do?" Ramirez growled.

"Taught you a lesson about the power of the press."

Ramirez scowled. The barmaid smiled. Ned picked up his Black and Tan. This time he sipped softly.

"And if you'd like to see that power work for you instead of against you, hear me out. You are the very heart of this investigation. It should have your name all over it. Yet as best I can tell, you have strategically positioned yourself as a minor footnote." A loud sigh followed this pronouncement.

Ned suddenly leaned into Ramirez. "But I can show you how to make the most of this," he said, his words quick and sharp. "I can show you how to elevate your status as one of America's best detectives quicker than you ever thought possible."

He paused.

"If, on the other hand, you're still of the mind to arrest me, I'll be happy to have the both of us driven back to your police station in a *News of the World* transport we used this morning. Let's make it the minivan," he said to the barmaid. She raised an eyebrow, and Ramirez realized she was one of Ned's cohorts in the hospital lobby.

"Just give me a minute to get my team ready to film me turning myself in. I might even do a live feed on the drive over. Could I get you to chime in? That would be brilliant."

The barmaid's gaze swiveled from Ned to Ramirez, only Ned continued talking. "You have single-handedly solved the biggest homicide on the planet. You should be the toast of the town. And you know what you've got to show for it?"

Ramirez didn't answer. Ned gestured at the bar.

"The worst cup of coffee in South Florida."

All three looked at the discolored mug.

"Tell me what you want," Ramirez said.

"It's not *what* I want, dear boy. It's *who* I want. Bring me Cesare Harrington."

"SO MR. WESTCHESTER CUP IS over in London doing whatever it is top-secret Army officers do," Bigelow said.

"Graduate studies at the London School of Economics," Hunt chimed in.

"And back home, he's got the most dazzling fiancée on earth. Ava Kenedy has got every bell and whistle a man could ever hope for. She's not just beautiful, but she's way more fun than he is, which to be honest, is not saying a whole hell of a lot. Of course, to a washed-up polo player like me, what stands out is the way she sits a horse. That gal was born to ride. Hell, right now she's on the short list to make the Olympic team as a jumper. And she's got her mother's looks, and I'm sure you know the Senator."

"I know of the Senator. But I've never been assigned to him," Cris said.

"A couple of years back, the governor appointed King to hold down the last few years of an unexpired Senate term. King agreed to serve only on one condition," Joe said.

"What was that?" the Secret Service agent asked.

"The minute his term was over, he got the hell out of Washington and back to the ranch," Bigelow said.

"Which is exactly what he did," Hunt added.

"Right on," Joe said. "The governor didn't stand a chance of getting him to change his mind, which is why the President gave it a shot. Had him to the White House. Took him and Lupe to Camp David. Didn't matter. King's mind was made up. And once that happens, it's all over. There's no changing his mind. That may be where Ava got her bullheadedness."

"May be?" Hunt asked no one in particular.

As their waiter returned to the table, he noticed the striking woman in the eye-catching outfit listening with rapt attention to the older gentleman. On the other side of the table, the younger man appeared lost in thought, his mind far from the conversation.

"Now, do I really want to hear what Rick did?" Cris asked.

"Count on it," Bigelow said. "'Cause as soon as you do, you'll realize why Ricky Ricardo needs all the help he can get."

"Let's cut to the chase," Hunt said. "Last summer, in London, I got a call from the embassy informing me that there was a single ticket available to the final of the Gentlemen's Singles at the All England Lawn Tennis Club. Sounds pretty good, doesn't it?"

A smile returned to Cris's face. She nodded in agreement.

"That's what I thought. I've been around the block enough to know that when a junior military officer gets a ticket to a Wimbledon final, it's because everybody up the ladder has passed it over," Hunt said.

"A ticket to the final at Wimbledon? Come on," Bigelow said.

"It's the Fourth of July weekend, Joe. Everyone from the embassy is in Chipping Norton or somewhere on the Continent. Any place but London. So Saturday rolls around, and there's a ticket left. I get the bid, and I don't mind. Would you?" Hunt asked.

Cris shook her head no.

"Ava thought it was the funniest thing on earth," Hunt said.

"Why's that?" Cris asked.

"I've never picked up a tennis racket in my life."

"Neither have I," Bigelow said. "What the hell for?"

"So I'm staying at Cavalry & Guards. I'm obviously representing my country, and I need to dress appropriately so I put on my uniform. Then I take the tube to Wimbledon. Present my ticket. And who do I find myself seated next to?"

"A lovely lady?" Cris asked.

"Not just any lovely lady but England's most eligible bachelorette," Hunt added.

"You've got to be kidding," Cris said.

Hunt shook his head.

"Did he mention that he was seated next to England's most eligible bachelorette on international TV in the Royal Box?" Bigelow asked.

"You've got all the pieces in place, right?" Hunt asked. "Royal wedding. Her sister. Every newspaper on earth? Well, from what I was told, the TV cameras spent more time focused on her comings and goings than on the match itself, which meant you-know-who got a hell of a lot of airtime."

"That you did, my man," Bigelow said. He took a swig of his Budweiser.

"So I gather from the fact that you are not yet a married man," she nodded at his left hand, "that you were unable to talk yourself out of this infidelity?"

"Talk himself out of it? That's the best part. He talked himself into it," Bigelow said.

Cris looked at Bigelow. Then she looked at Hunt.

"It's a little hard to explain."

"Please. Try me," Cris asked.

Bigelow could not contain himself: "He pocket-dialed his fiancée."

40

"YOU ARE OUT OF YOUR mind," Raul Ramirez said.

"Believe it or not, others have voiced a highly similar opinion."

"I believe it."

"So why on earth have you joined their number?"

"Point number one: What makes you think Cesare Harrington would ever agree to give you the time of day, let alone an actual interview, after the way you and those thugs of yours gang-tackled him this morning?"

"Please, continue."

"Point number two: What makes you think I would ever agree to give you access to Cesare after the way you and your thugs gang-tackled me this morning?"

"It's bloody simple. Because you tell him to."

Ramirez picked up his coffee mug. "And why would I do that?"

"Because we both know you have yet to resurrect your reputation."

Ramirez remained silent.

"Hauling that floozy up the front steps was good theater, but this is Palm Beach, old boy, not Covent Garden. Trust me on this one. Right now, all anyone knows is that you can pull off a spot-on perp walk. Do people know you are a man not to be trifled with? Do they know that no amount of money or prestige will save a miscreant like Kelly from her due? You know that. I know that. But do the Jack Dicks of Palm Beach know that?"

"What are you suggesting?"

"Obviously, I wouldn't want to impede your investigation."

Ramirez quietly placed the mug back on the bar.

"You? Impede an investigation?"

Ramirez's comment gave Ned pause. "I realize there have been times when I haven't been seen as of great value by various policing entities."

"You? Impede an investigation?" Ramirez asked a little louder.

"Point taken. On occasion, I haven't always been overly helpful."

"Overly helpful? Do you have any idea how long it will take to clean up the mess you made this morning? One patient was knocked to the ground. A couple of orderlies got dinged. Who do you think they're going to sue? The hospital? Some newspaper based in London? No, they're going to go after my police department, and they're going to go after me!"

Ned caved in. "You are absolutely correct. That was completely my fault. I wish I had known of some other way to get that story, but I didn't. My point is this: Cesare is the keeper of the flame. Everyone on earth wants to hear the memories only he can share: the insights on his brother's record-setting career, cherished moments from this private world that so few inhabit. As lead investigator, you of course would have full approval of all my questions. I'd require that you sign off on all aspects of the interview. In fact, I've already decided that I'll begin the interview with you."

"Me? Why me?"

"Don't you see? You are the heart and soul of this investigation," Ned said, laying a hand on the man's shoulder. "We'll open the segment with a live shot of Cesare and you on camera. The whole world knows Cesare, and I'd like to introduce you as the investigator who was thrown into this high-profile case, and then go into as much or as little detail as you feel comfortable discussing on how you cracked it open so quickly. You make the call. Any topics or details that come up off the cuff that prove unsuitable, we cut right there and re-shoot."

"And Cesare?" Ramirez asked.

"He's obviously dealing with the loss of his brother, and he's got a huge match tomorrow, so it would be a waste of time to approach him before then. I can only imagine how badly he wants to win this tournament for his brother and their family," Ned said. "Perhaps something Friday morning?"

"Friday morning?" Ramirez responded. The journalist knew much too much about his case. But he definitely didn't know everything. "The results of the autopsy are due back midmorning tomorrow, and as soon as they're in, the coroner can release his brother's remains. And with that the Harringtons will be off to Argentina."

"You mean, if Centaur makes it to the final on Sunday, he won't be playing?"

"You can forget about Sunday's final. Cesare told me that it was his family's wish for his brother's remains to be returned to Argentina as soon as possible. And he asked me point-blank if there was any way I could expedite the autopsy. He just wants to honor his brother, and I've done everything in my power to facilitate that. So, to your question, no, Cesare will definitely not be playing for Centaur tomorrow. Nor, do I imagine, will he be sitting down to an interview with you anytime soon."

Ramirez's revelation had its intended effect. For once, the rowdy journalist was stunned into silence. Ned could sense the greatest story of his career slipping through his fingers. He was *this* close to owning it free and clear. Only now he had to figure out how to corral or cajole Cesare Harrington into sitting down for an interview in Buenos Aires, of all places.

Who do I know down there? Who do we have in place that can assist?

A buzzing noise caught both men's attention. It was Ramirez's cell announcing an incoming text from one of his investigators:

10-19 to PBPD. Second suspect in polo murder.

Ned read it in tandem with the detective. He actually finished reading it *before* the detective did. And he instantly recognized its many implications. A triumphant smile on his face, the journalist placed an arm on his former adversary's shoulders.

"May I offer you a ride back to headquarters, old boy?"

41

AFTER GIVING HIS WIFE THE tongue-lashing of her life, Jack Dick stormed out of the interrogation room, a maddening list of To-Dos racing through his mind. His own team of investigators needed to get on the case ASAP. Not only would they have to clear his soon-to-be ex-wife's name, but their findings would be put to good use during his divorce proceedings. The investigators needed to liaise with the brigade of lawyers he just deployed. And the lawyers needed to coordinate the messaging that his P.R. team was pushing out to the Street. *The Street? How do I show the Street that this is just a minor detour, not a major roadblock? Maybe I green-light that takeover target.*

Strategically, the acquisition wasn't an ideal opportunity. The motion had been tabled at Centaur's most recent board meeting. *Who cares if that company is a mess? The patents they own are worth twice the price.* A quick thumbs-up would tell the Street that Jack Dick was definitely still in charge.

"This way, Mr. Dick," said the policeman who was escorting him from the interrogation room to the basement where his Bentley was parked. Dick gave the officer a quick nod. The escort directed him into a waiting elevator. The doors were closing when an arm thrust through the gap.

"Wait a moment, Mr. Dick." The doors reopened. It was one of the investigators who had been at the Centaur barn earlier that morning. "Would you mind answering a few questions about a suspect in the Harrington homicide investigation?"

"As a matter of fact, I would. I have nothing to say about my wife or her purported actions."

"Sir, I am not referring to your wife."

"Then who the hell are you talking about?"

"Sir, if you don't mind, please come with me."

42

AFTER MORE THAN AN HOUR and a half of questioning, the investigator was stymied by the smiling enigma seated on the other side of his desk. For starters, he couldn't figure out what it was that Rio Garcia actually did. To make matters worse, neither could Rio—at least in terms that he could convey. To begin with, he claimed to work for a polo team. There was a slight hitch. He didn't play polo, and he knew absolutely nothing about horses.

"OK. How about just the basics? What's your job title?"

"Whatever you wanting."

"Let me restate that, sir. What do you do for Centaur Polo?"

"Like I telling you—whatever you wanting."

"By 'you,' do you mean 'they' or 'me' wanting?"

"Why do you meaning 'they' or 'me'?"

"The ones asking you whatever you wanting."

"You the ones asking whatever you wanting!"

The language barrier was just the first stumbling block. The pint-sized Argentine was a master of the non sequitur. As the minutes stretched on, almost every line of questioning augured into complete bafflement. To the investigator's dismay, the few facts that did emerge were not at all germane. Rio possessed no degree, not even a high school diploma. He did have a valid Argentine passport, and he was able to produce a temporary worker's visa, but that's where his paper trail ended.

"So where did you live?"

"At Juancito."

"In Argentina or in Palm Beach?

"Yes."

"So you live in Argentina, at Mr. Harrington's house?"

"Not here."

"OK. Let's try this. You saw Mr. Harrington yesterday?"

"How I not seeing her? Don't I just telling you I live with her!"

"Yes, sir, you did. So how did your day begin?"

"In the morning."

"I fully understand that it began in the morning. I meant how did your day with Mr. Harrington begin?"

"With Juancito? No."

"So you didn't see Mr. Harrington yesterday morning?"

"No. I didn't seeing him. I driving him to polo. But not every morning. Sometime Juancito begin morning in the afternoon. Not yesterday. On yesterday, morning beginning in the morning."

"OK. So yesterday you driving him to polo …" and the investigator let out a frustrated sigh. One desk away, his partner chortled.

"Exactly! I driving Juancito to polo."

"Thank you. In what vehicle?"

Rio reached in his pocket and pulled out a set of keys. "Juancito Range Rover."

"You have the keys to his car?"

Rio stared at the detective. "Juancito never carry keys. She never carry wallet."

"Mr. Harrington didn't carry a wallet?"

"Why she need wallet? Everybody know Juancito."

The investigator flipped through his notes.

"So where did Mr. Harrington get his cash, his spending money?"

"The same place everyone getting her money . . . cash machine."

Rio opened his fanny pack and began rummaging around. The first card he pulled out was a charge plate for a country club that Jack Dick belonged to. It had his name on it, not Rio's. The second one was a platinum credit card with Kelly Dick's name on it, not Rio's. The third one was a bank card. The raised name read JUAN HARRINGTON. He plopped it on the investigator's desk. Next to it, he stacked bundles of tens, twenties, and hundreds.

"Do you mind if I have a look?" the investigator asked.

The investigator reached across his desk and picked up the debit card with the name JUAN HARRINGTON. He flipped it over. There was no signature. Not only was this Identity Theft 101, but it tied directly to a homicide investigation.

The two investigators sat back and let Rio ramble on about how he had driven Juancito to the Centaur barn. While the polo player worked his horses, Kelly had called him.

"You? Mrs. Dick called you?"

"She always calling me."

"Why is she always calling you?"

"Because she wants a little something from Juancito, no?"

"You mean, yesterday at the Brazilian Court was not the only instance when Mrs. Dick and Mr. Harrington had this type of rendezvous?"

For the first time in more than an hour, Rio did not answer a question. He was laughing too hard. It was enough of a cackle that he was incapable of speech. He simply shook his head from side to side.

"So am I to gather that this sort of rendezvous took place frequently?"

Rio's giggles continued. Only now he was nodding his head yes.

"Always at the Brazilian Court?"

Rio caught his breath. "The Brazilian Court. The Four Seasons. At the barn. At the airplane hangar. At the Centaur. She keeping Juancito very busy."

"So you confirmed to Mrs. Dick that you would be bringing Mr. Harrington to the Brazilian Court?"

Rio nodded.

Aiding and abetting a homicide, conspiracy to commit murder—the array of charges that were piling up against Rio were multiplying at an exponential rate. Yet he still hadn't finished describing the day's events.

The investigators eventually pieced together the rest of Rio's morning. Dropping Juancito at the Brazilian Court at around eleven thirty, he drove back to Wellington to retrieve a briefcase that Cesare had left at Juancito's condo. He fetched it, brought it back to Palm Beach, and met Cesare at the brothers' office. By this time, Rio and Cesare had left several messages on Juancito's cell for him to meet them for lunch at the Palm Beach Grill. When he failed to respond, they ate without him.

"Mr. Garcia, your lifelong friend, whom you had just driven fifteen or twenty miles from Wellington to Palm Beach, never called you back, and it didn't cause you the least bit of concern?"

"She doing this all the time."

"She did what? I mean, *he* did what?"

"Whatever she wanting."

"Let me rephrase that. Mr. Harrington told you he'd join you for lunch, and he doesn't show up. Then you drive back to Wellington without waiting in Palm Beach for Mr. Harrington to call and have you pick him up?"

"Maybe I waiting days in Palm Beach."

The two investigators looked at Rio. Then they looked at each other.

"You might be right about that," said one. The other picked up his phone and began to text Raul Ramirez to return to headquarters.

CRIS CLOSED HER EYES IN agony. "You pocket-dialed your fiancée when you were out on the town with another woman?"

"I cannot deny it. And let the record reflect that I didn't just pocket-dial her once."

"When it comes to technology, this guy is tops," Bigelow added.

"My ringer was off—you can't have your phone going off in the middle of the most important tennis tournament on earth—and Ava had been waiting and watching and saw me on TV. So when I pocket-dialed her, she thought I was calling to tell her about the great time I was having."

"Pal, you were having a great time. Just not with her."

"I had no way of realizing that I kept hitting redial, which meant she got to hear the two of us talk about polo, talk about the princes whom I had just played polo with at Sandhurst, talk about her royal sister, talk about London nightlife. The one topic she didn't hear me discuss—"

"Was her," Cris said.

"What makes it worse is that I was bragging on Ava. I talked up her success as a jumper, the fact that she was the Senator's daughter, and that we were engaged. But as fate would have it, those statements were not part of my global broadcast that afternoon."

"And you're supposed to be one of our best and brightest?" Bigelow asked. "How could you keep calling her like that and not know it?"

"Let's agree on one point. No one's ever accused you of being an expert witness on the fine points of military tailoring, have they, Joe?"

"Not yet."

"Then let me assure you that the Army's white service uniform was not designed to holster a BlackBerry. I had it tucked under my coat behind my belt. I must have pocket-dialed half the people on my speed-dial list. But let's face facts. I'm seated next to a beautiful woman, whom I didn't know I would be seated next to, watching the final of Wimbledon on international television. Is that a high crime or misdemeanor?"

"Forget your high crime smoke screen," Bigelow said. "What about that Facebook nonsense? What was all that about?"

A puzzled look crossed Cris's face. "You're not on Facebook, are you?"

"Of course not. But Ava definitely is. She has thousands of fans who follow her eventing and training and things like that. And in the two hours that the tennis match lasted, probably half of them posted pictures of me and 'my date' on her wall. Probably the same number asked her when we had called our wedding off."

"That must have gone over really well. So how did you apologize to her?"

"That night. The next morning. That next evening. Every chance I could."

"Let me rephrase that. What did you offer her on bended knee?"

Hunt shook his head. "Haven't seen her since."

"You've got to be kidding me."

Hunt sank lower in his chair.

"Cris, one thing I'll say about Ricky Ricardo is there are no ifs, ands, or buts with this guy. He is the master of the clean break," Joe said.

"Why haven't you seen her?"

"Cris, of all people? I expected some understanding from a Secret Service agent. I begged Ava to come to London. I offered to fly her over. Told her we'd go to Venice, tour the South of France, kick back in Cannes. She wouldn't have anything to do with me. She's got zero tolerance for anything less than her way. I was the one who screwed up, so I was the one who had to come calling. Like I had any downtime. That Monday, I got yanked out of class and escorted to the private residence of the American Ambassador in London."

"Winfield House?" Cris asked.

Hunt nodded. "It was during the G20 Summit. I ended up working five straight twenty-hour days for Ari Auerbach. That's how I ended up working at the White House today. By the time the G20 was over, so were my wedding plans."

"Wasn't the Westchester Cup in the middle of all this?" Bigelow asked.

"That didn't help my case at all."

"What's the Westchester Cup? And why do you keep calling him Mr. Westchester Cup?"

"'Cause he's Joe."

"'Cause the Westchester Cup is the mother of all polo trophies. For centuries, the United States and Great Britain have put their best players on the field to compete for that trophy. I never got a shot at it. Guess who does," Bigelow said, gesturing at Hunt.

Hunt nodded. "Right time. Right place."

"Pal, I've been married three times. And I don't mind telling you, and you," Joe said, looking at Cris, "that the reason each of those marriages ended was because I was right. I take that back. I wasn't right. I was damn right. Whatever it was that we were arguing about that pushed us over the edge, she wouldn't give, and I couldn't give. Because I had to be right. Not happy but right. And you know what I've got to show for being so damn right all the damn time? An empty bed. Some empty arms. An empty heart. I'm telling you this 'cause I don't want you to end up being right like me."

Cris picked up her Pimm's. "To not being right," she said.

The two men raised their glasses and joined the toast.

"To not being right!"

The table fell strangely silent. Hunt spoke first.

"What's the best way to get ahold of Mr. Australia?"

"The guy is old school. A complete holdout. No cell phone. No computer. Just pencil and paper. Best places to track him down are the Centaur barn or at the Chesterfield a block or two away from here."

Hunt nodded.

"So why are the Harringtons playing for Jack Dick?" Cris asked.

"If you want to win and can pay the piper, they're the best of the best. No one has dropped the kind of cash old Jack is paying in a long time. I'm talking Kerry Packer money, Prince Jefri dollars. Word is the Harringtons did their usual deal—five million apiece from New Year's to Easter—plus expenses: airfare, condos, cars, everything. And the string of horses that Jack has bought from them? Second to none. I promise you they've made another five million right there."

Hunt let out a low whistle. Bigelow nodded.

"He's had us over for a couple of scrimmages, and I mean to tell you, they pull out all the stops. When old Jack flies those Wall Street boys down to watch Juancito and Cesare trot around at a hand canter, you'd think they'd just seen Secretariat burning down the straight at the Belmont."

"How about you? You still playing?" Hunt asked.

"Don't need to."

"Don't need to or don't want to?"

"Don't have to."

"I've known you most of my life. You have to play polo."

"Why on earth does the Army keep promoting you? You got any ideas, Cris?"

A smiled curled across her face.

"Must be the way he wears those dress whites."

45

CONTRARY TO HIS FRONT-PAGE PROFILE in the *Wall Street Journal*, Jack Dick was no longer playing by his rules. And he was definitely not winning. Less than fifteen minutes after his wife was hauled off to the county lockup, Centaur's stock price dropped more than ten percent—from $147 to $129. The stock's hyper-volatility—which had long been considered one of its most compelling characteristics—had become its Achilles' heel. Automatic circuit breakers quickly kicked in, and trading was halted. During the break, more bad news hit the wire. A Palm Beach Police spokesperson confirmed that Centaur's CEO was being questioned about the murder of Juan Harrington:

> *At this point in time, Mr. Dick is not considered a suspect in the homicide investigation of Juan Harrington. However, given that his wife has been arrested for the murder of Mr. Harrington, and a personal employee of Mr. Dick's has been arrested on a series of charges relating to the unlawful possession of the decedent's personal property, investigators felt it necessary to question Mr. Dick.*

Centaur stock was in a nose dive. The collapse had nothing to do with the company itself. If anything, the exact opposite held true. Centaur Corporation's fundamentals were robust. Its revenues were at an all-time high and so was its bottom line. The Street could have cared less.

The instant the news broke that Kelly Dick had been arrested, millions of day traders began shorting Centaur's stock, betting its price would continue to plummet. This sell-off triggered high-frequency trading programs—called "freaks" by traders, analysts, and those in the know like Sullivan—which began automatically selling tens of thousands of futures contracts tied to Centaur's stock.

By using complex algorithms, freaks exploit microscopic price variances on different exchanges and profit from these discrepancies. When the news was announced that Kelly was being booked, the freaks detected that they were holding too many long positions, which not only accelerated the sell-off but also created a "hot potato" effect. The freaks began trading among themselves at lightning-fast speeds, pushing the price even lower and causing even more contracts to be dumped.

That's when the selling pressure migrated from the futures markets in Chicago to the NASDAQ itself. Arbitrageurs began buying the cheap futures contracts, selling actual shares of Centaur stock, and pocketing the difference. The enormous downward pressure on the stock became so intense that automatic circuit breakers quickly kicked in yet again. All trading came to a halt.

And with it so did Jack Dick's world.

46

HUNT STEPPED OUT OF THE luxury box elevator and led Cortés straight to the railing.

"Here it is—the Promised Land."

Cris stepped forward, grabbed the railing with both hands, and took in the spectacle before her. The two were perched at the topmost tier of the National Polo Stadium, overlooking the home of the US Open. With only minutes to go before the start of the day's sold-out semifinal, the grounds were a madhouse. At one end of the field, a matte-black helicopter was touching down as it ferried in some tardy muckety-mucks. At the other end, three hundred yards away, scores of horses—greys, chestnuts, bays—were bunched in different pony lines, some with saddles and others only bridled. Their hides twitched, and they pawed at the turf, anxious to be tacked and played. Dozens of grooms bobbed and weaved around and under the muscular Thoroughbreds, making last-minute adjustments. Both teams had taken the field, and each of the players was warming up on his own—putting a horse through its paces, bouncing a ball on the end of a mallet, slapping a shot downfield and barreling after it.

"Wow," said Cris. "I did a lot of event security when I was with Miami-Dade, but nothing quite like this."

Her comment barely registered with Hunt. The sight of the polo players pursuing their craft—the craft he once spent years striving to perfect—was mesmerizing. He hadn't realized how much he missed it—the field, the horses, the players, the camaraderie.

"You're looking at the largest playing field in professional sports, nine times the size of a football field. And each of those Thoroughbreds can gallop from one end to the other in the blink of an eye."

Cris's gaze drifted from the pony lines to the palatial marquees on the far side of the field to the grandstands below her. It was standing room only, and the dress code was decidedly theatrical: flouncy hats, dapper pocket squares, breezy chiffons, Madras trousers. One or two bordered on the absurd.

Like that guy needs a walking stick?

"These people all look like they're here to cocktail, not to watch a polo match."

Hunt snapped to. "Pretend you're here to do the same. Everyone will be talking about Juancito, Kelly, Kelly's husband, their team. Just go along with it. You'll hear a lot of innuendo and a lot of 'I told you so's.' These people have a dark side."

"They wanted Juancito dead?"

"No, but they certainly don't mind Kelly getting caught with her hand in the cookie jar. Or her husband's team facing elimination tomorrow. See if you can pick up anything that gives us more to go on than the police report this morning."

She nodded.

"Could be a horse trade gone bad or a loan that was never repaid, something completely incidental till it wasn't," he said as he escorted her down to the Rio Bravo box.

The moment they sat down, Hunt's radar zeroed in on the tension in the crowd. This was not an ordinary US Open. There was no magic, no festive air. Instead, an element of anxiety filled the stadium.

At the same time, the Secret Service agent's eyes jumped from clique to clique: the Bath & Tennis Club crowd in their chinos and button-downs gabbing noisily about whodunit, the young and the tattooed texting one another crime scene photos, a stylish gent sporting a Borsalino and a blue blazer pontificating about possible suspects with a group of cowboys in straw hats and starched jeans. Hunt noticed her stare tighten on a trio of tanned hunks wearing T-shirts and acid-washed jeans.

"Those are the Pieres brothers," he volunteered. "And every one of them is a 10-goaler. They've won this tournament. They've won the Abierto. They've won 'em all. And so did their father, Gonzalo. He won the same tournaments

44

AFTER MAKING SURE THAT THE Harringtons' two-bit twerp was booked on as many charges as possible, Ramirez turned his attention to his primary target: Kelly Dick.

He knew he had probable cause.

For starters, more than a dozen eyewitnesses identified her going to and from the Lancaster Suite.

On top of that, there was video footage from almost as many cameras.

And the amount of forensic evidence from the Lancaster Suite, the body of the victim, and the principal suspect was enough to build a case by itself.

But it was her silent pouting that made him pull the trigger. Kelly Dick was so spoiled that she refused to speak to him. It was beneath her.

Let's see if she gives her jailer the cold shoulder.

With his two investigators in tow, Ramirez paraded into the interrogation room and arrested the sexy socialite for the murder of Juan Harrington. Before her husband's defense team could even put in a cursory appearance, Kelly was escorted to the basement of the police department and readied for transfer to the county jail, where she would be booked, photographed, and fingerprinted.

As soon as word of her arrest reached the barbarian horde on South County Road, the throng of reporters swarmed the rear exit of Palm Beach P.D. They needn't have hurried. Her send-off was broadcast in real time, courtesy of Ramirez's new-found partner at the *News of the World*. Ramirez was conspicuously visible in the front seat of his SUV as Kelly was hustled over to the Palm Beach County Detention Center in a three-car convoy with sirens blaring and lights flashing.

Was there anything that could make matters worse?

At that very moment, Jack Dick was learning the answer was yes, yes, and yes. Centaur's CEO was informed that in addition to his wife, his personal chauffeur had also been arrested on matters pertaining to the homicide of Juan Harrington. And according to Walter Ned's blog at the *News of the World* website, "unnamed sources" confirmed that Cesare Harrington would not be playing for Centaur in Thursday's semifinal match. This last news item was more than just a crippling blow to Centaur's run at a US Open title. With both Harringtons out of the picture, Centaur's entire marketing campaign was officially in shambles.

This unending stream of bad news and worse press pushed Centaur's stock price over the edge. What had been a selling opportunity quickly turned into an all-out panic. On CNBC's *Street Signs*, the verdict was in: "Centaur's stock price hasn't just cratered. It's freaked."

with their uncle Alfonso. And Mariano Aguerre, another 10-goaler, is married to their sister, Tatiana."

"They sound like royalty."

"Exactly. Anyone who knows polo knows the Piereses, the Heguys, the Gracidas, and the Harringtons. That's why Juancito's murder is so shocking. That's why the White House wants this case closed. Juancito is a crown prince in Argentina. Down there, everybody follows him. He's like Pope Francis. You don't know the Pope because you're a Catholic. You know him because you're an Argentine."

Hunt looked out on the field. His eyes squinted. A slow smile crossed his face. He nodded in the direction of a rugged-looking horseman cantering a dappled grey in a figure eight. The man wore Rio Bravo's colors.

"That's him," Hunt said. "That's King. King Kenedy."

Cris recognized the familiar figure and noticed how at ease he was in the saddle. She found herself drawn to the grey the Senator was riding. There was a majestic quality to its carriage, something unhurried, purposeful but not forceful, focused yet calm.

"King plays back," Hunt said. "That's the position I used to play. Thanks to King, I was a pretty good back once upon a time. King taught me just about everything I know about this game. And what I didn't learn from him I picked up from your not-so-secret admirer."

"Joe? At Bice? He was just flirting."

"King also let me play his string. Playing one of King's horses is like driving a Ferrari. Quality-wise, nothing can compare to their responsiveness and handling, and cost-wise, they are *way* out of my league." Hunt pointed at the grey. "My entire salary couldn't buy her. Not that King would ever sell Terlingua."

"How do you know that horse's name?"

"I've played Terlingua many times. She's just like Juancito—royalty. Maybe even more so. Trace her breeding and you'll find A.P. Indy, Seattle Slew, and Secretariat. That mare, she *is* the game."

"Wait a minute. I haven't gotten past the fact that you know that horse's name. When was the last time you saw that horse?"

"The last time? How about I tell you about the first time I saw her—at Rio Bravo when I was a teenager. How about I tell you what it was like to play her in Midland when we won the Galindo Cup? She's got to be coming on seventeen or eighteen, and from what I can see, she's only getting better with age. The fact that King is warming up on her in the US Open says it all. Those two are ready to play high-goal."

Cris stared at her colleague.

"And to answer your question, the last time I played her was in Aspen at a snow polo tournament eight or nine years ago when I was still at West Point."

Cris's head arched back in laughter. "You've got to be kidding me. People actually play polo in the Rocky Mountains in the middle of winter with snow on the ground?"

"People play polo everywhere. And in every imaginable condition. They play it on elephants. They play it at the beach. They play it on snow. On King's ranch, they play it on fields that don't have grass. They call that a skin field. It's just dirt, and it's the best way to sharpen your ball-handling skills. I have no doubt that when this game got its start on the Asian steppes thousands of years ago, it was on a skin field."

Cris looked out over the lush field, the brightly colored banners, and the well-dressed crowd. "I don't see anything rough or rugged about today's match."

"There's a lot more going on here than meets the eye," Hunt began. "What you are witnessing today is a reunion of sorts, one that takes place several times a year at different championships in different countries. Polo is a closed set. Pick out almost anyone in this crowd and put them at Guards, that polo club in England, or at Palermo in Buenos Aires, and I promise you they're not going to know just one or two people. They're going to know a slew of people. And they'll be one person removed from dozens of others they already know. I've never been to Australia, or Kenya, or Chile, but if I went there tomorrow, through polo I'd have places to stay, friends to see, and horses to ride. And that's the real reason I was sent here. If Juancito's murderer is a jealous husband or some jilted lover in Palm Beach, then you and I just got a pair of free tickets to a US Open semifinal. But if someone in polo murdered Juancito, or if someone in polo had Juancito killed, odds are I know who that person is. And you know what else that means?"

"No. Like I told you, I know nothing about this game."

Hunt nodded. "What it means is they know me too."

47

HUNT TAPPED THE TOP OF Cris's hand and pointed to a polo player galloping after a ball. "That's SOB, warming up."

Down on the field, SOB stood up in his stirrups, cocked his mallet, and blasted the ball from 120 yards out. It sailed between the goalposts 10 feet off the ground.

"He's quite the player."

"I can assure you he'd agree with you."

They shared a laugh.

"You and Joe never told me how this friend of yours was gifted with such a flattering nickname."

"It's a genetic hazard among the O'Briens, although if your given name were Selden, you might actually prefer to refer to yourself as SOB. You'll meet him after the match. He's Rio Bravo's No. 1, their only 10-goaler, and from what Joe tells me, he's been playing 12 goals this season. Behind him, you've got the Gallego brothers as the team's No. 2 and No. 3," Hunt said, as he pointed to two polo players riding side by side. "King is at back. He's their No. 4."

"This morning you said that all polo players are rated from 0 to 10."

"That's right. But SOB is a scoring machine. Lights-out good. Been that way since we played junior polo. The official USPA handicapping system is from 0 to 10. So when someone like Joe says SOB is playing 12-goal polo, what he's really telling you is that the guy is playing off the charts."

"Sounds like you know him well."

"All too well. We were always at each other's throats, the bane of each other's existence. Growing up, I was the only back in junior polo who could stop him from scoring at will. And he was the only guy on the field who knew how to get past me. You won't be surprised to hear that Joe, the other coaches, and even King encouraged this cutthroat competition of ours every chance they got."

"On the polo field?"

"Everywhere."

"RICHARD!"

Down the stairs and into the Rio Bravo box stepped a stunning older woman.

Hunt immediately rose to his feet. "And here she is, the fairest of them all."

With a flourish, Hunt introduced Lupe Kenedy to the Secret Service agent.

"Lupe, may I present to you Special Agent Cristina Cortés."

"Not until you give me a big kiss, baby," Lupe replied.

As Hunt leaned in and kissed her on both cheeks, Cris took in Lupe's white Carolina Herrera button-down, her Ralph Lauren tailored trousers, the leather "H" Hermès belt, and her Ferragamo flats.

"What a pleasure to meet you," Lupe said, and she took Cris by the hand. "And look at you. The two of us are the best dressed at the match today. Come sit next to me."

Although she had witnessed countless VIPs up close and in person, the Secret Service agent was immediately taken with the gracious elegance that distinguished Lupe Kenedy.

"Why didn't anyone tell me that you two would be joining us today?" Lupe asked.

"Because no one told us either," Hunt said. "Both of us are on assignment, investigating the death of Juancito."

"Poor man," Lupe said. "Such a tragedy."

"The news still hasn't sunk in with me," Hunt lamented. "I heard about it last night in Buenos Aires, and I have no idea what time you got the call here in Florida."

"You don't want to know," Cris said.

"By midmorning, we were both in Palm Beach. Then I talked Joe into coming to town and grabbing a bite with us."

"At the lunch counter at Green's?"

"Believe it or not, I actually got him to meet us at Bice."

Lupe braced herself in her seat. "What sort of inducement was required?"

"I blamed it on this federal agent," Hunt said, pointing a thumb at Cortés.

"Nicely done, Richard. The man does have a roving eye," Lupe said.

The umpire blew the whistle to signal the end of the pregame activities. The eight players began to ride toward the two officials in the center of the field. One lagged conspicuously behind the others.

"Is Ernst Crutchman still playing?" Hunt asked incredulously.

"As bad as ever. I take that back. Worse than ever," Lupe said. "During their last match, in the quarterfinals, he T-boned one of his own players at a full gallop. Can you believe that? One of his own players. It was the worst wreck any of us had ever seen."

"Was anyone hurt?" Cris asked.

Sadness emanated from Lupe's kind face. "It broke my heart. They had to put that beautiful mare down. On top of that, he single-handedly took Piaget out of the playoffs."

Cris was confused. "But aren't they playing in today's match?"

"The team may be," Lupe said. "But their captain isn't." She pointed to the opposite side of the field. "Do you see that poor man with his arm in a sling?"

Cris nodded.

"That's the player that Crutchman T-boned, his own team captain. The accident ended his season and quite possibly his career. Only time will tell how his surgery went."

"That's certainly going to make life easy for SOB today. Joe tells me our boy has been having a whale of a season," Hunt said.

"Did he?" Lupe asked quietly.

"He sure did."

"Is that all José told you?"

"Of course not. We talked about Rio Bravo's season, how the team was playing, and a lot about Juancito."

"I mean about Selden."

Hunt paused. Lupe never referred to SOB as Selden. No one in polo ever referred to SOB as Selden. Not even SOB. Something was in the offing.

A moment later, a chill began to inch its way up his spine.

49

"HOW LONG?" HUNT ASKED.

He was staring down on the field, his eyes riveted on Rio Bravo's No. 1.

"How long what?" Cris asked.

Lupe rested a restraining hand on the Secret Service agent's arm.

Hunt closed his eyes. "How long?" he asked a second time.

The engaging smile on Lupe's face vanished. She pointed behind Hunt. "Grab him," she said. Cris turned and caught the attention of a passing waiter.

"A bottle of White Star, if you don't mind," Lupe requested. She motioned to her guests. "Captain Hunt may want something stronger."

"I'm fine, thank you," he said.

"That's what you think," Lupe said.

Cris took note of the change in Hunt's demeanor. He wasn't rude. He didn't seem angry. As best she could tell there was a complete absence of emotion. But his eyes betrayed his poker face. They were intently focused on their hostess, reading her every move.

"I've been dead-set against it from the very start, Richard," Lupe said.

"How long has SOB been dating Ava? Or should I say how long has Ava been dating SOB?"

"My daughter has always insisted on speaking for herself. This is one instance where I am more than happy to oblige." Lupe nodded down the steep stairwell to the bottom of the grandstand.

A group of photographers was stalking a tall, tan blonde in a boldly striped blue-and-white button-down, tight-fitting Wranglers, and the sort of paddock boots that equestrians, not polo players, wear. A bright orange Hermès belt was her lone nod to her mother's fashion sense.

In her arms, she carried a black Italian greyhound with intelligent eyes, alert ears, a narrow muzzle, and long, long legs. As they made their way up the stairs through the throng, they were greeted by noisy hellos and a sharp whistle or two.

Cris noticed one final point: Ava Kenedy was drop-dead gorgeous.

50

THE INSTANT AVA SAW HER former fiancé, the crowd jumped to its feet.

Down on the field, the game had just begun. King Kenedy connected with the opening throw-in. He tapped the ball across the midfield line and followed it up with a solid hit. His Rio Bravo teammates broke into a full gallop. SOB got to the ball first and whacked it downfield. It was a four-man cavalry charge chasing the ball to goal.

Up in the stands, their waiter returned, balancing a tray of Champagne flutes and a bottle of White Star on ice. Before they could say a word, the Italian greyhound that Hunt had given Ava leapt from her arms into his. Hunt caught the hound, but not before the dog hit the tray, knocking over the flutes, the bottle, the bucket, and the waiter, who collided with Ava.

"SOB, SOB, SOB!" the announcer yelled as the 10-goaler stroked the ball through the uprights.

The White Star exploded. The Champagne flutes shattered. Ice skidded everywhere. Ava's dog barked. Lupe screamed. Her daughter's eyes filled with fear. She was falling backward toward the stairway. At the last possible moment, Hunt threw himself forward and latched on to her hand. Fingers entwined, his grip tightened, he reeled her in and pulled her to his chest. They were face to face, just inches apart.

The stadium erupted in cheers. Ava let out an astonished gasp. The Army captain quietly smiled.

"You always did know how to make an entrance."

51

THE THUNDERING OVATION THAT GREETED Rio Bravo's goal prevented anyone but Ava from hearing Hunt's words. Yet sitting beside him, the Secret Service agent could tell he had hit his mark.

Bravo, Captain Hunt, Cris thought.

In spite of herself, Ava could not stop smiling. Her chest was heaving. Adrenaline coursed through her veins. For a long moment, she held her ex close. The applause was unrelenting. She closed her eyes, ignored her dog's excited yelps, and felt herself laughing a laugh that was more purr, one only her ex could hear and feel. She immediately sensed the many things that made this soldier so different from all the others: his scent, their fit, and the way he always held her so close yet so easily.

The moment Ava looked up and saw Bullet licking Hunt's smiling face, her body stiffened. "Those are the only kisses you're going to be getting in this company, Captain Hunt," she said. She poked him sharply in the ribs and pushed him away. "Unless, of course, your lady friend here is inclined to swap spit with you."

Ava turned to Cris and held out her hand.

"Ava Kenedy. Please forgive me my rudeness. But I will say, on my own behalf, that I've been waiting the better part of a year to sink a wooden stake through this man's heart, and wouldn't you know, when he finally gets the guts to show up to polo, he brings a date. And a beautiful lady at that." She leaned in closer. "Love your Jimmy Choos."

"Cris Cortés," the Secret Service agent replied.

"Mama, has this bad boy been misbehaving?" Ava asked.

Her mother slid over and took an empty seat, leaving room for her daughter next to the Secret Service agent.

"Of course he hasn't." Lupe was still beaming at the way her Richard had saved the day.

"Oh, that's right. You always did take his side. Maybe you should have married him."

Lupe gave her daughter a polite, measured look. In a quiet voice known only to mothers and daughters, she couched her response. "Your loss, not mine."

Oh my, Cris thought. Clearly, Captain Hunt was an emotion-charged topic, one previously discussed at length by her hostesses.

Ava noticed her Italian greyhound still loving on her ex. She made a quick clicking noise. The dog's eyes instantly sought out his mistress. "Quit giving him a lap dance." The dog immediately jumped out of Rick's lap, across Cris's, and into Ava's.

"You've certainly got him well trained," Cris said.

"The dog? Yes. The man? No. Never could get him housebroken. That boy needs a shock collar and a game fence. And now that we're no longer an item, I'd definitely have him fixed. Has he tried to mount you yet?"

"No, not yet," Cris said coolly.

"Don't put it past him."

Cris couldn't decide who had a better song-and-dance routine: the mother or the daughter. Although she just met both, the similarities were plain to see. The Kenedy women were naturals: natural beauties, natural wits, and both shared a complete inability to filter their comments. Ava definitely had an earthier, grittier side. She was no less refined than her mother, but she certainly came in a much stronger dosage.

"Since I picked him up at the Miami Airport this morning, I've been trying to learn as much as I can as quickly as I can about everybody and everything in polo. I had no idea this world existed."

Ava smiled sweetly. "Where on earth was he this time? London? Dubai? Kandahar?"

He can tell her if he wants. Cris leaned in and lowered her voice. "I assume he was overseas. He came through Customs."

"That figures. My ex only goes to fabulous places. He only gets fabulous assignments, meets fabulous people, and takes fabulous trips. He's got a fabulous life, and I never wanted to take that away from him. All I wanted was to be his fabulous girl. But the only way to get on his agenda is to get yourself listed as one of his fabulous priorities. Either that or be one of those ambassadors or princes he runs around with."

The Secret Service agent smiled.

Or princesses, she thought.

THE ROUT WAS ON—JUST AS Lupe predicted. By the end of the first chukker, the score was a lopsided 5–0. Without its captain, Piaget was hobbled, and Rio Bravo could do no wrong, scoring at will and stifling the few offensive threats its opponent mustered. The second chukker proved to be more of the same. After the teams switched goals and the umpire bowled in the ball, SOB got control of the throw-in, broke out of the pack, and went untouched all the way to goal. The crowd roared its approval, and none louder than Hunt.

"S-O-B!" he bellowed, both hands to his mouth.

After the crowd quieted down, Ava leaned forward and looked at her ex. "Make sure you don't pocket-dial anyone."

Hunt took his penance in silence. Cris exchanged glances with Lupe, and they chose not to acknowledge Ava's barb.

"He's quite the player," Cris said.

"Selden certainly is," Ava said.

"You don't call him SOB?"

"Richard uses that silly old nickname because he's a 3-goal amateur who never made it to the big leagues and Selden is a 10-goal professional at the top of the game. Everybody in polo knows Selden's talents. Those who can remember Richard's excel at Trivial Pursuit. Since Selden and I have been dating, I've insisted everyone on the team call him by his given name. Even Daddy."

Yes, ma'am!

Rio Bravo's next scoring opportunity was already taking shape. King intercepted a poor pass, turned the ball, and was moving it across the midfield line when Ernst Crutchman angled his horse directly in front of the Senator's. Then Crutchman attempted the feeblest of back shots. One of the field umpires called the foul.

"Did you see that?" Lupe asked.

Cris shook her head. "I did, but I didn't. Tell me what I missed."

"In polo, the safety of the horses is the paramount consideration. Players, even the best players, are a distant second. And what Mr. Crutchman just did endangered my husband's horse as well as my husband. The man crossed the line of the ball. Not only is it against the rules to impede play like that, but quite often it's the first step to inviting a wreck, which is why the foul was called. Let's see what King makes of it."

The Senator nailed the penalty shot and upped Rio Bravo's lead to 7–0.

Ava put two fingers in her mouth and let loose a shrill whistle. "Way to go, Rio Bravo!"

During the break between the second and third chukkers, the announcer's clipped British accent broke in over the public address system:

"Ladies and gentlemen, allow me to introduce some of the distinguished guests joining us for today's match. I'm sure you'll agree with me that no one is more welcome than our host in the Sunshine State, the Governor of the State of Florida."

The state's chief executive stood up and waved to the crowd.

"The accomplishments of our next VIP will undoubtedly thrill most of you, but his superlative performance in last summer's Westchester Cup pained all of Her Majesty's subjects here in Palm Beach, myself included. How about a round of applause for America's best-known soldier and sportsman, our very own Captain Rick Hunt."

Applause broke out as Hunt stood up. To Cris's surprise, the ovation was longer and more vocal than the governor's. Friends of Hunt's in the crowd shouted out his name—in English and Spanish—and he responded by gamely pointing and waving to them all.

After he took his seat, a quiet shrouded the Rio Bravo box. Hunt smiled.

"The only reason they know me is because at one time or another I've pocket-dialed every single one of them."

Now it was Ava's turn to sulk in silence. Lupe and Cris did their best to keep straight faces.

By the end of the third chukker, the match was a bona fide blowout. Rio Bravo had jumped out to a 10–2 lead. Less than a minute remained in the first half when a big hit sent the ball bouncing over the brightly painted wooden boards and out-of-bounds. One of the umpires reached down from his horse and grabbed the ball with a pickup stick. The two teams lined up for the throw-in. The umpire bowled the ball between them. It immediately became lost in a sea of horses' legs and polo mallets. In the middle of this melee, Ernst Crutchman boldly rode to the rescue and put everything he had into his best imitation of a roundhouse swing.

CRACK!

For the first time that afternoon, Crutchman connected—but not with the ball. The sharp sound that echoed across the field and all the way up to the Rio Bravo box was the hard head of his wooden mallet slamming against the gloved hand of another player.

53

A BLARING HORN SIGNALED THE end of the first half. The crowd surged forward, out of the stands and onto the field.

Hunt turned to his left. "Ladies?" he asked.

"Thank you, Richard. But I'm fine right here," Lupe said.

Ava turned to the Secret Service agent. "You want to learn about polo?"

"Absolutely."

"Then let's go," Ava said, pointing down to the field. "The divot stomp is where everything happens. People pretend to stomp in the clumps of grass that have been ripped up during the first half. What you're really doing is catching up with everyone about everything in polo, including the murder of you-know-who."

Cris nodded, and the two followed Hunt down the stairway. Almost immediately, the pace of their descent came to a complete halt as spectators poured out from both sides of the aisle. Family friends, old teammates and former foes, grooms and *patróns*—people of all ages and stations called out to the Army captain, shook his hand, and hugged him. The scene reminded the Secret Service agent of watching the President make his way into a fundraiser at the Fontainebleau a few months before.

"*¿Qué tal, Ricardo?*"

"Great to see you, Rick. Where have you been all this time?"

"Good on you for bringing the Westchester Cup back to the States."

Cris could see that Rick was back in his element. For a man who once hoped and dreamed of becoming a professional polo player, this was the closest thing possible to a homecoming. A smile lit up his face as he greeted friends. Out of the corner of her eye, Cris glanced at her companion.

Uh-oh. Ava's face was white. Then Cris turned and looked up at the Rio Bravo box. Lupe's smile was sublime, her eyes flitting between her daughter and Hunt.

"I don't have all day," Ava harrumphed. She picked up her dog and made her way across the row of seats and down another aisle. The Secret Service agent followed. When they reached the bottom of the stands, Cris took a final look. Hunt hadn't moved. He couldn't. The throng had only grown bigger.

"Where to?" Cris asked.

"I need some retail therapy."

"Count me in."

Ava made a beeline for the boutiques on the far side of the stands. Minutes later, the two strutted out onto the playing field in matching Ralph Lauren sun hats. Each was presented a glass of Champagne, courtesy of one of the tournament sponsors. Like everyone else, they gravitated toward a Maserati Gran Turismo parked at midfield by yet another sponsor. Dozens were gathered round the silver sports car; but they were standoffish, gawking but keeping a careful distance.

"What am I missing?" Cris asked quietly.

Ava strolled a discreet distance from the crowd. "Maserati sponsors the US Open," she explained. "And each year, the tournament's best player is given a convertible to drive the following season."

"Let me guess. Last year's best player—?"

"Was murdered yesterday."

No wonder the hushed voices and dark looks. Cris was struck by the irony of the bright colors, the sparkling Champagne glasses, and the strained whispers about Juancito's fast life and death.

"People actually do talk about polo during the divot stomp. But it's not always the game you're watching," Ava added.

More people stopped and stared at the Maserati. Cris could tell they were drawn to it, yet afraid to get too close.

"Trouble ahead," Ava said. Her eyes tilted in the direction of an overly tanned man in his seventies approaching them. Cris remembered seeing him when she first arrived at the polo stadium. He was dressed to the nines—a seersucker suit with matching pocket square, alligator slip-ons with no socks, and a pair of faux-tortoiseshell sunglasses. He reeked of old Palm Beach. She saw the cane he carried was definitely not a prop.

Ava went into whisper mode. "Trip is a dear friend of my parents, and he's a major power broker in Palm Beach County, but every woman in Palm Beach knows him as the Groper. He's got a lovely wife about half his age, but I bet he's so tired after pawing all of us that he never lays a hand on her."

"Hello, lovelies!" the Groper said.

"Trip! So good to see you," Ava exclaimed, picking up her dog. Cris watched Ava skillfully deflect her assailant's attempts to wrap his arms around her by shielding herself with Bullet. Still grinning, he set his sights on Cris.

"And who might you be?" he said as he approached the Secret Service agent with open arms.

"Someone with a touch of the flu," Cris said lightly.

The Groper stopped dead in his tracks. "The hip replacement I just endured almost did me in. I'm sure some Asian virus would be the coup de grâce," he said, looking aghast. "Now, where were we?"

"Cris and I were just talking about Juancito's murder."

"Who isn't!"

"You don't really think Kelly did it, do you?"

"There's no doubt in my mind that she is capable of rogering the poor boy to death. That woman is a carnivore, a sexual predator at the top of the food chain. But pulling the trigger, that seems a bit far-fetched, don't you think? The consensus at The Grill today was that there was no consensus. Our lone Argentine blamed it on the British. What a surprise. The Falklands, the Hand of God goal—those two countries always have it out for each other, don't they? Our British delegate insisted some jilted sheikh wanted Juancito drawn and quartered. I had no idea the Harringtons had been anywhere near the Emirates or Qatar or wherever it was they played. Where did they ever find the time? And since none of our Arab friends were present, they had no way of defending themselves against the scurrilous claims of my fellow reprobates."

"Are you still taking lunch at the Palm Beach Grill every day?"

"Since the day it opened, Ava dear. And don't think I've failed to notice that you have yet to take me up on my offer to join me for *le dejeuner*."

"Hold on," Cris said, suddenly alert. "Did you have lunch at the Grill yesterday?"

"I most certainly did. A superb *loup de mer* with sautéed spinach and a delightful Oyster Bay Sauvignon Blanc. I'm sure my tab indicated that several glasses were served."

"Did you happen to see Cesare Harrington?"

"How could I not? He was seated directly across from us at the bar. He showed up toward the end of the luncheon service at around one thirty with that Argentine leprechaun of his. That's early for them. Hell, some of those gauchos don't even think about dinner till midnight."

"So he's a regular there?"

"A regular? The Grill is his mess of choice, my dear. He's always lunching there with friends from polo or banker types or some other subspecies of moneylender."

"Did anything stand out in your mind about yesterday?"

"No, not really, my dear. I regularly eavesdrop on them. During my misspent youth, I spent several summers in Madrid perfecting my Castilian. Yesterday, they were yammering back and forth about Juancito's unexcused absence. Both of them called the poor man and left messages. When that proved useless, they ordered him lunch to go."

"That doesn't sound very out of the ordinary," Ava said.

"You're right. But in the middle of it all, something clearly caught Cesare's attention. He picked up and put down his phone who knows how many times, but I never saw him answer it."

A loud horn summoned the spectators back to their seats for the start of the second half. The trio turned and joined the hundreds of others migrating toward the grandstands. Without so much as a word, the Groper broke formation and zeroed in on a new target, a stylish young thing unfortunate enough to be walking by herself.

Cris followed Ava and Bullet up the stairs to the Rio Bravo box. There was no sign of Rick Hunt. Lupe was by herself. They both saw the troubled look on her face.

"What's wrong, Mama?"

Lupe nodded toward the playing field. Ava and Cris both turned to look. Both teams were gathered at midfield for the start of the second half. To Cris's untrained eye, nothing seemed out of the ordinary. But by the looks on the Kenedy women's faces, something was definitely amiss.

"Where's Daddy?" Ava asked.

"¡CABALLERO!"

Like a clarion, King Kenedy's voice carried across the din of the crowded pitch. Hunt was still a ways off from the team's tent, winding his way through the frivolity of the divot stomp, yet he could already hear his late father's best friend. Joe Bigelow was steps away. So too was Don Eliseo, King's lifelong groom. King's teammates, the Gallegos and SOB, were taking a breather under the tent.

All at once, the busy bodies and crazy colors on the field washed away from Hunt's mind. So too did the dark cloud of Juancito's murder. Instead, they were replaced by sights and sounds he knew deep in his heart: grooms racing against the clock, tack boxes and ice chests opening and slamming shut, a chorus of snorts and whinnies from the pony lines. Despite the red-eye from Buenos Aires, his run-in with Raul Ramirez, and the shock of the death of someone he knew and respected, Hunt was suddenly glad. He was back where he belonged. He had been gone far too long. This was Hunt's polo family.

"¡*Caballero!*" King called out again.

Hunt walked straight up to the Senator. "¡*Hola, señor!*"

King eyed Hunt's suit. "So where did the Chief track you down?"

Hunt smiled. "He busted me. I was AWOL from the embassy at one of B.A.'s finest *parilladas,* about to enjoy a plateful of grass-fed beef. Instead, I had the pleasure of a rise-and-shine breakfast at four o'clock this morning at 40,000 feet, somewhere over the Caribbean."

King nodded. "Good man, Ari."

"Thank you for reminding him of my ties to polo," Hunt said, voicing an unspoken truth. He knew why he had been hauled out of Argentina, and now he knew who the perpetrator was as well. The Senator merely smiled.

Rio Bravo's team veterinarian stepped into their midst.

"What have you got—a bowed tendon, navicular, colic?" Hunt asked.

"This might be Crutchman's only solid hit this season," King said, and he held out his mallet hand for Hunt to inspect. His right thumb was swollen to twice its normal size, the nail splintered. As Hunt eyed the injury, the vet threaded a fine needle. It was time to suture the wound.

"You sure you don't need a painkiller, Senator?" the vet asked.

King shook his head.

Hunt laughed. "Let me guess: no Novocaine, no tetanus shot, no nothing."

"Did Teddy Roosevelt need Novocaine when he charged up San Juan Hill?"

"TR didn't have three chukkers yet to play in the US Open. How are you going to ride out like that?"

"That's the best part."

"Sir?"

"I'm out," King said. "You're in."

Hunt's eyes widened. "I won't make you ask twice, but you do realize that I have not been on a horse all season."

Joe Bigelow strolled over and shook his head. Gone was the easygoing man who picked up the tab at Bice. In his place was a nine-time winner of the US Open gunning for his tenth crown. "Get in that trailer and get some whites on."

Hunt knew his marching orders when he heard them. He walked directly to King's trailer and stepped inside. Everything he needed was arrayed before him: a stack of folded white Wranglers, two sets of knee guards, four polo helmets, three pairs of boots, an unopened six-pack of socks, and half a dozen pairs of gloves. Hunt stripped to his skivvies and began donning a polo uniform. He was only half-dressed when the horn signaling the second half went off. He heard footsteps on the ramp and turned to see Joe.

"Thanks for the heads-up on Ava, amigo. Really appreciate your letting me walk into the Rio Bravo box flat-footed."

"Knew you could handle it. Now do yourself a favor and don't play Crutchman. We've got this game won. I don't want that one-man wrecking crew taking another one of us out. Got it?"

"Read you loud and clear. How about a jersey?"

"Go get it from King. Said he wanted to give it to you himself."

Hunt picked out a plain white helmet and walked out of the trailer bare-chested. In the distance, he could see the throw-in signaling the start of the second half. The vet was already bandaging King's wound.

"As good as new," the vet said. He snipped off a last bit of adhesive tape and packed up his kit.

"*Gracias*," King said, and he turned to Hunt. "I see this little mishap of mine as an opportunity, not a setback."

"Are you referring to what I think you're referring to?"

King paused and cleared his throat.

"It has been too long since a Hunt has worn these colors." He reached down with his good hand and scooped up a perfectly pressed black jersey with the number 4 emblazoned on the back. He placed his bandaged hand over the numeral. "You've earned the right to wear them, but I honestly thought you'd never get the chance."

Hunt nodded. "Neither did I."

"All too often, life proves us wrong," King said. "And today, that's a good thing."

With both hands, he presented his team's colors.

"Welcome to the high-goal polo. Now get out there and enjoy yourself."

HUNT STEPPED FORWARD AND STOPPED. He couldn't believe he was about to ride out in the Open, and on King Kenedy's finest mare. Terlingua pawed the turf. Don Eliseo smiled at her impatience and softly held the reins.

"*Ya esta lista,*" he said, revealing a golden tooth.

Terlingua breathed deeply and let out an exasperated sigh. Hunt heard her girth and saddle leathers stretch and strain. The noise had a hypnotic effect. It was just Hunt and his horse, this magnificent mare, once again.

With his left hand, he reached around her broad neck. King had already played her twice in the first half, but Hunt sensed she was still fresh. With his right he stroked her withers. As his hand stroked her softly, he felt her heat. He smelled her pungent sweat.

"What's the holdup?" Bigelow barked.

"Not a thing," Hunt said. He put his left hand on the pommel and deftly vaulted into the saddle. No step stand. No foot in the stirrup.

"*¿Vamos a ganar, Ricardo?*" Don Eliseo asked. Hunt knew the *vaquero* would not relinquish his mallet until Hunt confirmed that he was playing to win.

"*¡Tengo ganas!*" he said. Like a scepter, the mallet handle was placed in the palm of his hand.

Hunt immediately leaned forward and tightened his knees against the dappled grey. Terlingua rocketed over the boards and out onto the field.

High up in the grandstands in the Rio Bravo box, the three women saw a player in the black-and-white colors of Rio Bravo dash out to join the others.

"Ladies and gentlemen, we'll be seeing a change of lineup for Rio Bravo. I regret to inform you that during the final throw-in of the first half, Senator

Kenedy took a nasty hit and will sit out the remainder of the game with what, in all likelihood, is a broken thumb. Carrying 3 goals and riding in his place at back for Rio Bravo will be none other than Captain Rick Hunt."

The crowd let out a cheer.

"This can't possibly be happening," Ava said indignantly.

Lupe smiled serenely. "Oh yes it can."

Cris could only shake her head in amazement.

Down on the field, Hunt saw that SOB had taken control of the opening throw-in. Their team a man down, he was slowing the tempo of the game by dribbling the ball purposely and patiently. In a change of tactics from the first half, not one but two Piaget players were marking him. The first was the team's back. The other was Ernst Crutchman. Both were just feet from him. Hunt saw an opportunity. Fast approaching on Terlingua, he pointed her directly at SOB. Instead of slowing down, he sped up.

"What's he doing, Mama?"

Lupe's eyes focused. Cris leaned forward.

"Something's not right, Mama."

Hunt bore down on SOB with a half a ton of horseflesh. But SOB wasn't looking. He glanced at the two players marking him, glanced down at the ball, and tapped it again. By the time he looked up at Hunt, Terlingua was just a few strides away, her hooves pounding.

Hunt locked eyes with SOB. *Game on.*

"Stop!" Ava pleaded. "Before you kill him!"

Cris held her breath.

At the very last moment, Hunt executed a sharp turn alongside SOB's mount. Simultaneously, he reached down with his mallet and, with a flick of the wrist, plucked the ball away from SOB. Then he slapped it downfield with a nearside forehand.

"Would you look at that, ladies and gentlemen!" the announcer cried out. "Captain Hunt has stolen the ball from his own teammate!"

Hunt and Terlingua not only surprised SOB; the two caught everyone on the field flat-footed. The crowd jumped to its feet as Hunt spanked the ball a second time. It was a solid hit—straight and true—and it angled directly toward the uprights. Hunt spurred Terlingua into overdrive. She tore down-field, her furious strides going ever faster. This is what she lived for. This is what

Hunt lived for. With his left hand, he urged the mare forward. With his right, he readied his mallet. He didn't even think of glancing over his shoulder. The immense field spread out before him. No one stood a chance of catching them.

The three-inch white ball had come to rest directly in front of the goal-mouth. A feather would knock it in. But Hunt wasn't just playing polo. He was making a statement—to one of his teammates, to his former fiancée, and most of all, to himself.

Instead of tapping it over the line, Captain Rick Hunt rose out of the saddle, took his biggest roundhouse swing, and clocked the ball with all his might. The cigar-shaped mallet head slammed into the rock-hard plastic ball and sent it arcing into the sky like a shooting star. It was the boldest play of the game. It was the boldest play of the tournament, the ideal way to kick off another three chukkers of the best polo in America. The stands exploded with a roar.

"What a goal!" the announcer crowed.

"And not another player within a hundred yards. In his first seconds of play, the Army captain reminds each and every one of us what an up-and-comer he once was. And to think he set aside his polo career to serve his country. Clearly, the Westchester Cup champion still knows a thing or two about the game of kings. He just stole the ball from his 10-goal teammate and extended Rio Bravo's lead to 11–2."

THE FIRST SEMIFINAL OF THE US Open was no longer a polo game. It was a grudge match between Rick Hunt and SOB. And the grand prize sat grinning from ear to ear in the Rio Bravo box.

"I thought he was going to kill him," Ava said.

Lupe laid a hand over her daughter's. "He may yet."

"I know that, Mama. There's this side of Rick you never want to cross. And I may have done it last summer. Then I made it worse by going out with Selden this season. But he's got to learn not to cross me either. Oh, poor Seldie. He's the one I'm worried about."

The Secret Service agent was speechless. *Who are these people?*

On the opposite side of the field, Joe Bigelow was all smiles. "Got to hand it to you, King. Called that one right."

The Senator nodded. "Those two are going to be playing for keeps every minute of every chukker till that Open trophy is ours on Sunday. I guarantee it."

Down on the field, SOB and the Gallegos waited for Hunt to slow Terlingua, turn her around, and ride back onto the field. The crowd was still applauding his massive goal when he joined his teammates.

"Same old Rikki. Never knows his place," SOB said.

Hunt smiled back. "I appreciate your teeing that one up for me. Anyone could see that you were in a rut and needed some help with Crutchman's man-to-man coverage."

"Here we go," Roberto Gallego said. "You two are picking up right where you left off."

"I've got to be honest, Rikki. You've been more help than you can ever imagine," SOB said. "As long as I've known Ava, she always treated me like roadkill. I'd have never stood a chance of getting the time of day from her till you screwed the pooch last summer. I'm sure she's already told you that she's the one who called me, hasn't she?"

Roberto and Ramon were laughing out loud. "Take it easy, man. We can't have two murders in polo in one week," Ramon said.

Hunt reached down and patted Terlingua's sweaty neck.

"The only thing I know about Ava these days is that she's up there clapping for me like everyone else in those stands."

The four had arrived at midfield. It was time for the next throw-in.

"To be continued," SOB said as they took their positions.

As Rio Bravo's No. 4, Hunt lined up opposite Ernst Crutchman. He had never played against the financier before, and he quickly sized him up as he would any polo player.

Fire in his eyes? None.

Eager to play? No way.

In command of his horse? Not in the least.

The moment Hunt saw Crutchman put his mallet on the near side of his horse, he knew the man would be completely ineffective. There was no way that a player in the first position could make a play on the ball. His only conceivable play was to block Hunt, but he was too green to realize this. Hunt turned to the umpire, who had the ball hidden behind his back, and waited.

As soon as the ball was bowled in, Hunt positioned Terlingua in between Crutchman and the play, effectively cutting him off. Hunt waited for Crutchman to ride through him and follow the play. But he didn't. The man's polo skills were nonexistent.

Over the next sixty seconds, Hunt watched Crutchman cross the line of the ball, endanger the safety of his own mount, and then, when his horse slammed on the brakes to avoid a crash, almost fall out of his saddle. Hunt realized that the umpires were ignoring every one of Crutchman's minor fouls. Not only were none dangerous, but the match would have turned into a nonstop series of penalty shots if they had.

Hunt didn't think twice. He wheeled Terlingua around and galloped away from Crutchman. It had taken him a minute to digest the wisdom of Bigelow's instructions: keep an eye on the one-man wrecking crew aboard the leopard Appaloosa.

Now it was time to punish SOB—again.

Despite Hunt's bold goal, Piaget showed no signs of easing up its double coverage of SOB. That left Roberto and Ramon in man-to-man coverage and no one on Hunt. He seized the moment.

Whenever Hunt got control of the ball, he moved it downfield himself. Why hurry? Rio Bravo was way out in front, and the clock was on their side. Hunt picked and chose when he wanted to pass it to the Gallegos or if he wanted to carry it himself. There was no way he was going to let it go near SOB, which left his lifelong adversary fuming.

"Pass it, Rikki. Pass it!" SOB yelled again and again, but to no avail.

SOB had been white-hot throughout the tournament, scoring at will and buttressing his 10-goal prowess. Yet for some reason—a reason that was quite apparent to those in the Rio Bravo box—Hunt seemed capable of passing the ball only to Roberto or Ramon. The lone instance when SOB got control of a loose ball, he went straight to goal. He weaved in and around defenders, and his epic ball-handling skills led to a superb shot. But the roar of the crowd was replaced by a collective groan when the flagger signaled the shot was just inches wide, her bright banner fluttering from side to side beneath her waist.

By the time the final whistle blew, Rio Bravo had won in an 18–4 rout. Yet not one of the team's second-half goals belonged to its superstar. To make matters worse, 5 of Rio Bravo's 8 goals were credited to Captain Rick Hunt.

SOB made his displeasure clear to all of his teammates by riding off the field well ahead of them. By the time Hunt and the Gallegos arrived at the team's trailers, he was nowhere in sight.

Hunt dismounted, and was greeted by Don Eliseo's toothy grin. "¡Qué chingón!"

"Gracias a Dios," Hunt said, and he handed the vaquero his mallet.

Hunt walked toward the team tent. Lupe welcomed him with a warm embrace. "Your father would have been so proud of you today," she whispered.

"Thank you," he said, a quiet pride in his voice.

As long as the Boss's wife was speaking her mind, no one dared approach Rio Bravo's newest member. No one except Joe Bigelow.

"SOB sure thought you played some piss-poor polo out there. Said you were a ball hog with worse passing skills than he ever remembered. At least that's what I heard him grousing about to Ava when he skulked off to lick his wounds."

"I know it. Today was my one shot at the US Open, and I let it go to my head."

"No, it wasn't," Joe said.

Hunt stopped in his tracks.

"It wasn't your one shot at the US Open."

King spoke. "I'm not playing on Sunday. You are."

"Have I told you about my day job and who I report to?"

"Don't worry about Ari. I'll take care of him. As long as you stay on task, he'll honor my request."

A delighted grin crossed the Army captain's face. "So be it."

Latin music was playing over the stadium PA system. A festive vibe echoed throughout the Rio Bravo camp in the wake of the team's blowout. Hunt saw Cris walking over from the pony lines. In her bright dress and flowing hair, she was Palm Beach polo to a tee, and her new hat made her stand out even more.

"Nice lid," he called out and walked toward her.

She stopped and posed, a hand on either side of the sun hat.

"You wore yours today pretty well too," she said.

They laughed, and she walked up to the tent. As she arrived, Joe Bigelow playfully shoved Hunt right at her. Hunt caught her in his arms. Then he swiveled her, turned her, and dipped her backward, all to the beat of the music. As he pulled Cris upright, she let out a laugh.

"Just another day at the office, Captain Hunt?"

57

"I JUST WROTE YOU A million-dollar check, dropped it on your doorstep in a brown paper bag, and now you're telling me not to get my hopes up?"

Jack Dick stormed back and forth, his rant echoing the length of the ornate library. Before him, around a long conference table, sat a handful of his key advisors and their underlings. None dared to speak.

"I have big problems, and I need big answers. NOW."

The silence that filled the room only stoked Dick's anger, which he focused on the legal legend at the foot of the table.

As soon as Kelly's arrest was broadcast, Dick convened an emergency meeting of his War Council. It was an all-hands-on-deck command, and over the next six hours, Centaur's fleet of corporate jets ferried its out-of-town members to Palm Beach. By late Wednesday afternoon, his chief legal counsel, Centaur's marketing director, and the company's P.R. team had converged at the seaside estate.

Casa de los Santos was otherworldly—in size, in setting, and in design. On the inland side, a canopy of ancient banyan trees shielded the Addison Mizner masterpiece from prying eyes. On the ocean side, floor-to-ceiling windows framed views of the surf. As the War Council began, massive white clouds reached to the heavens over the Atlantic. It was a breathtaking vista, but no one thought to enjoy the view, especially the newest member of Dick's kitchen cabinet.

The moment Raul Ramirez dragged Kelly Dick up the front steps of Palm Beach P.D., every journalist knew who would get the call: Joshua Shapiro. Drug possession, drunk driving, tax evasion, manslaughter—the Miami-based trial attorney's well-heeled clientele had been tarred with countless salacious charges. Thanks to the talents of the renowned jurist, however, few ever did hard time. But setting in motion Shapiro's legal schemes took weeks, if not months. On rare occasion, years of preparation were required. Which is precisely why Dick was so angry—and Shapiro so measured.

Shapiro was more than just a brilliant litigator. His knowledge of procedural nuance was encyclopedic. For more than three decades, he had taught a course in advanced criminal evidence at the University of Miami. And his pretrial preparations were beyond exhaustive. His investigators, his jury selection specialists, the expert witnesses he paid handsome sums to testify—each was the best in the business. Thanks to his extensive media contacts, he enjoyed a unique ability to manipulate headlines. His critics claimed he orchestrated them. To further accentuate his extensive media presence, two twentysomething techies who specialized in social media sat nervously at the table.

"Do not expect a miracle tomorrow," Shapiro began. He answered Dick's hard questions in a soft voice, and he used the long fingers of his expressive hands to put the brakes on his client's expectations. "Due process cuts both ways. Over the next twenty-four hours, the State of Florida will be calling the shots. That's how the system works. Tomorrow morning, they'll hold a first-appearance hearing, and I can assure you we will be denied bail."

"Let me congratulate you for setting such a high bar for yourself."

"I realize it may come across that way, but at this stage in the case the primary driver is probable cause. I haven't seen a report from the crime scene, but from what I gather, there is more than enough circumstantial evidence for them to go for a first-degree murder charge. On top of that, given your resources, they'll undoubtedly label her a flight risk."

"I can assure you I will not let her out of my sight."

"That will be helpful. But not tomorrow. They're going to throw the book at her, toss the key, and then pat themselves on the back. As soon as they do that, I can step in and start to work. By then the police will have finished trashing the crime scene, and we'll get our investigators over there. Meanwhile, we can start setting up interviews with every one of the hotel's employees. We'll track down people who saw Kelly before she arrived, after she left, and of course, anyone who interacted with the deceased. We'll do a far better job than the State gathering evidence. But what we won't do is have a chance tomorrow morning."

"That's not good enough. We got slaughtered in the market today. And if tomorrow morning goes as you just described, it will be more of the same when the markets open."

The distinctive clicking of an all-metal door handle signaled the late arrival of the last member of Centaur's War Council. Into the library strolled a tall gentleman with thinning red hair brushed back over a freckled tan. He wore a Van Dyke peppered with red-and-white stubble, a windbreaker, and pressed khakis.

"Where the hell have you been?" Dick demanded.

"I was under the impression I was your polo manager, Jack," the man calmly responded in a breezy British accent. He plopped his straw fedora on the table.

"You were this morning. I'm not sure you will be tomorrow."

"And as your manager, that would be why I was watching a very impressive Rio Bravo team advance to Sunday's final." He greeted Dick's familiar retinue with a polite nod and extended a hand to Shapiro.

"Neville Haynes, at your service."

"A pleasure. Joshua Shapiro."

"Mr. Shapiro here has helped himself to a million of my dollars. The only catch is, he can't do a damn thing about Kelly till I'm flat broke."

"Got to give the man credit then."

"What the hell do you mean?"

"For getting paid in advance." Haynes winked at Shapiro and took a seat.

"You are not the least bit funny. Not today. Not in these circumstances, dammit."

"You're the one they call Mr. Australia, correct?" Shapiro asked.

"That you are. My father was a British cavalryman once posted to Australia. That's where I became smitten with horses. There's many a photograph of me at a young age in a felt hat with a feather plume, riding out with the Australian Light Horse Brigade."

"Perhaps you'd like to add something of value?" Dick demanded impatiently.

"It would be my pleasure, Jack. Much like us, Rio Bravo found itself a man down this afternoon. King Kenedy, actually. Broken thumb. Turns out they were able to replace him with a much stouter player. Army man. Quite good. They'll be formidable on Sunday."

"I don't care about *their* team. What about *ours*? What about tomorrow? Do we even have a team?" Dick demanded.

"I have contacted the tournament committee on a dicey rules interpretation that would enable us to draft into service a player who was ineligible to participate in the Open at its onset several weeks ago. I won't bore all of you with the particulars, but if this individual were deemed eligible and if Cesare Harrington could be convinced to play, Centaur could in fact field a team. Otherwise, we're out."

Shapiro's eyebrows peaked. "The show *must* go on," he said, looking directly at Dick. "It is absolutely crucial that you follow your day-to-day routine as though nothing out of the ordinary has taken place." He turned to Mr. Australia. "Part of what I just finished explaining to the group is that we must attack these charges on all fronts: in our pretrial preparations, in the courtroom, in the press, and I suppose, even on the polo field. Given what you just described, is that even possible?"

"Right now, our chances of fielding a team tomorrow are twenty-five percent at best."

"Twenty-five percent?" Dick bellowed. "They'd better be one hundred percent."

Haynes rested his chin on his crossed hands. "Am I to gather you're giving me carte blanche?"

"I'm not giving you carte blanche. I'm giving you an order. I'm telling you to do whatever it takes to get us a team!"

"Consider it done."

"You can start by picking up that driver of mine. At this very moment, the little twit's $100,000 get-out-of-jail-free card is being processed at the police station."

"What on earth did he do to deserve a $100,000 bail?" Mr. Australia asked.

"They're grabbing at straws, labeling him an accessory," Shapiro said. "It seems he had in his possession credit cards belonging to everyone affiliated with your polo team—Jack, Kelly, and both of the Harringtons—as well as a copious amount of cash."

"That's fraud, old boy, not murder. More to the point, that's polo. As Jack knows all too well, polo is all about other people's money," Mr. Australia said.

"And other people's wives," Dick added sourly.

Centaur's CEO abruptly stilled. His face began to contort. He grabbed the chair in front of him and gripped it tightly.

"Are you OK, Jack?" Shapiro asked.

"Take it easy, old boy," Mr. Australia said. He looked down the length of the table and pointed at one of Shapiro's techies. "You there. Alert the staff. Have them fetch a doctor."

"What the hell is going on?" Dick demanded.

"Take it easy, Jack. We'll ride out this storm," Shapiro said.

"Who are these people?"

Everyone swiveled in their seats.

A long line of heavily armed men could be seen infiltrating the grounds from the water's edge. Another troop spilled out onto the patio from around the opposite wing of the estate. Weapons drawn, they peered in windows and jiggled door handles. A thumping noise began to buffet the library's windows. Almost immediately, a police helicopter swept overhead.

Centaur's War Council stared in disbelief. Only one member had the presence of mind to speak up. He was also the only member with any actual combat experience.

"From the looks of it," Mr. Australia said calmly, "I'd say we are under attack."

58

WALTER NED WAS GRINNING FROM ear to ear.

No one enjoyed a better view than he: from the police helicopter hovering over the palatial estate. Down below, the department's SWAT team was storming the grounds from the beach. Arrayed in single file, they hustled past colorful sprays of bougainvillea as they rushed Casa de los Santos. Sheriff's deputies had encircled the main residence from the front and were securing the terraced gardens. Ned could see one of his videographers hot on their trail. The other one was grabbing aerial footage from the chopper alongside Ned's favorite still photographer. In the cockpit, next to the pilot, sat Raul Ramirez, coordinating his land-and-sea attack.

Within minutes of hauling Kelly in, the detective set out to secure a search warrant. By midafternoon, all available Palm Beach police officers and as many PBSO deputies as could be mustered were enlisted to scour the largest private residence in the Palm Beaches for the pistol that ended the life of Juancito Harrington. But Ramirez was not about to let hidden hands derail his case this time. His unholy alliance with Ned focused the glare of the Palm Beach press corps on his investigation. No safeguard was as strong as the public eye.

Sitting in the back of the chopper, Ned knew that he still owned the biggest story on the planet. In the space of a few hours, the brash journalist had gone from being Raul Ramirez's arch nemesis to his personal publicist. Some of Ned's co-conspirators were greedy. Others spiteful. Many craved the spotlight. But not Ramirez. Ned realized that embarrassing Kelly Dick and her husband gave Ramirez a visceral pleasure. That's why the detective delighted in dragging her up the police station steps. That's why he swallowed his pride and let Ned violate her privacy before a worldwide audience. That's why Ned just landed another scoop—the land-and-sea invasion of Casa de los Santos.

"Don't take no for an answer," Ramirez shouted into a handheld. "Barge right in. It's our legal right." Suddenly, he pointed to an opening door. "There he is!"

As he stepped out of his library, Jack Dick's all-black attire and distinctive silver mane made him easy to spot. Several members of his War Council were visible peering out at the spectacle from inside.

Ned grabbed his shooters and thrust them toward the open door. "Get him!"

Their timing was perfect. The look of surprise on Dick's face was palpable, even from the treetops. Dick looked up at the police helicopter and shook his fist defiantly. It was a made-for-TV moment.

Walter Ned had struck again.

59

"**HOW COULD I HAVE MISSED** him? I was just speaking with the desk sergeant not five minutes ago, and he told me that Mr. Garcia was still on the premises."

"That was me, sir. And he was right here. All I can tell you is now he's gone."

"Much obliged."

Mr. Australia made his way outside in the fading twilight and stood on the front steps of the Palm Beach P.D. He looked up South County Road. He looked down the winding boulevard and scratched the back of his head. Despite the media frenzy on those very steps earlier in the day, not a single pedestrian was visible, only the taillights of a distant taxi.

Where did he go?

A few blocks north at Royal Palm Way, the Yellow Cab stopped at a red light. On green, the taxi turned left. In the backseat, its normally chatty passenger was completely silent. As the cab passed Hibiscus Avenue, Rio eyed the wedding-cake white building where Juancito and Cesare had their offices. For an instant, he could see just a corner of the Brazilian Court a block behind it. Not a flower had been moved, not a blade of grass was out of place, yet everything had changed.

Rio Garcia was beyond scared. He was witless. Who would kill Juancito? *I next? They maybe murder me too.* Or would it be Cesare? *Why stopping with Juancito? Who can stopping them?* Had Kelly really killed Juancito? *She love him. But she loving a lot of polo players. They the worst, polo players, so jealous, so happy Juancito dead.* Or was it Jack? *That man hate everyone, especially himself.*

Rio pulled out his cell phone and tried to power it on. When the screen failed to light, he shook it furiously. The driver noticed and nonchalantly handed him a cell phone charger. Rio sighed and connected it to his phone. As soon as it powered up, dozens of chirps and whistles followed as voice mails and text messages registered.

"Shut up!" Rio yelled. "I'm not talking to you—or you or you or you!" The driver eyed him in the rearview mirror and maintained a grip on his own phone just in case.

They crossed the Middle Bridge and followed Okeechobee toward I-95. But instead of continuing back to Juancito's condo in Wellington—where dozens of members of the media were camped out—Rio instructed the cabbie to turn onto the interstate. He knew where to go. He knew where to find Cesare.

Cesare always know what to doing.

60

FEW CORPORATE TITANS HAD FALLEN so hard so fast. Jack Dick's star polo player, the very face of his company, had been murdered. Not only was his wife the prime suspect, but she had also been the dead man's lover. Those facts were the least of Dick's concerns. His company's stock price was in a nosedive. Billions in market capitalization had evaporated. To make matters worse, the police in Palm Beach were treating him like a punching bag while the press had turned his private life into a punch line.

Capping it off had been the arrival of a search party that violated every norm of decency. Like all of the Dicks' estates, security at Casa de los Santos was provided by Centaur Corporation. A single discreet call to the head of operations and a team of officers could have had the run of the grounds. Instead, Dick, his guests, and his employees were blatantly manhandled with no regard for their rights. And not a single one of them had been charged with a crime.

Late Wednesday evening, after all the police and every last employee of the *News of the World* had left, Dick found himself backed into the darkest corner of his career. In lightning-fast succession, he made two decisions. The first was strictly cosmetic. Per Joshua Shapiro, Centaur's end-of-the-season gala— the Polo Ball—would take place as scheduled that Friday night on board the *Centaur*. Only it would be bigger and better than any event Palm Beach had ever seen, a night to remember.

His second decision was strictly personal: Dick sought sanctuary. It was the only way he could put an end to the avalanche of bad press that was driving his company's stock price down. The longer he stayed in Palm Beach, the more likely he was to be subjected to the whims of a judicial system that was out to make him a scapegoat.

He wasn't the one on trial. He wasn't the one schtupping Juan Harrington. Yet at the police station, at his barn, and now at his own home, he had been the one who had been bullied. He had been the one who was belittled. And it was costing him millions.

Yet just twenty miles off the coast of Florida, one of the world's largest megayachts was en route from the Bahamas. The *Centaur* was completely self-contained. On board was everything he would need. Better yet, it was completely insulated from the press. Best of all, Palm Beach P.D. couldn't lay a finger on him while he sat parked in international waters. All his minions knew about the megayacht, yet none had thought to put it to use on their behalf. But Dick had, which is why, he concluded, they worked for him and not the other way around.

Less than an hour later, the ship's helicopter landed on the back lawn of Casa de los Santos. The embattled CEO walked outside and boarded it. Then, in a shroud of darkness, he retreated out to sea.

61

IN SOUTH FLORIDA, ONE PLACE and one place alone reminded the Harringtons of their homeland. Not the bright lights of Buenos Aires or the majestic views of the Andes but the sleepy sounds of the pampas where they had been boys: boys who loved horses, boys who lived for polo, boys in love with life.

Called Payson Park, the secluded compound sat just outside Indiantown, less than an hour's drive from polo yet light-years from Palm Beach. Hidden among groves of yellow pine along the banks of the St. Lucie River, it was built in the 1950s by a cadre of horsemen that included Bull Hancock, Michael Phipps, Christopher Chenery, and Townsend Martin. Although these men and their partners had the wherewithal to build their own Xanadu, they set their sights on a far loftier goal: creating the world's finest Thoroughbred training center. Payson Park's simple barns, plain dormitories, and spartan cafeteria emphasized their earnestness. Its mile-long oval proved their point. In the decades that followed, Payson Park's salt-kissed soil became recognized as the finest dirt track in North America. Numerous alumni—2- and 3-year-olds that trained on this oval—went on to win Graded races, Breeders Cup crowns, and even the Kentucky Derby.

Payson Park was built by horsemen for horsemen, which is precisely why the Harringtons were drawn to it. Their first visit proved indelible. Bill Mott was training a 4-year-old Palace Music stallion. The bay's catchy name—Cigar—overshadowed its good-but-not-great campaign as a 3-year-old. A new trainer was sought, Mott got the call, and his first move was to spell the horse at Payson Park. His new charge needed more than training. He needed confidence.

On a brisk spring morning, the Harringtons arrived at dawn and promptly joined Mott atop the viewing stand. Down below, Cigar was paired with a standout 6-year-old. The two breezed the first few furlongs. Once they hit the turn, however, the older horse muscled his way into the lead. A seasoned veteran, he hugged the rail and saved precious steps. Cigar's response was anything but expected. The younger runner shunned the challenge and slipped in behind his adversary, conserved his strength, and began stalking the pacesetter. Confidently. Only when the duo hit the home straight did Cigar swing wide. Now he had a clear view of the finish line. Now he was ready to make his move. He galloped his rival into the ground.

The hair on Cesare's neck was standing straight up.

"*Qué fabuloso*," Juancito said to his brother.

Cesare turned to Mott and told him to name his price. The Hall of Fame trainer laughed. Neither he nor the horse's owners, Allen and Madeleine Paulson, were about to let this one slip through their fingers. Later that year, Cigar began an unprecedented two-year-long winning streak that culminated with his victory in the first running of the world's richest race, the Dubai World Cup.

Now, more than a decade later, Cesare Harrington sat by himself atop that very same viewing stand. Only there were no runners. The trainers were gone, off racing their Triple Crown hopefuls at Aqueduct, Oaklawn, and the Fair Grounds. Cesare was by himself. He had been all day. After being assaulted by Walter Ned and his *News of the World* cohorts, Raul Ramirez refused to let him return to Wellington or to even consider staying in Palm Beach.

With its gated entrance and round-the-clock security, Payson Park was the ideal safe haven for Cesare to ponder the world without his brother the dreamer. The successes they built together—their polo team, their breeding operation, their global holdings—no longer existed. *They* were gone.

In the distance, the lights of an approaching car appeared. As it pulled up by one of the barns, Cesare recognized that it was a cab. A familiar silhouette emerged and waved the driver off. Then Rio disappeared into the cafeteria.

Cesare could feel the weight of the day returning to his shoulders. He took a last long look at the dark reaches of the track. Then he made his way down the stairs off the viewing stand, down the dirt road, and inside the building. Rio was face down at a table. He was sobbing. Cesare walked over and put a hand on his shoulder. Rio couldn't lift his head.

"What are we going to do?" he asked in Spanish.

"We are going to take our brother home."

"When?"

"It doesn't matter. Tomorrow. Friday. Whenever he can leave."

"But what about polo?"

"What about it?" Cesare asked.

"Aren't you going to play?"

"Of course. Maybe this summer. Maybe we take the summer off and wait to play in the Tortugas. What's the hurry? Juancito was the one who made it fun."

"Why wait so long?"

"To honor our brother."

A creaky screen door opened, and a solitary figure in a straw fedora stepped inside.

"May I suggest another way to honor your brother?"

DESPITE HER BEST ATTEMPTS TO pretty herself up, the jailbird jumpsuit was simply not Kelly's best look. That said, the fluorescent orange poly-cotton blend was a total eye-catcher. After spending the night in a see-through Plexiglas cell in the solitary unit of the county jail, she stole the show Thursday morning at eight o'clock as she debuted at her first-appearance hearing on the eleventh floor of the Palm Beach County Courthouse.

Outside Judge Singhal's courtroom, television crews from WPTV, WPEC, and WPBF were broadcasting live updates on the morning news. Inside, along the back wall, journalists and photographers from the *Palm Beach Post* and the *Sun Sentinel* sat shoulder to shoulder alongside reporters from the *New York Times*, the *Wall Street Journal*, and *Barron's*. Walter Ned sat well removed from his fellow journalists. At Raul Ramirez's invitation, he joined the detective in the front row immediately behind the State Prosecutor. Only a few feet away, right behind the defense table, sat Jack Dick and select members of his War Council.

Kelly seemed remarkably fresh-faced as she was led into the courtroom. Her poised demeanor was briefly shaken when she saw Ned. His smile repulsed her; his wink she found revolting.

A pit bull in a black pantsuit, State Attorney Ellen Roberts made it clear that her office possessed extensive proof of the suspect's criminal activity: video of Kelly's arrival at the Brazilian Court, eyewitness testimony of her presence in the Lancaster Suite, and forensic evidence of her presence not just in the suite but on all parts of the victim as well.

Considering the aggravated nature of the charges—first-degree murder—and the vast resources at the disposal of the accused—access to a private jet,

offshore residences, and an oceangoing vessel complete with its own crew—
Roberts asked Singhal to deny bail.

Shapiro's counterargument was masterful. It was a tour de force, a legal
primer, one that would have convinced almost any jury. Unfortunately, it did
not convince the court. Singhal denied bail and remanded Kelly Dick to the
Palm Beach County Detention Center.

As Kelly was hauled off, Jack Dick closed his eyes. His worst fears had come
true. Everything he had worked for was now working against him. Centaur's
head honcho was caught in a tectonic collision of sex and money and sports
and death. Only now, for the first time since he had become chairman and
CEO of a Fortune 500 company, he was powerless to alter the tide of events.
Lawsuits he could buy his way out of. Meddling analysts could be reassigned.
But the glacial workings of the judicial system? Not a chance.

At their first meeting, Shapiro made it clear that if Kelly were denied bail,
it would be weeks until additional steps could be pursued. Months might pass
before she was freed. But weeks and months were not the timeframe of the
Street. Even before the judge's decision was announced, gutsy traders were
betting that Kelly would be treated to an extended stay off Gun Club Road at
the Palm Beach County Detention Center.

In overnight trading, Centaur firmed up at $120. At the open, it bounced
around in a tight band from $119 to $122. The instant the judge's decision was
announced, it plummeted to new lows. Within minutes it had fallen through
the teens and was testing $112.

Centaur's free fall was an absolute panic.

IN A ROUTINE INVESTIGATION, THE officers on the case subsequently convene to discuss next steps. They consider the evidence, develop their conclusions, and put their findings in a document called an offense report. Yet on the Thursday morning after Juan Harrington's murder, it was anything but standard operating procedure at Palm Beach P.D. Standing room only was more like it. Not only were Ramirez and his investigators reviewing the evidence, so were a lieutenant, two sergeants, and several of Ramirez's fellow detectives.

Fortunately for Hunt, all eyes were fixed on an oversized, flat-screen TV when he stepped into the large conference room. The Army captain was late. Since his surprise selection as a member of Rio Bravo, he found himself shouldering the demands of a professional polo player, including reveille at o-dark-thirty followed by several hours riding sets at King Kenedy's polo barn. Roberto Gallego didn't show. Ramon Gallego wasn't there. Neither was SOB. Top-tier pros didn't ride sets at sunup. But Joe Bigelow was present and accounted for, and so was King Kenedy, who was inspecting his superb string of polo ponies when Hunt arrived.

By the time he finished showering and shaving, Hunt sensed he was cutting it close. As he strode out of the barn, he saw Ava pull into the parking lot. She drove a bright yellow '66 Bronco, and she was chatting with a wiry *vaquero* with a big moustache and a cowboy hat. Hunt immediately recognized Lalo, one of Don Eliseo's grandsons. More to the point, Lalo was Ava's groom. Her horses were his life, and this was especially the case with the Olympic trials just weeks away.

As a nationally ranked show jumper, Ava trained all year long. Compared with polo's lax schedule of twice-a-week practices, twice-a-week games, and some stick-and-ball, the demands she endured were brutal.

"Missed you after the match," he said as she neared.

"That's not the picture I got," she answered sharply and breezed past him.

Hunt knew that Ava was making a point. What sort of point, he didn't know. But her tone said it all. Her tone and her shirt. It was a man's shirt, custom-made in Houston by Hamilton, and it bore three initials embroidered on the pocket: SOB. Hunt recognized the Egyptian cotton. Ava had given him the very same one. She had woken up with SOB. She had gone to sleep with him. The two had dressed together. They had undressed together.

Not the picture I got?

Hunt knew the picture he was getting.

On the drive into Palm Beach, he alternated between fuming at himself, fuming at Ava, and fuming at the bumper-to-bumper traffic. Wellington, Lake Worth, West Palm—the sleepy little bedroom communities he remembered from his visits long ago had all grown up. Jog Road was a nightmare. Military Trail was under construction. And the Congress Avenue intersection? The worst.

There was no way he was going to be on time for his morning meeting at Palm Beach P.D.

64

HUNT WAS DEFINITELY RIGHT ABOUT his timing. By the time he finally arrived at the Palm Beach police headquarters, they were already screening the movie of the week: a highlight reel from the Brazilian Court's closed-circuit security cameras on the morning of Juan Harrington's murder.

Hunt slipped in and took a seat as Ramirez was updating all present on the particulars. "Here we see the victim stepping out of his Range Rover at 11:35 a.m. The driver of the vehicle is a lifelong friend of the victim who confirmed that he was going to meet the suspect. Notice that Mr. Harrington proceeds directly from the main entryway through the lobby to a large patio and court-yard adjacent to Café Boulud," he said.

The detective chose not to narrate a fast-moving series of black-and-white clips, short snippets that featured an outrageously good-looking Juancito or sometimes only his shadow gliding in and out of view through doorways and beneath ivy-covered arches. Every frame was time-coded; all were shown in sequential order. "The shots from this final camera show him entering the second courtyard where the Lancaster Suite is located."

"So there is no additional footage of the decedent?" Cris asked.

"That is correct," Ramirez said.

Kelly Dick starred in the next series of clips. "Here the suspect arrives at the hotel at 9:09 a.m. In these shots, she is making her way to the salon to have her hair blow-dried," the detective said. Then he paused. "Notice the large tote bag under her arm. We assume this is how she transported the murder weapon."

Everyone watched as Kelly greeted several individuals en route to the salon. Hunt was surprised that she made no attempt to mask her presence.

"Who is that man?" Hunt asked.

"The general manager of the Brazilian Court," Ramirez said.

Hunt looked across the table at the Secret Service agent. She had shed her colorful polo attire and reverted to the more somber Secret Service dress code with her hair pulled back. She caught his eye and nodded.

In the next series of clips, which began at 9:47 a.m., Kelly was seen leaving the Frédéric Fekkai Salon in a bathrobe and a pair of slippers. The same tote was slung over her shoulder. A long shot down a corridor featured her shapely silhouette as she sashayed to the Lancaster Suite. Despite the industrial quality of the black-and-white video, her dark tan glowed and her blonde tresses bounced with her every step. Hunt noticed that the entire room was staring in silence. They were star-struck.

"Dressed to kill," Ramirez said, an icy tone in his voice. No one else spoke.

Hunt kept watching the detective. All at once, it became clear. *This guy's got a grudge.* Hunt continued watching him watching her. Merely watching this woman soured the man. Hunt had rarely witnessed such venom. Now Hunt realized what was driving this investigation. *She's a have, and he's a have-not.*

"Do we know how she lured him to his death?" the lieutenant asked.

Hunt's brow furrowed. *We've already tried and convicted her?*

"Very discreetly," Ramirez answered. "Mrs. Dick was much too savvy to pick up the phone and call this guy. Instead, she might call his driver to arrange a rendezvous. Or she would have her stylist call Mr. Harrington, or her masseuse do it. If all that failed, they would set up a rendezvous by texting each other. Since the beginning of January, when he arrived in Palm Beach from Punta del Este, she has sent him hundreds of text messages."

"How many on the day she killed him?" the lieutenant asked.

"Four. Two from her, and two from him," Ramirez said.

"Tell me the timing," the lieutenant said.

Ramirez grabbed a printout from Kelly's cell phone provider. "The first exchange took place at 9:18. She reached out to him with an invitation to meet her at the Brazilian Court: 'need U NOW @ BC.' He responded at 9:19 by saying, 'Hold your horses while I'm riding mine!!!'—implying that he would be there as soon as he finished at the barn. An hour and a half later, at 10:57, a second exchange took place. This time our little princess was a little more insistent. Clearly, she wanted him to get a move on it."

"What did her text say?" the lieutenant asked.

"Need your body NOW!!!" Ramirez responded. He paused and looked up from the printout. "May I point out that the 'NOW' was in all caps. Beyond that, all it said was that she was in the Lancaster Suite at the Brazilian Court. His response was 'Si 30 min,' the Spanish word for yes along with an estimated time of arrival of half an hour. Thirty-seven minutes later, guess who we have on camera walking through the lobby of the Brazilian Court?" Ramirez asked.

No one thought it necessary to respond.

"A dead man," Ramirez said.

65

FOR THE FIRST TIME SINCE his arrival in Palm Beach twenty-four hours before, Rick Hunt truly understood why Ari had overnighted him from Argentina. It wasn't to monitor the fallout and report back to the White House. It was to solve the murder of Juancito Harrington *despite* Palm Beach P.D. No one got it: the crime, the victim, or the repercussions.

Hunt motioned to the text messages. "May I?"

Ramirez perked up. "Of course, Captain," he said, and handed them over. "For those of you not familiar with our guest, Captain Hunt is the White House liaison on this investigation. As we are all aware, the homicide of a foreign dignitary of Mr. Harrington's stature is a matter of national importance, which is why Captain Hunt and Special Agent Cortés of the Secret Service have joined us. In addition, we must all be sure to treat Captain Hunt as a dignitary in his own right."

"I'm not sure I follow you, Detective."

"Then let me be the first to congratulate you on your fine performance yesterday," Ramirez said. The sarcasm in his voice was noxious. Hunt scanned the group seated round the conference table and noticed that his Secret Service contact was doing an excellent job of keeping her eyes on her notes.

Hunt assumed that the snide comment was in reference to his performance on the polo field. Then Ramirez held up a copy of *InStyle* for all to see.

Splashed across the top of the front page was a color photograph of Hunt in a sweat-stained Rio Bravo jersey doing a tango dip with an unidentified woman in a sun hat. A banner headline gave the final score. Bold type described the Army captain's meteoric rise:

"FROM SPECTATOR TO GLADIATOR"

Now Ava's terse comeback at the barn made sense. *This was the picture she got.*

Fortunately, Cris's oversized hat preserved her anonymity. The fact that her colorful shift dress in no way matched what she was wearing when Hunt walked out on Ramirez earlier that day furthered the subterfuge. On the other side of the table, the Secret Service agent feigned disinterest.

Hunt knew Ramirez was challenging him. He couldn't back down.

"Never underestimate the skill set of a West Point graduate." He smiled proudly. A surprising number of laughs followed, much to Ramirez's annoyance.

Across the table, Cris alertly raised her pencil. "Could I ask you about any emails the decedent may have received yesterday morning or earlier in the week?"

"That's an easy one," Ramirez answered. "To the best of our knowledge, Mr. Harrington did not use email. If he did, his account was not linked to his cell phone. He used a Nokia flip phone for calling and texting. That's it. Here's his bill. No mention of any data plan." Ramirez held out a breakdown of the current wireless usage.

Cris held up her pencil again. "Could we have a look at the clips of Kelly leaving the Lancaster Suite?" she asked.

"There aren't any. It's off-camera, not on their security grid," Ramirez replied. "She planned this out to perfection. Gets her hair done, has sex with this guy on every piece of furniture in that suite—except, God forbid, in an honest-to-goodness bed—then serves him his last meal and puts a bullet in his head. The suite is located off the rear courtyard with direct access to Brazilian Avenue, so she skips out the back gate."

Hunt turned to Ramirez. "Do we know where she went?"

Ramirez nodded. "She had an appointment with a personal shopper at Tory Burch."

"What was her ETA?"

"Her appointment was at noon."

"Did the salesperson indicate that there was any mention or indication of what might have just taken place at the Brazilian Court?"

"We haven't been able to track her down. So far we've only spoken to her manager," the investigator said.

The tone and direction of Hunt's questions were clearly agitating Ramirez. "Let's get back on topic. Any other details about her Tuesday morning we need to know?"

"Yes, sir," said one of his investigators. "Prior to her arrival at the Brazilian Court, she made and received a total of three calls to a personal cell belonging to the manager of the salon. The manager confirmed that she always schedules all of Kelly's appointments."

Cris looked up. "Tell me about this salon manager. What did her background check show?"

The detective shook his head. "We haven't had time to go there yet," he said.

Hunt closed his eyes and breathed deeply. *You've got a key witness to a capital crime who spoke to the primary suspect three times the morning of the crime, and no one has even bothered to do a routine background check?* Out of the corner of his eye, he saw Cris frown. *I'm glad I'm not the only one who thinks this investigation is a farce.*

"What about other guests? How many were on the property the night before? Were there any suspicious check-ins or check-outs yesterday afternoon?" Hunt asked.

Ramirez raised his hand with mock deference. "Captain Hunt, if you don't mind, let's hear the forensics report that pertains to the accused murderer already in our custody before we start to consider your long list of suspects who may or may not have been hiding on the grassy knoll." There was an ugly pause as Ramirez's scorn soaked in. He turned to his longest-serving staffer, the balding crime scene investigator seated to his right. The man required no cue.

"It's her, all right," the investigator said. "Her hair, her fingerprints, her skin under his nails, her lipstick on his body. We'll get DNA results next week. Not that it will matter. The only thing that's missing is the murder weapon. She's totally clean. She's never registered a firearm, and she's never had any training. The Dicks have their own private security staff, a bunch of ex-FBI guys. We gave it a good go yesterday. Had twenty officers turning that place inside out and upside down, but didn't turn up a thing." There was a long pause as everyone pondered the fate of the missing murder weapon.

Hunt stood up and motioned for Cortés to join him outside.

"Can I help you, Captain?" Ramirez asked.

"No need to, Detective," Hunt replied. "You've done a superb job of convincing everyone in this room why Kelly Dick is your primary suspect."

"So am I to assume your assignment here is done?" Ramirez asked.

"Exactly the opposite. My assignment is just beginning."

"Now I'm not following you."

"I didn't expect you to."

Cris began to gather her things.

"Since you rolled out the red carpet for me yesterday morning, you have made it abundantly clear that you and I are not working toward the same end," Hunt said.

"Is that so?" the older man said smugly.

"Yes, Detective, that is so. Your goal is to close this case. Mine is to solve a murder. As best as I can tell, you've focused all your resources on a single suspect, and you're filtering all the evidence to support that case. I'm not about to fault you, but I won't applaud you either."

"You have my sincerest gratitude."

Hunt looked Ramirez directly in the eye. "Consider yourself lucky that you don't report to me, Detective. Yesterday morning, I would have read you the riot act for that charade you pulled on the police station steps. Everybody in this room knows that any defense attorney worth his salt is going to crucify the prosecutor who ends up assigned to this case because of the way you've prejudiced the jury pool. Given the amount of money Jack Dick will spend to defend his wife, his name, and his fortune, you're looking at a change of venue right off. Anyone here want to disagree with me?" Hunt asked. He looked right at the lieutenant.

Not a single person uttered a word.

"And yesterday afternoon, I would have taken you off the case for that stunt you pulled at Jack Dick's estate. What were you trying to do—serve a search warrant or stage a reality TV show?"

Ramirez was ready to go for Hunt's throat. But he couldn't. Not in front of a roomful of investigators and department brass.

"Today, however, after listening to the presentation you just made, I would put you on a leave of absence. It's one thing to build a case. It's a completely different matter to willfully ignore evidence that doesn't corroborate the case you're building. How many other leads have you chosen to overlook or not pursue?" Hunt asked.

Ramirez's seething turned into a snarl.

"You're placing a mighty big bet on just one horse, and quite honestly I can't afford to make the same gamble." Hunt grabbed his notes. "And just so everyone knows," Hunt paused and addressed the entire room, "if having Kelly Dick's DNA on your body were a capital crime, you'd have a dozen polo players up on charges at this very moment." He closed his leather portfolio.

"Go ahead and take the easy way out, Detective. I can't," Hunt said as he made his way to the door. "This is no ordinary homicide. It's an international incident, and like it or not, everyone in this room knows that all you've got is a suspect."

66

"SOUNDS TO ME LIKE SOMEONE is turning up the heat on you," Cris said.

"You're right," Hunt said. "Me."

The Secret Service agent and the Army captain walked down the front steps of Palm Beach P.D. and crossed South County Road. Ahead of them, long rows of palm trees lined both sides of the street. Pink and purple flowers clambered up arbors and over fences. A block away, the white awning of the Brazilian Court jutted into view.

"So what's your plan?"

"We're going to solve this case. Me and you."

"Count me in, Captain Hunt."

"So let me begin by asking you a question. Who commits a murder and then goes and buys shoes?"

Cris came to a dead stop. "You've got so much to learn, Captain Hunt."

"Excuse me?"

"Speaking from experience, most women would kill for the right pair of shoes."

Hunt grinned. "Right outcome, wrong scenario, Agent Cortés."

Cris laughed that sexy laugh of hers. Hunt was doing his best to keep the Secret Service agent at arm's length, but it wasn't proving easy. She was much more than just a looker; she was sharp, she had a certain style, she radiated a subtle animal magnetism. And she wasn't his ex.

Neither the time nor the place.

Cris resumed walking. "I definitely agree with you. Given the nature of the crime, a shopping spree isn't the sort of follow-up one expects."

The two were approaching the Brazilian Court. Hunt retrieved a schematic of the crime scene from his portfolio. The intersection of Brazilian and Hibiscus Avenues was distinctly highlighted. But instead of entering through the main entrance, he turned at Hibiscus and led the Secret Service agent to the back of the property.

Hunt now had his first view of the larger crime scene. The hotel was something special. A two-story structure, the Brazilian Court was painted a lemony yellow. It was an alluring contrast to the coral colors and whites that predominated on the island. A black wrought-iron fence framed an archway to one of the hotel's vast courtyards. It was wide open.

Hunt followed the Secret Service agent inside, beneath a stuccoed archway, and into a tropical oasis sprinkled with linen-covered divans and lazy deck chairs. A bathing beauty in sunglasses looked up from a canopied chaise. Her hair in a towel, her limbs cloaked in a robe, she was flipping through the pages of a glossy fashion magazine.

Must be nice, Hunt thought.

She looked up, and they exchanged glances.

"That's the route Juancito took," Cris said. She was pointing past a stone fountain. "This is the way we watched him walk in this morning."

Hunt nodded in agreement.

"Look over here," she said.

Hunt turned. Yellow crime scene tape cordoned off a stairwell. Cris put a hand on his arm and silently nodded toward the stairwell. Hunt agreed. She stepped over the tape and made a beeline up the stairs to the Lancaster Suite.

Hunt stayed put. He was all eyes and ears now. He turned and eyed the easy access off the street. He took note of the pace and the number of vehicles that drove by—a FedEx truck, a Mercedes sedan, a well-tanned businessman in a sport coat zooming by on a Vespa. The Brazilian Court was an urban oasis, but it was by no means off the beaten path.

Hunt turned again and looked from the quieter courtyard to the larger courtyard by the lobby and the hotel's main entrance. In his mind's eye, he visualized Juancito striding confidently toward him just as he had seen him doing in the closed-circuit video. For a few moments, Hunt's imagination brought Juancito to life. He watched the 10-goaler strut by the stone fountain. Hunt saw him toss off a quick hello to the bathing beauty on the chaise. Then

Juancito's grey ghost walked directly past Hunt toward the stairwell. Hunt was positive he saw the phantom polo player look him in the eye and give a quick nod back in the direction of his new acquaintance.

Hunt took his cue from the ghostly glance and started studying the intimate courtyard, the gurgling fountain, the stairway to the suite, and the ingress and egress off Brazilian Avenue. A curly-tailed lizard scurried across the stone pavers and caught his eye. No wonder Kelly had made the Brazilian Court her secret getaway. She could come and go as she pleased.

So could anyone else.

The lush gardens were brimming with birds of paradise. Hunt looked higher up at the canopy of banana trees and their leafy cover.

Why did she parade through the hotel? Why didn't she sneak in? The answer was obvious. She didn't come here to commit a murder. She came here to get her hair done and then to have Juancito mess it up.

The answers to all the questions Ramirez chose not to ask were right here at the Brazilian Court, hidden among the banana trees and the palm fronds. Hunt had no idea whether the detective purposely overlooked them or was simply incompetent, but he knew he had to uncover the truth. With Cris's help, he was sure he could.

"CAN I HELP YOU?" a stern voice asked.

Hunt turned and recognized the general manager of the Brazilian Court walking directly toward him.

"Captain Rick Hunt. I'm assisting with the investigation of the murder of Juan Harrington."

"And your affiliation?"

"I'm out of Washington, sir," Hunt said, purposely omitting his White House ties.

"May I see some identification?"

"You certainly can," a voice responded. It was Cris. She emerged from the stairway brandishing her badge. "Special Agent Cristina Cortés. Secret Service."

"Fred Motsch."

"You're the general manager here," Hunt said.

"That's correct," Motsch said. "And your name again?"

"Captain Rick Hunt, US Army, assigned to the White House." He handed Motsch his card. Judging from the look on Motsch's face, the White House logo had the intended effect.

"Would it be possible for us to have a look at the Lancaster Suite?" Cris asked.

"Certainly. I'm sorry to say, but there's not much to see anymore," Motsch said as he motioned them toward the stairs. "After the police finished tearing it apart yesterday, we had a crime scene cleanup team sterilize the suite."

Motsch made his way to the top of the stairs and led them inside. The living room was bare. Neat vertical lines from a thorough steam cleaning were visible on the carpet. The master bedroom and the master bath were also bare: no furniture, no linens, no accents, no amenities of any kind.

"I've taken the suite out of the room pool indefinitely. You would not believe the number of whack jobs who have already called and tried to book themselves in. TV shows, newspaper reporters—it's unbelievable the rush to get in here. Since Tuesday night, I've had a member of our security team camp out in the room downstairs around the clock," Motsch said.

"You've got a very affluent clientele. They bring their valuables, they bring other personal effects, and yet I just walked in right off the street and was standing just a few feet from one of your guests? Is it my imagination, or is it quite easy to gain access to these grounds?" Cris asked.

Motsch nodded. "You're exactly right. It's a part of our tradition. The hotel was laid out so guests can come and go without being funneled through a main entrance. That's why the Brazilian Court has been a favorite of guests like Marlon Brando and Katherine Hepburn. We guard their secrets well. And this being Palm Beach, a substantial portion of our business comes from locals. It is my staff's job to make them feel at home here too."

"I assume that strategy works," Hunt said.

"Yes, it does," Motsch said. "Speaking on background only, let me say that the Dicks are typical of our clientele. In Palm Beach, the Brazilian Court is their home away from home. Mr. Dick insists we maintain a vertical selection of Jordan Cabernets dating back to the original vintage, 1976. It's not uncommon for our sommelier to buy entire lots of *premier crus* at auction at Sotheby's, Christie's, and Zachy's. For her part, Mrs. Dick's monthly tab at the salon and spa easily tops $10,000," he said.

Hunt and Cris absorbed the sky-high numbers.

"From what I've read of the police reports, there was no record of a room reservation for this suite on the day of the murder. Am I to assume that you just told us how they gained access?" Cris asked.

An uncomfortable pause followed. The Secret Service agent's training with Miami-Dade P.D. had hit pay dirt.

"Please. On background only," she added.

Motsch nodded. "You would be correct," he said.

"How'd she get in?" Cris asked.

"With a key," Motsch said.

"From whom?" Cris asked.

"The front desk," Motsch said.

"But I just watched the video of her entering the property. She didn't stop at the front desk," Hunt said.

"She didn't have to. I imagine the room key was waiting for her at the salon."

Hunt did a double take. Motsch continued.

"To use the parlance of my counterparts in Las Vegas, Mrs. Dick is a whale. At the Brazilian Court, the world is her oyster."

The Secret Service agent and the Army captain nodded.

"Our drivers have chauffeured her down to South Beach for lunch with who knows who. Had nothing to do with our property. But when she asks, we deliver. Same with the impromptu pool parties she throws. Doesn't cost her a dime, and it doesn't cost us that much either. If a room is empty and she wants it, it's hers. We more than make up for it in other ways."

"But why here?" Hunt asked. "Why didn't she do all this at her own estate?"

"I know none of the staffing arrangements at the Dicks' residence. But I can assure you that her secrets were safe at the Brazilian Court. We know what our clients want the moment they arrive on the property. When Mrs. Dick schedules an appointment at Frédéric Fekkai, two or three appetizers from Café Boulud are sent over for her and her friends to nibble on. So is a bottle of Cordon Rouge, her favorite Champagne. I've seen nail technicians hand-feed her bite-size morsels of sushi while her fingernail polish was drying."

"So why has all this been treated as such a state secret?" Hunt asked. "Did these perks violate corporate policy?"

Motsch looked over Hunt's shoulder. There was no one in earshot. "Exactly the opposite, Captain Hunt. They are corporate policy."

"Then who is being kept in the dark?" Hunt asked.

"I'll answer your question with one of my own. What if it got out that there were other individuals, ones who weren't polo players in town for the season but locals who lived right here in Palm Beach, who might also have rendezvoused with Mrs. Dick on our premises?"

"And let's say some of these individuals were married," Cris volunteered.

Motsch winced. "Let's not say that. Let's not go there."

"If that got out, your hotel would be off-limits to more than a few of your best customers, and that would put a damper on your local trade," Cris said.

"Precisely," Motsch said coolly.

"Lucky for you Raul Ramirez couldn't care less about these other angles, isn't it?" Hunt asked.

Motsch gave a quick nod. "The only person who wants an open-and-shut case more than Detective Ramirez is standing right in front of you."

Hunt felt stymied. Downstairs, he had gotten a sense of Juancito's final moments. He could literally see the man breezing through the courtyard. But in the sanitized suite, he had no bearings. It was devoid of details.

Hunt looked at the Secret Service agent. Then he looked at Motsch.

"I need a favor," he said. "Make that two favors—one from each of you. And I need them fast."

THE WHITE HOUSE AIDE QUICKLY made her way to the basement of the West Wing and quietly entered the Situation Room. At the far end of the Sit Room, the Chairman of the Joint Chiefs was making a presentation on a key US military commitment in the Middle East. He was the least of her concerns.

The President, the Vice President, the Secretary of Defense, the Secretary of State, the Director of the CIA, the National Security Advisor, the Deputy National Security Advisor, the National Security Advisor to the Vice President, and the Director of National Intelligence were all in attendance. So too was Ari Auerbach, who sat at the end of the table closest to the door. She quietly placed a handwritten note in front of the Chief of Staff:

> "Palm Beach P.D. jumped the gun. Jack Dick's wife is a suspect but not—I repeat—not the only suspect. Can be reached on my cell at all times.
>
> —Hunt

The President watched Auerbach read the note. He watched him reread it and then fold it in half. Then the Chief placed it in his shirt pocket.

A NERVOUS TENSION RIPPLED THROUGH the capacity crowd.

Less than an hour remained until the start of Thursday afternoon's second semifinal in the US Open, and no one had seen a single sign of Centaur Polo. The team's tent was set up. Its horses were tacked. But with no one to mount, the team's Argentine grooms were sharing some *maté*. The only activity in the pony lines was Mr. Australia, who was meticulously inspecting the team's horses, patting their flanks, soothing their nerves, and gently massaging their tendons.

"Sign of a true cavalryman," said King, who was holding court in the Rio Bravo box. "Take care of your mount, and she'll take care of you."

To his left, Joe Bigelow nodded in agreement. "A good horse can tell you a lot of things, but not where it hurts. It wouldn't surprise me at all to see him find a hot spot and not play the horse on account of a torn tendon or a stress fracture."

"Like he did in the finals of the Gold Cup last month with Tesoro," Roberto said.

"Exactly," Joe said.

King turned to Hunt. "You looking after my string?"

"Me and everyone else in your barn."

"They better be. Those girls tell me everything, including who treats them right or wrong."

At the other side of the end zone, Los Dorados, the top-ranked José Cuervo foursome, wasn't even going through the motions. The entire team was at parade rest.

"Look at those slackers," SOB said. "Just praying for a bye to the final."

He and the Gallegos were seated in the second row of the team's box.

"No way," Roberto said. "I know those guys. They want to do it the right way. They want to earn it."

"Who put that locoweed in your feed?" SOB asked.

Laughter filled the box.

"That's not locoweed, *buey*," Ramon said. "That's good polo. Miss today's game, and it's a full week between the quarterfinals and the final. It might take the whole first half just to get up to speed on Sunday."

"No way, hombre," SOB said. "Your horses will be fresher, and so will your players. Am I calling it wrong?" He turned to Hunt. "Who's right, Rikki?"

"You guys are the pros. You make the call."

"Come on."

"I mean it. I never get to watch high-goal. I couldn't be happier that the game is about to get under way."

"Dream on," SOB said.

All eyes turned toward the players' gate. No cars had arrived.

"What do you got?" King asked.

"The grooms—they're the first giveaway."

All eyes turned to Centaur's pony lines. The entire contingent had descended to check the tack and tighten girths.

"And I don't know who those people are on the far side of Centaur's trailers, but it looks to me like they're putting up a rope line. See that?"

"Big deal," SOB said.

"You're right. It is a big deal," Hunt said. "The cavalry is about to arrive."

"Give me a heading, Captain," King said.

"One o'clock low, sir. Coming in at about 150 knots. ETA in about a minute."

King scanned the eastern horizon. "Got it."

A tiny speck was fast approaching the stadium. It quickly grew larger and more distinct. It was a helicopter, a huge helicopter. As it approached the polo grounds, the dull thumping of its rotors became a drumbeat. Then a roar. By the time it touched down, a logo featuring a stylized version of an ancient constellation was clearly visible on its tail.

"Look at those cockroaches scurry over there," SOB said.

Members of the media rushed toward the helicopter and were immediately ushered to either side of the rope line by a half dozen aides in Centaur polo shirts.

"Isn't that the bunch that shows up every time we scrimmage Centaur?" Joe asked.

"Sure is," Ramon said.

The rotors stopped turning, a door opened, and a triumphant Jack Dick stepped out wearing the Centaur colors. From behind the rope line, a volley of electronic flashes exploded in his face. And that was before Cesare Harrington appeared at his side. The two buddied up shoulder to shoulder and mugged for the press. A third player emerged: the team's 5-goaler, Daniel Ochoa. He too got star treatment, but it was nothing compared to the collective gasp that greeted the team's final player.

"No way," SOB exclaimed.

"Who is it?" Hunt asked.

"The bad boy."

"Martín?" Joe asked.

"That's right. Mr. Martín Harrington himself."

"Doesn't he play with his cousins in Argentina on El Toro?"

SOB nodded. "The Harringtons won the Triple Crown last year, and Martín is their enforcer. But he went a little too far last month during the Gold Cup. Got himself a month-long suspension for hitting another player's horse with his mallet."

"He's lucky he didn't lay a hand on one of my string," King said. "Fining a guy like that ten grand and banning him for a month was nowhere near the punishment he deserved. And today proves it. He'll probably pocket a hundred thousand for playing this afternoon, and if they make it to the final, the same for Sunday."

"At least," Roberto said.

A few minutes later, the players from both teams rode out to midfield. The sudden turn of events invigorated the stadium, and the crowd buzzed with energy. In no time both teams were lining up for the pregame introductions. All eyes turned to Centaur.

All four of Centaur's players were wearing black armbands and stern faces. Then, from the sidelines, Juancito's groom led a blood bay mare out onto the field. It was Nalgona, Juancito's finest and the winner of Best Playing Pony honors in two Argentine Opens. The muscular mare was as much a champion as the polo player himself. Her mane, her tail, her legs—she was black throughout with a hint of cordovan. The sight of her standing between the two teams with Juancito's boots reversed in her stirrups silenced the crowd.

"Viva Juancito!" a voice cried out from the stands. The second time it pealed, one or two others joined in. By the third time, hundreds of people chanted "Viva Juancito!" Cesare pumped his fist in unison with their cries, and the entire stadium responded in unison—chanting and clapping to honor the slain polo player.

Nalgona began to buck indignantly as she was led off the field.

"That girl wants to play some polo," Joe said.

As soon as she returned to Centaur's pony lines, the game was under way.

"I'LL NEED YOUR SUMMARIES FIRST thing Monday morning."

The Special Agent in Charge of the West Palm Beach Secret Service field office peered over his glasses. "On second thought, make that Sunday night." He pursed his lips and nodded his head. Then he closed his portfolio and exited the conference room.

In the silence that followed, one agent spoke up.

"Will someone remind me what weekends are for?"

"Those are the two days of the week when you can work from home without interruption," a colleague responded. He stood up to leave, and so did the rest of the group, including Special Agent Cortés.

She walked straight back to her office. From the Special Agent in Charge's office, the vista reached all the way from Mar-a-Lago down south to the cluster of buildings that made up Worth Avenue to the Middle Bridge and Bankers Row straight ahead, and then to The Breakers and as far north as Peanut Island. Cris's view was South Florida contemporary: one boxlike office tower after another, some new, others mildewed, and all stacked neatly along the Intracoastal Waterway from West Palm to Miami.

Her office was spartan. Other than her bike and a gym bag, the only personal item was a photo of her crossing the finish line on the National Mall in the Marine Corps Marathon 10K. She went directly to her desk, punched in the password, and logged in to the Palm Beach P.D. database. LIVING ROOM, MASTER BEDROOM, MASTER BATHROOM, GUEST BEDROOM, VICTIM. She copied the folders from the server to her laptop and then from her laptop to her iPad.

A timer appeared on her screen as the hundreds of high-res files began to transfer. On her desk in a manila folder was the investigator's report that had been handed out that morning at Palm Beach P.D. It would tell her all she needed to know—not about the murder of Juancito Harrington but about the accuracy of the investigation itself.

She opened it to the first page and began to read. When she reached the last page, she turned back to the beginning, clicked on the first folder on her iPad, and began her postmortem. She had learned the procedure from a detective's detective at Miami-Dade. Phase one was to match photos to notes. Phase two was to match photos to interviews. Phase three was the most critical—and the most difficult: scrutinizing the crime scene photos that no one paid any attention to.

They were the ones that told the story no one had heard.

CENTAUR WAS A TRAIN WRECK. From the very first throw-in, it could do nothing right. Jack Dick was his team's own worst enemy, getting tagged for penalties and tripping up his own teammates. Cesare hoodwinked a defender and burst into the open field only to watch Martín's pass bounce out-of-bounds.

"Didn't I tell you, hombre?" Ramon asked SOB.

"Come on. He's been off for a month. That's a lot different than getting a bye to the final."

"He's going to be off a lot longer if his team doesn't get it together," Roberto said.

Centaur fell behind 3–1. By halftime, Los Dorados had increased its lead to 7–3. The two teams traded goals in the fourth chukker, which ended with the score 9–5. The fifth chukker was a scoreless duel.

"Man, they know how to eat up that clock," Joe said to King.

"Watch out!" SOB yelled.

Jack Dick reached out with his mallet to hook one of the Los Dorados. Instead, his stick caught in Cesare's reins. The blunder took both players out of the play and led to the only goal of the chukker. Cesare castigated his *patrón* loud enough for all to hear.

"It looks like it was five against three out there," the public address announcer joked. "Los Dorados holds a commanding 10–5 lead going into the final chukker."

Cesare rode over the boards and began barking at Mr. Australia. The 10-goaler pointed at his *patrón* and gestured at the scoreboard. His coach calmly shook his head and folded his arms.

"Will you look at that? I bet he wants Jack out of the lineup," Joe said.

Both Roberto and Ramon nodded.

At midfield, the umpire held up a polo ball to begin the chukker.

On the sidelines, Cesare pointed to Juancito's beautiful blood bay. Juancito's groom led her over. The 10-goaler vaulted from his mount to Nalgona without touching the ground, wheeled her around, and bolted onto the field.

"Give me an alley," the umpire yelled out. The two teams created a path, and the umpire bowled the ball in. It scooted past all seven players into the open field. Nalgona, who had yet to reach midfield, bore down on it. Cesare went to the near side, tapped the loose ball with his mallet, and took off with it. His next hit was a brutal lash, a line drive that rose a few feet off the ground and rocketed more than a hundred yards directly at the goal. It hit the turf and skidded into the goalmouth as the flagger waved her red banner above her head. Cesare stood out of his saddle, pumping his mallet hand in the air. His teammates were ecstatic, his opponents in awe, and his mare not even winded.

"Hail Cesare!" the announcer called out.

Gone was the master strategist who waited and watched. Instead, a completely different No. 3 emerged, one who dominated play: on offense, scoring at will from all points on the field; on defense, stealing the ball and snatching errant passes. Cesare and Nalgona scored six times, single-handedly erasing his team's deficit. Centaur triumphed 11–10.

"Hail Cesare!" the crowd chanted.

High in the grandstands, Hunt joined his teammates in the standing ovation.

How the hell are we going to stop him? Hunt wondered.

Joe leaned forward. "You're going to have your hands full on Sunday."

"Me?" Hunt asked.

"That's right. He's your man on Sunday. You'll be marking Cesare."

Hunt laughed a low laugh. "Ay, Chihuahua."

SOB gripped his teammate's shoulders. "Glad it's you not me, Rikki!"

"If you can hobble Cesare, Centaur doesn't stand a chance," King said. "Keep him off his game, and the Open is ours."

"Need you guys on the field by nine thirty tomorrow morning. Practice begins at ten," Joe said.

SOB stood up and patted Hunt on the shoulder. "*Mañana, amigo.*"

"*Hasta mañana.*"

The Gallegos said their good-byes and followed SOB down to the field.

Hunt turned to King. "Guess where I'm headed tonight?"

"You got me."

"The Chesterfield, to meet that man." Hunt pointed across the field to the Centaur tent. The players and the grooms were celebrating their stunning comeback. But one man was off by himself, checking his team's horses.

"I thought I would get some background on Juancito from Mr. Australia."

King turned and looked over at Hunt.

"You also might want to ask him how to cover Cesare."

72

MOST PEOPLE ARE DRAWN TO polo; Neville Haynes was born to the game. Haynes's father was no ordinary British cavalryman. Born in England, schooled at Sandhurst, and posted to Australia, he was singled out on his return for royal service as an equerry, an aide-de-camp in service to one of the Royal Family's most iconic members, Lord Louis Mountbatten: Admiral of the Fleet, First Sea Lord, last Viceroy of India, and the Supreme Allied Commander in Southeast Asia during World War II.

Lord Louis's equerry shadowed His Lordship, assisted him, and advised him at every step along the way, including those times when he chose to play polo with and against a long list of celebrated cronies, including a former cavalryman by the name of Winston Churchill as well as the most popular celebrity on earth during the 1920s and 1930s, the dashing Prince of Wales.

It was Lord Louis who encouraged his nephew Prince Philip to take up polo. The Duke's eldest son, Prince Charles, continued the family tradition, and so did Neville Haynes, who relinquished his Army commission to serve as polo manager to the Prince of Wales. Mr. Australia's tenure as Wales's polo manager came to an ignominious close late one night when the dapper lieutenant colonel was photographed escorting a gorgeous dish in a sequin number from one of the tony London clubs favored by the Army and Navy crowd. Of more importance to readers of *The Sun* and *The Daily Star* the following morning was that that his lovely companion was not Colonel Haynes's wife of 32 years.

Mr. Australia's next steps were strictly by the book.

By sundown, a terse statement detailed his resignation as polo manager to the Prince of Wales. Then the debonair colonel vanished. Only those at the uppermost echelons of the British Army—and the Royal Family—were aware that the former cavalry officer had reenlisted with his old regiment: the Queen's Royal Lancers. Known in military circles as the Death or Glory Boys, the historic cavalry regiment had long been lionized in song and verse and was immortalized by Tennyson in "Charge of the Light Brigade."

A century and a half later, the Death or Glory Boys were again dispatched to the far side of the globe. Only this time it was to the Asian steppes, where they were dropped behind the front lines of the War on Terror in Afghanistan. Much like their predecessors in the Light Brigade, the joint Anglo-American task force that Haynes commanded was given a daunting assignment. But the regiment's greatest similarity to its predecessor came when, at the dawn of the new millennium, its soldiers rode out to challenge their enemies on horseback. More than any other element of the campaign, that's what Haynes remembered.

So did a newly minted second lieutenant from West Point who reported directly to the colonel.

73

THE LEOPARD LOUNGE EXUDES A certain civility that sets it apart from the hustle and bustle of other Palm Beach watering holes. Despite an epidemic of catty fabric, the bar at the Chesterfield emits a bespoke aura, a difference Hunt sensed the moment he arrived for his rendezvous with Mr. Australia.

He scanned the dining room. Several well-dressed couples were enjoying an early dinner, but there was no sign of the British cavalryman. At the bar sat an older woman whose dress was too short for her years and her ample thighs. She was engaged in a boozy chat with a well-manicured younger man. A smile crossed Hunt's face. He couldn't help but notice that Beau Brummel was wearing a kilt.

Clan Stewart has gathered in Palm Beach for the Highland Games.

"Hey, good-looking," she called out.

"Hello there," Hunt replied. There was no way he was going to get sucked into this shootout. He looked over at the bartender, a rail-thin character rattling a cocktail shaker with an industrial rhythm.

"Captain Hunt?" the man asked in a decidedly Scottish accent.

The lady turned to her companion. "Did you hear that? Gorgeous is a captain," she said.

"Yes, sir," said Hunt to the bartender.

The barman's brogue completed the picture. The carved elephant heads, the shiny brass lamps, the profusion of gins, the buckets of Champagne, the barman's Glaswegian accent—the Leopard Lounge was as British as the changing of the Guard.

"Colonel Haynes would be in the Cigar Room, sir. I'm putting the final touches on his gin martini. May I prepare you a refreshment, Captain?" he asked.

"The same," Hunt said. "Dirty, please."

"Very good, sir," the bartender said.

"The dirtier, the better, right, Captain?" the woman said.

Hunt nodded and smiled. Then he pointed a thumb at her companion. "My money is on Braveheart to win tonight's bagpipe competition."

The howl of her laughter filled the Leopard Lounge as he exited the bar.

In the center of the lobby, a mind-boggling bouquet of roses anchored a gilded table. Hunt dodged the towering arrangement and made his way down a hallway to a quiet corner of the hotel. He opened a door and was greeted by the rich aroma of fine tobaccos and foul language.

"Dammit!" An English accent filled the air. Mr. Australia was grousing about something, his back to the door. Hunt stepped inside and saw his former commanding officer hunched over a backgammon table. He was obviously getting thrashed by his mustachioed opponent.

"Over here, my boy. Captain Hunt, you've arrived too late to distract the luckiest backgammon player on the planet. Say hello to Sunny. The bastard has just gammoned me," he said, as his opponent picked up his last checker.

Hunt extended his hand. "Pleasure to see you again, Your Grace."

The mention of his title gave the Duke of Marlborough pause. He looked up from the backgammon board and did his best to place Hunt's face.

"The Westchester Cup gala at the palace last year," Hunt said.

"Ah, yes. Army man, aren't you? Correct me if I'm mistaken, but didn't you have some Sloane Ranger glued to your hip for the better part of the evening? Do I have that right?"

"Your memory serves you well, sir," Hunt said.

"She better not have been glued to anything of yours," Mr. Australia said to Hunt. He turned to the Duke. "His lovely date was my beloved daughter."

His Grace let out a chortle.

"I trust you did a thorough inventory of the flatware at Blenheim Palace prior to having this Philistine removed from the premises," Mr. Australia said. "When he's not trying to mount your daughter, rest assured he's pocketing your silver."

"Isn't that the line you use with our Argentine brethren?" Hunt asked.

"Hunt—I've always admired your consistency. Per usual, you are wrong yet again. With that bunch of thieves, my standard interrogatory would be 'When does an Argentine become a Spaniard?'"

Hunt and the Duke exchanged glances.

"When he marries your daughter," Mr. Australia said.

The Duke roared with laughter. Mr. Australia saw fit to continue the bonhomie when the barkeep showed up with a silver tray bearing two martinis.

"Here you go," Mr. Australia said. He deftly presented his martini to the Duke.

"No, you don't," the Duke countered.

"Take it, man. Woodcock—fetch me another!" Mr. Australia demanded.

His Grace shook his head in dismay. "I have no idea how on earth he gets away with this bloody awful behavior of his. But I do take comfort in knowing that he inflicts himself like this on people of the highest station."

"I've seen that with my own two eyes, sir," Hunt said, recalling the caustic comments Mr. Australia directed at Wales at Sandhurst.

The casual comment gave the Duke pause. He looked more closely at Hunt.

"You did say Hunt, did you not?"

"Yes, sir."

A thought eluded the older man—but not for long.

"He's the one, is he not?" the Duke asked Mr. Australia.

"That he is, Sunny."

"Forgive my forgetfulness," the Duke said.

Hunt was the odd man out. "The one what?" he asked.

"You mean, he doesn't know? After all these years?" the Duke asked.

"He most definitely does not," Mr. Australia said.

The Duke turned to Mr. Australia. "Then it's about damn time someone told him."

"Not until I get my martini. WOODCOCK!"

74

THANKS TO THE TEAM'S DRAMATIC comeback victory, the air at Centaur Polo was electric. Loud laughter and louder music echoed throughout the barn, but what made the celebration truly come alive was Cesare Harrington's shape-shifting transformation. The 10-goaler hugged everyone he encountered. He thanked one and all for their support. He reiterated to every member of the organization how his brother had inspired each of them. His warmth was a radical departure from his usual distant bearing, and it fueled the festive mood. Sharp yells and loud whistles punctuated the few moments of calm.

In the midst of this pandemonium, the members of Centaur's marketing team darted in and around the barn, coordinating interviews and setting up photo ops with the team's pros. Jack Dick, however, was nowhere to be seen. As Joshua Shapiro dictated, there was little to be gained and a lot to lose by putting the company's chairman on display in a celebratory mood. Despite his team's success on the polo field, his wife was still incarcerated for the murder of Juan Harrington. The day's goal had been a simple one: to field a team in the semifinal. That Centaur Polo had triumphed in a storybook finish was beyond belief. Now at least the company's marketing machine could combat the week's never-ending stream of bad press with some good news of its own.

As the day drew to a close, the members of Centaur's War Council recognized the possibility that Centaur's costly bloodbath might be stanched. Per Dick's explicit instructions, his War Council now had its own War Room on board the *Centaur* that was staffed by members of the company's in-house legal team under Shapiro's direction. Updates were sent out in an email bulletin that was issued every hour on the hour to all council members, with one exception. Without a cell phone or an email account, Mr. Australia was exempted.

The closing detail of each bulletin was Centaur's share price. Early that afternoon, savvy day traders, who had grown cautious about the stock's massive sell-off, tested a new bottom below the $100 level. It was short-lived. Following the surprise appearance of Cesare Harrington at Jack Dick's side in the semifinals, shares rose to $105 at the close. In after-hours trading, this upward trend strengthened. By the time the match concluded, Centaur was hovering around $114.

This small move barely made a dent in the two-day sell-off. Since Raul Ramirez hauled Kelly Dick into police headquarters, the company's stock had lost more than one-third of its value. Centaur's market capitalization had fallen more than $15 billion, and so had Jack Dick's fortune. The man was no longer a billionaire. By some estimates, his net worth had dropped to around $760 million. But the bleeding had stopped.

Centaur's formidable marketing team had encamped at the site of their triumphant *InStyle* photo shoot in the barn and was facilitating interview after interview with Martín Harrington and Daniel Ochoa. Journalists and reporters from newspapers and TV stations all took a number as they waited for an opportunity to spice up the slow news day. Those who wanted to speak to Cesare, however, were destined to be disappointed.

The man of the hour had been whisked away to the sanctum sanctorum: Juancito's tack room. There, in this most intimate of settings, surrounded by countless mementos of his brother's career, Cesare was giving an animated one-on-one interview to the *News of the World*'s Walter Ned.

And he was doing so at the request of Raul Ramirez.

75

"HIS COURAGE. HER BRAVERY. THEY** were beyond magnificent. I cannot begin to tell you how honored I was—and still am—to have witnessed such gallant conduct. You should be too," the Duke said.

Hunt's eyes were sparkling. "Thank you, sir."

Mr. Australia smiled broadly, raised his martini, and in a quiet voice, toasted Hunt's father. "Death *and* Glory."

"Death and Glory," Hunt and the Duke replied in unison.

As the moment passed, the three set their empty glasses down.

"Me, on the other hand, I will no doubt endure some horrifically boring demise, one devoid of honor or duty," the Duke said. "I can see the write-up in the *Mail*. 'According to eyewitness reports, he was dining on a particular brand of sushi known as *saba* when he choked to death.'"

Mr. Australia threw his head back in laughter.

The Duke continued. "And all the chaps at my club will be saying, 'Serves him right, eating bait at his age.' Now, if you'll both excuse me. I must pop off. *She* is waiting." He stood up and wagged his index finger at Mr. Australia. "I've got you and that lovely lady of yours down for dinner at the club at six o'clock sharp Saturday night. In the meantime, have your accountant arrange a payment plan to cover your losses this evening." He turned and extended his hand. "Best of luck on Sunday, Hunt. Be sure to watch your back with this character and that bunch of thieves in his employ."

"I certainly will. And Your Grace," Hunt paused.

"Yes, Hunt."

"Thank you."

"My pleasure, Hunt."

The Duke exited the Cigar Room, and Hunt sat himself down in the green leather chair he had just vacated. He quietly began rearranging the board to start a new game.

"And what do you think you're doing?" Mr. Australia asked.

"I'm about to find out whether or not you threw that last game," Hunt said.

Mr. Australia's face burst into a brilliant smile. "Always liked that about you, Hunt. You read between the lines. You make smart decisions *fast*."

"Sounds like you and His Grace bump into each other quite often."

"That we do. We both delight in berating the staff at Ta-boo as only an exiled Englishman can. Out of this mutual contempt, our bond has become implacable."

"Aren't you a little out of the way over here? I'm in Palm Beach only for a week, but the commute to Wellington can take a toll. How do you put up with it all season long?"

"I gave up on Wellington ages ago. Far too plebeian. Here at the Chesterfield, I'm a block to Worth, a block to the Brazilian Court, and five or ten minutes to almost anywhere I need to be. Out there, I was a thousand miles from nowhere. Believe it or not, it's just three turns in my Defender from the bell stand to the barn. Take a left at Banker's Row, cross the Middle Bridge, and it turns into Okeechobee. I scoot down to Southern, and by six-thirty sharp I've arrived in Wellington. Takes me twenty minutes on a good day. Thirty minutes if I mistime the drawbridge. Same story when I come back at two or three. Catch a short nap, and by five o'clock I'm at my post in the Leopard Lounge or over at the Everglades Club with Sunny, enjoying a cocktail and eyeing his gorgeous new girlfriend. What a stunner! One of those exotic creatures from India, the type that hypnotized Alexander. That's it! I must tell him that. She's Sunny's Roxane. It's a shame you missed her."

"Word in the barn is that you're playing above your handicap as well."

"Right you are. Gorgeous South African jumper. Magnificent body. And takes off her kit at the drop of a hat. I've been on life support since we first bumped into each other. I give my word—no matter the circumstances, I will die a happy man. And from what I gather, you'll be back on board with King's daughter in no time flat."

"What do you know that I don't?"

"As I've told you time and again, a hell of a lot, my good man," Mr. Australia said. There was conviction in his voice and a smile on his face. "I've had the pleasure of chatting with Ava several times this season. What a Thoroughbred. Look at her pedigree. I go right to the dam: her mother, a classic beauty and a great horsewoman. And her father, such a splendid man. She's well above your teammate's station. Thoroughbreds like Ava require a stayer, not a sprinter. O'Brien breaks well from the gate. I'll give him that. But he's bound to fall off the pace. Six furlongs is his limit. That's one season here in Palm Beach. He's about to pull up."

"You're not out to spoil my team's esprit de corps, are you?" Hunt asked.

His colleague leaned back and laughed. "Not in the least. But now that you've brought up that topic, let me impart one bit of advice. As your former commanding officer and a dear friend who admires you greatly, do watch yourself on Sunday."

Hunt bit his tongue.

"You're a damn good horseman and an excellent polo player. If you stick to your game, you won't have a thing to worry about. But I doubt your marching orders will permit that. Knowing King Kenedy and Joe Bigelow as I long as I have, your talents won't lie fallow. Hunt, you're able. You're aggressive. I can tell you grew up playing polo because you understand what cannot be taught. I'm quite confident that you can cause a lot of trouble for my team. Rio Bravo has all the firepower it needs with O'Brien and the Gallegos. They won't engage you in their scoring schemes. Most likely, they'll use you to trip up Martín or have you pester Cesare. And that is where you must be *en garde*. Not if but when the occasion arises for you to pester Cesare, prepare yourself to face the consequences, old boy."

"You've witnessed his wrath?"

"That I have. The man is lethal on horseback, one of the Four Horseman of the Apocalypse. In the Hurlingham—I believe it was the quarterfinals—a defender was marking Juancito. Then he would switch and mark Cesare. Mark one and then go to the other. Juancito's response was to run circles around the poor boy. His older brother responded in an altogether different manner. Cesare swung his horse's head like it was a sledgehammer.

"Gave him the bit?"

"I'd say. Broke the man's hand. Took him out of the game. Ended his season.

Afterward, Cesare's only comment was that the man 'needed to be taught a lesson.'"

The two eyed each other silently.

"Hunt, you and I are amateurs. We're good enough to hold our own, but at the end of the day we are still amateurs. Cesare plays a game of which you and I are not familiar. And as evenly matched as our teams are, I believe the fates will decide who faces death and who tastes glory."

Mr. Australia took a sip from his martini.

"King must have told you that I was sent here by the White House to get a fix on this mess."

"He did."

"Tell me about yesterday. Where did you find Cesare?"

"Out at Payson Park."

"Of course. A perfect place to regain your wits. How did you get him to stay? From the reports I got, he was escorting Juancito back to Buenos Aires today."

"Initially, I thought it was going to take wads of cash. Cesare drives the hardest bargain of any man I've met. He'd fit right in with our good friend Jalaluddin Haqqani. I imagine the two of them would hit it off as founding members of the Khyber Pass Polo Club."

The two started to laugh. It was a ludicrous notion, the thought of the urbane Argentine 10-goaler butting heads with the wizened Afghan warlord beneath the tassled roof of a windblown tent.

"I can already hear them haggling over which one would have to provide the elephants for the Haqqani polo team," Mr. Australia said.

"Each would insist the other mount the team," Hunt chuckled.

Mr. Australia administered the coup de grace. "And each would require the other to employ as many of his family members as possible."

Neither man could speak for the laughter.

"Hunt, I must confess I can't believe the both of us made it out of that hell-hole alive. Since the days of Alexander, able-bodied soldiers from all over the world have met their maker north of the Khyber. Yet somehow we managed to not join their number."

"Perhaps it was because you engineered one of history's great getaways?"

"Make that one of history's hastiest retreats."

"So true," said Hunt. "What about Cesare?"

"Oddly enough, money didn't matter to the man. Honoring his brother was his only interest. As for Martín, he said his cousin would be privileged to play in his brother's stead."

"Good for them."

"If I hadn't been so surprised, I'd second that."

"What do you mean?"

"The only time I ever saw Cesare and Juancito go at it was over money. It was toward the end of the British Season, and Juancito had disappeared for a week or so. He was off chasing some heiress on the beaches of Ibiza. While he was gone, Cesare traded away an older mare. Her playing days were well behind her, and she was too old to carry a foal. Of course, she was a favorite of Juancito's, and the instant he set foot in the barn he noticed her absence. He went through the roof, and so did Cesare. The two almost came to blows."

"What happened?"

"You'll never guess who saved the day."

Hunt paused. "Rio."

A broad smile blazed across Mr. Australia's face. "How right you are. That may well have been the only time I've ever seen that ne'er-do-well earn his keep. He paraded that old girl back to the barn like he had just ridden her home upsides in the Derby. Truth be told, I'm a lot more like Juancito—old-fashioned and out of date. He has this cell phone he never used. I never even bought one of the bloody things. You want to get a hold of me, come see me at the barn, meet me at my club, leave me a message at the front desk of my hotel. I'm the same when it comes to my mares. I'm a natural cover man myself, if you know what I mean. And I say that knowing full well that the wave of the future has left me behind. Why wait and see what sort of offspring Nalgona will produce at the end of her playing days when a skilled technician can take care of an embryo transplant here and now while she's playing lights-out polo? That's the smart way. That's the profitable way. But it's not my way. I'm a British cavalry officer, not a genetic scientist. I'd rather run a barn with ten horses who know my scent and the sound of my step than a laboratory with hundreds of embryos plucked from the world's finest mares. But that's how Cesare's mind works. He's all business all the time."

"The exact opposite of his brother."

"Which is why they made such a damn good team. Try to play them clinically, and Juancito would decimate you. Take a wait-and-see approach, and Cesare would pick you apart," Mr. Australia said.

"Would you mind telling me what you can recall about Tuesday morning? Anything unusual happen at the barn?" Hunt asked.

"Not in the least. When I pulled up at six thirty, Cesare was already out riding. The man is a true horseman. Shows up bright and early and schools his string in the cool of the morning. Always admired him for that. Day in, day out, high goal, low goal, no goal—he knows his horses cold. Right after he wrapped up, Juancito showed up. I assume his boy drove him over. The police tell me it was approximately a quarter till nine when they arrived. I'll take their word on the timing. I doubt if the three of us spent more than five minutes chatting about a few minor loose ends regarding today's match. Ten minutes at the most. When Juancito went off to ride, Cesare and I sketched out our plans for the British Season. As we talked, I placed a few calls to England. I was on the phone, off the phone. We talked in between calls, and then, as he always does, he left for his office here in Palm Beach. I've walked over and met with him several times myself. It's only a couple of blocks away from here," Mr. Australia said.

"What's the story in England?" Hunt asked.

"I'm trying to figure out a way for Will or Harry to play with us in one of the high-goal tournaments. What a treat for everyone—the boys, Charles and Camilla, their grandparents. But as anyone who has taken a look at the Court Circular knows, their appearance schedules are merciless. I still think it would be absolutely brilliant if I could arrange to have one of them play in the Queen's Cup with El Toro. A lot of work to do on that one, but from the sounds of it I just might be able to make it happen."

"I noticed in some of the crime scene photos that Juancito wore his boots and britches to the hotel," Hunt said.

"No surprise there. He always showed up ready to ride. They both do. Neither uses his tack room to change or to shower. When you've got a house a few minutes from the barn, why on earth would you?"

"And that was the last time you saw him?"

"Actually, Juancito stopped in just before he left. I was finalizing some stabling arrangements at Royal Berkshire. He popped in, grabbed his wallet and his phone. Then he was gone. I doubt I even waved good-bye. We certainly didn't say a word to one another. I wish we had. I'm embarrassed to tell you that I didn't give the poor bloke another thought the rest of the day. After polo, I came back here shortly after two, took a nap, freshened up, and then met Sunny and Lily at the Everglades Club for an early dinner. Little did I realize what had happened just steps away from where we sit."

His Q&A finished, Hunt looked down at the backgammon board and grabbed a leather cup. "Care to take my challenge?" Mr. Australia responded in kind. The two rattled their cups and threw their dice. Two sixes appeared.

"Boxcars, my boy," Mr. Australia proclaimed. Hunt proceeded to turn the doubling cube from two to four.

"Have we discussed a wager?" Mr. Australia said.

"As I recall, one of us is still in arrears. If memory serves me, he owes his opponent a bottle of Grange," Hunt said.

"Damn it. You're bloody right!" Mr. Australia declared. "With accrued interest, I must owe you a case by now. I've got to win it back—and more— here and now."

As they rattled the dice for another throw, the door to the cigar room swung open; the barman from the Leopard Lounge stepped inside.

"Where the hell have you been, Woodcock?" Mr. Australia demanded. "Hunt and I were under the impression you'd taken other employment."

"Still looking, Colonel," Woodcock said dryly.

"Is another round a possibility, or have you come to submit your resignation?" Mr. Australia asked.

"For Captain Hunt, I believe another beverage could be arranged. But not for you, Colonel," he said.

"Go on," Mr. Australia said.

"The maître d' at Renato's informed me that a young lady is taking your name in vain. It seems that you were expected at seven o'clock sharp," he said.

Mr. Australia jumped to his feet. "Woodcock, how could you let this happen?"

"Entirely my fault, sir," said the barman. "I hope you don't mind, but I took it upon myself to learn that she was enjoying a Santa Margherita Pinot Grigio and requested an order of smoked salmon and toast points. Perhaps that will buy you enough time to make amends. The maître d' also informed me that she just ducked out and can presently be found eyeing several items at Barzina."

"Excellent! A little baksheesh from Barzina could well save the day," Mr. Australia said. "Woodcock, you not only own up to your faults, but you make a credible effort to rectify them. I applaud a man who knows his limitations. Hunt, my apologies for leading you on, but instead of shellacking you in backgammon, I'd prefer to get lucky with someone else."

THE DISTANCE FROM THE CHESTERFIELD to the Brazilian Court was not even a block, but Hunt didn't hurry the short walk. He had temporarily shelved the mystery of Juancito Harrington's murder. Instead, a much different secret had presented itself. Not about Juancito but about his own father.

Thanks to King Kenedy, Hunt knew a good bit about his father's exploits. Way back when, the two met as teens on a dusty polo field at the New Mexico Military Institute. After graduating as second lieutenants, they enlisted, went to Ranger School together, and were shipped off to Viet Nam. After the fall of Saigon, their career paths diverged. King was sent to the Army War College and then posted to the Pentagon, where he reported to General Hal Moore. Hunt's father joined the staff of the Ranger School at Fort Bliss, where his only son was born. All the while, military transports ferried both to and from polo matches out West, in the Virginia horse country, and even overseas. Shortly before his father's death, they were paired on a US Army team against Royal Navy at Cowdray Park. King returned to Washington and the Pentagon. Weeks later, Hunt's father returned to Washington—and Arlington National Cemetery.

Now the Duke of Marlborough had upended that story's ending. If what he had just said were true—*Why wouldn't it be?*—the implications were beyond belief.

Why the hell didn't Mr. Australia ever share that damn story?

Hunt stopped and stared across the street at the entrance of the Brazilian Court. Under the awning, he could see Cris Cortés talking with Fred Motsch. She looked up. Hunt knew it was time to get back to work. Taking a deep breath, he crossed the street.

77

THE OFF-DUTY POLICEMAN DID A quick about-face. Just as quickly, he nodded to Fred Motsch as the general manager escorted his two guests into the back courtyard.

"Anything this evening?" Motsch asked.

"No, sir. Just more flowers."

Motsch turned and looked at the back entrance to the property. So did Cortés. Hunt walked up to the padlocked gate. On the street side, bouquets of flowers blanketed the ground, covering the sidewalk.

"Do you smell that fragrance?" Cris asked. She followed Hunt over.

"It's the red ones—the ceibo. You see them everywhere in Argentina." Hunt leaned into the steel bars and pulled himself closer. He inhaled the scent of the distant land he left just two days before. He and Cris stared at the makeshift altar, sharing a moment of silence. It was littered with handwritten notes, cards addressed to Juancito, and pictures of Juancito. Hunt turned away, and they silently rejoined Motsch.

Hunt lifted the crime scene tape and followed Cris as she ascended the steps to the second floor, where the G.M. was awaiting them in the entryway to the Lancaster Suite.

"Captain Hunt, you asked me to give you an insider's perspective on the crime scene. With that in mind, I suggest we begin in the guest bedroom. It's the only portion of the suite that is completely intact."

Motsch turned and walked into the smaller of the two bedrooms. A queen-sized bed with an elaborate silk canopy dominated the left side of the room. Beside it, a doorway led to the bath. In the opposite corner, an upholstered loveseat was angled toward the center of the room. Brazilian Avenue was visible through the windows.

"During the Roaring Twenties, South Florida was mesmerized by a wizard of an architect named Addison Mizner, who found his inspiration in the Italian Renaissance, which is why the Brazilian Court is so special," Motsch began. "What you see in the quiet elegance of this suite is the sublime touch of Rosario Candela. Instead of the heavy hand of the Borgias or the Medici, Candela preferred a New World sensibility."

Motsch ran his fingers along the wooden headboard. "Notice the mahogany shutters, the doors and the door frames, also of mahogany, and the windows and this beautiful bed." He stroked the silk comforter and turned to the Secret Service agent. "Weren't your eyes drawn to the beautiful duvet and the golden canopy that crowns this lovely bed?"

Cris nodded.

"That's because the dark mahogany frames the room so elegantly. The Brazilian Court is not palatial. It's not ornate. It is elegant. We say more about our sense of style by bathing ourselves in the warm citrine hues that color our walls than by transplanting the same Old World motifs found on college campuses."

"Pardon me, sir."

"Yes, Captain Hunt?"

"I was with you right up to the part about those warm hues. That's when this Army officer threw in the towel."

Cris burst out laughing. "You're a better man than I, Rick Hunt. I was not about to admit that."

Motsch chuckled. Hunt was smiling.

"Your candor is a welcome trait, Captain Hunt. Citrine is our hotel's distinctive yellow color. It's very Dutch Colonial, is it not? Think the Netherlands Antilles, Bonaire, Curaçao—so different from the Mediterranean tones that predominate here in Palm Beach. It's one of the many reasons I love this property. And I love sharing its story. Unfortunately, I can only share a fraction of it today. Please follow me."

Motsch retraced his steps out of the guest bedroom and through the entryway. "The Lancaster features an L-shaped configuration. We're at the bottom of the L. The living room, the master bedroom, and the master bath form the upper portions." He stepped into the living room. "Et voilà!"

Just as at noon, not a stick of furniture remained. Even the curtains had been removed from the floor-to-ceiling windows overlooking the courtyard.

Hunt looked to his colleague.

"I guess that's my cue," Cris said. She reached in her tote and retrieved an iPad. "I've already opened the LIVING ROOM folder." She previewed several images from the crime scene investigation. Each showed the spacious room in its full glory two days before.

"There," Motsch said, pointing to a wide shot.

The Secret Service agent tapped on the image and expanded it full screen.

"This room is ideal for entertaining. It can easily accommodate half a dozen guests plus whatever service you might require from our staff, such as a barman or a light buffet. According to the investigators, a lot of activity took place here on the morning of the crime. There was sexual DNA on the sofa, which would be right here directly in front of us, and also on the ottoman, which would be here, to the right of the sofa. Another chair belongs at the other end of the sofa. There was no evidence of any activity there. Once the police finished, I had all the furniture removed, including the coffee table in front of the sofa and the desk set against that wall. The entire suite will be redone."

Cris held out the iPad and positioned it in the general area of the room where each photograph was taken. The empty Champagne bucket, some bronzer stains on the seat cushions, and single strands of blonde hair on the sofa, the ottoman, and the floor all indicated a vigorous welcome by Kelly.

"So the thought is they started here in the living room," Hunt said.

"And they made their way to the bedroom, where she rips off his clothes," Cris said. She opened another folder, one that documented Juancito's shirt, his boots, his socks, and his riding pants strewn on the floor at the entrance to the master bedroom.

Motsch proceeded into the master bedroom, but Hunt did not. He was looking at the empty room and where Juancito's clothes had fallen. Then he walked into the master bedroom. It too was absolutely empty.

Motsch continued. "Over there, against the far wall, was a king-sized canopied bed much like the one in the guest bedroom, with nightstands on either side and a scalloped end-of-bed bench at the foot. Against this wall, a dresser with mirror. All done in mahogany, and all sent off to storage except the mattress and the linens, which I've had destroyed."

The luxurious bed, the matching nightstands, the end-of-bed bench, and the mahogany dresser—Cris swiped from one photo to the next in the MASTER BEDROOM folder. The three stood silently as she opened the VICTIM folder. They viewed Juancito from afar; Juancito much closer, the entry wound clearly visible; Juancito the homicide victim. The photos of the left side of his face—where the bullet had entered his temple—looked almost placid. The right side, however, was nightmarish, swollen and distorted by the force of the bullet as it plowed through his skull.

"A classic entrance wound. Based on the stippling and the gunshot residue at the point of entry, I'd say the range of fire was extremely close. Less than two feet," Cris said.

The next shots featured Juancito's personal effects lying on the nightstand: a Reverso watch and a beat-up Nokia cell phone. On the far side of the bed were the room service tray, plate empty and wine glass drained dry. A pressed napkin lay folded on top.

"A housekeeper found him?" Hunt asked.

"That's correct," Motsch said. "She came in to do the nightly turndown service and saw the foil from the Champagne bottle on the living room floor. There was more on the sofa. As soon as she saw the empty Champagne bucket sitting on the wet bar she knew something was wrong. We had a check-in scheduled Tuesday night, and the suite wasn't close to prepared."

"Then she sees his clothes at the entrance to the bedroom," Cris said. She was reading from the crime scene report.

Motsch nodded in agreement.

"She approaches the entrance to the master bedroom, announces herself, sees the victim, and immediately leaves," she said.

"That's it?" Hunt asked.

"There's much more than that," Motsch said. "After recognizing Mr. Harrington and realizing his condition, she ran out of here in hysterics. She was barely coherent Tuesday night and almost incapable of giving the police a statement. I've put her on full medical leave."

"So sad," Cris said.

"It turns out the porter whom she had contacted to retrieve the Champagne bucket heard her screams, found Mr. Harrington, and radioed hotel security."

"How long do you think the housekeeper was here in the suite?" Hunt asked.

"A minute sounds about right, don't you think? Two minutes seems too long."

Cris nodded. Hunt listened.

Motsch walked across the room. "On the far side of the bedroom, at the top of the L, we have the master bath."

Cris started to follow, but Hunt stayed put. He was eyeing the progression of Kelly and Juancito from the living room to the bedroom and the bath.

"Who delivered the Champagne?" Hunt asked.

Motsch paused midstep. "Vicente. He also delivered the luncheon service. As a matter of fact, I believe he is working in the lobby bar tonight."

"Could you arrange for us to speak with him?"

"My pleasure. Give me a moment."

As Motsch pulled out his radio, Cris and Hunt walked into the master bath and stood side by side. The towels, the toiletries, everything was gone. All had been replaced by the stench of a harsh antiseptic.

Cris positioned the iPad so that objects magically reappeared in place: on the vanity, a monogrammed hand towel with black mascara streaks; blonde hairs in the Jacuzzi; by the tub, a lipstick-stained Champagne glass.

"This is where the bottle of Champagne ended up," Cris said. She and Hunt looked at a picture of the bottle of Veuve Clicquot framed by two flutes: the one with lipstick on it was empty, the other untouched.

"Notice that someone didn't touch his Champagne," she said.

"And someone else definitely did," Hunt said.

Hunt swung open the shower door and looked inside. Cris peeked, too. There was nothing worth noting.

Motsch walked in. "How are we doing in here?"

Cris and Hunt looked at one another. The tour was over. "I think we've seen all that we need to see," he said.

"Excellent. I have to break away to say hello to some key clients in the café, but I've made arrangements for Vicente to talk with the both of you. Will that work?"

THE ARMY CAPTAIN AND THE Secret Service agent were seated at Fred Motsch's favorite table, one that not only featured a perfect vista of the inviting courtyard but also offered a discreet view of the other patrons.

Hunt stared at the gurgling waters that gave the Fountain Courtyard its name.

"Anything you'd like to share?" Cris asked.

"For starters, there's not a polo player on earth who would walk into that suite, make passionate love in the living room, and then get undressed in the bedroom."

"Why do you say that?"

"The clothes Juancito was wearing are for mounting a horse, not a woman."

"Go on."

"In polo, you use a flat saddle."

"So?"

"With a flat saddle the stirrups are attached by a long, thin leather strap that can pinch your legs worse than anything you can imagine. To protect themselves, polo players put the cuffs of their pants in their socks and pull their socks over their calves and then wear knee-high boots. Long story short, pulling your pants down while your boots are on is the wrong way to go about it."

"What you're telling me is that the two of them didn't fool around in the living room and then go back to the bedroom."

"Exactly. It may have been as simple as him getting undressed in the bedroom and then going back into the living room. That's one possibility. To me, the more likely scenario is that they went from the bedroom to the bath.

That's the direction the clothes were coming off, weren't they? Shirt, boots, socks, pants."

Cris nodded. "You've got a point there."

"And we've got a waiter here," Hunt looked pleased. "*Hola, Vicente.*"

A slight Filipino man in a Café Boulud uniform approached their table.

"Good evening, madame. Good evening, Captain Hunt. Mr. Motsch asked me to assist you with any questions you might have. But first, he insists that I bring the both of you your beverage of choice."

Cris smiled. "The Service doesn't encourage this sort of behavior, but given that I'll never have an assignment quite like this again, make mine a Champagne."

"Make that two, Vicente."

"Certainly," he said and retreated to the bar.

"So if it's bedroom, bathroom, living room, were there any water stains on the living room furniture?" Hunt asked.

"No. Other than the bathroom, the only water stains the police identified were on the carpet by the front door."

"Well, this is going nowhere."

"What do you mean?"

"You've just taken off my clothes in the bedroom. Next up, we fool around in the bathroom—on the vanity, in the tub or the shower or wherever. Now, for round three, where are we going to fool around next?"

"The living room?"

Hunt shook his head.

Cris's eyes widened. "Of course not. We're going to do it in the bedroom."

"Exactly. Why would we go to the living room?"

"When there's a perfectly fabulous king-sized bed right in front of us."

Hunt held his arms up and his hands out as he nodded in agreement.

"It doesn't mean we can't have sex in the living room. We obviously did have sex in the living room. But that leads me back to the question that's been eating at me all day long: *Why didn't we have sex in the bedroom?*"

Hunt enunciated his final words so distinctly that Vicente paused a few feet from the table.

Cris burst out laughing. "I bet you overhear way too many things, Vicente."

A broad smile filled the waiter's face. "La Grande Dame 2011," he said as he presented a bubbling flute to Cris and a second one to Hunt. "When it comes to our guests, Mr. Motsch insists that we hear nothing but notice everything."

"Which is exactly why we appreciate your joining us," Hunt said. "Tell us about Tuesday morning—delivering the Champagne, delivering lunch, any other details you can remember. Did you speak with Mrs. Dick? Did you speak with Mr. Harrington? Things like that."

The waiter slipped his tray under one arm.

"The Champagne service was a routine request. Quite often, the salon calls and has something delivered to a guest's room as a special favor or a thank-you. I didn't take the call but was informed that the Champagne service was to be presented at 10:30 sharp. So I selected the bottle, put it on ice, and arrived at the Lancaster Suite at 10:30 promptly. I rang the bell twice. Then I knocked once. No one answered. I was about to let myself in when Mrs. Dick opened the door."

"Tell us about her," Cris said.

"Of course, madame. She was wearing a robe from the salon. She had obviously just gotten some treatments. Her hair was pulled back. Her face was still flushed. As always, she was very attractive."

"What happened next?" Cris asked.

"Nothing unusual. When she opened the door, she said, 'I'm so glad it's you!'"

The memory of her warm greeting made him beam. "I like to think I'm her favorite. We all do. I always look forward to taking care of her." He paused. "And Mr. Dick, of course."

"Please continue," Hunt said.

"I brought in the service and asked her if the wet bar would suffice. She was fine with that. But when I began to open the bottle, she requested I leave it be. Which of course I did."

Hunt turned to Cris. "What time did Rio drop off Juancito?"

"11:35."

"That makes sense. Still an hour to go. Was there anything else about the room that you can remember? Was the TV on or something like that?"

"No, sir. It was all quiet. Except for the Jacuzzi. I could hear it filling."

"That explains the water stains at the front door," Cris said.

All three paused and listened to the loud lapping of the fountain.

"What about the luncheon service?" Hunt asked.

"Mr. Harrington actually called it in himself just before noon."

"How did you know it was him?" Cris asked.

"He identified himself when he called. That was his manner."

"So you've served him before?" Hunt asked.

"Yes, on one or two occasions. As always, he was most gracious. He ordered a pepper steak well-done, a side of *pommes frites*, and a glass of Malbec."

"Did you speak in Spanish to one another?"

"Yes, we did."

"*¿Un filete bien hecho con papas fritas?*" Hunt asked.

"*Exactamente.*"

"When did you deliver lunch?"

"About 20 minutes later."

"How did he seem?"

"Actually, I didn't see him. Mrs. Dick answered the door. She was dressed, and if I were to guess, I might say she was applying her makeup. I could tell she did not expect me."

"What do you mean?"

"She wasn't aware that Mr. Harrington had ordered lunch. That happens quite often. One guest places an order, and the other doesn't know about it."

"And then what?"

"I asked her where I should I set up the luncheon service. She asked if I would put it on the dresser in the master bedroom, and I obliged. I asked Mrs. Dick if I could be of further assistance, and she said no."

"And Mr. Harrington?"

"I could hear him in the shower, singing in the shower. He was such a happy man. When she told him his lunch had arrived, he thanked her for being so thoughtful."

"Did you sense any anger on her part, anything that would lead you to believe she would commit the crime she is charged with?" Hunt asked.

"Not in the least."

Vicente waited for his next question, but neither Cris nor Hunt spoke.

"I don't mean to hurry off. I do close the bar tonight. So if you have some more questions or would like another Champagne, it would be my pleasure to return."

"Give me one more minute, Vicente," Hunt said.

"Certainly."

"The police interviewed you, correct?"

"They certainly did. Yesterday morning in the ballroom."

"Would you mind telling us what they asked?"

"They asked me if I had seen Mrs. Dick in the Lancaster Suite on Tuesday, and I told them that I had, the two occasions I just mentioned to you."

"Did they ask about speaking with Mr. Harrington or overhearing him in the shower?"

"No, sir. They did not."

"Thank you, Vicente."

"My pleasure, Captain Hunt. Good evening, madame."

79

HUNT STEPPED INTO THE RIO Bravo barn just before nine thirty on Friday morning and was greeted by the nonstop clip-clopping of a dozen horses being fetched from stalls, tacked up, and led out to the pony lines. The team's Thoroughbreds had been pointed at Sunday's final for better than half a year, and Friday's practice at King Kenedy's barn was the final opportunity to prep them for the big match. Each would be played hard—but only for a chukker. The first two or three minutes would be to get some air in their lungs. The last few minutes would be casual loping at a hand canter. Saturday would be more of a tune-up than a workout—stopping, turning, and maybe some short work off the fence—just enough to keep them razor sharp. On game day, all forty Open horses would be warmed up and breezed the length of the field two or three times. Then it would be six short hours till showtime.

Quick steps and sharp commands filled the long hallway between the stalls. Today's scrimmage would be a tougher test for Rio Bravo's grooms than Sunday's final. In the championship, each member of the team would play his best horses—four, maybe five. Most would be played in different chukkers; the best would be doubled in the same chukker. But Friday's practice would be a relentless relay race with all forty of Rio Bravo's Open horses played one after the next.

Tendons were wrapped. Blankets were thrown over horses' backs and quickly smoothed out. Saddles were hoisted into place. Staccato chatter stoked the electric tempo. Rio Bravo's grooms spiced up their Spanish with a menu of terms that Hunt hadn't heard in ages—*yegua, montura, cincha, martingana.*

In the middle of this frenzy, Don Eliseo was the lone constant, the team's magnetic north. Hunt watched the old *vaquero* as he eyed the horses being led outside. Occasionally, Eliseo would hold up a hand, and a horse would be stopped. A minor adjustment to a throatlatch, a pat on the shoulder, and it got the green light. He snapped his fingers and pointed to a wrap. It wasn't undone. But it needed to be redone.

Don Eliseo saw Hunt and waved him over.

"Zapata, Quanah, Lobo, Comanche, y Marfa, *mi capitán*." As he named each of Hunt's mounts, Don Eliseo held up a leathery brown finger.

"*Andale*," Hunt said, as he high-fived Don Eliseo. The slapping sound startled several of the high-strung Thoroughbreds.

"Hey!" one of the grooms yelled out.

"Hey!" three or four responded.

"*¿Vamos a ganar?*" Hunt demanded of them all in a loud voice.

"*¡Vamos a ganar!*" The barn resonated with Don Eliseo's mantra.

We are going to win!

Hunt smiled and walked briskly to his tack room. He ditched his watch, his phones, and his wallet, changed into jeans and boots, strapped on his knee guards, and put on his helmet and gloves. When he stepped outside, Zapata awaited him, and he mounted up.

Hunt leaned forward and rode out of the cool barn into the bright tropical morning. He followed the sandy path to the edge of Rio Bravo's two practice fields, pausing to take in acre upon acre of the greenest grass framed by a long line of palm trees. Higher up, white clouds smudged the baby-blue sky.

Behold the road not taken, he said to himself.

At the far end of the pitch, the Gallegos were stick-and-balling. *Tap, tap, tap*—each wielded his mallet like Merlin. One hit, two hits, three hits, four, in the air and on the ground, each wooed and caressed a polo ball, doing the seemingly impossible, again and again and again.

Neither knows how to miss.

Hunt shook his head at the liver chestnut speeding down the field at a full gallop. It was SOB.

No patience then. No patience now.

Hunt was unable to identify the two players at the opposite end of the pitch, but the pair parked at midfield needed no introduction. He pointed Zapata at King and Joe and cantered toward them.

"*Muy buenos dias.*"

King reached up and tipped his cap with his bandaged thumb. A whistle was draped around his neck, and in his lap he balanced a pickup stick, the tool referees use to reach down and pluck a polo ball off the ground.

"How the mighty have fallen," Joe said, teasing the Senator.

"Not ashamed of my injuries. Just embarrassed by who inflicted them on me," King said.

"Polo is like war," Hunt said. "Sometimes your most dangerous enemy is the one you least expect."

"*On War*?" King asked.

Hunt shook his head. "Close. Yours truly. It's a dream of mine to teach a course at West Point called *Polo: The Decisive Leader's Secret Weapon*. We'd study military leaders who played polo, like Churchill and Patton, to see how the game of kings influenced their thinking and strategy, and I'd weave in classics, like Clausewitz's *On War*."

"Win yourself a US Open on Sunday, and you'll be a step closer toward making that course a reality," King said. "Now, what did you learn from our esteemed adversary last night?"

"Not much. When I showed up at the Chesterfield, he was playing backgammon with the Duke of Marlborough. After His Grace left, Mr. Australia chose not to give me the keys to the kingdom despite our longstanding ties. But since everyone already seems to know that I'll be marking Cesare on Sunday, he did suggest that my chinstrap be on extra tight."

"Mighty kind of him," Joe said.

"Then he ran off. Had a hot date with some South African jumper."

Joe let out a whistle. "I'd be running after that one too."

"How was Sunny?" King asked.

"Fine form. Excellent spirits."

King lifted his whistle to his lips and gave a short blast.

"What about you, cowboy?" Hunt said to Joe. His polo gear included a pair of well-worn leather chaps. "I knew you wouldn't shirk my challenge at Bice."

The former polo great grinned. "I don't go taking suggestions from you, pal. I take orders from this guy." He pointed at King.

"You're going to be covering José today," King said.

"A little taste of Sunday?" Hunt asked.

"No, sir," Joe said. "A heaping helping of Sunday."

Hunt kept an eye on the players at the far end of the field.

"By Jove," Hunt said, adopting a British accent. "Where did you dig up those gits?"

"I ran into them at dinner last night in Palm Beach," King said. "Lucky for us. Neither Piaget nor José Cuervo could scrimmage this morning. A lot of the best players have already left. So when Lupe and I bumped into your Westchester Cup rivals, I made them an offer they couldn't refuse. They'll be watching the final from our box."

The Ashton brothers rode up. Each wore the telltale signs of a proper British polo player: soft hands, perfect posture, and heels down.

"We have come to avenge last summer's tragic loss," James announced.

"Or at least that's the story we've told everyone back at Ham," Geoffrey added.

"Bring it on," Hunt said enthusiastically. "Glad to see you."

Joe extended a hand. "I'm Joe Bigelow. I'll be lining up against Rick. We're going to have you two lining up against the Gallegos."

"Excellent. Just like last summer," Geoffrey said.

"Who's lining up against SOB?" Hunt asked.

"Here she comes, right on cue," King said.

From under the archway, Ava rode out in black boots, a black shirt, a black helmet, and a pair of scarlet britches that lit up the morning. Her blonde hair was pulled back in a ponytail, and she was riding Terlingua, the odds-on favorite to win Best Playing Pony in the US Open. Silence ensued as she guided the grey onto the field. Each was a sight to behold; together the two were a matched pair.

"So if that happens to be whoever is lining up against SOB, would you mind explaining to me what it takes to be an SOB? Because if it were at all possible, I'd prefer she cover me," James said with a straight face.

"Point of fact, I've been told I'm an SOB quite often—by you, of all people," Geoffrey said.

King eyed the two Londoners. Joe and Rick shook their heads in silence.

"Given that I'm your older brother, doesn't that make me the bigger SOB?"

"You two are neck and neck for the crown," Joe said as Ava rode up and joined the circle.

"Hello, Daddy."

The Ashtons' stares turned to cringes.

"Senator..." Geoffrey began.

His older brother interrupted. "If you don't mind, Senator, that sort of behavior is intolerable. With your permission, I'm going to excuse my brother from attending Sunday's final."

SOB and the Gallegos rode up right as King, Joe, and Rick were laughing.

"You can forget that idea," Ava declared. "On Sunday afternoon, I'm going to show you two the time of your lives."

The Ashtons' ears turned even redder.

"What am I missing?" SOB said.

Everything, Hunt muttered to himself.

"Pardon me," James said. "And you are?"

"Selden O'Brien."

"We were supposed to have met last summer, were we not?"

"I don't think so."

"In Westchester Cup play. Weren't you selected to make the challenge?"

SOB hemmed and hawed.

"What happened? We saw neither hide nor hair of you."

"Well," he began. His eyes looked to the ground. "I ended up getting bounced off the team. Happened the week before we were supposed to fly over."

"Sorry to hear that," James said. A long pause followed. "So I guess that's how you came on board the American squad, am I right, Captain Hunt?"

"I never got the lowdown on that, and I don't think I'm about to get it here either," Hunt said.

SOB shot Hunt his dirtiest, most disgusted look.

"You couldn't have picked a better stand-in, especially the part where Hunt lost a stirrup in the final chukker yet still managed to pull off a superb steal. A fine bit of horsemanship, and in front of the Royal Box no less. Would that be why you and Her Majesty enjoyed such a lengthy chat at the awards ceremony? The way you two were carrying on, we were all positive you were in line for a knighthood."

"Not at all. We were discussing a fabulous runner of the Queen's, a brilliant mare named Estimate that had just won the Gold Cup at Ascot." Hunt turned to the gorgeous player in red and smiled. "Remember her, Ava?"

The Olympic hopeful nodded. "An Irish-bred from the Aga Khan Studs. Trained by Sir Michael Stoute."

"And how about the memorable finish of the Gold Cup?"

"How could I forget, Captain Hunt?" Ava paused. She was looking directly at him. "There must have been half a dozen horses in contention as they turned for home. Estimate was running fourth or fifth. The Gold Cup is the ultimate test of a stayer—two miles four. And her jockey, Ryan Moore. Do you know him?" she asked the Ashtons.

"Who doesn't?" Geoffrey said.

"He managed to keep *just* enough in her tank. She pulled ahead with, oh, two lengths to go. Couldn't have timed it better. She won by a neck. It was pure Ascot, one of the most sensational finishes I've ever seen. The Queen must have been over the moon. I certainly was. I had £100 on the lucky lady to beat the boys."

"Look at you!" James crowed.

"You mean you were at Ascot?" SOB asked. He was clearly perturbed.

"Yes," Ava said hesitantly. "I went with Rick."

"Royal Enclosure, old boy," Hunt added.

"But you told me you didn't go over for the Westchester Cup?" SOB asked.

"I didn't, Selden. After Ascot, I stayed for a little bit of Wimbledon, and then I flew back to the States to compete."

"This is the one who you were talking up last summer, is she not?" Geoffrey asked Hunt.

"The one and only," Hunt said.

"You two did get married, didn't you?" James asked.

"We did not," Hunt said.

"I'm dating her now," SOB said icily.

James Ashton looked at Hunt, then SOB, then Ava and her father.

"Hunt, I must say that only a true polo player would think you got the better end of that deal."

80

JOE BIGELOW AND RICK HUNT collided at ramming speed. Both were riding at full gallop, and the impact robbed each of his breath. Yet neither slowed. Instead, each did his best to elbow the other off the line of the ball. Both were out to make a point—Bigelow, that he was still hardy enough to play high-goal polo, and Hunt, that he was up to the task of marking Cesare.

The ball rolled out-of-bounds, and the two broke formation. Joe rode up beside King as they made their way back to midfield.

"This is the most fun I've had in years."

"You like working him over, don't you?"

"Always have."

"He'll be feeling that last hit in a day or two."

"Sure hope so."

"Last throw-in," King yelled out. "Give me an alley."

The two teams lined up, and King bowled the ball in. Joe got control of it—for the umpteenth time. He had been red-hot all morning long, playing with twice the energy and the enthusiasm of someone half his age.

"Look, listen, and learn," he bellowed proudly.

Joe took a long, lazy swing, and the ball rocketed downfield. Ava spurred her horse into high gear and bolted after it. Hunt blazed after her. As the team's back, it was his job to shut her down. Everyone else pulled up and watched the final duel of the day.

"Dust his ass," SOB said to no one in particular.

Hunt was about to pull even with her but Ava wouldn't have it. As he leaned in to ride her off, she gave it gas and pulled away. Nearing the ball, she cocked her mallet, leaned far enough forward out of the saddle to evade Hunt's coverage, and let loose a picture-perfect neck shot right under her horse's head. The ball took off straight for the goalmouth. The final goal of the morning was hers. A blast from King's whistle ended the practice.

Ava slowed her mount and looked over her shoulder. A smile lit up her face. But Rick was already gone, loping his horse back to the barn. SOB rode up.

"Ten-goal shot, babe."

He followed up his compliment by hooking a finger through one of her belt loops, pulling her closer, and giving her an unexpected kiss.

81

"WHAT ON EARTH?"

James Ashton was gobsmacked by the sizzling asado that awaited the play-ers in the barn's center courtyard.

"I haven't seen a spread like this since last year's Abierto," his brother said.

"*¿Cual es esto?*" James asked the groom working the pit.

"*Bife de chorizo, señor,*" he said, as he pointed with his tongs to the New York strips at the center of the fire. Farther out, hefty *ojo de bifes* rested off the flames. The thicker rib eyes, which took longer to cook, had been seared to perfection and were slowly finishing. At the edge of the fire, loaves of French bread browned and crisped.

"King does it right, doesn't he?" Hunt said.

"Every time," said SOB.

James and Geoffrey shot each other puzzled looks.

"Am I the only one who finds you two a bit odd: you dating his ex-fiancée, you stealing his glory in the world's most prestigious polo match, and the both of you now playing on the same polo team?" James asked.

SOB let out a laugh. "Me and Rikki have lined up against each other for most of our lives."

"Neither of us ever had much of a choice," Hunt added.

"That's where you are wrong, hombre. You did have a choice. And you chose West Point over professional polo. You could have made it to 10 goals easy, Rikki. You're way better now than when we were 5-goalers. You're 6 goals no question. On the right team, you'd be lock at 7. You could have gone all the way to the top. Still can."

Hunt smiled. "What makes you think I'm not there already?"

SOB rolled his eyes.

"You two should take this variety show of yours on the road," James said.

"They already have," Ramon said. "And we were their chaperones."

Roberto nodded. "Once we were at a tournament in Paris, and my phone started ringing. It was Joe. 'You seen SOB? The hotel manager says he hasn't checked into his room.' This was two days after the team landed. I said not to worry. 'I believe he's getting an intensive safety briefing from an Air France stewardess at her flat!'"

SOB took the throaty laughs as a compliment.

"Joe worked you extra hard that week, did he not?" Roberto asked.

"So did she," SOB said.

Everyone was laughing—except Hunt.

"Oh, Rikki. Always the All-American, so God and country. I take it back. You belonged at West Point."

"Go ahead. Change the topic. You and I both know you were this close to putting us in the losers' bracket."

"We won the World Championships, didn't we?"

"We did?" Hunt asked pointedly. "As I recall, the only riding you did in our first match was on the bench."

"I suppose you're going to point out that's what happened last summer too."

Hunt smiled. "The only thing better than playing with you in the Westchester Cup was playing in your place."

"Ohhhhhhh," James exclaimed. "That stung."

SOB wore a cocky smile. "That's kind of the way I see it with me and Ava."

"Ohhhhhhh," Geoffrey exclaimed. "That scalded."

Hunt threw an arm around SOB's shoulders, and they headed to the table together. "You might have a point there," Hunt said under his breath.

At the far side of the fire pit, Don Eliseo approached the grooms in charge of the asado. He pointed to several cuts of beef. Then he pointed to some bread and a bottle of vino. He was not serving himself. It was for King. For some reason, the Senator was taking his meal in his tack room. So was Joe Bigelow.

"*Hola, Eliseo*," Ramon said.

"*Hola, Ramon*," Don Eliseo responded. "*Caballeros*," he added and tipped his hat to the rest of the table.

"*¿Algo a comer?*" Hunt asked, inviting the *vaquero* to dine with them.

"*Muy amable,*" Don Eliseo responded as he turned down the offer. "*Mi capitán, el Rey le gustaria hablar con usted.*"

"*Cómo no,*" Hunt said and nodded.

Hunt had been summoned by the Senator.

He stood up and turned to his teammates.

"Gentlemen, I shall return."

82

THE HEEL PLATES ON HUNT'S boots echoed sharply as he marched down the long stall-lined hallway that led to King's lair. As he approached the door, it swung open and Ava stepped out. Bright-eyed and sweat-stained, she quickly closed the door behind her and held up a hand.

"Would you give me a minute before you go in to talk to Daddy?"

"Of course I would, Ava. I loved that last shot of yours."

"But why were you in such a hurry to get away?"

"Because what I really want to say to you I couldn't say out there."

"You can say it now," she said shyly.

Hunt paused. "Ava, I want to apologize for what happened last summer. When you left, we were on top of the world, weren't we?"

She nodded.

"Then I let the Chief, the President, the Summit, and a lot of other things take over my life."

"You mean take over our lives."

"You're right—our life. We had a good thing going, and I blew it. I see that now. It was entirely my fault. I'm especially sorry for what happened after Wimbledon."

Ava looked at her ex. She bit her lower lip. Hunt reached out and put his hand on her shoulder. It slid down her sleeve. Her soft smile began to emerge, a smile he hadn't seen in almost a year.

Before either could utter another word, a voice bellowed from inside the Senator's tack room:

"Get in here!"

HUNT WAS NO STRANGER TO the Oval Office. He had been to Windsor Castle, flown on Air Force One, and been welcomed into the tent of one of the world's most powerful warlords. Yet each time he stepped into King Kenedy's tack room, he found it an incomparable experience. It wasn't because his lair was lavish or historic. On the contrary, it was spare. Yet it was emblematic of the equestrian tradition that Hunt had been brought up to respect and to revere.

Over the centuries, horsemen of all stripes had encamped at Rio Bravo. Conquistadores, Comanches, *pistoleros*, Texas Rangers—the artifacts of each were meticulously documented by the ranch archivist. One of his other charges was to rotate artwork from the Kenedy Collection at the ranch to the family's Georgetown brownstone, their home off Turtle Creek in Dallas, and the Senator's Palm Beach polo barn. Hunt took a moment to inspect the new installations.

One, two, three Paul Browns. Next up was a Western sunset. *That Peter Hurd must be of the Ruidoso Valley.* He came to a full stop in front of an elegant oil of a well-muscled chestnut. *How the hell did he get his hands on an original Stubbs?* The last paintings by George Stubbs that Hunt had seen were on a private tour of the Royal Collection at Windsor Castle. *No telling.* Hunt spied a pair of stainless steel spurs on King's rolltop desk. He picked them up and fingered the rowels. *Bayers 218s.* As he did, he noticed the smallest portrait of all. It was a simple sketch, done in ink on cloth, of a young woman's face. A bold signature and the date—7.7.70—were the only other elements. The dark ink had begun to blot, but the beauty of the subject was indelible.

All his life, Hunt had heard about this Picasso, the one that the artist had sketched the moment he set eyes on Lupe. She and King were honeymooning on the Côte d'Azur. One day, they made their way to Aix. By chance, she spied a café. Little did she know it was a favorite of the Spaniard's. While King parked their Peugeot, she stepped inside. The maestro must have been close to ninety. Not that age had dulled his keen eye. He seized on her and did his best to entice the young bride to be his new muse, but she was much too in love to be seduced by the promise of immortality. By the time King arrived at their table, her portrait was complete and the artist's hopes crushed.

At the far end of the spacious room, the Senator was seated on a tufted leather sofa with a bold Navajo chief's blanket draped across the back. Next to him sat Joe Bigelow. At their feet, a muscular greyhound lay sprawled on the floor. The breed was one of the Senator's passion projects. He had long made a practice of adopting greyhounds off the track.

Another set of eyes fixed on Hunt. Ava's Italian greyhound had been snoozing on King's lap. In a flash, the lightning bolt sprinted across Joe, vaulted onto the back of the couch, and planted his paws on Hunt's chest. Hunt responded with a back-scratching that soothed the not-so-savage beast.

"Let's take it from the top," King said.

Bigelow hit PLAY and the breaking news story began again. In the first frame, Kelly could be seen in a baggy prison jumpsuit.

"In an unexpected turn of events in Palm Beach County, bail was set at $10 million this morning for accused murderer Kelly Dick. Just yesterday, the wife of Centaur chairman Jack Dick attended a first-appearance hearing after being arrested for the shooting death of her husband's star polo player, Juan Harrington, following a lovers' quarrel at the luxurious Brazilian Court Hotel."

The tawdry *InStyle* portrait of Kelly sandwiched between her lover and her husband flashed on the screen. "Although she was initially denied bail at her bond hearing, this morning state prosecutors softened their position following a personal plea from the murder victim's brother."

A clip of Cesare ran full frame. "It is absolutely impossible that Kelly murdered my brother. A preposterous notion." There was sweat on his brow and a towel around his neck.

Hunt was riveted to the screen. Ramirez's case had just taken a direct hit.

Only one person on earth could resurrect Kelly's reputation, and he had just done so.

"Must have been right after yesterday's game," Joe said. The caption at the bottom of the picture indicated that Cesare was being interviewed in Wellington by the *News of the World*.

Poignant mementos of his slain brother's storied career were visible on the walls behind him: a photo of the Harringtons at Guards accepting the Coronation Cup from Her Majesty, a dashing shot of Juancito and Cesare in black tie, a faded black-and-white of a young boy holding an infant at an asado.

"Are you saying that the State of Florida has wrongfully imprisoned Kelly Dick?" an English-accented voice asked.

"Absolutely," Cesare said. "Her arrest and detainment are a miscarriage of justice. There is no doubt in my mind that Kelly had nothing whatsoever to do with my brother's death. Kelly is a wonderful woman and a close friend of our family. And she's equally generous with strangers. I can't begin to count the number of charities she supports. Anyone lucky enough to have met her knows that she should be set free."

In the next series of clips, reporters and cameramen hindered the progress of a chauffeur-driven Cadillac Escalade as it whisked Kelly from the Palm Beach County Detention Center.

"Only minutes ago, Ms. Dick was spirited out of a West Palm Beach correctional facility and driven to her family's estate on South Ocean Boulevard. In addition to posting a $10 million bond, Judge Singhal has set a lengthy list of conditions regarding Mrs. Dick's pretrial release. According to the court, she must surrender her passport and remain in Palm Beach County. She is also required to wear a tamper-resistant ankle monitor at all times, and to check in with the court twice a week. And her attorneys have agreed to pay all costs associated with maintaining a team of security personnel to monitor her whereabouts and ensure that she poses no flight risk. Our sources tell WPTV that this service starts at $100,000 per month and can easily cost twice as much."

84

JACK DICK COULDN'T DO IT.

Joshua Shapiro couldn't do it.

The only one capable of freeing Kelly Dick was Cesare Harrington—with a little help from Walter Ned.

The moment Cesare described Kelly's arrest for the murder of his brother as a "miscarriage of justice," Ned knew that Raul Ramirez and the State Prosecutor had lost their absolute authority. Until that point, all the evidence pointed at Jack Dick's wife. So had all the witnesses. There was no question as to who had perpetrated this heinous crime. But as soon as Cesare said those fateful words, an iota of doubt entered the equation. Ned's eyes lit up. His mind began to race. Cesare's statement was by no means an exoneration, but a counter theory had emerged, one brought forward by the most credible of sources. The journalist had to stifle his impulse to halt the interview and transform those sound bites into gold. Cesare's statement was more than an opinion. It was a precious asset, one that would rapidly depreciate in value. Within twenty-four hours, it would be old news.

The moment the interview concluded, Ned excused himself and stepped out of the tack room to place a call. The Centaur barn had never been busier. Grooms paraded shimmering horses back to their stalls. Cesare's teammates were taking other journalists' questions. A quiet corner was nowhere to be found. Ned shook his head. A quiet corner wasn't necessary. No one was paying any attention to him.

He speed-dialed Joshua Shapiro's cell.

At that very instant, only a handful of people knew of Ned's stop-the-presses interview with Cesare. And they all worked for him. It would be hours before the footage was cut and ready to upload to the *News of the World* website. The video clip that Ned had taped with his iPhone? It was good to go.

"Can you send it to me now?" Shapiro asked.

"All I need is a king's ransom and your lifelong fealty," Ned responded.

"I'll throw in my firstborn," Shapiro said.

Within the hour, Kelly Dick's lead attorney was demanding a hearing.

"I've just reviewed a statement from the victim's brother, and based on what he said, we definitely need to revisit the idea of granting her bond. My next call is to Judge Singhal's judicial assistant," Shapiro said.

"There's no way I'm going to let that happen," the State Attorney retorted.

"Of course you don't want it to happen. Then the public will see that there are two sides to this story, and my client's side is not being told," Shapiro countered.

"I know what you're doing, Josh. I know what you're trying to pull here," the State Attorney said.

"What I'm doing is trying my best to secure the treatment my client deserves. And that begins with the hearing I'm demanding first thing tomorrow," Shapiro said.

"OK. In lieu of a hearing, what would you accept?" the State Attorney asked.

The moment he heard those words, Shapiro knew his client was going home.

IT WAS DUCK-AND-COVER TIME AT Palm Beach P.D.

From securing every shred of paperwork related to Kelly's release to confirming the ETA of the genetic material from the forensics lab, Raul Ramirez's subordinates readied themselves for the deafening tirade all were sure to endure.

The first hint of what was to come rushed up the stairs and spilled down the halls like an angry squall. As his sharp steps approached, Ramirez's roar crystallized into a non-stop stream of profanities. Bits and pieces of his rant crescendoed as he neared.

The bullpen door flew open, bounced off its stopper, and slammed shut. Ramirez kicked it open a second time, barged in, and stared menacingly at the first investigator.

"They released that spoiled brat because a paid employee of her husband's vouched for her innocence?"

The investigator took a deep breath. A second one squeezed his eyes closed as though he was about to be slapped. The crime scene photographer hid his battery packs and anything else that could be thrown.

"Since when has anecdotal hearsay outweighed hard evidence?"

The first investigator made the briefest of eye contact with his boss and then quickly refocused on his computer monitor.

"And now she's back in that damn palace, living like Marie Antoinette!"

Ramirez didn't wait for a response. Instead, he stormed into his office and slammed the door shut. It bounced open, and everyone in the bullpen froze again. A moment later, he kicked it closed with an anguished howl.

86

"EXCUSE ME BUT I'VE GOT to check my BlackBerry," Hunt said as the special report concluded. "I'm sure I've got a dozen emails on this already."

"No, sir," King said. "Your first responsibility is to call the Chief."

"I gave the Chief a heads-up yesterday. Told him that the case against Kelly was very weak."

"*Now*," King said.

"He's on his way to the UN with the President."

"You let Ari decide what's the best time. You let Ari decide the importance of your information. When it comes to intel, he calls the shots, not you. At his level, that's the way the game is played. If the President is talking his ear off, if he's in the middle of an important meeting he can't break away from, if he's tired of talking to you—that's no concern of yours. Your assignment is to be ready, willing, and able. Got it?"

Hunt nodded and walked over to the rolltop desk. He hit the speaker button on the telephone and dialed the main switchboard at the White House.

"White House."

"This is Captain Hunt calling for the Chief."

"One moment, Captain."

"Office of the Chief of Staff," a second voice said.

"Captain Hunt, checking in, ma'am."

"There you are, Richard," a pleasant voice said. "The Chief has gone to New York with the President for his UN address. Let me see if I can catch him."

The line went dead for a few seconds, then a half a minute, then a full minute. Bigelow muted Walter Ned's interview with Cesare.

"Is that you, soldier?" a voice suddenly boomed out of nowhere.

"Yes, sir."

"Can't talk right now. We're on FDR Drive about to pull up at the UN. Thanks for the update yesterday. The President and I were on Air Force One this morning. Watched her get released. Good call there. He's very interested in how this situation develops. I want a complete update tomorrow."

"10-4," Hunt said. Then the line went dead.

Silence enveloped the sanctuary.

"Point taken, sir," Hunt said.

King nodded. "Here's your next step." He handed Hunt an embossed envelope with a handwritten inscription:

Captain Richard Hunt & Guest

"Go ahead and take a look," the Senator said, gesturing at the envelope. Hunt opened it. It was the most sought-after invite of the entire polo season: The Polo Ball on board the *Centaur*.

For the past five years, on the Friday night before the final of the US Open, Kelly had thrown an over-the-top party aboard her husband's sleek megayacht. In the early years of Centaur Polo, back before the Harringtons signed on, there hadn't been much to celebrate in the way of major tournament victories. But given her long-standing ties to the best-known players in the game, Kelly was able to convince and cajole the biggest names in polo to attend. Her former beaus were more than happy to oblige. Most were already in town for the final, and what better way to see her than at Jack Dick's expense.

Kelly's two personal assistants spent months focused on the project: booking the hottest celebrity chefs, piecing together an extravagant goodie bag, and flying in a columnist from *Page Six*. Thanks to the success of Kelly's Polo Ball, Jack Dick's profile easily overshadowed the marginal reputation of his polo team early on. And that was before Centaur began to win.

"As a member of the Rio Bravo team and a finalist in the US Open, your attendance is mandatory. Mess dress, jeans, tux—your call. There's one other stipulation."

"What's that?"

"Lupe expects you to bring that Secret Service agent you introduced her to at Wednesday's game."

"I ASSUME YOUR OFFICE MONITORS Centaur trading on a daily basis?"

Phone to her ear and pen in hand, Cris Cortés listened intently to the answer. It was midafternoon at the Secret Service West Palm Beach field office, and her computer screen featured a list of pending cases concerning the manipulation of Centaur's stock price. The first involved a potential insider trading violation. The second dated back to the previous summer when word of a blockbuster acquisition was mysteriously leaked. Key officers and board members of both companies had been investigated, but the culprit was never discovered. The news had a tumultuous effect on Centaur's stock price and sent the market into a tizzy.

"That's so different than the work we do. The scammers we track down push counterfeit paper. They hack credit card numbers. They forge signatures. You can't get more straightforward than that. But manipulating the price of a major publicly traded company?"

She listened to her contact at the SEC.

"Give me a for instance."

Her contact continued.

"I get it. Now what about this week?"

She nodded her head as if the woman were in the room. Listening some more, she wrote the words down on her legal pad and underlined them twice.

Nothing this crazy since Enron imploded!

Over the course of the next fifteen minutes, the Secret Service agent filled several pages with notes on Centaur's trading volume since the news of

Juancito's murder broke—its usual hyper-volatility on Monday and Tuesday followed by the racing insanity of Wednesday, Thursday, and Friday, and the intense scrutiny that the aftereffects of the murder were drawing from SEC investigators.

"What about a tip from an investigator or a first responder? Could that have given someone a jump on the market?" Cris paused and listened.

"No, I can confirm that the news of the murder was withheld overnight by Palm Beach P.D.," she explained. "That's a hell of a head start for the right person or persons."

She continued to listen and filled up another page of notes. Flipping to a blank page, she scribbled OPTIONS and COMMODITIES FUTURES TRADING COMMISSION. As her SEC contact explained the intricacies of puts and calls, Cris began to realize how contracts on the most extreme positions could go from worthless to worth millions in a single day. She made a final note:

Even a tiny ripple can create enormous profits in a big pond.

"You wouldn't mind pinging the CFTC for me on this, would you?" Cris asked. She listened a moment. "Of course. The afternoon got away from me too. Yes, thanks so much. You've been extremely helpful."

Cris hung up the phone and picked up her BlackBerry. The message light was blinking, just as it did all day long. She scrolled through several system-wide Secret Service alerts and then switched to texts. She stopped scrolling when she saw the one from Captain Rick Hunt:

"Meet me at Breakers at 5:45. Resort casual."

DESPITE BRIGHT SPLASHES OF COLOR—THE handcrafted mallets, the red and blue and black balls, and the lollypop-colored center pegs—the only person paying attention to the duel on the croquet lawn was Rick Hunt. Dressed in a blue blazer, open-collared shirt, and cavalry twill trousers, he was sitting on one of the cushioned chairs at the edge of the lawn. Back and forth, his gaze alternated between the two players lining up their shots and the long line of cars queuing up to park. It was early Friday evening, but the sun was high above the horizon. It was that breezy blue part of the day in Palm Beach—not too hot, not quite cool, absolutely perfect.

What game is she playing?

The thought had been gnawing at him most of the afternoon.

Cars pulled up, doors slammed, valets sprinted back and forth—The Breakers was in high gear. Except on the croquet lawn where the two players were quietly, carefully strategizing.

She certainly isn't trying to set me up. She knows better than that.

Getting a bid to The Polo Ball was one thing. But insisting that Cris tag along as his date added a curious element of intrigue.

Does she think Cris might catch SOB's eye?

Hunt considered his teammate's modus operandi. Then he considered Cris. Not a chance.

With a delicate but decisive tap, one player knocked the other's ball hopelessly out of play. A moment later, Hunt saw Cris drive past the lawn and park. An attentive valet pounced on her car door and opened it with a flourish. A toned calf emerged—then another—as she stepped out in a form-fitting floral chiffon dress. The bell stand came to a halt as one by one the valets all turned to check out the new arrival.

Cris looked spectacular. Walking toward him, she held his gaze.

"You do good work in a hurry, Agent Cortés."

Cris accepted the compliment with that smile that kept dazzling him.

"Heading out to sea on a ship like the *Centaur* is bucket-list material for a girl like me, Captain Hunt."

"Even if we are on the clock, an evening like this will be a night to remember," he said. He offered her an arm and led her in the direction of a black Lincoln Town Car.

"What did I miss today?" he asked.

"The case against Kelly is at a complete standstill, yet Ramirez refuses to consider any other suspect."

"No surprise there. He hates her. He hates her kind."

"That's not enough in a case like this. Not without a motive, a murder weapon, or any record of violent behavior on her part. And she's got one hell of a character witness in Mr. Harrington's brother."

"So much for Ramirez's open-and-shut case."

"On top of that, the list of Kelly's lovers here in Palm Beach makes you wonder when she sleeps. She's been a busy girl. Once Ramirez ducked out, there was a lot of discussion about which one or ones might be potential suspects."

"Any front runners?"

"Not yet. The first task is to figure out who was in town on Tuesday. I gather a lot of the polo players have already left."

"Correct. We had to change up practice this morning because so many of the best players are gone. King ended up recruiting a couple of friends of mine to scrimmage against us. Brits I played against last summer."

"Sounds like fun."

Their driver held the door for Cris.

"Actually, it was something special for me," he said as he slid in from the other side. "Once upon a time, I wanted to be a professional polo player. Today, I got to see what it was like."

"Mixing work and pleasure?"

"It was a morning I won't forget for a lot of reasons. But the bubble burst when I learned about Kelly getting sprung. What's your take on that?"

"I wasn't surprised. You've got the wrong guy in charge. He's built his case solely on circumstantial evidence."

"I'm talking with the Chief tomorrow. Anything else I can brief him on?"

"According to my contact at the SEC, they are alert but not alarmed about Centaur stock. Jack Dick has incurred enormous paper losses—well into the hundreds of millions—but to the best of her knowledge, those losses haven't set off any triggers that would materially affect him or the company."

"He's bruised but not battered?"

"Exactly. And his board is definitely on his side. If it hadn't been for Kelly's arrest, this week would have gone down as one of the best in the company's history: record earnings, increased market share, and on track to make the most of several substantial opportunities."

"Did she suggest who might have gained from Centaur's nose dive?"

"Everyone. Centaur's trading volume has been staggering. From day traders to hedge fund managers and sovereign funds, hundreds of thousands of traders have been buying and selling Centaur as it tanked and while it bounced back. Today was another roller-coaster ride. This morning, before Kelly made bail, it opened at \$112. By noon, it had jumped to \$127. And it closed at \$138."

"Remind me what it was on Wednesday before Kelly was arrested?"

"It opened at \$157 Wednesday morning. Then the sell-off began."

They turned off South County Road and were headed down Australian Avenue toward the docks. In the middle of the second block, they passed the Brazilian Court. In the distance, the sun silhouetted the huge hull and sleek lines of one of the world's most expensive yachts. Directly in front of them, South Lake Drive was clogged with a long line of cars bearing guests for the Polo Ball.

"You mind a short stroll?"

"Not at all."

"We'll walk from here," Hunt told the driver.

He cracked the door handle and stepped outside. He turned, extended a hand, and helped Cris to her feet. She stood up, and they came face to face.

"It's showtime!" she whispered. She wrapped her bare shoulders in her pashmina. "Who do you want me to be tonight? A damsel in distress? A fairy-tale princess? What's our story?"

"Local girl. Mutual friends. New to polo. Eager to learn more."

"That's easy enough," Cris said, slipping her hand in his arm.

A few feet behind them, a horn honked loudly.

"Park this car. That's an order, Captain," a plummy voice boomed.

It was Mr. Australia behind the wheel of his Defender. Seated beside him in the khaki-colored Land Rover was the gorgeous young South African jumper he had run off to meet at Barzina.

"Higher priorities tonight, sir," Hunt said as he snapped off a smart salute and kept walking. Cris squeezed his arm with a slight smile.

"What do we have here?" she asked.

A daunting reception committee greeted guests. Guarding the gate to the dock were three uniformed police officers, two sheriff's deputies, and an assortment of plainclothes security. Presumably a portion of this contingent was Kelly's court-ordered security detail. A gaggle of photographers had staged themselves just feet away; all lenses were trained on Raul Ramirez, who was berating a gate-crasher sporting a top hat, a loud plaid jacket, and shocking green trousers.

"I don't care who you claim invited you. I am uninviting you. This dock belongs to the Town of Palm Beach, and I am denying you access," Ramirez shouted.

He motioned for the gate-crasher to be removed, and a madcap scuffle ensued, one punctuated by fast footwork and more than a few expletives. Two of Palm Beach's finest had little problem carting off the Mad Hatter to a waiting patrol car.

"Any idea what we just saw?" Cris asked.

"Not yet."

The couple glided toward Kelly's personal assistants. Hunt presented his invitation to the tallest of the three Valkyries.

"Welcome to the *Centaur*, Captain Hunt."

The first confirmed Hunt's name on the guest list, the second radioed his arrival, and the third waved them through the gate, where the couple joined the flow of guests proceeding down the long dock. On either side, dozens of boats were moored. The one-hundred-meter behemoth at the end overshadowed all of them.

Hunt could feel Cris's excitement. Her eyes lit up. Her step quickened. Sea breezes ruffled her chiffon dress; the setting sun glinted on the yellows and reds. He watched her pick out the ship's namesake constellation boldly stitched on the colorful awning that greeted guests.

"This *will* be a night to remember," she said. She looked over at Hunt and her brow furrowed. "What are you thinking about?"

"I'm asking myself the same question I asked you at the bar last night."

She thought for a moment. Then she nodded.

Why didn't they have sex in the bedroom?

KELLY DICK GLIDED ACROSS THE pool deck in five-inch-high gold Manolo Blahniks with gold grommets, her toned body barely concealed by an Eres two-piece white bikini with a silk Versace wrap. One of her husband's eye-catching gold Rolexes dangled on her left wrist. A gold Bulgari chain hugged her surgically enhanced tatas. But the showstopper was her court-ordered ankle monitor. Instead of covering it up, Kelly had blinged it with hundreds of Swarovski crystals. It was impossible to overlook—just like the woman who wore it. She reached out with both arms and greeted Hunt with air kisses on both cheeks and a wet one on the lips.

"Ricky, I am so disappointed I missed your amazing performance on Wednesday. I can't quite remember, but something came up and I missed your match." She started to giggle.

Appearing at her side, Jack Dick only smiled at her behavior. "Captain Hunt is a man of many talents. Let's hope that Wednesday's match will be his only amazing performance in the Open," he said as he shook Hunt's hand.

Hunt introduced his date to the Dicks. The two women immediately eyed each other up and down. Kelly's keen eye picked out the fact that this was Cris's first time on board a ship such as the *Centaur*. No woman in her right mind would go out to sea in floral-print chiffon. If she had to make a guess, she'd wager it came from Calypso Christiane Celle. She gave her style points for the designer look-alike flats—probably from Steve Madden—but the pashmina needed to go overboard. It was so last year.

The Secret Service agent's gaze was one of mild awe. Gone was the shell-shocked suspect at Palm Beach P.D. In her place, the sassy hostess had reclaimed her throne.

"How do you like this new little something Jack got for me?" Kelly asked, showing off her sparkling ankle monitor.

Hunt turned to his host. "Jack, is this the model that comes with the obedience-training option?"

Dick's eyes brightened. "If I'd have known one were available, I would have ordered it years ago!"

Kelly threw back her head and laughed. "Baby, I wouldn't if I were you. This one cost you a fortune, didn't it?"

Dick turned to the Secret Service agent. "Can you believe her? I'm down $400 million, and she's making a joke about it?"

The Secret Service agent shook her head. She could not.

"Baby, that's why I married you," Kelly said. "You're going to make those millions back, and then you're going to make millions more." Her voice switched into baby talk. "And then you're going to let me spend one or two of them, aren't you?" She had planted her arms around him, and her blonde locks were resting on his chest. Jack Dick was beaming. He loved the way she loved him for his money. She didn't hide it. She flaunted it.

Another guest had arrived. "And whom do we have here?" Dick turned.

Hunt sensed it was time to move on. With a parting wink to Kelly, he guided Cris onto the crowded main deck.

"Is she always that brazen?" Cris asked.

"What you see is what you get," Hunt said. "Just like this guy."

Joe Bigelow was walking directly toward them.

"Hello there, gorgeous. How's our boy holding up?" Joe asked.

"You're in big trouble," Cris said, a friendly smile on her face. "You and that paparazzi nearly got the two of us in some very hot water yesterday."

"I liked that pretty picture in the paper. I knew we could get an honest day's work out of him. And if that's your idea of hot water, then believe you me, you just stuck your toe in it. I've been married three times. And each time, it was a whole lot like crawling in a hot tub."

"What do you mean?" Cris asked.

"After a while, it ain't so hot," Joe said, and he clapped Hunt on the back.

An abbreviated conga line began to throb to the live music. At the front of the line was a sultry Cuban model wearing next to nothing and wearing it well. Dancing right behind her was an elf-like creature who alternated between spanking her and issuing a trilling squeal at the top of his voice. He was put-ting on as good a show as she was.

"I hear the conga calling," Bigelow said. He bolted into the fray with his arms over his head and his boxy hips knocking from side to side.

"Do you want to take a guess who that might be?" Hunt asked Cris.

"You mean the spanker?" she asked.

Hunt leaned into her. "The last person outside of the Brazilian Court to see Juancito alive," he whispered.

"Rio?" she asked. "Rio Garcia?"

"Juancito's right-hand man," Hunt said.

"I'd say he's ambidextrous, not right-handed," Cris observed wryly.

At that moment, Rio had both of his hands on the *cubana's* curvaceous hips. He was rattling her cage as though she were a giant maraca. She loved it. He loved it. Everyone watching loved it.

A sharp whistle pierced the air. Hunt and Cortés both turned. It was SOB, dressed to the nines: tweed jacket, rep tie, silk pocket square—the works.

"Live from Palm Beach, it's SOB!" Hunt proclaimed.

The 10-goaler was holding down the bar by himself. As the couple made their way toward him, his eyes gave Cris a once-over.

"Working at the White House has been good to you, Rikki."

"Cris Cortés is actually a colleague of mine here in South Florida."

"Sure beats the colleagues I'm stuck with."

"Cris, may I introduce you to America's finest polo player, the one and only."

"SOB," she said, offering her hand.

SOB smiled at her recognition. "My pleasure. How about I offer you a drink?"

He had two margaritas in front of him. One was partially drained; the other was full to the brim.

"You double-fisting it tonight?" Hunt asked.

"Nope. Just waiting on Ava to get done with her mother."

Hunt followed SOB's gaze. Just off the dance floor, the Kenedy women were engaged in serious chat. Ava looked up, saw Hunt and his date, and immediately began making her way across the main deck. Hunt watched her every step. Her outfit was stunningly simple—a chambray shirt over a lace maxi-dress—and she wore it with Kenedy panache. He also noticed that Lupe was watching him watching her. She nodded, and Hunt returned the gesture.

"Don't you look fabulous," Ava said as she walked up to Cris. She stroked the chiffon. "I love this!"

Lupe winked discreetly at Hunt and slowly turned away.

Now he knew—*Lupe wanted Ava to see him with a catch like Cris.*

Someone else had been watching Ava as well.

"Hello, lovelies!" the Groper said as he stepped forward.

"Trip!" Ava said, greeting the man with mock enthusiasm. She took a step backward, and Cris edged closer to Hunt. Both had assumed a defensive posture. "And Lori! So good to see you. I love this look," she added.

The Groper's wife trailed her husband into their midst. They were the oddest of couples: he in his seventies, in yet another seersucker suit; and she, a stylish brunette in her forties, in a Chanel cocktail dress.

"So lovely to see you, Ava," she purred.

Lori Capra was a soft-spoken soul, and Ava made a point of introducing her to everyone. When she came to her former beau, Lori interrupted.

"I've already met Captain Hunt."

"Oh, really?" her husband asked.

"Well, almost. Do you remember stopping by the Brazilian Court yesterday morning?"

"Of course I do."

"I was on a chaise in the courtyard when you met the general manager."

"Yes, I remember you now, Lori," Hunt said. "You had your hair up in a towel, and you were wearing some Jackie O's and a white robe."

"That's my girl, all right," the Groper said. "Now, how about we all meet there? I'd love to host a luncheon for you ladies."

As Ava launched into a gushing apology, Lori leaned toward Hunt. "Could I talk to you privately?" she asked. "It's about that polo murder."

"OF COURSE. LET'S MEET . . . " Hunt paused for a moment and looked around the crowded deck. "Let's meet on the Upper Deck. It will be quieter up there. How about we catch up in five or ten?"

"That sounds perfect. See you in a minute."

Lori left without acknowledging her husband. Nor did he notice her departure. The Groper was still endeavoring to lure Ava and Cris to the Brazilian Court. Hunt listened as the lecher tried to coax, entice, and beg the lovely ladies. His first gambit was lunch. When that failed, he shifted to poolside. Then dinner. Then drinks. Then a private screening of a film he had helped finance. Hunt could see that Lori had reached the stairwell and was making her way to the Upper Deck. He caught Cris's eye and gestured that he was taking off. She nodded.

The sun was setting, the light dimming, and in less than half an hour the events of the evening would get under way: the introduction of the finalists and a speech or two from the team *patrons*. Who knew what Kelly would add to the mix.

The Main Deck was packed. Polo players, past champions, Palm Beach socialites—all had caught conga fever, thanks to Rio. Hunt had never seen the little man exert such concentrated effort. The truth was he'd never seen him lift a finger. Instead of wading into the crowd, Hunt circled its perimeter. Halfway around, a firm hand latched on to his shoulder.

"There you are," Mr. Australia said. He was not alone. Standing next to him was King Kenedy. A magnum of Penfolds Grange had been decanted. Both held a glass of the wine-dark elixir. A third glass sat on the bar. It had already been poured. King reached over and presented it to him.

"Take it," the Senator said.

Hunt was trapped.

Mr. Australia cleared his throat. "Thanks to His Grace, you were apprised of certain events that took place decades ago, events that I swore never to divulge. Given the fact that Sunny is a personal friend of Her Majesty and saw fit to violate that oath, I no longer feel duty bound. Monday night, you'll receive a full debriefing. I've already contacted Sunny, and he's agreed to host the four of us at the Everglades Club."

Before Mr. Australia could say another word, his stunning South African date barged in on their conversation. She was half his age and perhaps a quarter his IQ.

"What are you boys up to, darling?"

"We are celebrating a life well lived."

"I'm going to run have a look round the ship, love."

"You do that," Mr. Australia said.

He picked up right where he had left off and hoisted the remarkable Shiraz. "Death or Glory!"

"Death or Glory," the two Americans responded.

Hunt took a single swallow and placed his glass on the bar.

"Don't go drinking it all," Hunt said. "I'll be right back."

He didn't wait for either man to respond. Almost ten minutes had passed, and he had yet to catch up with Lori. If the Chief ever found out about this dereliction of duty, his head would be in a bowling bag.

When he reached the base of the stairs, Hunt could not believe who was descending: Cesare Harrington himself.

"Cesare," Hunt exclaimed.

"Ricardo," Cesare said.

The two shared a warm *abrazo*.

"My heart goes out to you, my friend," Hunt said. "It was my privilege to watch you honor your brother yesterday. That was the performance of a lifetime."

"May I tell you something privately?" Cesare said.

"Of course," Hunt said.

"Last summer, after we played at Sandhurst, Juancito told me that it was such a shame about you."

"I'm sorry?"

"Forgive me. What he meant is that so often the amateurs we play with and against, they barely comprehend the game we love. You, on the other hand, you required no introduction. You know polo, you grew up in polo, and Juancito instantly recognized that about you. He would be overjoyed to see you lining up against us in the final."

Hunt was speechless, and Cesare sensed this. He clapped him on the shoulder.

"*Suerte*," he said, as he wished him good luck in Sunday's match.

"*Suerte*," Hunt replied as the two parted ways.

91

HUNT STEPPED OUT ON THE Upper Deck, his mind in a fog. *What courage.* Despite the loss of his brother, Cesare had not only rewritten the record books, but the man was beyond gracious. *He's complimenting me? I'm the one supposed to be reaching out to him.*

Then he snapped to.

"Lori," he called out. There was no response.

The sun had set, and the deck was dark. Only a few sherbet rays colored the western horizon. He looked down and searched the crowded Main Deck below. The Groper's wife was nowhere to be seen. The lights from the boat flickered on the dark water.

Where could she be? He paused. *The loo?*

Hunt made his way down one flight of stairs and then another below deck. There had to be a lounge or a powder room close by. He went up one hallway and down another and found himself at a dead end, facing two sliding doors. He slid one open. A large dark room spread out before him. He reached out to find a light switch, and his hand bumped into a hard metal object. It was tall. It was thin. It was oddly textured and very cold. Whatever it was, it was perched on some sort of base or stand. Hunt's hand spidered up and down it several times, yet he still couldn't make it out.

He found a light switch. A single solitary beam emerged. It didn't illuminate the room. Its sole focus was the bronze that Hunt had been fondling.

"Good God."

He remembered the news of Christie's $141 million sale of the Giacometti before him. It set a record for a contemporary sculpture. The name of the buyer was never revealed, nor its ultimate destination. Now Hunt knew both.

The dim rays of the single spotlight barely illuminated the rest of the room. Hunt turned and looked around. On the walls facing the portholes were a series of whiteboards; each was covered in neatly printed black block letters. On the first, below a header that read Brazilian Court Employees, there was a list of names. Next to it, under the heading of Frédéric Fekkai, there was a second roster of names—stylists, colorists, and clients. A third list, the longest by far, featured only women's names. Juancito's name was atop that one. To the side of some of the women's names, there was the occasional male name.

Husbands?

Hunt had stumbled upon the Centaur War Room. An elaborate time line ran the length of the far wall. Another board featured a Distribution List. Atop it was Jack Dick's name. Then came Joshua Shapiro and Neville Haynes. For contact details on Mr. Australia, it said NTKB.

Need-to-know basis. Hell, they couldn't track him down if they tried.

Off by itself, he noticed a name that was asterisked, underlined, and in red: RICK HUNT. Beside his name, also underlined, also asterisked, it read US EMBASSY ARGENTINA.

Hunt thought back to Jack's first words to him: "Captain Hunt is a man of many talents." So too was Mr. Dick. Hunt took a closer look around the War Room. There were stacks of papers, files on every name. Hunt started looking for a dimmer or a light switch when he sensed someone approaching. He cut the light on the Giacometti.

A man's voice filtered down the corridor. Then he heard a second voice, a female voice with a cheery lilt. In the crack between the sliding doors, Hunt could see two shadows heading down the hallway toward him. *I'm busted!*

Then he realized it was SOB who was traipsing down the hall. Like fleas, his fingers were jumping all over the dress of . . . Mr. Australia's date. And she was not swatting them away. Hunt watched SOB slide his hand down her backside and guide her into a guest room. SOB turned and looked toward the stairwell. The coast was clear. Then he looked down the hallway directly at Hunt. Hunt knew he couldn't be seen. Not with the lights out in the War Room.

Hunt's last glimpse of his teammate was SOB undoing his belt as he entered the guest room. As soon as the cabin door lock clicked tight, Hunt stepped into the hallway. He quietly slid the War Room doors closed just as he had found them. The wall-to-wall carpet muffled his next steps. Not that anyone in the cabin was listening. Hunt could hear her giggles as SOB took her clothes off. In the back of his mind, a voice echoed:

"O'Brien breaks well from the gate. I'll give him that. But he's bound to fall off the pace. Six furlongs is his limit. That's one season here in Palm Beach. The man is about to pull up."

He noted the placard by the cabin: Guest Room Number Six. Right next to it, there was a fire alarm.

How convenient.

Hunt shook his head. This wasn't his fire to put out.

Neither the time nor the place.

He walked down the hallway, still intent on finding Lori. When he found no one, he bounded up the stairs to rejoin the party and carefully scanned the crowd.

No luck.

On the other side of the deck, Lupe and Ava were locked in conversation.

If they only knew.

King and Mr. Australia were still nursing their Grange and chatting with the Ashton brothers.

Monday night will be something special.

"¡*Che*!" a squeaky voice called out.

Hunt turned to see Rio prancing toward him.

"¡*Che*!" he said, echoing the Argentine greeting. "That was quite the performance you put on out there on the dance floor."

"La cubana, she always wanting more. Just like Kelly wanting Juancito."

"*Era un animal?*" Hunt asked.

"*Sí!* You not believe! She never stop calling him, calling me, calling the car, calling the barn, calling Cesare, always saying she hot for Juancito. Now Juancito dead, and she partying."

There had to be more to Rio's story, but Hunt didn't get the chance to ask. A slow reggae ballad was playing. "¡*Ven pa'ca!*" the Cuban model commanded. She was sweating and smiling, and she grabbed Rio's hand and pulled him back onto the dance floor.

"¡*Ciao!*" Rio yelled as she dragged him away.

The Jamaican music, the ruckus of the crowd, the sounds of the big boat—this was the life Hunt thought would be his. As strange as Palm Beach was, he belonged here—at least during the high-goal season. Whether he liked it or not, it was a part of him and he a part of it. A member of the crew walked past, and Hunt vetoed an earlier decision.

"May I make a small request, sir?" he asked.

"How may I be of service?"

"Do you see that lovely lady in the lacy dress?" He was looking directly at Ava.

"Of course, sir."

"Would you ask her to meet me in Guest Room Number Six?"

"It would be my pleasure, sir. And your name?"

"Selden O'Brien."

The crewman departed, and so did Hunt. There was no way he was going to be identified anywhere near Guest Room Number Six. He heard a throaty laugh. It was Kelly, flanked by two of her Valkyries, returning to the party in a stunning off-white Luca Luca ensemble.

"Your date is an absolute dish, and a spicy one at that," Kelly said.

"Some like it hot, Kelly."

She glanced at her husband kibitzing with a few of his friends and then cozied up to Hunt, smoothly slipping an arm through his. "Makes me wish you had gotten to 7 goals."

Hunt chuckled. "Not a chance, Kelly. You've always been out of my league."

"I would have made an exception for you. Carrying 5 goals was enough. But you were never a taker, Ricky. Not like everyone else in this town."

Hunt could see the crewman relaying his message to Ava. He watched as she cut short her chat with her mother and headed for the stairs. Locking Kelly's arm in his, he guided her straight out to the dance floor and the reggae love song. He took her in both his arms. Kelly's eyes lit up.

"It's been a long time, Kelly."

She pulled him tight. Her body swayed in his arms. Her hips and her chest pressed against him. She wasn't dancing with him. She was enticing him. "Go ahead," she said. "I can tell something is bursting inside you. Say what you want to say, Rick."

This woman knew how to cast a spell. "Friend to friend?" Hunt asked.

She nodded and breathed deeply. They were cheek to cheek.

"I know you didn't kill Juancito."

Hunt felt Kelly's body snap taut. She tried to step back. But he held her tight.

"What are you keeping so secret, Kelly? Why won't you talk to the police?"

"I can't," she said as she buried her head in his shoulder. "Jack would kill me."

Jack used his own wife to have Juancito murdered?

"I'm not buying that. There's no way your husband would have —"

"You've got it all wrong, Ricky."

Kelly's hands clutched his back as she pulled herself against him. Hunt was turning over the possibilities in his mind when he felt a tap on his shoulder. He looked up and found himself face to face with Jack Dick.

How much has he overheard? How much does he know?

"May I?" Kelly's husband asked. His voice was brusque, but there was a smile on his face.

Not too much, Hunt thought.

"Why of course, Jack."

As Hunt handed his dance partner over to her husband, her free hand traced its way down his sleeve. "Thanks for the dance, Ricky."

Over Kelly's shoulder, Hunt could see Ava descending into the stairwell. He smiled and saw Cris standing with Joe by the bar. He beckoned her to join him on the dance floor. She glided into his arms. For a moment neither said a word as they found their rhythm. The moment became two.

"Did you see where that woman Lori went?"

"Hold that thought a minute. I don't get many chances to dance on a yacht."

"We don't have a minute. I've got to find her. She said she had something to tell me about Juancito's murder."

"You didn't catch up with her?"

"Couldn't find her. She said she would meet me upstairs, but when I got there I was the only one on the Upper Deck."

"I noticed you managed to find someone else."

"Kelly's got all the answers, but I couldn't get her to say word one. She knows a lot more than she wants to tell. But she also knows better than to talk."

"Palm Beach rules," Cris said. "She knows them very well."

"You're right," said Hunt. "And I ran into Rio. He told me that Kelly was always hot for Juancito, calling everyone all the time, trying to track him down."

"Wait. I forgot to mention something to you about Lori's husband at the divot stomp."

Before Cris could say another word, an earsplitting siren terminated their conversation. Crew members hustled to their stations. Plainclothes security personnel poured out of the bridge.

"What's going on?" she asked.

Hunt shrugged his shoulders. "Sounds like a fire alarm." He turned and looked at the Main Deck. Out of the stairwell marched Ava.

Her mouth was set. Her eyes were hard.

I know that look, he thought.

"Party's over," Joe shouted. "Bartender says we're headed back to shore."

92

"DID WE JUST WITNESS THE Great Escape?" Hunt asked.

The two were driving down an almost deserted South County Road. They had just spent the last half hour in the darkened Lincoln Town Car surveilling the onesies and twosies exiting The Polo Ball. There were no conga lines as the once boisterous crowd straggled off the Australian Dock as if mourning the ball's abrupt end.

"How could we miss her?" Cris asked quietly.

"There's got to be an explanation," Rick replied. "Maybe she has a friend at the marina on one of the other yachts. I could see her popping in for a quick hello."

"Without her husband?" Cris asked.

Hunt laughed. "Wouldn't you?"

The Secret Service agent swatted him playfully. "I don't care how rich that cad is. You have to wonder why she married him in the first place. She could have done much better."

Neither spoke as the Town Car left the city center and disappeared into a dark stretch of tropical foliage. Hunt was lost in his thoughts. The Polo Ball seemed so ripe yet proved so fruitless. Rio said a lot but offered little. Kelly knew something she would never tell. And the one woman who could have shed light on what happened at the Brazilian Court was nowhere to be found.

Looking out the window, Cris's thoughts drifted back to Hunt's crazy question:

Why didn't they have sex in the bedroom?

ANY SOUL WHO STROLLS INTO a crowded bar on a busy night knows that the best bartenders, the ones who pocket the most tips, silently communicate with a select clientele. It is a system that is not taught. It is not teachable. Its essence is embodied by the move Rick Hunt made the moment he stepped inside the Seafood Bar at The Breakers.

The barkeep recognized Hunt's slight head feint and answered by signaling an open seat directly before him. Hunt countered by holding up two fingers. The barman motioned to his right. Hunt proceeded to the far end of the bar precisely at the moment a couple stood up and vacated two seats.

"Right here, Captain Hunt," the barman sang out as he picked up the paperwork from their bill. "Thank you so much for joining us." Then he turned in the direction of the gentleman in the solitary seat at the end of the bar: "And may I introduce to you one of the stars of our small universe here at the Seafood Bar, Walter Ned."

Hunt uttered a polite greeting and took his seat.

"If it isn't the brave new face of polo," the journalist proclaimed.

Hunt immediately recognized Ned's British accent. This was the bloke who had interviewed Cesare Harrington the day before. There was a top hat at the end of the bar, and the man wore an obnoxious plaid jacket. Hunt realized he was also the man that Raul Ramirez had disinvited from The Polo Ball.

Hunt knew he could respond abruptly. He could also respond submissively. Or he could assert himself silently. He chose to ignore the journalist and scrolled through the list of incoming emails on his BlackBerry. None from the White House.

"Don't be alarmed, old boy. I've been looking forward to the day our paths would cross."

"Why is it that I haven't been looking forward to the same, and yet I've only just met you?"

"So many say you only get one chance to make a first impression. I, on the other hand, pride myself on my unique ability to overcome the bad impressions I invariably make. It's one of my greatest gifts. You, on the other, have no need for this talent. You always make the right impression with the right people, don't you now?"

Hunt set his BlackBerry on the bar and looked at the odd character to his left.

"Last summer, my colleagues across the pond were ringing me morning, noon, and night trying to get a bead on a certain American Army captain. All they could tell me was that you were spotted with the President of the United States, with his Chief of Staff, leaving Winfield House, entering the American Embassy, at the G-20, and on the tarmac with Air Force One. How the hell you managed to secure an invitation to the VIP reception at the British Museum was beyond everyone's comprehension. Come to find out, you're on a first-name basis with the Royal Family, and you were able to snag the best seat in the house at the Gentlemen's Final at the All-England Club. Needless to say, after hearing about your standout performance in the US Open on Wednesday, all I can say is *fantastique*."

"Sounds like you work for Scotland Yard, Mr. Ned, not a newspaper."

"Not *a* newspaper, Captain Hunt. The world's greatest newspaper. The *News of the World*. Quite frankly, there's not much that goes on that our network of reporters, staffers, and well-placed sources aren't privy to."

Ned chose not to reveal what he knew about his employer's underhanded techniques and its murky ties to the Metropolitan Police Service.

"As I was saying, all anyone in London could dig up on you was some perfunctory information from a West Point alumni website: your name, rank, and graduating class. Here in South Florida, I was able to locate a couple of ancient mentions about you winning this tournament or that in the archives of the Museum of Polo. But not a single scintillating detail could be found that explained how you managed to get so many people interested in you."

"Such as?" Hunt asked, taking Ned's bait.

"I doubt it would be too difficult to put together a short list of general officers who were more than displeased by your standout performance at the G20 Summit last summer in London," Ned said.

Two seats down, the bartender finished serving a whiskey sour. He turned to Hunt, only it was Ned who caught his eye. The journalist held up two fingers and motioned to the bottle of Champagne he had on ice. The barman grabbed two flutes.

"Please allow me," Ned said to Hunt. "Pol Roger's Churchill Cuvée is a dreadful weakness of mine. During the week, I repent by drinking only Black and Tans, but once the weekend arrives, I must pay my respects to Sir Winston. His civilizing effects more than make up for the hoi polloi that are my daily bread."

"Tell me again how I became Public Enemy Number One?" Hunt asked, still curious.

"Figure it out for yourself, old boy. How many full-bird colonels were in London last summer mixing and mingling with the powers that be, only to find out that they were displaced by some junior military officer? I'm not sure if it was a British staffer or one of your American compatriots, but somebody somewhere definitely wanted dirt on you. They obviously couldn't find it in your dossier. You went to West Point. You graduated with honors. So what? You're a nobody, a captain. There's nothing in your vitae that makes you stand out. But your father? He was standout material: a highly decorated warrior, and if memory serves me right, a groomsman in a certain lieutenant's wedding long before King Kenedy was appointed to the United States Senate by the Governor of Texas. I know how you ended up playing on the most famous polo team in the United States. But what I don't know is why you are here in Palm Beach in the first place."

Hunt focused his attention on the man before him. Before he could respond, he picked out a subtle shift in Ned's concentration. Hunt turned and looked in the direction of Ned's gaze: Cris was walking into the bar.

After their outing on the *Centaur*, Hunt's driver ferried the couple back to The Breakers. "Come in for a nightcap?" Hunt asked.

"Love to. I was hoping you'd ask."

The two had entered The Breakers via the ornate main lobby, but as they made their way to the Seafood Bar, Cris broke formation.

"Pardon me while I freshen up," she said and ducked into the ladies' room.

Now Hunt stood up. He knew he had to intercept her. As he walked toward her, he saw that she had combed out her hair, put on fresh lipstick, and fluffed up her chiffon. She looked like a million bucks. Cris slowed as he approached, and he put his arm around the small of her back.

Then he kissed her full on the lips.

"A BIT OF BAD LUCK," Hunt said.

He brushed his lips across her face and then whispered in her ear.

"We've been seated next to some gossip columnist covering Juancito's murder, and he's already identified me. We've got to do everything possible to stay off his radar screen."

Special Agent Cortés responded by squeezing him closer. "I love undercover work."

Hunt wheeled her around and walked back to the bar with her hand in his.

"Cris, I'd like you to meet Walter Ned with the *News of the World*."

"Ah, yes," Ned said, as he took Cris's hand. "The lovely lady beneath the big floppy hat."

As Ned stood up, his elbow knocked over his Champagne flute.

"Bloody hell," he cried. He grabbed the loose items on the bar and called the bartender for a towel.

"Such a lout I am. We'll clean this mess up in a jiffy."

The barman grabbed a towel and began mopping up the spill.

"You are that lovely lady, am I not correct?"

"How right you are."

Hunt and Cris took their seats. When he let go of Cris's hand, she grabbed it and pulled it back into her lap, and gave him the slightest of winks. They would convince this Fleet Street legend that neither had anything to do with the investigation into the murder of Juancito Harrington.

"And what about you? How do you pass your days?"

"'Fools' names and fools' faces are always seen in public places.' That picture of us in the *Post* was an absolute disaster, wasn't it?" she asked Hunt. He turned to answer, but she was nibbling on his ear. He pulled back, and stared into her eyes for a long second. She didn't look away, then blinked and grinned.

So that's how Captain Hunt climbed the ladder of success, Ned thought.

"Your secrets are safe with me, my lady. I give you my word," he said, and he pledged his honor by directing two freshly poured glasses of Pol Roger to his new acquaintances.

"The two of you wouldn't by chance be returning from the soirée aboard the *Centaur*, would you?"

Hunt slid his free hand across Cris's back and began drawing large lazy circles.

"First things first," Cris said as she sipped from Hunt's flute. "Might you be the character we saw being forcibly removed from the Australian Dock by the police tonight? I'd recognize those electric green trousers anywhere."

Ned broke into nervous laughter. "Rather unfortunate, my reception this evening. Kelly's end-of-the-season bash has become *the* party on the Palm Beach social calendar. Unfortunately, I was blacklisted from this year's festivities because of some rather boorish behavior on my part. If memory serves me right, it was a little something on the courthouse steps earlier this week."

"Boorish?" Hunt said. "I'm surprised you didn't waterboard the poor girl."

"I must apologize to dear Kelly. Certainly not my finest hour. But from a professional standpoint, my conscience has endured far greater shame. On top of that, I played a pivotal role in springing her from jail. Did you know that? By the time I finished interviewing Cesare yesterday afternoon, Joshua Shapiro was already badgering the state's prosecutors for her release."

Hunt twirled one of the brunette curls that cascaded down over Cris's shoulder. Although he was staring at her locks, he was hanging on the man's every word.

Ned and Shapiro. Ramirez and Cesare. Ned and Cesare?

"So you were banned from the party?" Cris asked. Now she was running her fingers through his hair.

"Not exactly. I was prohibited from entering it. My interview last night with Cesare Harrington was arranged by a certain detective at the Palm Beach constabulary whom I had labored long and hard to convince of my trustworthiness. Once Cesare concluded his comments about Kelly's innocence, I was designated persona non grata."

"So this detective denied you access to the *Centaur*?" Cris asked.

"Exactly. So close yet so far," Ned said.

Cris began forcefully kneading the Army captain's neck.

Raul Ramirez and Walter Ned were thick as thieves. Or at least they had been until Ned blew Ramirez's airtight case out of the water.

Ned took a sip of Champagne.

"So tell me, Captain Hunt, how is it that a White House Fellow just happened to be in the stands when the call to duty came? You must have been a bit flustered when you found yourself playing in the US Open, weren't you?

"Ask any professional polo player, and they'll tell you that high-goal polo is the safest polo there is. Everyone knows what they are doing."

"Everyone except Juancito Harrington," Ned muttered.

Hunt's senses went on high alert. Ned was dangerously close to zeroing in on his assignment in Palm Beach. They had to leave immediately. He put his hand on Cris's thigh and looked directly in those deep dark eyes. But she didn't move. Ever so slowly, she met his stare. She draped a leg over his.

Then she smiled the sort of smile a woman smiles when she shares a secret with a man.

"You'll forgive us if we drink and dash, won't you?" Hunt asked as he stood up.

"My dear boy. I'm surprised you wasted this much time on me in the first place."

95

FROM A FOURTH-FLOOR SUITE AT The Breakers, sunrise overlooking the Atlantic is a magical spectacle. Or at least it should be. For Rick Hunt, it was a mad dash from unconsciousness to utterly confused. The sound of bare knuckles pounding on the door of his suite at six fifteen jump-started the Army captain and the Secret Service agent into high gear. Both were very naked. Each was a tad hungover. And neither paid attention to their nudity or what it implied about their night together.

"Oh my God," the Secret Service agent exclaimed. "Look at you!"

A black-and-blue mark the size of a grapefruit stained one of Hunt's thighs. War wounds from Wednesday's polo match and Friday's one-on-one bout with Joe Bigelow covered his arms, his chest, and his legs.

A second volley of loud knocks shook the door of the suite.

Who ordered that Champagne? Hunt wondered as he bumped into a bucket with a half-empty bottle beside the bed.

That's right. After he and Cortés had torn off each other's clothes, the bartender from the Seafood Bar arrived with yet another bottle of the Sir Winston Cuvée as well as Hunt's BlackBerry, which he had managed to leave behind as the two made a beeline to the suite.

Cris hurried into the bathroom.

"Hand me one of those robes," Hunt yelled.

A plush cotton robe caught him square in the face.

Hunt untied it, put it on, and closed the bedroom door as he stepped into the sitting room. It was a yard sale. Cris's bra was hanging off a doorknob. Clothes were strewn on the floor and on the furniture. He gathered all that he could find and stuffed them in the room's only closet.

A third round of impatient knocks followed more quickly.

"Captain Hunt," a stern voice called out.

Hunt hurried across the room. Through the peephole, he could see an older man with some sort of badge hanging around his neck. Hunt cracked the door open.

"Captain Hunt," the man said. "Bud McDaniel. FBI. May I come in?"

"Certainly," Hunt said.

As he gestured to the seating area, he noticed a purple thong caught on the corner of an end table. Hunt deftly snagged the underwear, stuffed it in the pocket of his robe, and took a seat in the chair beside it. He looked up to see the FBI agent staring directly at him.

"Captain, we have reason to believe that you were compromised last night."

96

THE LONG STRETCH OF SPARKLING sand beneath The Breakers was absolutely spotless. Which was unfortunate, at least in the mind of the Palm Beach County Deputy eyeing the pristine setting. An ex-pilot from the Florida Highway Patrol's Aviation Section, he was seated in front of a bank of monitors at the Palm Beach Sheriff's headquarters off Jog Road. Each morning, it was his duty to pilot a drone the length of the Palm Beaches and identify any narcotics that washed ashore, dumped overboard by smugglers fleeing the Coast Guard.

In the wrong hands, the bricks of cocaine or bales of marijuana could be worth millions, which is why the South Florida Task Force funded his job and his drone. But drugs weren't his sole focus. European tourists were also a high priority, especially the topless ones. They required particular scrutiny not only by the pilot but by his dozen or so colleagues in the data center. So were couples coupling. Some did it in the open. Others had the sense to take cover under the mangroves that lined the beach. Not that it mattered. The optics on the newest drones were phenomenal. His only disappointment was that the current generation of drones was not fitted for audio. Yet.

Flying north, he passed over the Palm Beach Country Club at 200 feet. The early-morning walkers were out and about—all retirees. The more clothes they wore, the better. At the top of the island, he banked left at the entrance channel to the Port of Palm Beach. Through this narrow mouth flowed all the commercial ships, all the private yachts, and every other vessel entering or leaving the Intracoastal Waterway.

The undercurrents from these boats sucked in all sorts of debris, which is why he always detoured away from the shoreline and paid particular attention to the inner channel and the turning basin. The slips at the port were an aquatic dustbin. So was the southern shore of Peanut Island. The three landmasses framed the entrance channel and were routinely littered with jetsam.

The northern reaches of Palm Beach were clean. So were the turning basin and the port. Peanut Island was the last stop before heading north to Jupiter Island. Suddenly, he sat up straight and steadied the joystick. Hovering, he descended to one hundred feet and then to fifty. Then to ten. He held his position and zoomed in on the object on the beach. It had no doubt washed ashore overnight during high tide. He turned a knob on his control panel and zoomed in on her open eyes. She was dead all right.

"We've got a floater on Peanut Island," he announced to the room.

97

"SIR?" HUNT ASKED WITH A straight face.

"We have reason to believe that you were compromised last night," the FBI agent said again.

This was exactly the sort of prank that Joe Bigelow was capable of. Or was Mr. Australia behind this charade?

Peals of laughter came from the bedroom. The FBI agent raised his eyebrows.

"Please ignore her," Hunt said.

"I'm afraid I can't," the FBI agent said. "This is a matter of national security involving the White House."

This was no prank. Something was afoot. Something important. Hunt stood up and walked to the bedroom door. He opened it and poked his head in. "Would you mind joining us on some official business with the Federal Bureau of Investigation? It might help if you brought some identification."

Cris was nowhere to be seen. Nor did she reply.

"Did you hear me back there?" Hunt asked slightly louder. A tinge of irritation crept into his voice. He shut the bedroom door and rejoined the FBI agent, who was about to speak. Hunt cut him off.

"One minute, please," he said and picked up the room phone to call room service.

"What would you like for breakfast?" he asked the agent.

"Nothing, Captain. Thank you."

"And I don't want to be eating breakfast with you either. Now, what can I get you?"

By the time Hunt finished putting in a breakfast order for himself and his two guests, Cris had made her way out of the bedroom. She too was wearing only a robe. And her badge. She broke into laughter.

"Nice to see you, Bud."

"Always on the job, Cris. Love that about you."

Hunt was the odd man out.

"Fabulous. Now that we all know each other, would you mind if we got down to business? What's got you knocking on my door at six fifteen?"

The FBI agent looked at his counterpart from the Secret Service. "Is he always so much fun at this hour of the day?"

Cris smiled. "Honestly? I couldn't tell you, Bud. This is the first time we've been on night maneuvers together."

Both agents laughed.

Hunt summoned his most professional demeanor. "My apologies to the both of you. You've caught me at a weak moment. Perhaps a cup of coffee will save the day."

At that very moment, a gentle knock filled the room. Hunt held up both of his arms in the hallelujah position. He rose to his feet and made his way to the door and opened it. Standing before him was a porter holding a black duffel bag.

"May I help you?" Hunt asked.

Cris scooted in between Hunt and the porter, gave the man a five-dollar bill, and took the duffel with the Secret Service tags. "Thank you, sir." She walked into the bedroom and left Hunt standing in the empty doorway. "I'll be out in a minute, boys."

Hunt went back to his chair. Before he could finish sitting down, there was another knock at the door. Hunt held up a hand and indicated to his guest to stay put. He walked over to the door, opened it, and greeted a second porter. The man was wheeling a room service cart.

Hallelujah, Hunt thought. "Please come in," he said.

As the porter arranged the breakfast service, Hunt could hear Cris humming in the bedroom. She emerged in an eye-catching heavy-duty field uniform: black shirt, black cargo pants, and lace-up boots. It was a tad Goth, the exact opposite of the cushy white robe she had just been wearing. Hunt and the FBI agent had poured themselves coffees and were preparing their plates. On the coffee table, Cris's breakfast already awaited her.

"Captain Hunt, I owe you an apology. Maybe you are a morning person."
She sat down like Eloise at the Plaza and looked at her perfect plate: fresh
fruit, a croissant, some fluffy eggs with a hint of feta. She smiled at Hunt,
opened her napkin, and her thong dropped in her lap.

"There you are," she said, and looked up to catch a wink from Hunt.

98

"SIR, CIVILIAN CRAFT HEADING OUR** way," the lieutenant barked to his captain.

His binoculars were fixed on an overloaded seventeen-foot jon boat. Designed for two fishermen, it was carrying five.

The two Coast Guard officers were assigned to Marine Safety Detachment Lake Worth. Both men stood on the beach on the hard sand just below the tide line. At their feet, cloaked in a grey blanket, lay the drowning victim. Their thirty-three-foot special purpose craft with its two-man crew was anchored just offshore. Powered by three 300-horsepower outboard engines, the speedy craft topped out at forty-five knots and was used on counter-drug missions as an interceptor. It was also deployed to support local law enforcement efforts along the water's edge.

"Sir, I'm going to have to ask you to remain offshore," the captain shouted.

Walter Ned promptly jumped out of the fishing boat and began wading ashore in waist-deep water. His arrival was an absurd take on MacArthur's return to the Philippines: the hungover journalist, unshaven and bleary-eyed, garbed in the same shocking-green trousers and loud plaid jacket he wore the night before and shielding his eyes from the rising sun with his Bond Street brolly. He was trailed by a videographer holding his gear high overhead, a still photographer proceeding in the same manner, and the Irish barmaid from O'Shea's. Still in her kilt, she was the only one with enough sense to not get her shoes wet. She had no shoes.

Ned made land and walked directly toward the officers, brolly in hand. "Didn't quite catch what you said?"

"Sir, I'm going to have to ask you to return to your boat."

Ned turned and looked at the owner of the small boat. Then he raised a hand and made the "OK" sign. The fisherman gunned the engine and took off for his original destination with two crisp hundred-dollar bills buttoned in his shirt pocket.

"I'm afraid that's not possible," Ned said.

The two officers stepped forward to intercept Ned and his retinue.

"Aren't you supposed to serve and protect?" Ned queried.

"Yes, we are, sir," the captain responded coolly. "And in this instance, it is our duty to assist local law enforcement by securing this crime scene until they can begin their investigation."

"Well, you're not serving me, and you're definitely not protecting her," he said, nodding at the body by the water's edge.

The captain placed his hands on his hips and sized up the character before him. He was a pushy bloke, used to getting his way, but the captain knew the moment he was in custody the others would do precisely as they were told. He put his whistle to his lips and let out a piercing blast. On the special purpose craft, one crewman jumped down and began hustling toward them through the surf.

"That's really not necessary," Ned said.

The captain did not respond. The seaman drew closer.

"Seaman Murphy," he began.

He was about to order Ned's detention when the other seaman let out a shout.

"Here they come, sir."

A patrol boat from Palm County Sheriff's Marine Unit was fast approaching.

"Perhaps they'll be more helpful," Ned said indignantly.

He looked more closely.

"Then again maybe they shan't."

At the prow of the patrol boat stood Raul Ramirez.

99

"LATE LAST NIGHT," THE FBI agent said between mouthfuls, "a series of phone calls were placed from an encrypted number to the cell phones of several key government officials, including the President's Chief of Staff, the American Ambassador to Argentina, the American Ambassador to Great Britain, and Senator Kenedy. In each instance, repeated attempts were made to hack into their voice mailboxes. As you may have already surmised, when this was attempted with Mr. Auerbach's cell phone, the FBI was alerted."

"And my connection?" Hunt asked.

"NSA analysts reviewed the call records of each of these individuals, and over the last week the only number they have in common is assigned to your government-issued BlackBerry. You haven't lost your BlackBerry or had it stolen, have you, Captain Hunt?" McDaniel asked.

"No, sir."

"May I see it?"

"Of course," Hunt said. He got up, retrieved his smartphone from the bedroom, and presented it to McDaniel. The FBI agent accessed the Manage Connections feature. He scrolled down past Mobile Network and Wi-Fi to Bluetooth.

"Bingo," he said.

"What do you got?" Hunt asked.

"It's what you've got—a burner phone linked to your BlackBerry via a Bluetooth connection."

"Someone connected to my BlackBerry with their burner and then accessed my contacts?"

The FBI agent nodded. "Exactly."

"How did they do that?"

"Not long ago, hackers used a police scanner to listen in on conversations. What we're seeing now is far more sophisticated. Have you ever paired your phone with another device like a car's sound system?"

Hunt and Cortés both nodded.

"All you need is a four-digit numeric code, right?"

Hunt and Cortés both agreed.

"With the right app, today's handheld devices can crack that four-digit code in a nanosecond. Somehow someone got a hold of your phone. Then they paired it to their Nokia and accessed your contacts. The technology is grade-school level. The tricky part is isolating your phone and manually inputting the correct Bluetooth code. When was the last time you were not in possession of your BlackBerry?"

Hunt thought back over the last twenty-four hours. "I guess at polo practice yesterday morning. Nobody ever rides out with a phone. I left mine in my tack room, and it was there when I returned after lunch. Someone could have easily gotten hold of it. But everyone at the barn already has King's number. Maybe not the others. But they all have King's," he said.

"Last night!" Cris cut him off.

"I kept my jacket on the whole time I was on board the *Centaur*."

"Not the *Centaur*. The Seafood Bar. When I walked in."

A pained look crossed Hunt's face. He had been had. "That dirt bag."

Walter Ned only *pretended* to spill his Champagne. Instead he used the spill as a ruse to snag Hunt's BlackBerry. Hunt had been in such a hurry to get Cortés in the sack that he had offered up his phone on a silver platter. Sending it up with the bottle of Pol Roger was the perfect way for Ned to cover his tracks.

"Tell me about this guy," McDaniel said.

"Journalist. Works for the *News of the World*," Hunt said.

"British?" McDaniel asked.

"Definitely," Hunt said.

"Bingo again," McDaniel said. "London's tabloids have raised phone hacking to an art form. It's an epidemic over there. No one is immune. It's the twenty-first-century version of the bubonic plague. Our London office is astonished by the lack of response by British law enforcement at every level. Over here, taping, tapping, hacking—they're federal offenses. Hell, look at Watergate. We took down a president for crossing the line. But in Britain, it's a free-for-all. This is not the first time we've seen some of this stuff creep over here. But it is the first time we've seen it at this level."

"What do you suggest I do?" Hunt asked.

"You'll be turning your BlackBerry over to the agent in charge of the investigation in Washington. I gather you'll be meeting with him this morning at the White House."

Hunt put down his coffee cup. "What time am I flying out?"

The FBI agent looked at his watch. "My orders are to get you to Palm Beach International by eight o'clock sharp. You're expected at the White House by noon."

100

THEY WERE SPEECHLESS, ALL OF them, mesmerized by her pleading gaze. Her eyes beseeched them. Her mouth was wide open, ready to speak, to shout, to scream.

"It's like she didn't drown. She died of fright," the Coast Guard captain said.

Raul Ramirez stood at the feet of the drowning victim. He chose not to notice the fear in her eyes or her plaintive cry for help. Instead, he was fixated on the diamond sun pattern of her wedding band and the necklace she was wearing. It too was lightly sprinkled with diamonds, only they didn't glitter. They were encrusted with sand, just like her lips, just like her eyebrows. The sight of these golden baubles made the detective sour. So did her dress. It was fancy, too fancy.

Why are you doing this to me? Ramirez asked himself.

"No identification, sir," one of his investigators said.

"Not to worry," Ramirez said. "We'll get her one way or the other."

Ramirez's crime scene photographer was all over the body. He snapped shots on his knees. Then he was on his belly. He straddled the corpse and carefully scooted down the length of her body, clicking away. He took numerous shots of her hands. She was mature, but not old. And she was definitely well cared for. There were no callouses on her fingers. Her fingernails were flawless.

The photographer's devotion to his work and the fieldwork of the other investigators had an unintended consequence: Standing thirty feet away, Walter Ned's shooters couldn't get a good shot. The *News of the World* journalist and his cohorts were on the far side of a line in the sand Ramirez had drawn with Ned's brolly.

"Any of you cross this, and you're all going to jail for tampering with a crime scene." Perhaps it was the hour of the day. Maybe it was their level of sobriety. But all of them stepped meekly to the far side of Ramirez's line.

Now Ned was beside himself. He fidgeted and craned his neck for a better glimpse of the victim.

"Go tighter," Ned demanded. His still photographer zoomed in on the victim's face. "Pan the high-rises, move to the waves, and focus on her lying out there," he told the videographer. "Show me the high life, the low life, and then death."

He was so busy ordering his underlings that he failed to see Ramirez walk up.

"You've got this knack for showing up uninvited," Ramirez said.

The journalist wheeled around, startled.

"Wednesday morning at St. Mary's. Last night at the docks. Right now at an empty park. Funny how you always show up at the wrong time."

Ned laughed a bit nervously. "After a long night on the town, I can't think of a better way to savor a hangover than sunrise on Peanut Island with a beautiful woman who has washed ashore." He was not about to reveal his source in the Communications Center at PBSO.

"Furthermore, it's not a knack, Detective. It's what I do. It's my business to know. And like it or not, this morning it's my business to be in the wrong place at the right time. On average, that would be several hours before any of my competitors has the slightest inkling that a story is breaking. Which is why the *News of the World* puts up with me. And it's why I hope you put up with me to whatever extent you can."

"Did you sleep in those clothes?" Ramirez asked derisively.

Ned glanced at his plaid jacket and trousers. "My valet has no imagination."

Ramirez nodded and grew silent.

"I could be of assistance, you know," Ned said.

"Like you were with Cesare?" Ramirez laughed loudly. "What makes you think I'd let you play me for a fool a second time?"

Ned started scraping away the detective's line in the sand. "You couldn't ID her, could you?"

"No, not yet. But it won't take long. We've already uploaded her facials to a statewide database. If she's got a Florida driver's license, I can tell you all you need to know about her by lunch."

"This time of year, you know how many foreign nationals are in Palm Beach?"

Ramirez shrugged.

"On top of that, how many visitors are here from out of state?"

Ramirez shrugged again.

"Why don't you make things a whole lot easier for yourself?"

"And do what?"

"Ask me her name."

"WASHINGTON?" KING KENEDY BARKED INTO his cell phone. "I need you in Palm Beach. I need you in the final of the US Open tomorrow."

"It's just for the day," Hunt said. "The Chief wants to meet this afternoon. I'm booked on a flight to Dulles, and I'll be back this evening. You'll have to count me out on any team activities."

"Cancel your flight," King said.

"Sir?" Hunt felt caught between a rock and a hard place.

"Cancel your flight. You're flying to Washington on my plane. Be at the hangar at eight thirty."

102

THANKS TO KING KENEDY'S GULFSTREAM, the 800-mile flight to Washington took less than two hours. After turning in his BlackBerry and undergoing a brief but intense interrogation by two FBI agents, Hunt arrived at the E Street security gate at eleven. He made his way through the lobby of the West Wing, past the Vice President's Office, to the Office of the Chief of Staff.

Hunt knocked on the door and let himself in. The Chief was seated at his desk on a call. For a moment, Hunt considered taking a seat on the comfortable-looking sofa. He could feel the tiredness in his bones. It started with the beating he took at practice, courtesy of Joe Bigelow. How much alcohol had he downed on board the *Centaur*, at the Seafood Bar, and then upstairs with Cris?

And how long did the two of us go at it?

Then there was the early wake-up call, courtesy of his bacon-and-eggs buddy from the FBI. Hunt set his personal iPhone and his leather briefcase down on the long conference table adjacent to the Chief's desk and took a seat in a hard wooden chair.

This ought to keep me awake.

The Chief hung up the phone. "It's time," he said. He hadn't looked up.

His boss's tone said it all.

"You mean that time?"

"Yes. I'm firing you just as quickly as I hired you."

Hunt paused. "I understand, sir."

"I'm glad you do. I like you, Hunt. Learn from your mistake. At the level you and I operate on, you've got to keep your eye on the ball."

"And I didn't."

"I'm not talking about you keeping an eye on the ball. I'm talking about me. Serving the President requires all that I can muster. There's no margin for error in my position. The moment someone comes along and throws in a security breach involving the White House and I don't know how many US embassies and ambassadors, it's time for me to cut them loose."

"Understood."

"On top of that, do you have any idea how much mileage the press could get out of this? According to the FBI report I just read, the reason one of my direct reports left his government-issued BlackBerry at a resort hotel bar was because he was preoccupied with a young lady who spent the night in his room, correct?"

Did Bud McDaniel include Cris's name in his report? Hunt wondered.

"That's true, sir. I did leave the bar with a woman who spent the night in my suite. In my haste, I left my BlackBerry."

The Chief let Hunt swing in the wind for a few moments.

"Do you have any idea why no one in Washington gives a rat's ass about the clusterfuck you created last night?"

"No, sir."

"Because everyone is trying to figure out why a prominent socialite, the wife of a very big donor, washed up on Peanut Island this morning," the Chief said. He waved his iPad at Hunt. The screen featured a frozen image of Walter Ned doing a news report on an empty beach.

Hunt snapped to.

"It's Lori. Lori Capra. Isn't it?"

The Chief wordlessly eyed Hunt.

"Nobody knows about this. Not even her husband. How the hell do you?"

"Last night I was on board the yacht that Jack and Kelly Dick own, and Lori approached me. She said she wanted to talk to me about Juancito's murder."

"Why did she come talk to you?"

"She recognized me."

"What do you mean she recognized *you?*"

Hunt knew he should have made a beeline for the Upper Deck. Instead, he let himself get detoured by Mr. Australia and King.

What was she going to tell me?

"How the hell did she recognize you?" the Chief demanded.

"I had gone to the Brazilian Court—that's the hotel where the homicide took place—and was scouting the crime scene. She overheard me introduce myself to the general manager. Come to find out, she wanted to tell me something about the murder. We agreed to meet in a quiet corner of the yacht, but I never was able to find her."

"What is going on in Palm Beach? On Tuesday, the world's most famous polo player gets murdered. And on Friday, the wife of one of South Florida's most prominent philanthropists goes to a cocktail party and ends up dead?"

At that very moment, the sound of wind chimes filled the office. The Chief heard it. Hunt definitely heard it. His iPhone was for his personal use only. Outside of immediate family and a few classmates from West Point, almost no one had his private number. And as best as he could recall, only one of his contacts had a personalized ring tone—his former fiancée.

Hunt realized that this was no ordinary call. His ex had swallowed her pride and reneged on her year-old vow never to call him again. He knew why. He was the one who lured Ava to SOB's love nest. And now she was turning to him. Hunt looked at his iPhone. Her profile picture featured the two of them on horseback at Rio Bravo astride bay mares, Folsom mares.

Right then, right there, in the Chief of Staff's office in the West Wing at the White House, Rick Hunt knew what he wanted. He wanted Ava back. He looked the Chief in the eye.

"Sir, if you don't mind, I've already been canned. I'm taking this call."

The Chief's jaw dropped.

"Hello, gorgeous," Hunt said. It was a greeting he hadn't used in a year.

Her voice was thin and fragile. "Rules are meant to be broken, Captain Hunt. And I'm breaking one of my own by calling you right now. Is this a good time to talk?"

Hunt felt her voice washing over him. "Anytime you call me is a perfect time to call, Ava. I promise." Hunt looked directly at the Chief. An astonished look covered his boss's face.

"Ava Kenedy?" the Chief asked under his voice.

Hunt nodded.

"Don't worry, Ava," the Chief blurted out. "Nothing much ever goes on here at the White House. You call whenever."

Hunt sensed a smile crossing her face. "Honey, I know there's a lot of bad press about the Chief's short temper and his politically incorrect vocabulary, but the guy is really a pushover."

"He sounds like one."

"The truth is he'll probably fire me for taking your call, but you're worth it."

"Don't blame her for my canning you," Ari said forcefully.

Before Hunt could respond, the door to the Chief's office opened.

Hunt was on his feet before the President of the United States finished entering the room. As a White House Fellow, he had sat in on presidential meetings. But he hadn't met with the President like this: one-on-one, in the middle of a personal call.

The President was in Camp David mode—khakis, a tennis shirt, and a blue windbreaker featuring the Presidential seal—and he gestured for Hunt to take his seat. Hunt's sole mission in life was to end Ava's call as quickly as possible.

The Chief's lone goal? Exactly the opposite.

"Mr. President, I hope you don't mind, but Captain Hunt is taking a personal phone call. So if you could keep your conversation with me to a minimum, the captain would certainly appreciate it."

It was the funniest remark the President had heard all day long.

"Who's he got on the line?"

"The one and only Ava Kenedy," the Chief said.

The President perked up. "Senator Kenedy's daughter?"

The Chief nodded.

The President turned to Hunt and gestured for his iPhone.

Hunt could hear Ava pouring out her soul. It was their first heart-to-heart conversation in almost a year. She was confused, she had been abused, and her ex was her only lifeline. Only now, the President of the United States wanted to interrupt her. Hunt slowly reached out and handed over what was left of his career to his Commander in Chief.

The President mouthed a tacit "Thank you." Then he turned on the charm. "Excuse me for interrupting your call, Ava. This is the President," he said.

Hunt held his breath.

"That's right, Ava, I screen all of Captain Hunt's calls," the President said. "It's part of a program of enhanced security procedures that have been developed here at the White House during my Administration. Given all the bickering on Capitol Hill, however, I wasn't able to get any funding for this initiative, so I am personally overseeing its implementation."

Hunt couldn't believe his eyes. His boss, the biggest hard-ass in Washington, was actually smiling. The First Family was about to take off for Camp David, and here was the President enjoying himself on a no-brainer of a call.

"And on light days, when I'm not hosting visiting heads of state or meeting with my National Security team, I valet a couple of cars out front, including the captain's," the President said. He turned to Hunt. "What are you driving these days?"

"My in-town vehicle is an M1 Abrams, sir," Hunt said, referring to the Army's main battle tank. "I paid a little extra for the sport package. Comes with a sunroof. And a much better sound system. It's perfect this time of year here in the District."

The President gave Hunt a thumbs-up.

"Ari, make a note. We may need to get Captain Hunt over to OMB. This guy has cost containment hard-coded into his DNA. With him as our point man, we could be on our way to a balanced budget in a year."

The Chief could not have been happier at his boss's jolly mood.

"Ava, one of the disappointments of my Administration is that we haven't seen you here at the White House. I assume that's not your fault," the President said. He listened to her response. "You're right, Ava. Another black mark on Captain Hunt's record. This guy requires full-time adult supervision, which is why I've got him under the Chief's thumb."

A wicked smile crossed the Chief's face. His eyebrows raised menacingly.

"Yes, I've noticed that myself," the President said, as Ava continued talking his ear off. "And that too," the President added.

Without warning, the President let out a surprisingly strong laugh. On the Ed McMahon scale, it registered a full five out of five. Hunt had forgotten how much of a pro Ava was.

"You are so right," the President said. "I would if I could—it's a generous offer—but I've got a previous commitment. We're leaving for Camp David in a few minutes. But I do want to thank you for inviting us to tomorrow's match. I can assure you that everybody in the White House is rooting for our man in Palm Beach. No, I will. I definitely will. I promise. At your family's ranch? What a great idea. I'd love to go there, and that would be a great way for me to see my first polo match. Let's act on that."

Hunt could not believe his ears. Ava was not letting the President get a word in edgewise.

"You've got my word," the President said. "How about this? Would it be all right if I sent the Chief in my place to tomorrow's final?" The President looked at Ari. "Are you up for this—a day trip to South Florida to watch our man in Palm Beach carry the flag for the Senator's team?"

Before Ari could answer, Ava piped up yet again.

"Hold on," the President said and held out a hand to the Chief. "What's that? Captain Hunt flew up here on your father's Gulfstream?" There was an immediate lull in the conversation. Both the President and his Chief of Staff gave Hunt the eye.

And I thought I got kid-glove treatment, the President thought.

He put the phone to his chest and turned to the Chief. "I had a great call with the Senator. He's ironing out a few details with the guys at National Security, but it might be a good idea for you to follow up with him privately tomorrow."

Ari nodded.

The President put the phone back to his ear. "That's perfect, Ava. The Chief will accompany Captain Hunt to Palm Beach and attend the final of the US Open. Now it's my turn to make you an offer. In a few weeks, I've got a state visit to Argentina, and I insist that you and your parents join me as my guests on Air Force One."

The President began listening to Ava's response.

"No, no, no, I understand. I understand completely," the President said. "Ava, I completely understand. If I were you, I wouldn't make Captain Hunt's attendance mandatory. I've seen those Ralph Lauren ads myself. Everyone knows how drop-dead handsome those Argentine polo players are. You may want to fly down on Air Force One as a free agent and see what sort of company you can scare up after you arrive." The President looked at Hunt. He was enjoying tooling the younger man. "Then again, you may not. The guy drives a tank to work. The choice is yours."

Ava was talking his ear off. The President was smiling and nodding.

"Let me give you back to Captain Hunt. I've wasted much too much of his time, and I have no idea what his cell phone plan is. Given his reputation as a cost cutter, I wouldn't be surprised if he asked me to reimburse him for the minutes I just used. That's so kind of you to say, Ava. Here's Rick," the President said and gave Hunt his iPhone.

Hunt heard a happy sigh on the other end of the line.

"Where were we?" he asked.

"I don't know about you, but I'm on cloud nine. I can't tell you how much it means to me that you took my call, especially with the President right there."

"You don't have to say a word," Hunt said. "See you at the barn tomorrow?"

"Deal."

The call ended. The room was silent. The Leader of the Free World and his right-hand man were eyeing the lowly Army captain.

The President slapped his hands together and pointed directly at Hunt. "When I grow up, I want to be you. Got a gorgeous girl. Jetting around on a Gulfstream. Playing polo in the final of the US Open. But you know what the most impressive part is?"

"No, sir."

"Even I don't get to take personal phone calls when I'm meeting with Ari. How'd you manage to pull that one off?"

Ari laughed the loudest at the President's quip.

"I promise you, Mr. President, he doesn't cut me any slack either."

Before the President could respond, the Chief butted in. "Guess what, *paisan*? Today just might be your lucky day. There is a one-in-a-million chance that I will cut you just enough slack to keep you on the end of my leash here at the White House."

The President grinned. But both Auerbach and Hunt knew that his recent termination was now under review.

"Has Ari brought you up to speed on Senator Kenedy?" the President asked.

"No, sir," Hunt said.

"We're in the final stages of bringing him on board in my Cabinet. He's a key player on so many levels. I rank him right up there with a Jimmy Baker or a Lloyd Bentsen. Appointing him to my Cabinet will send all the right signals. It lets people in my own party know that I'm a centrist. It makes it that much harder for my opponents to label me as an extremist. And he'll waltz through the confirmation hearings."

"Do you mind my asking what post you are considering?"

"His extensive military background and experience on the Senate Defense Appropriations Committee make him a natural to head up the Pentagon." The President paused. "Now, where were you two when I came in?"

"I was telling Captain Hunt that he needed to up his game," the Chief said.

"Just so you know—Ari tells me the same thing," the President said.

"He can't fire you, sir," Hunt said.

"I'm not so sure of that," the President cracked.

"You're right!" the Chief exclaimed. He wagged a finger at the President. "I am firing you . . . for the next thirty-six hours. I want you and the family to get to Camp David and have a great time, *kapeesh*?"

The President smiled and nodded. "What did I tell you?" he asked Hunt. Then he stood up. So did Hunt.

"Would you mind escorting me out to Marine One?" the President asked Ari. The Chief nodded and stood up.

"Good work, Captain. See you back here next week."

"Thank you, Mr. President."

103

DURING THE BRIEF FLIGHT FROM Washington to Palm Beach, Hunt updated the Chief on the latest developments into the Harrington murder investigation. Then he gave his boss a crash course in Polo 101.

"OK, one more time—from the top."

"Size of the field?"

"Over nine acres."

"Length and width?"

"Three hundred yards by one hundred and sixty yards."

"What is a team's sponsor called?"

"*Patrón.*"

"Number of players on a team?"

"Four."

"After every goal?"

"Teams switch sides."

"Best players are called?"

"10-goalers."

"How many 10-goalers are there worldwide?"

"Less than a dozen."

"Where do most come from?"

"Argentina, Mexico, and the US."

"You'll do fine."

"I'd better!"

As the Gulfstream crossed the island on its final approach to Palm Beach International, Hunt stole a glance out the starboard window. He immediately picked out the Brazilian Court. It was a completely different angle on the crime scene — a checkerboard arrangement of gardens and homes boxing in the hotel. Hunt noticed its proximity to so much of Palm Beach and the number of broad boulevards close by—Worth Avenue, A1A, and Bankers Row. As the jet crossed the Intracoastal, it occurred to him that he had been so focused on whodunit that he hadn't considered who *could* have done it. The possibilities brought to mind the piercing quote that taunts every soldier in military intelligence:

There are known knowns. These are things we know that we know. There are known unknowns. That is to say, there are things that we know we don't know. But there are also unknown unknowns. These are things we don't know we don't know.

Kelly's derelict behavior, the never-ending stream of Argentine polo players who flocked to South Florida, the loose millions jingling in people's pockets in Palm Beach—these were the known knowns, checklist material for anyone trying to pinpoint Juancito's murderer. The known unknowns—professional rivalries, petty differences, personal scores—these possibilities branched off the checklist of known knowns.

But the unknown unknowns? They metastasized from that very same list. Who wanted something that no one else knew of, something that only Juancito possessed or controlled or determined? And what was that something? The man was a global figure with ties to dozens of countries and people and clubs. How could his death be of value in some sort of warped way? Was there a void he created, one that was almost impossible to discern?

Less than a minute later, the Gulfstream taxied into King's hangar. The two-man Secret Service detail traveling with the Chief exited the plane first. The Chief went next. Hunt grabbed his briefcase and followed last. Halfway down the stairs, his quick step slowed to a crawl. There, on the tarmac, stood the third member of the Chief's Secret Service detail: Special Agent Cristina Cortés.

Cris was all business: a dark suit, no slinky chiffon, no eye contact with Hunt, and no conversation with the Chief. Hunt did his best to read the scene. From what little he could tell, the Chief had no idea that the newest member of his detail was a key influencer in Hunt's dereliction of duty the night before. Cris grabbed the Chief's luggage and loaded it into the black Suburban.

"Thanks again, guys," the Chief said to King's pilots.

Hunt walked directly toward Cris.

"Were you given a heads-up on the Flagler Steakhouse, Agent Cortés?"

"Everything is in order, Captain Hunt. Welcome back, sir."

"Thank you. I should have known you'd be on top of it." Hunt was grinning.

Cris cracked a smile and made her way around the driver's side of the Suburban.

The Chief was on the phone the entire drive to The Breakers. Hunt jumped out first, made his way into the steakhouse, and hurried up the rich wooden staircase. He was still talking with the maître d' when his boss arrived.

"It will be my pleasure, Captain Hunt," the maître d' said. "May I escort you gentlemen to Table 102?"

Hunt raised a hand and slowed the maître d'. "An adult beverage at the bar?" he asked his boss. The Chief nodded.

Hunt ordered a couple of Red Stripes. Auerbach grabbed his beer, raised it, and toasted Hunt.

"L'chaim," Ari said.

"L'chaim," Hunt replied.

They each took a swig, and Auerbach put his glass down.

"OK, cowboy. What's the deal? I saw you drop that C-note back there with the maître d'. Why are you busting everyone's chops to get Table 102?"

Hunt breathed a sigh of relief. The Chief was taking names and kicking ass. That meant he was definitely back on the team. He took another swig of his Red Stripe.

"I've done my share of advance work, and I know what it takes to get things right. That's what this is all about—you."

An exasperated look crossed the Chief's face.

"You think I'm falling for this table-for-two routine? Then think again. For the life of me, I can't figure out this whole polo deal—you and private jets and concierges and princes. And now the President's rooting for you. The guy calls me from Camp David and tells me to keep an eye on you. So instead of shit-canning your ass like I thought I was going to do this morning, I'm telling the President that I agree with him—you're one of our best and brightest. On top of that, King Kenedy thinks you hang the moon. For the life of me, I don't get it."

"That surprises me."

"What are you talking about?"

"You're usually not this slow to pick up on things."

Before the Chief could lay into him, a hand landed on his shoulder. The Chief looked in the mirror behind the bar. King and Lupe Kenedy had just arrived for their standing Saturday night dinner date. Ari looked Hunt in the eye.

"Let me guess—Table 101?"

"I knew you were a quick study."

The Chief nodded his head ever so slightly. "You play well under pressure. I like that about you, Hunt. I need to turn the heat up on you more often."

The Chief wheeled around and gave the Senator a long-time-no-see bear hug. Then he and Lupe traded air kisses.

Hunt stood up and took Lupe by the hand. "I need some quality time with this quality dame."

"Have at her," the Senator said.

"You can have all you want, baby," Lupe said, and she took the arm that Hunt graciously held out. He escorted her through the dining room and outside to Table 101. As he held her chair, Hunt looked in the window. He could see Ari loosening up, enjoying himself with the Senator. King was ordering a drink. The Chief's gaze strayed out the window to Hunt's table. He watched the White House Fellow sit down opposite Lupe. In that moment, Ari slapped his hands together and pointed right at him. Hunt knew the words the Chief was mouthing: the same ones the President had uttered a few hours before:

"When I grow up, I want to be you."

WALTER NED WAS IN A sullen mood. He was seated by himself at his usual perch at the bar at O'Shea's. It was a slow Saturday night, and he had picked his way through an order of fish and chips. He belched and pushed away the half-empty plate. Kelly's arrest and detainment were already blowing over, and Lori's story had grown cold much too quickly. He needed a new angle. Both women had been on board the *Centaur*. Both had ties to polo. But that was all that Ned could find in common. His next move eluded him.

He picked up his smartphone and started scrolling through the list of contacts he had purloined from Hunt the night before. The young Army captain was impressive, all right. He was still a kid, not even thirty, yet his Rolodex was chockablock with senators and generals and White House staffers. The lad was clearly on the make.

Without his phone, Ned said to himself with a chuckle.

He continued scrolling through Hunt's contacts absentmindedly. Then he stopped.

"Hello," Ned said aloud. "Who do we have here?"

He reached in his coat pocket and pulled out a dog-eared six-page document. Atop the first page was the embossed logo of an ancient constellation. It was the guest list for The Polo Ball. One of Kelly's Valkyries had an insatiable fondness for *la vida loca* in South Beach. Fortunately for Ned, she lacked the means to fund it.

The team rosters for Centaur and Rio Bravo were both listed on the first page. By each player's name was his contact information and RSVP status. Another line featured the name of the guest accompanying the player. Hunt's guest was discreetly listed as "Ms. Cortés."

In Hunt's contacts, there happened to exist a certain Special Agent by the name of Cristina Cortés, and her affiliation was USSS. It took Ned a moment to decode the abbreviation: United States Secret Service. He had no problem deciphering her home number. Or recalling her fondness for a certain West Point graduate.

"Nicely done, old boy."

A SELECT NUMBER OF TABLES line the southern veranda on the second floor of the Flagler Steakhouse. Each offers a stunning view of the Ocean Course, the nighttime skyline of West Palm Beach, and the glowing façade of The Breakers.

Note to self, Hunt thought. *If this is good enough for King Kenedy and his best girl, then it's much better than I deserve.*

He turned to Lupe. "How is she holding up?"

Lupe sighed. "Whenever life doesn't suit my darling Ava, she throws herself headfirst into whatever project suits her. Last summer, when she decided against her parents' best judgment to call off her wedding, Mr. O'Brien became her project. I don't know if you're old enough to recall Audrey Hepburn's performance in *My Fair Lady,* but I believe Ava had hopes of casting herself in the role of Henry Higgins. As I told her last night, it only made a bad decision worse. Now her sole focus is the Olympic trials. They are less than two weeks away in Lexington. She is absolutely determined to make the Olympic team this time around."

A waiter approached the table. "Champagne, madame?"

"They know us so well here," Lupe said. "King and I adore Pol Roger. We always split a bottle on date night. We shouldn't, but we do. King loves it because I always end up telling him things I shouldn't say."

"Do you have the Sir Winston Cuvée?" Hunt asked.

The waiter nodded triumphantly.

Lupe was delighted. "The Army has served you well."

Hunt pleasantly smiled to avoid the foul truth. *I will ring that journalist's bloody neck if I ever set eyes on him again.*

Lupe had long been impressed with the young man before her. And that was before he became a professional soldier and was posted to the White House. She reached out and placed a hand on Hunt's.

"I must thank you for what you did last night. Ava has put an unbelievable amount of pressure on herself, and it all came crashing down, thanks to that time bomb that was so conveniently triggered on board the *Centaur*."

Hunt elected not to respond.

"What an unfortunate turn of events — my dear daughter making her way below deck precisely when her date was in the arms of another woman. It's a shame Ava never considered why that porter invited her. Then again, maybe it isn't."

The waiter returned and presented the Sir Winston Cuvée to Hunt. He nodded. Lupe remained poised, ever alert.

Their Champagnes poured, she raised her glass.

"Welcome back, Richard."

Their glasses clinked.

"Don't get me wrong. I am certainly not about to condone Selden's behavior, but Ava played no small part in running Selden out of her life just as she did with you."

"Well, the good news is she's got a new best friend in the President."

"I can only imagine. Her father was aghast when he learned that they had had what sounded like a lengthy conversation."

"It was not short, but it was sweet."

"King puts such a value on that man's time. Quite often, after they speak, and the President requests a call back, he rings back Ari or one of his advisors. He does that simply out of respect for the office."

Lupe and Rick had a bird's-eye view of the Senator and the Chief. Both men were at the bar, and each was far removed from the day-to-day travails that crowded their lives. For Hunt, watching the two enjoying themselves was a moment in itself.

"I gather he's going back to Washington."

"I'm afraid so." A smidgen of resignation was evident in her voice. "From the way they describe things, you'd think the whole ship of state could be righted by my husband."

"What are their chances?"

"I've tried to talk King out of going to Washington and into taking an ambassador's post instead. I say Bermuda. He says Beijing. I say Canberra. He says Court of St. James. The current Secretary—such a lovely man—is a holdover from the previous Administration. What am I telling you this for? You already know everything there is to know about DOD. You're such a dear, letting me rattle on about all these topics. Here I am already rambling, and I've barely had a drop of Champagne. You must forgive me, Richard."

106

THE SOUND OF HIS VOICE gave Cris the willies. She sensed her right hand instinctively creeping toward the Glock in her shoulder holster.

It was after midnight, and she had just arrived at the one-bedroom apartment she called home after dropping off the White House Chief of Staff and his security detail at the West Palm Marriott. She hit Pause on her answering machine and cut him off. But the silence offered no comfort. He knew who she was. He knew what she did. He knew where she lived. She craned her head backward, and let out an agonizing moan. He had watched her and Hunt spontaneously combust the night before.

He could torch the both of us in an instant.

She hit Repeat, and Walter Ned began again.

"Pardon me for calling you on your private line, but the two of you took off so quickly that I never got the chance to bid you a proper good-bye. It was a pleasure meeting you. I have no doubt that you were a hit at the Polo Ball. You're elegant. You're enchanting. And you're *tres dangereuse*. But that's our little secret, isn't it, Special Agent Cortés? Now, should anything ever come up where you require the services of a discreet journalist with an inability to recollect a source's name and a vast knowledge of the comings and goings of the high and mighty as well as the lowest of the hoi polloi, I am at your service, my lady."

Cris hit Stop and cringed.

The biggest sleazebag in South Florida had just solicited her to join his web of informants. And it was all because she tried to lead him on at the Seafood Bar. If she had only come out and told him that she worked for the Secret Service and to mind his own business, this would not have happened.

Her eyes flashed back and forth. Then again, she wouldn't have ended up spending the night with Captain Hunt.

The price we pay.

She looked at the time. She thought a moment about the long, long day, hers and his. She looked up a number and called it.

"It's a beautiful night at The Breakers Palm Beach. How may I assist you?"

"This is Special Agent Cristina Cortés calling for Captain Richard Hunt. He's expecting my call."

"Certainly, ma'am. I'll put you through."

Cris expected Hunt to pick up by the second or third ring. She was wrong.

"Hunt here."

"Cortés here."

They both laughed.

"So this is how it is when your boss is in town."

"What gave it away?"

"You tackled your phone on the first ring."

"What did you think of the Chief?"

"He's everything you said he was. How did it go in Washington?"

"I got my ass singed. But it's still there. You saw the Chief in action. He's beating me up just like he always does. That's a good sign. I'm still on the team. Here's another good sign: I don't think your name came up regarding my missing BlackBerry."

"It did."

She heard the sharp intake of his breath.

"I've been outed."

"Who ratted you?"

"Walter Ned. He called me at home."

"That guy is everywhere on this case. He's a virus that won't stop spreading."

"A snippet in his paper, and we'd both be toast. Should we be worried about him?"

"Play me his message."

Cris hit Play again and put her BlackBerry next to the answering machine. For the next half minute, Ned had the run of her one-bedroom apartment, his presence echoing off the walls and inhabiting its darkest corners. After his final "my lady," she brought the BlackBerry to her ear.

"Well?"

"This is a lot worse than I thought," Hunt said.

"What do you mean?"

"It's apparent to me that you should come back to The Breakers right away, Agent Cortés."

Cris burst out laughing.

"The only known cure for anxiety like yours is a nightcap at the Seafood Bar."

She was smiling from ear to ear.

"That's enough, Captain Hunt. I've had my chukker with you. I think both of us will be safe right where we are."

"Sleep tight, Agent Cortés."

"That I will, Captain Hunt."

WIN OR LOSE, HUNT KNEW his Cinderella story was coming to a close. No matter the outcome of the US Open or the investigation into Juancito's murder, he would soon be back in Washington, continuing the career he had chosen for himself. Which is why he showed up at the Rio Bravo barn extra early on Sunday morning and asked Don Eliseo to tack up a horse that wasn't playing in the Open. He wanted to ride out just one more time.

Although he carried a mallet, Hunt didn't plan to stick-and-ball. All he wanted was the moment: to taste it, to treasure it, so he could somehow recall it in the months and years to come, in Washington or wherever he was posted.

It was a completely calm morning—no breeze, no clouds, not even the call of a throaty songbird. The lone sound was the drumbeat of pounding hooves. The grooms were breezing the team's horses. It was a show of shows, one prized Thoroughbred after another, opening up eagerly and effortlessly. The short sprints teased the bold runners. Each wanted more, and they would have it— that afternoon. Till then, the grooms did their best to keep their headstrong charges in check. It was an enviable task for a horseman. Hunt could see them smiling and laughing as they tempered their mounts.

The timeless echo of the galloping horses stilled Hunt's mind.

There are known knowns. Hunt knew the ins and outs of the case better than anyone. *There are known unknowns.* Kelly was in the middle of it, yet somehow she wasn't. Hunt was certain Kelly would never kill Juancito. Yet when he asked her what she was hiding as they danced together on board the *Centaur*, her fierce reaction was practically a confession that she had a hand in his death. *But there are also unknown unknowns.* Perhaps she couldn't tell him what she herself didn't know.

HUNT AND HIS MOUNT WERE perfectly still. The grooms had finished breezing Rio Bravo's horses, the polo pitches were empty, but his mind was racing.

"So, Lieutenant Hunt, is it your opinion that the assassination of Archduke Ferdinand did not trigger World War I?"

The West Point classroom fell silent as the professor clicked to a slide of a motorcade route in Sarajevo in 1914.

"Yes, sir," the young cadet replied. "The Serbian nationalists who tried to assassinate the Archduke failed miserably. One got stage fright and watched the motorcade pass by. Another lobbed a grenade that bounced off the Archduke's car and exploded in the street. By midmorning, all six of the assassins had either been captured or called it quits. The grand plan was an absolute failure."

Hunt's taut defense of his bold position riveted his fellow cadets.

"That is why I credit the Archduke's driver for starting World War I. Leopold Lojka was not from Saravejo. So when a more secure parade route was selected, Lojka took a wrong turn, got stuck on a side street, and stalled the car directly in front of one of the would-be assassins. The targets were five feet away. All that was required was to point his pistol and shoot twice.

"Now tell me—who bears greater responsibility for the start of World War I? The Serbian nationalist whose best efforts failed, or the inept chauffeur who delivered the royal couple to their deaths?

"Every one in this hall recognizes the name John Wilkes Booth. But almost no one can recall the name of Abraham Lincoln's bodyguard, the one who left Ford's Theatre for a drink at a nearby tavern. We study the great leaders who change

history. Yet real people can effect change as well, men and women such as Leopold Lojka, an unsuspecting agent of change whose wrong turn triggered the start of the Great War."

Did Kelly somehow trigger Juancito's murder? Is that how she fit into the case? But why? What was behind it all? A personal vendetta? To shame Jack Dick? Derail Centaur's US Open hopes? Or to brutally end the career of the world's greatest polo player?

Hunt's musings ended when a black Suburban drove through the gate and headed to the barn.

109

HUNT LEANED FORWARD AND RODE toward the SUV. By the time he arrived, Ari had emerged. So had Cris and the other members of the Chief's detail.

"How late did you and King stay out last night?" Hunt asked from on high. Out of the corner of his eye, he could see a smile flash behind Cris's dark sunglasses.

"I refuse to answer that question on the grounds that it may incriminate a future Cabinet secretary," Ari said.

Hunt dismounted. "So you got him on board?" Hunt asked.

"We're pretty damn close," the Chief said, nodding his head. "That's all there is to it. I've got more security clearances than anyone on earth, and I'm scrambling to keep up with the things he reels off the top of his head. We need him on our team. That's what I told the President this morning."

"Do you mind my asking what the President said?"

Ari's eyebrows peaked. "He kind of surprised me."

"How's that?"

"He said King would be good VP material."

Hunt let out a surprised laugh. "Forget I asked."

The Chief nodded. "Forget I told you."

Joe Bigelow ambled out of the barn.

"José, say hello to Ari Auerbach, my boss at the White House."

Bigelow put a hand over his heart. "My condolences, sir."

"You too?" Ari asked. "Hell, the more I get to know this guy, the more I realize that he's not working for me. I'm working for him."

"Welcome to my world," Bigelow said. "You want proof?"

Ari nodded.

"I got proof. Follow me."

"No you don't," Rick said.

"Yes I do," Joe said.

"Yes he does," Ari added.

Hunt mounted up and rode back to the pony lines. Then he hurried into the barn. Joe and Ari were standing outside his tack room.

"Let me tell you one thing, Ari. King and I won the Open three times together. The East Coast Open, the Pacific Coast Open, the Gold Cup—we've won them all, and we won some pretty big tournaments over in England and down in Mexico. But I've never seen what I'm about to show you right now."

Joe grabbed the handle to the door of Hunt's tack room and opened it with all the aplomb of a bellman at the Plaza. Before them, bouquets of flowers of all sizes covered the benches, the table, and the chairs.

"Are you opening on Broadway?" Ari asked Hunt.

Joe pointed to a horseshoe-shaped arrangement. "That one is from the Superintendent at West Point. I gather the big John Hancock is the superintendent's, and the others are the members of West Point's equestrian team." He pointed to a patriotic arrangement of red, white, and blue roses. "These are from your coworkers at the White House."

"You want to guess who didn't sign the card?" Hunt asked.

Ari opened it. It was signed by every one of the White House Fellows as well as the program director. There was one additional signature: the President's. The Chief's signature was nowhere to be seen.

"The President has time to sign, but you don't. I get it. I read you loud and clear."

"No one even told me this card was making the rounds," Ari bellowed.

"The one from The Breakers is my favorite," a female voice said. "It's that gorgeous one over there, the green and white peonies."

Ava Kenedy had arrived. For match day, she was wearing a knee-length dress of Hermès scarves stitched together. It was a bright, bold equestrian pattern, and she jazzed it up with some dazzling Ralph Lauren alligator pumps. Ava bent down, picked up Bullet, and cuddled the Italian greyhound in her arms. She was beyond fetching.

"OK, Hunt. I get it. Now I see why you took her call," Ari said.

"What call?" Bigelow asked.

"You know Ava, Joe," Hunt said. "She's always making new friends."

"Next time, I'm going to dial you directly," Ava whispered to Ari. "So I can keep an eye on you-know-who."

The Chief let out a sharp laugh. "Please do. I need all the help I can get in that department."

A bright bouquet caught Hunt's eye, one that had been overlooked. It was the smallest. But it was also the most distinctive. It sat in a sterling silver vase. In the center of the arrangement, the note card bore an unusual insignia: three ostrich feathers.

Hunt shook his head in amazement. He was flabbergasted at the thoughtful touch. He read it to himself, and then he read it aloud.

"'Sir, mind the windows.' And it's signed Charles, Will, and Harry."

Hunt took a moment to cherish the memory of Juancito ribbing Wales the summer before at Sandhurst.

The Chief was shaking his head. "I give up, Hunt."

"Give up on what?" Hunt asked.

"Look at your fan club: the Prince of Wales, the President of the United States, the Superintendent at West Point. There's no way I can ever be like you when I grow up. Ava, has your father shown up yet?"

"First one at the barn this morning."

"Would you mind taking me to see him? I think I'd feel more comfortable hanging out with someone on my own level."

Ari and Ava and Bullet turned and began walking down the long hallway. Neither Bigelow nor Hunt were invited to join them. Both could hear her charming the Chief.

Joe smiled. "If I so much as catch you even thinking about her today . . ."

"You'll put me in the back of a horse trailer headed for Cimarron, New Mexico."

They both laughed.

"I haven't heard that threat in I can't tell you how long."

Joe winked an eye, clicked his tongue, and walked away, leaving Hunt to himself in the quiet of his tack room with just hours to go before the biggest showdown in American polo.

110

THE F-15 EAGLES SCREAMED OVER the capacity crowd at 500 feet before pointing their noses skyward and disappearing into the big bright blue. But Hunt and his teammates missed the show. They were seated beneath the Rio Bravo tent, getting their marching orders from Joe Bigelow.

"And remember: nobody covers Dick. Do not mark the *patrón*. Always play him for a miss." Hunt and the Gallegos and SOB all nodded. They didn't have to be told, but they were being told. So they nodded.

From across the playing field, an air horn blasted. The grandstand was a sea of sunglasses and floppy hats, and thousands of fans began clapping in unison.

"Welcome to the granddaddy of them all, the US Open," the announcer crowed.

King Kenedy held up a hand in the tent.

"One last thing, boys. You're in the final of the US Open. You're about to ride out and play for the greatest prize in American polo. Joe and I have done this before, and we'd give anything to do it again. So go out there, give it your all, and have yourselves a great time."

Hunt and his teammates rose to their feet. He walked over to where Don Eliseo was holding Zapata. Barring an act of God, how well he played, and how well he hindered the play of Cesare Harrington, would determine the outcome of the most coveted crown in American polo. Everyone knew it, including Don Eliseo.

The old man drew in his spit in a sucking sound.

"*¿Poquito miedo, no?*" Eliseo asked.

"*Quítate, hombre,*" Hunt responded.

Don Eliseo held out Hunt's mallet. "¿*Vamos a ganar, mi capitán?*"

Hunt looked him right in the eye. "¡*A la chingada!*"

Don Eliseo rewarded Hunt with his mallet and a golden smile. Hunt rode out and caught up with his teammates as they approached midfield. All four lined up side by side, facing the grandstands. So did their opponents. The two field umpires parked themselves directly in the middle of this long line of horsemen.

"Ladies and gentlemen," the announcer began. "It's time to introduce the lineups for today's Open championship. Playing at No. 1 for Centaur and carrying 10 goals, the winner of two Argentine Opens, Martín Harrington." A polite round of applause greeted Martín as he rode toward the grandstand and then began a lazy loop back to his place in the lineup. "Centaur's No. 2, Daniel Ochoa, known as *El Portero*, 'the Doorman,' for his uncanny ability to lead the way for his teammates' scoring strikes."

Hunt paid no attention. His focus was on the stands. In the Rio Bravo box, he could see the Chief seated between Lupe and Ava. And to Ava's left sat James and Geoffrey Ashton. *Those wankers.*

"And now a man who needs no introduction, Centaur's captain, the incomparable 10-goaler, Cesare Harrington!"

The crowd rose to its feet.

Helmet in hand, Cesare graciously nodded as the applause rained down.

"Hail, Cesare! Hail, Cesare! Hail, Cesare!"

Hunt watched his man effortlessly canter before the adoring crowd. Then he refocused on the Chief's Secret Service detail. The two White House agents had stationed themselves at the top of the grandstand. Cris was harder to find. *There she is.* She was directly in front of him, almost at eye level, at the foot of the long stairway.

Uh-oh.

Only a few feet away, Walter Ned stood in the midst of a gaggle of photographers and videographers. Hunt tilted his head in the direction of the tabloid journalist. Cris gave him a subtle nod and what he liked to think was a wink.

"And at back, carrying a 1-goal rating in his first US Open final, Centaur's patrón, Mr. Jack Dick."

Thin applause greeted Centaur's CEO.

"Leading the charge for Rio Bravo at No. 1, the American 10-goaler, Selden O'Brien."

Hunt's lifelong rival rode forward into a chorus of "SOBs." Hunt noticed he rode faster than anyone else and returned to the lineup almost hurriedly.

"Playing No. 2, a six-time winner of the US Open, Ramon Gallego."

The former 10-goaler rode out coolly and quietly, just the way he played.

"At No. 3 for Rio Bravo, another six-time winner of this very tournament and a two-time MVP of the US Open, Roberto Gallego."

The applause for Ramon hadn't stopped, and it only grew louder as his older brother followed him.

"And now our last player. It's been many years since we've had an opportunity to watch Rick Hunt play in Palm Beach. Welcome the Westchester Cup champion to his first US Open final. Let's give Captain Hunt a hand!"

As he rode forward, the loud whistles and shouts of "Go Army" and "Viva Ricardo" startled Hunt. Now he knew why SOB circled round so quickly.

The accolades ended the moment the umpire bowled the ball in. Unlike Friday's practice, when Joe Bigelow met him head-on, Cesare Harrington was an elusive target. His stops, his turns, his horse's acceleration—Cesare's game was lightning fast. Hunt could barely keep his horse within a length of Cesare's. The Argentine rode two, sometimes three horses in a single chukker, switching mounts at a moment's notice when the ball bounced out-of-bounds or a penalty was called. Meanwhile, Hunt and his tuckered mount were left in no-man's-land. He could hear Bigelow's voice booming from across the field, berating him and scolding him as Cesare pulled away.

His first taste of success came in the middle of the second chukker. Hunt brought Terlingua to a full stop in front of Cesare's horse, cornering them against the boards. The play turned without the 10-goaler. Cesare cursed and rode out-of-bounds. Hunt continued to block his way as he tried to cross the boards and come inbounds again. By the time he skirted Hunt's block, Roberto was going to goal.

During the next throw-in, Hunt brought Cesare's game to a virtual standstill when he and Terlingua barged in between Cesare and the ball. Again, Rio Bravo capitalized. Hunt found marking the 10-goaler the most physically demanding challenge he'd faced since combat. Yet as he became more effective, the tempo of the game subtly shifted. Early on, the lead had seesawed between the two teams, but by the end of the second chukker, Rio Bravo was up 5–3. Rio Bravo's 3-goaler couldn't stop Centaur's 10-goaler, but he was learning how to trip him up. He stayed on task.

By the half, Hunt's ability to keep between Cesare and the ball, to pester and antagonize him, was the deciding factor in Rio Bravo's 7–4 lead. Hunt knew it. Riding back to the sidelines, the Rio Bravo team knew it. And so did everyone on Centaur's side, including Cesare Harrington. There was only one nonbeliever.

"What the hell were you doing out there?" Bigelow demanded.

"Marking my man," Hunt answered.

"Like hell you were. Just a minute ago, I watched Cesare take his time, turn the ball, and pass it upfield to Martín. And nobody was covering him."

"Somebody was covering him. Somebody had his eye on the clock and knew that time was about to run out. Somebody forced him to pass it, even though that wasn't what he wanted to do."

"Somebody needs to get his ass in gear. Somebody needs to put his horse in Cesare's face the exact same way I did to you half a dozen times during Friday's practice. Somebody needs to remember this is the US Open. I don't want your best. Now is the time to play better than your best."

King and his daughter were close enough to get an earful of this ass-chewing. Ava paid absolutely no attention to her godfather. The whole time Bigelow was giving Hunt an earful, she was giving SOB the evil eye. By the time Bigelow was finished, Hunt's pride was only slightly bruised, but his determination was doubled, which Hunt knew was precisely his coach's intent.

In the quiet that followed, King walked over and handed Hunt his phone. "It's for you." Hunt was flummoxed. Halftime in the final of the US Open was no time for chitchat. "Take it," King said.

He put the phone to his ear. "Hunt speaking."

"This will only take a minute, Rick."

Hunt immediately recognized Cris's voice. "Where are you?"

"In a marquee down on the field. But that's not why I'm calling. My contact at the SEC called back."

"And?"

"She hit the jackpot."

"Mount up!" Bigelow yelled out. Halftime was coming to a close. Only three chukkers separated Rio Bravo from another US Open crown.

"You've got to make it fast, Cris. What did she find out?"

"They've identified a trading account based on the Isle of Man that shorted Centaur stock."

"Thousands of traders shorted Centaur, Cris."

"Not on Tuesday, Rick. Not before news of the murder broke."

Hunt was the only player not on the field.

"Whoever engineered these trades made a killing. Their $800,000 invest-ment returned $38 million in two business days."

Before Hunt could ask another question, King's phone started to vibrate. "I've got to go. Let's pick up on this after the match," he said and hung up.

"Incoming," he said as he handed the phone to King.

The Senator looked at the text on the iPhone screen. "Not to worry." He turned to Ava. "Your mother has requested that you and I join her and the Chief for lunch in the marquee. Why does she do this to me?"

"Do what?" Hunt asked.

"Send me these silly messages and expect me to respond with a broken thumb," he said. He turned to his daughter. "Do me a favor. Let her know we're coming right over." He handed Ava his phone for her to text his reply.

"That's it?" she asked.

"Tell her we'll stop in on our way up to the box. Hurry! We've got to get across the field before the second half starts."

Ava handed Bullet to her father and began keying in his message. As she did, Hunt's mind went into overdrive. A moment ago, he was trying to process what Cris said about the massive position accumulated before anyone knew of the polo player's death. Someone had used Juancito's affair and his subsequent murder in Kelly's suite to secretly make millions.

Now, as he watched his ex, he realized how it was done.

By the time Ava hit Send, Hunt was riding out onto the field.

HUNT HAD A PREMONITION THAT all his years of military service were going to be put to the test in the final half of the US Open. And he relished the opportunity. It would be war on horseback: a clear-cut outcome born of strategic nuances and tactical challenges.

Hunt began to put Zapata through the most basic of maneuvers, guiding her through a series of figure eights while making her change leads again and again. The routine would prepare both for battle. But his mind was not on polo. He was putting together the pieces of what he had just seen and heard. Neither he nor Zapata noticed another horse and rider interrupting their tango until Cesare Harrington parked himself directly in their path. Like a condottierie trained in the art of war, he was fearless and stood fast. Hunt reined in his mount to a quick stop.

"I must commend you, Ricardo, on an excellent first half," the superstar said.

"That's high praise, Cesare, coming from you. These next three chukkers, I promise to even better my performance."

Harrington laughed. "That won't happen. Let me tell you why."

Less than sixty yards away, a battery of photographers was positioned in the center of the end zone. Each was armed with a telephoto lens the size of a bazooka. They sensed a moment. The clicking cameras caught the split second when the Argentine began moving his mare closer to his opponent's. They captured each jab of his index finger as the 10-goaler tried to intimidate the 3-goaler. But they couldn't capture the cold-blooded threat in Cesare's final words.

"Stay out of my way or I'll run you over, Ricardo. I'll put you down. I'll kill you."

Hunt repressed a smile and adjusted his reins. "Did you give Juancito a similar warning before you took his life at the Brazilian Court? Or don't you extend such courtesies to family?"

Harrington inched his mare even closer. His furious stare was fixed on the Army captain. Hunt didn't budge.

"I've got to give you credit. Last summer in the Hamptons, Kelly must have been the best imaginable source for insider information on Centaur that anyone could ever get their hands on. She didn't need the money. She never made a trade. And that made your trades completely invisible. But that all came to a halt the moment your brother charmed her out of your arms and into his, didn't it?"

Like the line of the ball in polo, Hunt was controlling the play. Cesare's failure to respond told him so.

"The worst part must have been when you told Juancito about your arrangement with Kelly and how much money you had been making. It went in one ear and right out the other, didn't it?" Hunt laughed right in Cesare's face. "*Que hombre*. What a man your brother was. Tell me, Cesare. How many millions did Juancito cost you? Because I already know how many he made you last week: thirty-eight million and counting. I guess those offshore accounts on the Isle of Man aren't as secret as they used to be."

The reins in Cesare's hand tightened in his fist. "You sound awfully sure of yourself, Ricardo."

Hunt was about to respond when an umpire blew his whistle, summoning the players to midfield for the start of the second half. Neither man moved.

"But the way you baited Juancito with Kelly. That was too good. Where did you hide? In the guest bedroom?"

Hunt turned his horse and began to canter to midfield. He knew that if Cesare were truly guilty, his curiosity would compel him to find out how much Hunt really knew. An innocent man would simply play polo.

The boisterous crowd was on its feet, clapping in unison, thrilled to witness such a classic matchup, urging man and beast to challenge themselves to give their all, as polo players have done for thousands of years. Hunt looked over at the crowded grandstands and let their cheers buffet him. This was the moment he would take back to the White House.

This was the time and the place.

The glow evaporated as soon as Cesare galloped up alongside him and slowed his mare to match Hunt's canter. The 10-goaler said nothing. His silence gave Hunt his answer. They approached midfield, and both slowed to a walk. Hunt held up his polo mallet. But instead of gripping it, he began tapping out an imaginary text message on the flat side of the handle. It was exactly the size of a cell phone keyboard.

"I finally figured out how you murdered your brother. With his cell phone." A shrill whistle blew. "Let's go, you two. It's time to play," the umpire said. Cesare rode up and took his place. So did Hunt.

"*Suerte,*" Cesare said.

KING'S BROKEN THUMB HAD PREVENTED him from responding to Lupe's text. But as Hunt had witnessed, it had not prevented Ava from responding in his stead. And whoever received that text undoubtedly presumed that the message had come from King Kenedy. The text had come from King's phone—but not his hand. Only when he saw it with his own eyes did Hunt realize what had taken place on the morning of Juancito's murder.

According to every account, Juancito and Rio arrived at the barn at 8:45. The moment they pulled up, Juancito's string was readied, his first mount prepped, and his helmet and gloves were brought out along with an assortment of mallets. Simultaneously, Juancito proceeded to Mr. Australia's office, where he encountered his brother and their polo manager.

Mr. Australia said that he doubted "the three spent more than five minutes chatting . . . ten minutes at the most." Sometime during this interlude, Juancito took out his wallet and his cell phone and set them down in Mr. Australia's office. Hunt knew from firsthand experience that this must be true. Not only did Mr. Australia say that Juancito stopped by to pick them up before he left for Palm Beach, but all polo players, including those at the highest echelon, knew how easy it was to lose a set of keys or a cell phone while playing. The smart ones did it only once.

By Hunt's reckoning, all this must have taken place before 9:00. So when Kelly sent her text from the Frédéric Fekkai Salon at 9:18 inviting Juancito to the Brazilian Court, the man she was inviting could not possibly have texted a response the very next minute. Not only did Juancito not have his cell phone handy, but he was in the middle of schooling a world-class Thoroughbred.

Juancito's past behavior confirmed this. All week long, in the back of Hunt's mind, he could hear an echo that countered everything everyone was saying. But it wasn't Juancito's voice he heard. It was Cesare's, and it was last summer, that summer day in Surrey. They were at Sandhurst, chatting with Prince William and Prince Harry, and Cesare was poking fun at his younger brother:

"It's a miracle if Juancito ever looks at his cell phone."

There was no way on earth that Juancito would have responded to Kelly's text inviting him to the Brazilian Court. It was Cesare who saw his brother's phone light up in Mr. Australia's office. It was Cesare who responded while Mr. Australia was tied up on a call with Royal Berkshire. It was Cesare who convinced Kelly that she was texting Juancito. She had no way of knowing the difference between the two. Then Cesare deleted both messages from Juancito's cell phone.

Until she opened the door to the Lancaster Suite wearing only a La Perla negligee, Kelly had no idea that it was Cesare, not Juancito, who had received her enticing invitation. Not that she minded. The two were anything but shy about reacquainting themselves—on the sofa, on the ottoman, and on the vanity in the bathroom. Then something must have preoccupied her. Maybe she drew a bath. While her attention was elsewhere, Cesare was able to grab her cell phone and send a text to his brother, the one that said she needed his body NOW.

By then, Juancito would have finished his morning workout. He'd be with Rio, and he'd have his cell phone handy. Maybe Cesare even prepped Rio by telling him that Kelly was in heat, begging Juancito to service her. When Juancito texted back that he would be at the Brazilian Court in thirty minutes, Cesare deleted both messages from Kelly's cell. She never knew about this secret exchange. Then Cesare disappeared.

When Vicente arrived with the bottle of Veuve, Kelly was wet from the bath and in a robe. She wasn't expecting Champagne. She was expecting Cesare to return from who knows where. To Kelly's surprise, the next knock at the door was Juancito in his britches and Faglianos. For the second time in less than an hour, she welcomed a Harrington into her arms as she stripped off his shirt, his boots, and his britches on their way back to the bathtub where she'd been lounging and the shower where they scrubbed each other squeaky clean. When Vicente surprised them with Juancito's final meal, the one Cesare ordered while mimicking his brother's voice, it was Kelly who answered the door. Cesare's lurid sense of civility mandated that he order his brother a meal from Café Boulud: a well-done steak *au poivre* with a side of *pommes frites*, and a single glass of Malbec. It was the Harringtons' wine of choice at family events—christenings, weddings, and in this instance, a last supper. Kelly served his lunch in bed and finished dressing as he was eating his last meal. By the time he set it aside and dozed off, she had probably already kissed him good-bye.

Never once did she stop to think where Cesare had gone. But if she had, she might have realized how easy it would have been for Cesare to hide in the suite's second bedroom, sitting on the divan as he listened to the two chase each other right into his trap. After she left, he emerged, silencer in hand. As he approached the master bedroom, he could hear his brother's soft snores. At that moment, Cesare knew that neither his brother nor their lover would ever divulge the secrets of the Brazilian Court.

HE MAY HAVE BEEN A murderer, but on the polo field Cesare Harrington was a man of his word. Over the course of the final three chukkers of the US Open, he committed himself and his team to ending Rick Hunt's life. And unlike the secretive murder of his brother, he did so in broad daylight in Palm Beach with thousands of witnesses watching his every move. It was an audacious plan, and if anyone were capable of making it happen, it was the brilliant 10-goaler.

Before the umpire could bowl the ball in to start the second half, Cesare jumped off his horse and feigned a problem with his horse's girth. As he adjusted it and repositioned his saddle, he beckoned Martín and *El Portero* to assist him. Then he issued his marching orders. Moments later, during the throw-in, Ramon Gallego connected with the ball. It landed a few yards in front of Hunt, and he bolted after it. El Portero got there first. The Argentine hit a perfect nearside back shot and turned the play. Then, without warning, he cranked his horse to the left. Hunt didn't stand a chance.

El Portero's horse's head peeled him off Zapata and dropped him flat on his back on the turf. As soon as he sat up, he felt a searing pain in his right thigh. Hunt looked down to see a six-inch tear in his whites and blood spewing out of his thigh. He pinched the wound between his thumbs to stop the bleeding.

SOB quickly dismounted. "You all right?"

"Direct hit."

"The shank of his double bridle got you good," SOB said. He looked over at the EMTs driving across the field and gestured for them to hurry. The medics spent the next five minutes butterflying closed Hunt's wound and wrapping his pant leg.

A few minutes later, the ball squirted out of a throw-in and skidded toward the grandstands. Martín Harrington pounced on it. He tried to turn it upfield, but SOB was on fire. He reached out and hooked Martín's mallet. The ball continued on, bounced against the boards, and ricocheted back into play. Thanks to the timely hook, a new line had been created, one that sent the ball toward Hunt. The play was his, and he rode straight for the ball.

Only Martín didn't check his horse. He could have. He should have. But instead of slowing down, he plowed right into Zapata, knocking her off her feet. Hunt had only a fraction of a second to launch himself out of the saddle and out of harm's way. The moment he did, his horse landed on her back and tumbled over, narrowly missing him.

Play immediately halted. Whistles blew. Martín was already protesting. "It was my line. He should have let me clear the play!"

His pleas fell on deaf ears. As Zapata was led off the field, Rio Bravo was awarded a Penalty 4. Although the mare seemed perfectly fine, she would be untacked and sent back to the barn to be examined. Don Eliseo led Terlingua out onto the field.

Roberto Gallego had no problem converting the Penalty 4. As Rio Bravo rode back to midfield, he pulled up his horse alongside Terlingua.

"*Oigame*, Ricardo," Roberto said. "*Hay algo en su espalda.*" He motioned to Hunt's back.

"*¿Qué?*" Hunt asked.

"*Una equis*," Roberto said, and he drew a large X on Hunt's back. "You are a marked man. Watch yourself, Ricardo."

As the second half progressed, Martín and *El Portero* continued to cut Hunt out of plays and thwart his attempts to harass Cesare. Several polo balls went whistling by his head at Mach speed. Only his years in polo and his lightning-quick reactions prevented him from getting beaned.

The gap between Rio Bravo and Centaur began to close. By the end of the fourth chukker, Centaur had narrowed the Rio Bravo lead from 7–4 to 8–6. The two sides traded goals throughout the fifth chukker, but midway through the final chukker, they were tied at 10.

Momentum shifted to Centaur, and so did the big breaks. A go-ahead goal for Rio Bravo was called back because of a minor penalty. Then a superb defensive play in front of the Centaur goalmouth came to naught when the ball bounced off a horse and came to rest directly in front of Martín. A quick tap and Centaur took a 1-point lead.

Hunt galloped to the sidelines to spell Terlingua. He knew she would be going all out the final three minutes of the championship. Even a short break would be invaluable. Joe would have nothing of it.

"Stay on her! She can handle it!" he yelled. Hunt wheeled her around and galloped back onto the field.

The ball was thrown in, and Cesare got control of it. He slapped it toward the boards. Hunt took off after him. Terlingua pulled even with Nalgona and then edged out in front by half a head. The ball bounced off the boards and rolled directly toward them. With Cesare on his right side, Hunt's only play was to lean to his left and swing his mallet under Terlingua's neck. Cesare's only shot was the exact opposite — to lean out to his right and swing his mallet under Nalgona's neck.

Neither was able to execute his difficult neck shot, and both players rode right over the ball. As their horses cleared the boards and went out-of-bounds, Hunt did his best to check Terlingua. But he didn't have a good seat. And she wasn't slowing down. The steel struts of the ESPN TV tower loomed dead ahead. On his right, he was boxed in by Nalgona, charging ahead at full speed. Cesare's horse not only cut off this escape route, but she was pushing his to go too fast. Hunt had only one option: an abrupt left turn into the Cartier marquee.

Teak chairs snapped like matchsticks as Terlingua barreled into the flower-filled tent. A fully set table launched into the air and knocked over a server. There was no way out. An enormous service bar ran the full length of the marquee, and tables filled every available space. There was only one thing Hunt could do, a maneuver known to only the most skilled equestrians: He dropped his reins.

Whatever happened next was strictly up to Terlingua. He had put his life in her hands. It was the sort of faith that the best horsemen put in the best horses, and she rewarded her rider by digging in her heels and executing a flawless skid stop just inches from a four-top with two elderly couples.

Terlingua's rapid breathing was the only sound in the tent.

"Please accept our apologies," Hunt told the table as he backed Terlingua up.

When they rode out from under the tent and back into play, the grandstands welcomed them with an enthusiastic round of applause.

"Ladies and gentlemen," the announcer cried. "Only two minutes remain in the final of the US Open."

Both teams waited as Hunt rode to the throw-in. He could sense his teammates' determination to even the score. One look at his opponents, however, and he saw that Cesare, Martín, and *El Portero* were still circling. The only thing they wanted more than the Open crown was to end his life.

Hunt joined his team's lineup, and the umpire bowled the ball in. It landed directly in front of him, and he cracked it with his mallet. It ricocheted off a horse's hoof and skidded behind Hunt and his teammates. Cesare jumped on the ball and was flying downfield before anyone on the Rio Bravo team could respond.

"And there goes Cesare, galloping to goal," the announcer yelled. "It's Cesare all by himself. Cesare on his own! HAIL CESARE!"

Hunt felt an enormous pit yawing in his gut. With just over a minute to play in the match, Rio Bravo was down by two goals, 12–10.

The crowd welcomed Cesare back to midfield with a standing ovation. Cries of "*bravissimo*" and "*coloso*" rained down on the man. Hunt watched in disgust as Cesare basked in the adoration.

On the next throw-in, Jack Dick lined up incorrectly. His ineptness created a moment of confusion for his teammates just as the umpire bowled the ball in. It squirted out of the throw-in toward the Rio Bravo goal, and SOB backed it downfield. Terlingua accelerated after it, and Hunt made the next hit. He caught all of the ball. Both he and Martín flew after it. As both players closed in on the ball, Cesare and Nalgona swooped in from the right and cut down both players' horses, spilling the riders and sending their mounts somersaulting. The ground was littered with horses and players.

An eerie stillness filled the stadium as ten thousand people held their breath. The quiet was broken by the umpires' whistles. EMT trucks sped out onto the field. The umpires immediately penalized Cesare by ejecting him from the game for the rest of the sixth chukker and awarding Rio Bravo an automatic goal. Centaur's lead had narrowed to just one goal, 12–11.

As seconds turned into minutes, the two Thoroughbreds eventually regained their feet. Hunt and Martín were slower to come around. A long break ensued as both players were carted to their tents to be examined and given new mounts.

With less than a minute to play, Rio Bravo was down by a single goal. Thanks to the Penalty 1 against Cesare, the ball would be bowled in directly in front of the Centaur goalmouth at the 10-yard line. And because Cesare had been sat down, Rio Bravo fielded four players to Centaur's three. The seven lined up.

"Remember the World Championships, Rikki," SOB yelled.

Hunt nodded and positioned his horse directly in front of Jack Dick's. Just before the umpire was about to bowl the ball in, he shifted left and created a hole. SOB spurred his horse and claimed Hunt's spot. Now Rio Bravo's best player was lined up opposite Centaur's worst. The ball left the umpire's hand and never touched the ground. SOB slapped it straight into the goalmouth.

The score was 12–12. The Open was going into sudden-death overtime.

114

"WIN THE LINEUP, AND WIN the game," was Joe Bigelow's lone counsel.

SOB, Ramon, Roberto, and Ricardo all nodded in agreement. Nothing more needed to be said. In overtime, whichever team controlled the offensive tempo would win the US Open.

Simultaneously, in the Rio Bravo box, King Kenedy was telling Ari Auerbach how his team would win—or lose—its next US Open championship:

"Win the lineup, and win the game."

"What does that mean?" the Chief asked.

"You determine your destiny right from the throw-in."

"Score, and you've won the game," Ava said.

The Chief nodded again.

"Let's go, Bravo!" Ava yelled at the top of her lungs.

The players lined up in the middle of the field, but now Cesare was back in the Centaur lineup. The umpire bowled the ball in. Neither team was able to gain control. A whistle blew, and the umpire picked up the ball.

The crowd bristled with anticipation as both teams lined up again. Only this time, Cesare quickly got possession of the throw-in. He advanced it, slowly and artfully, one tap at a time, all the while scoping out the field of play. Then his eyes came to rest on his true opponent.

For a moment, Hunt hesitated. He knew the master strategist was preparing his ultimate play—just as he planned his murders. And it was Hunt's job to put an end to this. It was time to play better than his best. He urged Terlingua forward and parked her directly in front of Nalgona, forcing Cesare to go either to his left or right but not straight ahead. But instead of going to the side, Cesare tapped the ball forward yet again. Hunt stayed perfectly still, and Harrington came to a halt.

It was the great polo player's fatal mistake.

Throughout the game, Hunt had abided by King Kenedy's instructions. He had played his man, not the ball. But now it was time to play by his own rules. The instant Cesare stopped, the Army captain lunged for the ball and flicked it with his mallet. And with that tiny tap, Hunt created a new line. He wheeled around, took another swing, and knocked the ball across midfield.

Cesare raised his mallet indignantly. He had been fouled—at least in his own mind. But by the rules, the moment his horse stopped moving, Cesare gave up the line, and Hunt knew it. So did the umpires. They dismissed Cesare's appeal without a second thought.

Hunt dug his heels into Terlingua, and the standing-room-only crowd jumped to its feet. The sharp crack of his next shot sent the ball eighty yards downfield. Terlingua accelerated directly toward the goalmouth. Hunt could feel her opening up. The mare had such a big heart. It was clear sailing ahead. All Rio Bravo needed was for Hunt to connect with that little white ball just one more time—maybe twice—and the US Open was theirs.

"Hit it! Hit that goddamn ball!" Ari yelled.

"Go, Rick!" Ava screamed. She was about to tug the Chief's arm off.

Hunt pegged the ball, and it scooted directly toward the gaping goalmouth. He leaned forward onto Terlingua's neck. She was all in. So was he.

Hunt could hear the hellhounds tearing after him. Behind him to his left, *El Portero* was closing fast. And a length behind *El Portero*, Martín was whipping his horse like a demon. Hunt didn't look—he knew better—but he could hear the thunder of their hooves. As he readied himself for his one last shot, he purposely avoided taking a full swing.

Neither the time nor the place.

He would finesse it. Hunt leaned forward, reached out with his mallet, and gently coaxed the ball over the line.

The US Open was over, and the winning goal belonged to Rick Hunt.

The crowd erupted in cheers. Hunt had stripped the ball from one of the world's greatest players and followed it up with a flawless attack on goal.

In the Rio Bravo box, Lupe jumped out of her seat. Ari and Ava high-fived and hugged. The Ashtons gripped each other madly. Everyone in the box was cheering wildly. Everyone except King Kenedy. The Senator was yelling at the top of his voice:

"Look up, son! Look up!"

115

WHAT KING COULD SEE THAT Rick could not was the thousand-pound Thoroughbred on his tail running blind. Hunt had no way of knowing this. His eyes were glued on the ball, not his opponents.

As soon as he scored the game-winning goal, Hunt instinctively veered to his left to avoid the cavalry charge behind him. Less than a length separated his horse from Martín's. Hunt naturally assumed that his opponent would guide his horse straight ahead.

But Martín did not.

He was incapable of checking his horse or slowing it down. The raw-boned gelding was beyond exhausted. It had already played two and a half chukkers: the first, the fourth, and the last half of the sixth. Now, in the overtime chukker, when Martín mercilessly flogged it to catch Hunt's breakaway play, he pushed it over the edge—and Martín knew it. The horse was what polo players called running blind. Its legs were galloping at full speed, but its brain had turned off. Martín knew he couldn't stop it. He knew he couldn't control it. But he could steer it, which is how he T-boned Hunt at full speed, just as Cesare had instructed him.

Terlingua slammed to the ground and rolled over her rider. She immediately sprang to her feet and stood over the Army captain, as she was trained. The only action in the end zone was Martín's runaway mount, galloping at full speed. The mindless gelding raced back onto the field and never slowed down till he reached the pony lines and the safety of the herd. The EMTs scrambled to respond. But they were at the opposite end of the field, more than 300 yards away. They would not be the first on the scene.

That honor belonged to Cesare Harrington.

Cesare raced into the end zone, catapulted off his still-moving horse, and rolled head over heels before regaining his feet. As he rushed to Hunt's side, his eyes were on fire, his breathing shallow and hurried. In front of thousands of shell-shocked fans, he skidded on his knees and came to a stop at Hunt's side. He reached down and put one hand under the unconscious polo player's head. Then he cradled his next victim in his arms. With the other hand, he reached into Hunt's mouth.

In a bad wreck, it's rarely the impact that proves lethal. It's his own tongue that chokes the fallen rider to death. The polo aficionados in the stands knew that Cesare was grabbing Hunt's tongue to prevent him from swallowing it. But he was actually doing the exact opposite. Cesare was burying his fist in Hunt's throat, blocking his breathing. Already winded by the fall, the unconscious polo player began to suffocate.

Cesare felt the life leaving his victim. Killing Hunt on such a grand stage was far more thrilling than winning another Open. He pushed harder, and Hunt began to convulse. Cesare's forearms strained as Hunt's body fought for oxygen, his torso buckling and twisting. Death was at Cesare's fingertips. Then it slipped away.

Cris Cortés shoved the 10-goaler aside and tilted Hunt's head back to open his breathing passage. The Secret Service agent put her mouth on his and filled his lungs with life-giving breath. She put her ear on his chest. Hunt's heart was pounding violently. A series of sharp coughs was music to her ears. Seconds later, the EMTs arrived. One put an oxygen mask on the downed player's mouth. Two more arrived with a stretcher and backboard.

Slowly, surely, the color began to return to Hunt's face.

Slowly, surely, Cesare began planning his nemesis's death.

116

THE SOUND OF NEWSPAPER PAGES stirred the fallen polo player. As the light of consciousness gradually seeped in, he recognized a sensation. It wasn't a sight or a sound. It was much deeper than that. It was a touch. Someone was holding his hand. Despite the depth of the trance that he was emerging from, he had a damn good idea whose touch it was.

He squeezed once. She squeezed back once, twice, three times, and a fourth. Without a second thought, he quickly clenched her strong hand three times. It was their secret code—I love you—and by any measuring stick it was the best way Rick Hunt knew to return to the land of the living.

The moment he attempted to smile, he realized his predicament. An oxygen mask was strapped to his mouth. His facial expressions were limited. He couldn't speak either. He opened his eyes to see Ava leaning over him. Not the gorgeous Ava Kenedy that bowled over everyone she met. This was the Ava Kenedy that few got to see: her hair in a ponytail and wearing not a bit of makeup. She was beyond beautiful. She was real. She was his again.

Although he wouldn't know it until he got up to full speed, his former fiancée had spent every minute of the previous forty-eight hours by his side at Wellington Regional Medical Center. Her mother had brought her fresh clothes as well as something to eat. But she barely touched her food. Joe Bigelow had checked in on Hunt and on his goddaughter. The Gallegos stopped by three times. SOB even made a timid cameo.

"Houston, do you copy?" a voice asked.

Hunt let out a groan and looked left. It was King Kenedy. Like his daughter, the Senator had been standing watch over the downed player. It had been his phone call that got Hunt into this mess. He was the one the White House had turned to for insights, ideas, and answers regarding the diplomatic nightmare surrounding Juancito's murder. He was the one who suggested that Hunt be reassigned from the advance team for the President's State visit to point man on the investigation. Hunt was a protégé, his best friend's son, and for those reasons and many others he stood over him through his darkest hour in intensive care. The only time he had left Hunt's side was to escort Ari Auerbach back to Washington on his Gulfstream. After his meeting in the Oval Office concluded, he left the White House for Palm Beach and Wellington Regional. King folded the newspaper he had been reading.

"Doctor says you'll be enjoying a nice little hangover for the next couple of days, if not longer."

Hunt nodded and immediately winced. A dull sensation thudded behind his eyes.

"That runaway of Martín's really pounded you into the ground. Knocked your lights out. They put you under as soon as your MRI came back. Good news is, you're alive and kicking. Better news is, Terlingua won Best Playing Pony."

Hunt held up a hand to the grey mare's breeder and owner. King high-fived him.

"And the best news is …"

"You are a US Open champion," Ava crowed.

Hunt's oxygen mask, though cumbersome, could not prevent a smile from breaking out across his face. He gave King a thumbs-up.

"Good job, Major Hunt," Ava said.

What? Hunt thought.

He tried to pull the oxygen mask off his face, but Ava made him keep it in place.

"You heard right," King said. Hunt noticed Ava beaming. Then he noticed the burly gatekeeper in the dark suit standing by the door of his ICU room. Then he remembered the purpose of the Chief's trip to Palm Beach.

"It would be a breach of protocol for a military aide to the Secretary of Defense to carry a captain's rank," King said.

Hunt smiled and nodded.

"The President offered me the position yesterday morning. You're not going back to the White House. Your next assignment is to help me prepare for my confirmation hearings before the Senate."

Ava squeezed his hand. She was ecstatic. The idea of her ex-fiancé reporting directly to her father cut through the clutter that had derailed them the year before. Yet Hunt noted a bittersweet look on the Senator's face.

He must be disappointed to be leaving the ranch and going back to Washington.

"Got to give you credit. You called two things right," King said. "The first was overruling my direct order and stealing that ball from Cesare. That old boy was so used to you playing off him that he practically invited you to make that steal."

"You were so amazing," Ava said, interrupting her father. "You waited and waited and waited. You waited so long that Cesare forgot you were right there in front of him. Then, when he was ready to make his move, you pickpocketed him in front of everyone and took off down the field. It was the most amazing play any of us had ever seen. No one who was there will ever forget you. Me especially."

"And your second call was on target. You were right about Juancito's murderer," King said. He held up his copy of the *Palm Beach Post*. A crime scene photo anchored the front page of the paper. From the cramped confines of a horse stall, Detective Raul Ramirez peered out. Sprawled at his feet lay the torso of a man. His head wasn't visible, but the blood that spilled from it was pooled in dark, shimmering puddles.

"ASSASSIN TAKES HIS OWN LIFE"

Cesare Harrington killed himself?

Hunt could not believe his eyes. Cesare must have realized that the weight of the evidence piling up against him was overwhelming.

King shook his head. "None of this makes any sense at all. Says here he even used the same gun he murdered Juancito with to take his own life."

The most disturbing part of the picture was the amount of space Raul Ramirez took up. This was no news photo. It was a glamour shot, a press release. Like a hunter with his kill, the detective was hamming it up for the camera.

Walter Ned taught him well, Hunt thought.

The closer Hunt looked, the more he realized something didn't make sense. In the photograph, a lone arm was visible. It was pale, not tanned. It couldn't be Cesare.

Hunt couldn't speak, but he could point. He mumbled into the mask. Then he pointed again.

King nodded.

"That's not Cesare," said King. "That's Mr. Australia."

117

THE MOMENT HE HEARD THE metal shoe pounding against the wooden door, the British cavalry officer knew it could only mean one thing: a cast horse.

It was well after nine o'clock, and the most famous finale in the history of the US Open seemed eons ago. After the match, Centaur Polo broke camp. Dozens of horses were bathed, and each was checked for injuries. From bridles to cinches and saddles, every piece of tack was inspected and cleaned and stored. Saddle blankets were washed and dried. Part-timers were given their final wages and sent down the road. By ten o'clock, the only occupants of the barn were the fifty-six horses scheduled to be trailered to Jack Dick's polo farm in the Hamptons. And Neville Haynes.

Mr. Australia had been running on empty. He took a moment to recharge, closed his eyes, and instantly started snoozing. The sound of the colicking horse brought him to his senses. Whichever one it was, he could hear it in pain, its stomach in knots, kicking the wall of its stall at the far end of the barn.

"God Save the Queen," he muttered to himself.

He grabbed the arms of the old oak banker's chair, swiveled forward, and stood up. Quickly, he strode out of his office and through the barn to locate the stall of the ailing horse.

Judging from the sound, whichever horse was colicking had to be near the players' tack rooms. His intuition was confirmed by dozens of Thoroughbreds. Roused from their slumber, they had poked their heads out of their stalls. Several quiet snorts were followed by a long comedic whinny.

"Quiet in the ranks."

Then he heard the sharp crack of the metal shoe against the wooden door again. It was coming from near Juancito's tack room.

Nalgona! Could this team have any more bad luck?

Mr. Australia hurried toward the stall, lifted the latch, and slowly stepped inside. There stood Nalgona in the back of her stall, her dark silhouette virtually imperceptible. He slowed to a stop, squinted to better see her, and reached out to put a hand on her side.

"Easy, girl."

Neville Haynes never felt the bullet that ended his life. He never saw the man who pointed the gun at his head as soon as he stepped inside the stall. No one could have. Mr. Australia's long walk through the Centaur Stable had been bathed in bright light, yet, as soon as he set foot in Nalgona's stall, he descended into a world of shadows, the world where Cesare Harrington dwelled.

After Centaur's spectacular overtime loss, Cesare demanded Rio drop him at the barn. In a rude snit, he dismissed his brother's lackey. Rio meekly obliged. He knew what a poor loser the elder Harrington was. Cesare proceeded to his tack room, shed his uniform, and showered. Then, courtesy of his brother, he disappeared. After toweling off and changing into his home clothes, Cesare unlocked the door to his brother's adjoining tack room, stepped inside, and locked the door behind him.

Since Juancito's murder, Juancito's tack room had been off limits: at first, at the request of the Palm Beach Police; and then, after Kelly's arrest, per Cesare. After settling down on a big leather couch, Cesare set the alarm on his cell phone for nine o'clock and proceeded to doze off. By the time it began to vibrate, he was certain the barn would be empty except for one man. Cesare knew that on game day the ever-diligent British colonel would be the first to arrive and the last to leave.

At any moment during a match, Cesare could pinpoint the exact location of every player on an opponent's side as well as his own, and he did this without so much as a second glance. More importantly, he knew what each player was thinking. Most importantly, he knew what all were capable of.

Cesare then got up and made his way back to his own tack room to fetch the Browning Hi-Power 9 millimeter he had cached since arriving from Argentina at the start of the season. Getting his hands on the single-action semiautomatic had been a breeze in Buenos Aires. The Browning was standard issue in the Argentine Army. What made it an even better choice was that it was standard issue in the British Army as well, and that made pinning Juancito's murder on a retired British officer all the easier. Smuggling the

Browning and its silencer into the States was a nonissue. He simply hid it in the buckets of tack that he and his brother airfreighted from Argentina with their horses. Customs could have cared less about the mountains of equipment they brought with them. All they ever worried about was getting the ag inspectors to check the ponies for equine flu.

After quietly confirming that the grooms had called it a night, Cesare made his way to the great mare's stall. He knew the punctilious Englishman would spend far too much time tying up loose ends the last night of the season.

Cesare passed the next half hour in the corner of the stall savoring his newfound passion. Killing his brother had been beyond easy. Both Juancito and Kelly were utterly predictable. Each was a child: so spoiled and self-indulgent. Only patience was required with those two. Much like playing polo, committing the perfect crime was a seamless combination of impulse and instinct. Unfortunately, there had been a loose end.

As his brother silently shuffled off his mortal coil, Cesare made a point of studying the spacious courtyard beneath the Lancaster Suite. From the suite, he could see almost all of it, and for twenty long minutes he waited and watched to see if and when any of the staff or guests came or went. Housekeeping had finished its morning rounds. No maintenance men appeared. The only soul who had departed was his brother's. The deserted wing of the Brazilian Court was perfectly still. Cesare safetied the Browning, tucked it in the back of his pants, draped his shirttail over it, and exited the suite.

Down the stairs he skipped. All that was left for him to do was make his way through the wrought-iron gate that led to Brazilian Avenue and get back to his office. Unfortunately, an unexpected surprise awaited him: Lori Capra, sunning in her favorite chaise. She had arrived after Cesare surprised Kelly and before Rio dropped off Juancito, and her favorite perch was exactly in Cesare's blind spot. He couldn't see her from up above, but now she saw the world-famous polo player as he skipped down the stairs. He was caught.

"*Hola*," she said.

Cesare knew that he had been identified. And it was far too public a setting for him to do anything but carry on.

"*Hola*," he replied.

Without so much as another word, he walked out the gate, across the street, and down the two blocks to the alley off Bankers Row. He entered the El Toro office via the back stairway, sat down behind his desk, and pondered his next move. Only one possibility emerged. Just as he planned, he began to make the bewildering number of trades that would ready his portfolio to profit from a precipitous drop in Centaur's stock price.

Prior to this chance encounter, Cesare had staged the morning's events like a maestro: guiding Juancito and Kelly into his trap, baiting Rio to make sure Juancito got to the Brazilian Court, and then showing up himself and having his way with Kelly. He even bolstered his own alibi by making sure that Rio returned to Wellington to pick up his briefcase before meeting him for lunch at the Palm Beach Grill. All eyes would be focused on Kelly. All eyes, that is, except for the beautiful brown ones that belonged to the lounging lady who had seen him depart the scene of the crime.

On board the *Centaur*, Cesare's eagle eye immediately picked Lori out. He watched her approach Hunt and saw the two talking, which only furthered his resolve to tie up this loose end. Then she made a quick U-turn and proceeded to the Upper Deck. An opportunity presented itself, one born of chance and a master plan. Cesare immediately cut short his conservation and made his way to the stairs. As he started to climb up, he turned and looked for Hunt. When he picked him out, goose bumps of anticipation sprang from his flesh. Hunt had been sidetracked by Haynes and Kenedy. She would be his and his alone.

For the life of her, Lori couldn't understand why she had seen one Harrington enter the Lancaster Suite and the other one leave. Was she imagining things? She couldn't make sense of the situation. Like everyone else, she was incapable of putting two and two together. But she knew the Army captain from the White House might know what happened, and she endeavored to tell him.

Only now she was alone at the top of the stairs, and Cesare was approaching her. He was so excited he could hardly speak. He sensed her uncertainty at his sudden appearance and gently took her by the hand.

"*Hola*," he said, sharing her preferred greeting.

"*Hola*," she said in a soft, scared voice.

He led her to the railing along the starboard side of the yacht. She had no idea what game he was playing. Or the stakes.

She was about to speak, but he silenced her by putting a finger to her lips.

She wasn't one to cheat on her husband, but she became mesmerized by the strange force enveloping her. Only a minute ago, she was trying to understand why this man had been at the Brazilian Court the day of his brother's murder. And now he was brushing the hair off her face.

Cesare swept her off her feet, lifted her up, and perched her on the railing. She felt off-balance and instinctively wrapped her legs around his waist. He began to kiss her. Not her mouth. Not her face. But her neck and her shoulders. She found herself indulging in the moment, looking skyward into the bright stars that flooded the night sky. She could hear choppy waves slapping against *Centaur*'s hull and loosened the grip of her legs around his waist. She could feel Cesare's hands descending lower and lower down her back. This was going too far, but he moved so softly, so sensually, that she had no chance to notice that she was drifting out of his arms.

As he launched her into the night, Cesare was transfixed by her startled gaze. She tumbled into the Atlantic, her hair streaming over her face, her mouth open but not a sound coming out. The thirty-foot drop knocked her unconscious. She never felt her lungs fill with seawater. Just like his brother, just like Neville Haynes, her life had ended when she least expected it, in the shadows of another glorious day in Palm Beach.

118

HUNT BOLTED UPRIGHT AND GRABBED the newspaper out of the Senator's hands.

Anchoring the bottom of the front page was a photograph of Raul Ramirez fielding questions at a packed press conference. A quote attributed to the detective made it clear that the Englishman had been his primary suspect throughout the course of the investigation.

Hunt yanked his oxygen mask off, snapping the elastic band that kept it in place. "Why would Mr. Australia have possibly wanted to kill Juancito?"

"According to this detective, Neville had been skimming a little cream off the top: double-billing expenses, getting kickbacks on feed, things like that," King said.

"Are you kidding me? We're talking about a British cavalry officer, a public servant whose career was spent in dedicated service to the Crown. He didn't care a whit about padding a feed bill. What sort of proof did they provide?"

"None," Ava said.

Hunt turned to her. "What do you mean?"

"All the evidence is in Argentina," Ava said. "That's where the Harringtons' breeding program is based. That's where this detective said all the wheeling and dealing took place. According to him, when Juancito figured things out, Colonel Haynes murdered him at the Brazilian Court and then slinked back to the Chesterfield."

"That's impossible. Juancito could never have figured out anything like that. The guy barely knew how to operate a cell phone. He had absolutely nothing to do with the Harringtons' financial affairs. That was all Cesare."

In addition to the trophy shot of Ramirez crouched over Mr. Australia's bloody body, a smaller photograph was inset. It showed Juancito and his polo manager on the sidelines during a preliminary match in the Open tournament. The two were in the middle of a heated exchange.

"A groom found Neville Monday morning," King said. "Nalgona had wandered out of her stall. From what Joe tells me, the groom was bringing her back in when they discovered Neville's body."

Although he was still groggy from the sedatives, Hunt's mind was whirling. With Cris's help, maybe some federal agents could bring Cesare in to elaborate on some of the particulars, and they could force a confession out of him.

"Can we get Cesare in for questioning?" Hunt asked.

"Not unless you go to Argentina," King responded.

"What do you mean?" Hunt asked.

"Juancito's funeral was postponed till today," King said. "Cesare and the boys flew out on the red-eye from Miami last night."

ON STREET CORNERS AND ALONG the avenues that crisscross the capital, the special edition of *La Nacion* devoted to Juancito sold out. The Archbishop himself conducted the funeral mass at the Catedral Metropolitana de Buenos Aires. The President and her husband attended, as did thousands of *porteños*. Every seat in the cathedral was taken. The Plaza de Mayo was packed. Not only was the service broadcast live outside the cathedral, but it was transmitted to all of Argentina on every major news channel.

Few who saw the spectacle would ever forget the precise moment when polo's greatest champion was borne on the shoulders of his teammates between the tall Greek columns that guard the gates of La Recoleta Cemetery. Night had fallen. Hundreds of torches lit their path. Thousands thronged the route. To many, their most poignant memory was not the casket draped in the Argentine flag. The defining moment was the tear-stained face of Cesare Harrington leading his younger brother to his final resting place.

The two brothers had blazed a path together. Now Juancito was destined to spend eternity not alone but in the company of giants. Scattered among La Recoleta's wide walkways and narrow side paths are the mausoleums of Argentina's greatest heroes: Formula One champion Juan Manuel Fangio and, of course, Eva Perón. But as Evita's followers soon learned, her status as the cemetery's most popular celebrity was soon to be eclipsed by her dashing new rival.

IT WAS THE SORT OF communiqué that changes the course of human events.

Lab technicians analyzing the DNA samples submitted by Palm Beach Police pertaining to Case No. 823453274 identified genetic material from not two but three individuals at the crime scene: one female and two males. Moreover, it was "highly probable" that the two unidentified males were related.

Unfortunately, neither the email nor any of its attachments were ever opened, let alone read. They arrived two days after Detective Raul Ramirez closed the book on the Palm Beach polo murder.

Ramirez's forensic technician took one look at the subject line, clicked on his Closed Cases folder, and dragged it straight to the subfolder labeled HARRINGTON.

121

THE NINE-PAGE FAX SPIT OUT of the printer and landed on the floor of the conference room on board Air Force One. Hunt got up from his seat and walked over to clean up the mess he had just made. The cover sheet was easy to pick out. It featured the insignia of the United States Secret Service. The sender was Special Agent Cristina Cortés—West Palm Beach Field Office. The recipient was identified as Major Richard Hunt—Office of the Secretary of Defense—Air Force One.

Three hours remained on the twelve-hour flight from Andrews Air Force Base to Buenos Aires, and the newly minted aide-de-camp to the Secretary of Defense was briefing his boss on the murder of Juancito Harrington. Although the case was officially closed, Hunt was adamant that Palm Beach P.D. had gotten it wrong.

"Sir, you and I both know that Mr. Australia was incapable of defrauding the Harringtons of the trivial sums they accused him of. That's not how he played. The Duke of Marlborough put me in touch with the executor of his estate. Colonel Haynes had been buying and selling top Thoroughbreds for decades. The man was worth millions. Saying he was fleecing the Harringtons for a thousand here or there is nonsense. The idea that he murdered Juancito is completely out of character, and so is the notion that he took his own life. I know for a fact that he was orchestrating an opportunity for Prince William and Prince Harry to play high-goal polo at Royal Berkshire this summer. And wasn't he planning on meeting us at his club for dinner Monday night with His Grace?"

King nodded. He was seated at the head of the table, in the President's chair, his arms crossed and his eyes focused on Hunt. The Secretary of Defense wore a houndstooth suit, and his junior aide was in his service uniform, a gold aiguillette on his left shoulder. It was just the two of them at the long table, which was covered with reports that Cris had gathered in the weeks since the US Open final.

Thanks to the Town of Palm Beach's traffic cameras, Cesare's early arrival at his office on Bankers Row Tuesday morning was chronicled down to the minute, as was Juancito's arrival with Rio at the Brazilian Court ninety minutes later. So was Rio's round-trip to fetch Cesare's briefcase. But the most crucial clips documented Mr. Australia's return to the Chesterfield after four thirty when he crossed the Middle Bridge en route to his hotel. According to the coroner, Juancito's estimated time of death was approximately noon. Based on this evidence alone, Mr. Australia's guilt was completely unfounded.

Just as damning were the reports from the SEC on the Isle of Man trading account linked to Cesare. In addition to the $38 million he grossed when Centaur tanked Wednesday and Thursday, he made another $17 million on Friday when it rebounded. The following week, the monies were swept out of his anonymous Isle of Man trading account, and a $55 million credit was posted to another offshore account linked to him.

Hunt handed King the report that Cris had just faxed him. "These documents prove Cesare's guilt beyond the shadow of a doubt."

"What am I looking at?"

"On the day of the murder, we've been able to track Cesare's whereabouts in a piecemeal manner through eyewitness testimony and a few traffic cameras."

"What am I looking at, Major?"

"My apologies, sir. It's a summary from the Secret Service on the metadata that Cesare Harrington's cell phone transmitted on the day Juancito was murdered. Metadata doesn't tell us who he called. It tells us where his cell phone was. That's because cell phones constantly ping the closest towers and say, 'Here I am. Route all my calls to this number here.' Now look at this page."

Hunt flipped to the second page of the report.

"You can see, Cesare spent the night and woke up in Wellington. This shows when he went to the barn at six thirty. And this is when he left for Palm Beach just before nine thirty. Now watch the trail he created when he drove down Lake Worth Road. Do you see he is handed off from tower to tower?"

King nodded. "I do."

Hunt flipped a page.

"Right here, just before ten, he arrives at his office on Bankers Row. That matches what we saw with the traffic cameras. But notice this: He only stays there for nine minutes. Then, for the next three hours, he moves a few blocks south and shifts to a tower closer to Worth Avenue. It's the very same tower that tracks Juancito's cell the minute he arrives at the Brazilian Court."

King nodded again. Hunt flipped to another page.

"And it's the same tower that tracks Kelly's cell from just after nine, when she arrives at the Brazilian Court, until just before twelve thirty, when she leaves."

King leafed through the rest of the report.

"There are a lot of other threads that tie this case together, but these facts are irrefutable. Cesare claims he was in his office all morning and all afternoon. He says he only left to go have lunch at the Palm Beach Grill. This proves otherwise. He's a liar. He's a murderer, a double murderer. And this proves it, sir."

His presentation concluded, Hunt leaned back in the comfortable leather chair and watched King flip back to the beginning of the metadata summary. He paged through it slowly. Then he studied the map that showed Cesare's whereabouts and the time of day. After setting it aside, he studied the different traffic camera images, flipping the pages back and forth.

"This is good work, Major. It's why I recommended you when Ari called with the news of Juancito's murder. He asked me flat out if your lack of police training would be an impediment. I told him that your insight into the world of polo would guide your efforts, and you would be able to handle any learning curve related to the investigation. And I was right. Well done."

"Thank you, sir."

King sat in silence, neither looking at the reports nor at Hunt.

"But now you're going to ask me to stand down, aren't you, sir?"

The Secretary of Defense nodded. "I was afraid it was going to end like this," King said.

"You mean tabling the investigation?" Hunt asked.

"No, I mean a ton of evidence pointing to Cesare. It would have been one thing if you had come back with a case built on innuendo and hearsay. That would be easy to dismiss. You and I know the charges against Neville were malarkey, and the rest of the world be damned, right?"

Hunt nodded.

"But these documents are not hearsay."

Hunt swiveled in his seat. "Then why are you ordering to me to walk away from this case?"

"Last month, our Commander in Chief requested I join his cabinet. You were among those present when I swore an oath to faithfully discharge the duties of this office. Since then the enormity of our task has become all too clear. Has it not?"

"Sir, it has."

"As much as we both detest it, I believe we must set aside any plan to clear our friend's name. We have far greater responsibilities to fulfill. Do we not?"

"Yes, sir."

Their conversation ended with a knock on the door.

"Come in," King said.

The President's military aide stepped into the conference room.

"Pardon me, Mr. Secretary. But the Chief of Staff has requested that Major Hunt join him in the President's office. There is a potential change in the President's schedule this evening, and Mr. Auerbach wants the major to weigh in."

King turned to his underling.

"Get in there."

Epilogue

POETS, OLYMPIANS, NOBEL PRIZE WINNERS—a Who's Who in Argentina cashed in their markers and elbowed their way onto the guest list for the State Dinner honoring the President of the United States. Not since the triumphant return of *el Papa* to Buenos Aires had such a coveted invite existed.

In the receiving line, the President of Argentina greeted the newly minted US Open champion with effusive praise. A lifelong polo fan, she complimented his now-famous performance and extended a personal invitation to join her in the Presidential Box at Palermo at the final of *el Abierto* later that year.

"For what you did last night, you deserve to be more than just my guest. You will be a guest of all of Argentina!" she said.

"Madame President," Hunt began.

"I will not allow you to disagree, Major Hunt. The President of the United States journeys to my country, and on his busy schedule he has one free evening. What does the man do? Does he spend it at the embassy like so many other heads of state that come to my country? Does he go to the estate of some corporate *jefe* like so many other leaders do? No, he does not. What does the most powerful man on earth do when he comes to my country?" Her question hung in the air.

"Madame President, it was only appropriate that he and the First Lady see and taste Argentina's wonderful culture for themselves."

"Appropriate?" she said incredulously. "It was inspired. Did you see the front page of every newspaper this morning?"

Hunt smiled. "Yes, ma'am. I did."

"And so did everyone at your embassy and in my office and around the world. The President and the First Lady looking like lovebirds, cooing in that crowded steakhouse, drinking Malbec, trying the *mollejas*, enjoying the *chorizo*, *ojo de bife*, and *lomo*. My countrymen see in your President a true Argentine. And from what my sources tell me, he has you to thank for this. He is fortunate to have you in his service."

Hunt was hard-pressed to answer such a statement.

Someone else was not. "I couldn't have said it better myself, Madame President," Ava said, springing into action.

"Hugo, the owner, was running up and down that staircase, serving the President and the First Lady and my parents himself. Rick insisted he let one of the waiters take care of us, but Hugo wouldn't stand for it. The man was beside himself, he was so happy."

The two ladies enjoyed a laugh, and so did Rick Hunt. His right eardrum was still ringing from the peals of joy that blared in his ear when he called Hugo from Air Force One and asked if it would be possible to reserve the entire second floor of La Brigada for the President's private dinner party. Given Hugo's screams of delight, Hunt could only assume that the answer was yes.

How many times had Hunt endeavored to dissuade Hugo from the cockamamie notion that he had any pull at the White House? Yet the minute he was called into the President's office on Air Force One and informed that a change of plans was required, Hugo was proven right. The private dinner at the Ambassador's residence was out. Something truly Argentine was in order.

Like true *porteños*, the President and the First Lady enjoyed a meal that lasted well past midnight. By sunup, the Internet was flooded with pictures of the Leader of the Free World, posing with patrons of La Brigada, gripping and grinning with the kitchen staff, and arm in arm with his new best friend, Hugo.

"But your attendance at *el Abierto* is conditional," the Argentine President added.

"Ma'am?" Hunt asked politely.

"This lovely member of the American Olympic team must accompany you."

In a breathtaking Sarah Burton gown, Ava was turning heads left and right. In addition to her chat with the President of Argentina, the daughter of the new Secretary of Defense enjoyed a lively conversation with the President of the

United States, whom she invited yet again to her father's ranch. When he found out that it boasted an asado that rivaled La Brigada's, the deal was cinched.

"After the midterms?" the President asked.

Ava paused. "I can make it happen."

"Ava, if you can make it happen, I can make it happen. I'll get it on the calendar."

After making their way through the receiving line, the couple glided into the Grand Salon. Uniformed waiters greeted them with a superb sparkling rosé of Malbec. Hunt snagged two flutes and turned to Ava. After a year on the rocks, their relationship was back on track. During that span, Hunt's career had accelerated into high gear: first, at the White House, and now at the Pentagon. But he paid too steep a price, and he knew it. Hunt raised his flute to toast his girl.

All of a sudden, the hair on the back of his neck stood up straight. Then he heard the voice: "To the new US Open champion!"

Hunt turned and faced not one but two startling surprises. There before him, holding his own glass of sparkling, stood Cesare Harrington in black tie. For the first time since the final of the US Open, Hunt was face to face with the elegant assassin, a murderer who had eluded justice and taken two, three, how many lives?

To make matters worse, Hunt couldn't believe who was on his arm: his long-lost dinner date. Anastasia looked equally if not more attractive than when he left her so abruptly at La Brigada. Only now the Spanish model, like so many others, was under Cesare's spell. Hunt felt his stomach turning. He could only imagine her fate in his hands.

"It's a shame I never got to congratulate you after the final, Ricardo. That donkey of Martín's spoiling your superb steal and brilliant goal. That was 10-goal polo, my friend." Cesare reached out and took Ava by the hand. "This man here, he taught me a thing or two about my own game. Juancito would have been proud of him."

"So would Neville Haynes," Hunt said coldly.

Ava caught her breath. She couldn't believe Rick's callous remark.

A deliciously sinister smile crossed Cesare's face. Although he was still gazing at Ava, his eyes slowly shifted to the one man who knew so many of his deepest darkest secrets.

"I can't wait till we meet again between the boards, Ricardo. Maybe this summer in England, no?"

The End

The Perfect 10 is the first work of fiction by **Eric O'Keefe.** Over the course of his career, this Texan has interviewed Clint Eastwood, Willie Nelson, Russell Crowe, Julia Child, Ted Turner, and T. Boone Pickens, among others. His introduction to the game of kings came as editor-at-large for *POLO* magazine. In addition to covering matches around the world, he has profiled such legendary 10-goalers as Adolfo Cambiaso, Mike Azzaro, and Memo Gracida, winner of a record 16 US Opens.

The instantly identifiable style of **Robert McGinnis** graces movie posters such as *Breakfast at Tiffany's*, *The Odd Couple*, and the James Bond films *Thunderball*, *You Only Live Twice*, *Diamonds Are Forever*, and *Live and Let Die*. Since the 1950s, he has created paintings for more than a thousand paperback books—detective novels, tales of the Old West, thrillers, and murder mysteries such as *The Perfect 10*. In 1993, the award-winning painter was elected to the Society of Illustrators Hall of Fame.